PENGUIN

Th
Beautiful
Mother

Katherine Scholes was born in Tanzania, the daughter of a bush doctor and an artist. When she was ten the family left Africa, going first to England, then migrating to Australia. She now lives in Tasmania with her husband and two sons, but makes regular trips back to her first homeland, where many of her books are set.

She is the author of international bestsellers including *Make Me An Idol*, *The Rain Queen*, *The Stone Angel*, *The Hunter's Wife*, *The Lioness*, *The Perfect Wife* and *Congo Dawn*. She is particularly popular in Europe, where she has sold over two million books.

Her novel *The Blue Chameleon* won a New South Wales Premier's Literary Award, and *The Stone Angel* was longlisted in the International Dublin Literary Awards. Her work has been translated into over a dozen languages, and includes children's titles as well as novels for adults. She has also worked as a documentary filmmaker.

katherinescholes.com

The Hunter's Wife

'*Out of Africa* meets *White Mischief* . . . A bittersweet, entertaining mix of Hollywood, obsessive love and the unbearable longing for what is not possible.' *Australian Women's Weekly* Book of the Month

'Beautifully written.' *Herald Sun*

The Stone Angel

'Full of passion, fine writing and interesting observations about the way potent events that help shape one generation have an impact on the next. Wonderful stuff.' *Australian Women's Weekly* Book of the Month

'A beautifully descriptive read and a soul-searching take on human relationships.' *New Idea*

'Scholes crafts her fiction with such care and subtlety.' *Weekend Australian*

'Scholes has masterfully captured those fateful moments that can change the course of many lives. *The Stone Angel* touches the senses with its rich descriptions of coastal Tasmania and emerges as a lovingly crafted account of a home we can never run away from.' *Good Reading*

'A truly absorbing book filled with secrets and conflicts.' *Woman's Day*

'Scholes shows a rare ability to understand people in their specific geographical context and find within them the great surging passions of humanity.' *Sunday Tasmanian*

Make Me An Idol

'A superb novel.' *Cote Femme* (France)

The Perfect Wife

'*The Perfect Wife* takes readers on an exotic journey, exploring the struggle between duty, desire, jealousy and freedom in another era ... hard to put down.' *Weekly Times*

KATHERINE SCHOLES

The Beautiful Mother

PENGUIN BOOKS

PENGUIN BOOKS

UK | USA | Canada | Ireland | Australia
India | New Zealand | South Africa | China

Penguin Books is part of the Penguin Random House group of companies
whose addresses can be found at global.penguinrandomhouse.com.

First published by Viking, 2020
This edition published by Penguin Books, 2021

Copyright © Katherine Scholes, 2020

The moral right of the author has been asserted.

All rights reserved. No part of this publication may be reproduced, published, performed in
public or communicated to the public in any form or by any means without prior written
permission from Penguin Random House Australia Pty Ltd or its authorised licensees.

Cover design by Louisa Maggio © Penguin Random House Australia Pty Ltd
Cover photograph by Rohit Borkar/EyeEm/Getty Images
Typeset in Fairfield LH by Midland Typesetters, Australia

Printed and bound in Australia by Griffin Press, part of Ovato, an accredited
ISO AS/NZS 14001 Environmental Management Systems printer

 A catalogue record for this
book is available from the
National Library of Australia

ISBN 978 1 76104 510 3

penguin.com.au

For Freya

This story is set in 1970 and reflects archaeological research and other factual information as it was understood at the time.

Your children are not your children.
They are the sons and daughters of Life's longing for itself.
They come through you but not from you,
And though they are with you yet they belong not to you.

— Kahlil Gibran

ONE

1970
Tanzania, East Africa

Essie leaned back in her chair, a mug of black tea resting on her knee. She gazed out through the open front of the tent. In the early morning light the rocky plain below the camp was painted in smudgy tones of brown and grey. Away in the distance she could see the silver gleam of the lake. Rising up behind it was Ol Doinyo Lengai. A wreath of cloud drifted across the summit, hiding the cap of strange white lava that looked like snow.

From overhead Essie heard weaverbirds calling between the thorn trees. The air was cool and still. She tried to draw it inside her, so that she would feel it there later on, when the sun blazed from a sheer blue sky and a hot wind blew in from the north-east.

'That's the last of the marmalade.'

On the other side of the dining table Essie's mother-in-law was scraping out a jar with a teaspoon. Her actions were slow and precise. She could have been removing specks of earth from a fragment of fossilised bone. A faint frown marked her brow as she worked.

'There's no more, you know.' Julia spoke in her usual matter-of-fact tone, even though Essie knew that marmalade was one of the few luxuries she cherished, along with Scotch whisky and cigarettes.

1

Essie passed over a glass dish of dark-gold local honey. Julia shook her head, preferring to spread her slice of bread with the meagre amount of marmalade she'd collected. As she began to eat, she reached across to a wooden tray piled with stones at the far end of the table. She picked out a large grey pebble – water worn, with one end broken off. She stroked the edge with her finger. Essie guessed she wanted to make some comment about it, but was waiting for her son to reappear.

Ian was over in the Administration Hut where the radio was set up. He was expecting to talk to the Head Ranger at Serengeti. The call had been arranged last night, but there'd been no clue as to what it was about. It was rare, these days, for anyone to need to get in touch with the Lawrences. Since the Ranger's office some-times acted as a local contact for other authorities, including the Department of Antiquities, they all felt a bit uneasy.

A sudden nudge at Essie's elbow made her spill her tea. She gasped as the hot water soaked through her shorts. Reaching behind her, she pushed away the muzzle of a young gazelle. 'No, Tommy!'

The animal took two steps backwards, then stood still, head lowered, staring reproachfully at her. With his eyes so dark and shiny he always looked to be on the brink of tears. Relenting, Essie called him back and scratched his ear. The sun glanced off the silver buckle on his blue collar.

'He's getting horns,' Julia stated. 'He'll be impossible to manage.'

Essie said nothing. She knew Julia was tense because of the radio call. And this was on top of the fact that she had never approved of Tommy being at the camp. He'd been found six months ago by one of the local workers, abandoned by his mother only weeks after his birth. When Tommy had been brought to the Work Hut, Julia had instructed the worker to put the hungry animal out of its misery.

'No, wait,' Essie had intervened. The baby looked so frightened, his cry almost silent as if his voice had run out. 'Let's keep him. I'll take care of him.'

'That's not a good idea,' Julia had said firmly. 'You might think you're being kind, but you're not. It's very hard to rehabilitate a wild animal that's become tame. He'll never belong anywhere.'

She'd gone on to talk about the cost of milk powder and other practical issues. Then she'd started on her more serious concern. By rescuing the creature Essie would be interfering in a natural process – survival of the fittest.

Julia had looked to her son for support, but Ian had surprised both women by taking Essie's side. 'I don't see what harm it can do. One little gazelle.'

Essie had fallen in love with Tommy. She often buried her face in his fur, breathing his smell. She felt a rush of affection when she saw him sitting in the shade with his legs folded away so neatly, and she smiled at the sight of his tail flicking constantly from side to side. Now, Tommy was half-grown and grazing independently, but he was showing no sign of wanting to return to the wild. Instead, he still liked to stay as close to Essie as possible. He would sidle into the tent and stand – like he was now – right at her side.

Avoiding Julia's gaze, Essie tore off a hunk of bread and fed it to Tommy, watching the quaint sideways movement of his jaws as he chewed.

'You'll have to let him go in the end,' Julia said.

Essie took a breath. 'I know that.' There was a short silence. Essie noticed a smear of marmalade on Julia's chin. She found herself rubbing her own chin as if that could remove it.

Into the quiet came the sounds of footsteps – brittle leaves and twigs being crushed. Essie looked up to see Ian striding over.

There was a focused look on his face, as if his thoughts were racing.

'Is it good or bad?' Essie couldn't help asking. On the other side of the table Julia waited quietly for a report. Her stillness felt like a reproof – a reminder that her daughter-in-law hadn't yet spent enough time at the Gorge to learn how to take each day, month, year as it came.

Ian let the quiet stretch out for a few seconds, then he grinned. 'Guess who I've been talking to.'

Julia watched him, saying nothing.

'Frank Marlow,' Ian announced.

Julia's eyes widened. 'You mean – Frank Marlow himself?'

Ian nodded. 'I could hardly believe it.'

Essie had heard the name Marlow but couldn't place it, so she just raised her eyebrows to show she was impressed.

'He's staying at the Lodge,' Ian continued. 'Yesterday he flew to Olduvai to see their museum. Leakey took him round all their sites – showed him what they are working on.' A shadow of dismay crept into Ian's voice. The Leakeys were another family of archae-ologists who worked in a gorge about half a day's drive away. A year ago they'd managed to secure funding for a museum at their research base. It had been a real coup – and it was hard not to feel envious of them. The moment passed, though, and Ian's smile returned. 'Now he's coming to Magadi.'

'He wants to see what we're doing!' Julia clasped her hands together like someone offering a prayer of thanks.

'Not exactly,' Ian said. 'He wants to bring his wife here. It's a surprise. For their wedding anniversary.'

Julia mouthed his last words as if they made no sense. At Magadi Camp, Christmas was celebrated and birthdays warranted a cake, if the ingredients could be found. But wedding anniversaries were barely mentioned. Ian and Essie's had come around four times; they'd married within a year of her arrival at Magadi. Essie always wished they could go away somewhere together to mark the occasion – perhaps to Serengeti. But the date occurred in January, during the intense digging season of the Short Dry when no time could be spared.

Ian cleared his throat. 'He wants to have sundowners served at the Steps.'

Julia's lips parted, but she didn't speak. Essie could see her struggling to come to terms with the famous archaeological site being used as nothing more than a romantic backdrop. She was annoyed enough by sightseeing planes that flew low over Magadi Gorge so that tourists could peer at the Steps on their way to view the volcano.

'He's asked as a favour,' Ian continued.

Julia drew in a breath as if preparing to be brave. 'So we have to say yes.'

'Who exactly is he?' Essie asked carefully. If she let the conversation run on any longer, it would only get harder to admit her ignorance.

'A Canadian millionaire. He made his money in mining. The Marlow Trust funds private archaeological research all over the world.' As he spoke, Ian looked in the direction of the Steps site – down on the plains, out of view behind a rocky outcrop. 'Frank's going to bring everything with him from the Lodge. Glasses. Folding table and chairs. And food as well. Trays of canapés. We don't have to provide anything.'

'That's just as well,' said Julia dryly.

Essie imagined the Marlows at the Steps, sipping champagne and nibbling caviar on crackers as they gazed out over the lines of footprints that had been captured in stone nearly four million years ago. Preserved beneath layers of ash and lava, the impressions were made on a muddy plain by the first of our ancestors to walk on two legs. The footprints of the Australopithecines – a species that was part-ape, part-human – led across the plain in the direction of the volcano. There was a man, followed by a woman and a child walking side by side, the distance between them regular as if they might even have been holding hands. The connection with deep history and long-lost people would be almost tangible. The visitors were lucky with their timing: the flamingos had recently arrived in Magadi for the breeding season. Essie had got out of bed to watch them fly over the Gorge, on their way to the salt lake where they, themselves, had been hatched. The birds made the journey from other regions of the Rift Valley, travelling during the course of a single night, lit by a full moon. Now there were tens of thousands of them milling around the lake. Along with the pyramid of the volcano, they would provide a stunning backdrop to the Steps. Essie pictured pink birds, pink sky, pink lake, even pink desert roses growing nearby. It would be unforgettable.

'When are they arriving?' Julia asked.

'The day after tomorrow.'

'Where shall we put them up?' She glanced towards her personal tent, and then at the one Essie shared with Ian. 'Yours is the biggest.'

'Frank has his own plane. His idea was to fly in and fly out. Get back to Serengeti before dark.'

'But there won't be time to show him around,' Julia protested.

Ian lifted his chin. 'I convinced him to come earlier in the day. I promised him a flint-knapping demonstration.' He turned to Essie. 'I told him we have Arthur Holland's daughter here.'

'He's heard of Dad?' Essie was surprised. Professor Holland, along with his unique collection of stone tools, was known in academic circles but he was hardly a household name like the Lawrences were.

Ian nodded. 'He actually mentioned the Tasmanian flints. Marlow's not just a rich sponsor. He's an amateur archaeologist. He knows who's who.'

Essie swallowed. She liked the idea of being useful, but didn't want to feel responsible if the man was unimpressed by her knapping skills. Flint could be unpredictable in the way it broke. Striking a worked edge could destroy a nearly completed tool. She didn't want to end up with a failure. She'd be letting down the Lawrences and her father, both at the same time.

'We can lead on from that to a tour of the dig,' Ian continued. 'We have to be careful, though. I've heard he doesn't like to be asked directly for money.'

'Of course, we wouldn't beg anyway,' Julia said. But there was a note of doubt in her voice. So far, the large-scale excavations that had been funded by the Steps' success had failed to produce any significant finds at Magadi. In one of the sites there were some promising undisturbed living floors – buried surfaces containing evidence of occupation – but after an initial discovery of a hominid tooth nothing more had turned up. Grants had petered out and funds were alarmingly low.

Essie's eyes strayed to the empty marmalade jar. Running out of a treasured luxury might not matter, but there were lots of other empty things here at Magadi Camp. Petrol drums, kerosene tins, whole shelves in the storeroom. Even the Indian ink they used to mark numbers on specimens was running out. If nothing changed, they'd soon have to start cutting the already reduced number of local staff. Then the excavation sites and the camp would be almost empty as well.

'There's just one more thing.' Ian looked cautiously at his mother. 'Marlow wants to create a sense of celebration, for the occasion. He'd like us to dress up.'

Julia looked blank. 'What in?'

'Evening wear.'

'He can't be serious,' Julia responded. 'This is a working camp, not a sideshow!'

'I said we would,' Ian stated.

'We could wear our town clothes,' Julia suggested.

'That's not what he wants.'

Essie knew better than to join in a debate between mother and son. While she waited to hear the outcome, she looked down at the three dogs that had slunk in to lie under the table. The mingled bodies formed a patchwork, with the stark black-and-white spotted hides of the two Dalmatians, Rudie and Meg, set against the tawny coat of a hound that belonged in the staff camp.

'I haven't got anything suitable, anyway,' Julia said.

'There's that dress you wore in London.' Ian pointed to a framed black-and-white photograph perched on top of the bookcase in the rear of the tent. The picture had been taken at a royal reception held to mark the discovery of the Steps. It showed a much younger Julia shaking hands with the newly crowned Queen, both women wearing elbow-length white gloves. There was a glimpse of Julia's dress – an elaborate gown in a pale tone, embellished with lace. When Essie had first seen the image she hadn't recognised her tough, no-nonsense mother-in-law. The person in the picture looked elegant and fragile – vulnerable, somehow. Julia would hate to know it, but she reminded Essie of a gazelle.

8

Ian turned to Essie. 'What can we do about you?'

Essie didn't reply straightaway. The fact was, she had a silk evening dress that would suit the occasion perfectly. It was hidden away in her suitcase along with the winter clothes she'd been wearing when she left England. Her father had advised her to pack a formal gown when she'd set off to work in Tanzania. 'White people in Africa love to dress up,' he'd told her. He'd made two expeditions there himself, so he knew what Essie should expect. In the five years she'd spent at Magadi Gorge, however, there had been hardly any trips away from the remote camp – and definitely no dinner parties or dances in Arusha. So Essie had never revealed the dress to her husband. Now, as Ian and Julia waited, she tried to think how to answer without giving away the fact that she'd envisaged a different life here. Ian and Julia might think there was another, frivolous, side to her. On the other hand, she didn't want to be a problem.

'I've got a dress somewhere,' she said vaguely.

'Good,' Ian responded. Essie expected more questions but he turned his attention to the field notebook he'd removed from his pocket. After a brief pause, he spoke again. 'We'll have to stop the digging and concentrate on getting ready.'

Julia raised her eyebrows. Magadi ran on a strict schedule. The local staff as well as the Lawrences worked every day except Sundays. Even during the rainy season, the teams achieved whatever they could.

'There's a lot to do.' Ian swung one arm, taking in their immediate surroundings, and then gestured towards the open doorway with its view to the rest of the camp.

Essie scanned the tent, her gaze passing over the sideboard with the gramophone player; the neat stacks of books, their dust jackets faded in the harsh sun; the Persian carpet that was well worn but swept clean. Kefa worked hard to keep the place presentable. The effort he put into polishing silver, waxing furniture and laundering linen sometimes felt to Essie like a reproach to the Lawrences with their shrinking resources. Even though his official title was 'houseboy', the man was in his sixties. He had been employed by the family, on and off, ever since Julia and her husband, William, first came here, nearly forty years ago. Kefa liked to place on the top of the magazine pile an old *National Geographic* from 1956 with William on the cover, standing proudly at the Steps. The photograph was taken only four years before his death. The magazine had come to symbolise everything the man had achieved. It had to be dusted daily to maintain the glossy shine.

'The place isn't too bad,' Essie ventured.

'It has to look busier,' Ian explained. 'We need to get things out of the store. Fossil eggs. The giraffe skull. Snake skins. Anything interesting. And I want a few of the guest tents erected, nets hung and beds made up, in case we end up giving a tour. We want it to appear as if they've caught us in a slow moment, but we're expecting company.' Ian paced back and forth, making small detours to avoid Tommy, who kept standing in his path.

Essie smiled at her husband. He looked more wide-awake and alive than she'd seen him in years. Then she felt a twist of anxiety. Was he getting carried away? What if Frank Marlow and his wife came here to enjoy their romantic interlude, and then just flew away, never to be heard from again?

On the other side of the table Julia had turned around to peer at a map of Magadi that was pinned on a noticeboard. A grid had been drawn in red pen, dividing the Gorge, and the smaller gullies – called *korongos* in Swahili – into zones.

'We could begin work somewhere completely new,' she said. For someone so practical, she seemed to be getting ahead of herself too.

Ian nodded, following her gaze. 'A fresh start.'

With Tommy dogging his steps, Ian came back to the table. He stood behind Essie, placing his hands on her shoulders. His thumb rested on her neck. The touch sent a warm current through her body. She leaned back against him, feeling the hard mould of his muscles through his shirt. Perhaps their luck really was about to change. There would be more times like this – carefree and bright. Suddenly, Tommy's bony head butted in from the side. Sitting up straight, she pushed him away. She glanced across to Julia, waiting for a critical look.

But the other woman hadn't been watching. She was staring out towards the volcano. The flush of excitement had vanished from her face, but her usual calm expression had not returned. In her eyes was a look of fierce longing. The lines around her mouth and across her brow were drawn tight as if she was in pain. Essie felt uncomfortable, looking on. It was as though Julia's mask had been torn away.

The emotion was too raw to be connected with the Lawrences' quest to solve the puzzle of the human family tree. Essie guessed Julia was thinking about something that was even closer to her heart: the child she had lost.

Ian's little brother, Robbie, had gone missing when he was only four years old. Julia had been doing fieldwork over in the foothills of the mountain. The two boys were playing near her when they'd wandered off and become lost. Their absence had not been noticed for some time, with Julia and her assistant both focused on their work. After a frantic search Ian was located, but he'd become separated from his brother. No sign of Robbie had ever been found. It had taken months after Essie became close to Ian for him to talk about the tragedy. Even then the story had come out in small painful pieces, not all of which made sense. Julia kept up a wall of silence on the topic, as if it gave her a place to hide. The Africans in the camp hardly ever talked about Robbie. If they did, they never used his name. He was *mtoto wa siri*. The hidden child. Visitors to Magadi understood not to mention the lost boy, even though the case was well known; the fruitless search had been covered in newspapers, here in Tanzania and abroad. More than thirty years had passed since Robbie's disappearance, yet his presence – absence – still haunted Magadi Gorge, like the echo of a cry that had never been heard.

Essie understood why Julia would be thinking of Robbie now. Perhaps Ian was too. A grant from the Marlow Trust would mean the Lawrences could continue to live and work here. But if this bid failed, they might well have to leave, cutting off their last link with Robbie. It would also be the end of an extraordinary era. The Lawrences had been researching in the Gorge since the 1930s – during the dry season only, at first; then full-time. After the interruption of the Second World War they'd returned here again. Where the Marlows' visit was concerned, the stakes were high.

As if aware of being observed, Julia turned around. As she did so, Essie saw her take possession of herself again. Feature by feature, like an artist correcting a faulty painting, she rearranged her face. When she spoke, her voice was almost bright.

'Where shall we begin?'

Ian went to sit next to Julia. Frowning with concentration, he ran one hand back through his hair, leaving it standing up in dark tufts. He looked across the table. Caught in the brightening sunlight, his eyes were a piercing blue. 'I'll start with the landing strip. You two deal with things here.'

Julia watched her son intently as he spoke. It seemed to complete her recovery. Essie saw a look of renewed excitement pass between the two. She presumed they were thinking of the days when Magadi Camp was at its peak – when William was alive, with Julia working at his side, and Ian a young graduate already making his own name in their field. At that time, Essie was still a schoolgirl in England, looking forward to university. The thought made her feel like a newcomer all over again. Though it was childish, she wanted to push her way in, like Tommy. She gazed down once more at the dogs under the table. Rudie had moved closer to her chair. Essie watched his spotted chest rising and falling. He'd already begun to pant, his long pink tongue draping onto the worn threads of the rug. The day was fast warming up. A first trickle of sweat moved slowly down her back.

Essie tied up the mosquito net neatly and straightened the pillows. She smoothed the sheets and tucked them in – Ian slept badly and his tossing and turning always left the bed rumpled by morning. Next, she picked up items of clothing and dropped them in the laundry basket. She could have let Kefa deal with the tent, but she still felt it was an invasion of her and Ian's privacy having him do this, regardless of what Julia thought.

Essie had already spent several hours in the Work Hut this morning, helping Julia rearrange the tables and lay out collections of specimens – careful not to separate items that belonged together or to dislodge anything that was in the process of being assembled. Julia was now preparing a 'typical day's find' on a tray. Frank Marlow was very knowledgeable about archaeology, but Julia pointed out that his wife might be completely ignorant, for all they knew. She might be completely uninterested too, Essie thought. But she didn't say this – Julia would find it hard to imagine that anyone could fail to be fascinated by the topic.

Ian was down on the plains, supervising the clearing of bushes that had grown up on the landing strip. The place hadn't been used in years. The Lawrences could no longer afford to fly supplies in to Magadi. Instead they radioed their orders to Arusha and the items were sent to Olduvai Camp on one of the Leakey's regular chartered flights. From there, they were collected by Land Rover. None of the Lawrences took part in the pickups. Their friendship with the Leakeys – which had led to the gift of the two Dalmatian puppies some years ago – had been neglected. Ian pretended the Lawrences were too busy to make the trip to Olduvai, but Essie knew he found the contrast between the camps too humiliating.

After kicking a pair of old sandals out of sight under the bed, Essie crossed to the cupboard. She took out Ian's cream linen suit and his matching shirt. A faint smell of mould clung to them, but she could see no sign of any green-black blemishes. She hung the garments up to air from one of the tent cross-poles, then she took down her suitcase and laid it on the sisal matting. After working open the corroded locks, she lifted the lid. The smell of musty wool and lavender rose up. She stroked her grey jumper with its coloured band of Fair Isle knitting – the one she'd worn since she was a teenager, out collecting with her father. A wave of longing washed over her.

The two had spent so much time together, especially once the family moved from Tasmania to England. Essie had been seven at the time. At first, Arthur had had no choice but to take his young daughter with him on field trips when her mother wasn't well, or if Essie didn't want to spend the day shopping. There was no one else to look after her. But soon the pair had become a team. They were able to communicate without words, one passing over a tool the other needed, or lending a second pair of hands. They even liked the same cheese-and-tomato sandwiches for their picnics. Essie wished she could make a visit home. Or just talk to Arthur on the phone. He was not in good health and she worried about him, living by himself, relying on a part-time housekeeper for support. He wanted Essie to be here at Magadi – he was proud that she'd married into the Lawrence family and was pursuing her career in Tanzania – but she knew he was lonely without her company. Corresponding by mail was frustrating; the time between sending and receiving was so long that news was always out of date. (Reports on world events were slow to filter through, as well; last year, when Neil Armstrong became the first person to set foot on the moon, the Lawrences didn't know about it for months.) Even if the postal service had been more efficient, letters were still a poor replacement for being able to see someone and hug them or even just hear their voice.

Reaching into the corner of the case, Essie's hand hovered over the bundle of orange silk. Letting herself give in to the lure of memories, she closed her eyes. She was back in the kitchen at home, going through her packing list. Her father was nodding as she read out each item. There was a look of anticipation on his face as if he was the one who would be travelling. The next item on the list was the formal dress.

'You don't need to buy a new one,' Arthur said. 'Heaven knows there are enough to choose from here.' A wry smile offset the bitter edge to his voice. 'Come on.'

Essie followed him into the guest room at the end of the hallway. She avoided looking in the direction of the bed – it was too smooth, with just a satin coverlet on the bare mattress. Her eyes skimmed past an empty dressing table balled with dust.

Arthur walked stiffly beside her, crossing to a huge antique wardrobe. It seemed to be crouched there, set on bulbous carved wooden legs that ended in lion's feet. Both doors creaked faintly as he opened them, letting out the smell of new fabric and cardboard shopping bags.

Essie took in the array of dresses – bright cotton prints, pastel chiffons, midnight-blue satin, black lace. It was a jumbled collection revealing no sense of one person's taste, as if Essie's mother had been hunting desperately to find her own style. Most of the garments looked as though they'd barely been used. Some even had their shop labels still attached. Essie scanned the options quickly, choosing by colour and length. She took out an orange silk dress.

'I'll take this,' she said to Arthur. 'It'll fold up to nothing.'

It was one of the new gowns – unworn but for the brief touch of skin on fabric in the changing room at Harrods.

Arthur checked the label. 'Made in France. Fifty-five pounds.' He shook his head helplessly. 'I remember when your mother bought this. It was for a faculty Christmas dinner. When the time came around, of course, I went on my own.'

'At least it'll go to some use now,' Essie said, managing a bright voice.

She hadn't thought, then, that it would be another five years before she had any need for the gown. Luckily, she hadn't changed size. The spare weight she'd once carried had simply turned into muscle.

She held up the dress, shaking it out. The skirt billowed, then fell into soft folds. Here in the tent, far from that room in Cambridge, it seemed to have been set free to become beautiful. Even the dim, green-tinged light of the tent could not dull the glowing orange. When Essie hung it up beside Ian's suit she could imagine how they would both look, all dressed up. She pictured them standing near the Steps, chatting and laughing with their guests. The thought brought a smile to her lips. But then she reminded herself how important the occasion was. How wealthy the Marlows were. How hard it would be to ensure she didn't make the wrong remark at the wrong time, while avoiding being a bore by saying nothing at all.

Essie now wished she could leave the sundowner party to Julia and Ian. Perhaps she could make some kind of excuse – pretend to be unwell. After all, she knew how that was done; for a good part of her life she'd watched the performance played out over and over again. She knew every small detail. How a footstep became heavy and slow. A chair was dragged, not lifted. Then came the crackle of an aspirin packet. Deep breaths that didn't seem to help. A quick lie down in a dimmed bedroom. A headache that grew worse, not better . . .

But Essie was never ill. She never complained or avoided hard tasks. That was why she was good at fieldwork, and why she'd fitted in so well with the Lawrences here at Magadi Gorge. She lifted her head. This was no time to lose her nerve. Crossing to a chest of drawers, she removed a black silk purse. Unzipping the top, she took out a lipstick and mascara, an eye shadow and a powder compact in a tarnished gold case. She carried them over to where a mirror was propped up on an old tea chest, forming a makeshift dressing table. There she laid the items out like instruments ready for surgery. The lipstick, she knew, had broken off; the top was stuck inside the lid. The powder cake had fractured into small pieces. The mascara was half dried out. It would be wise to have a practice run.

She wiped the sweat from her face and smoothed back her hair. Then she rubbed the broken stub of the lipstick over her lips, painting them a deep orange red. She paused to pick off a few dried clumps. She went on to shade her eyelids, darken her lashes and powder her nose and forehead. When she was done, she stared at her reflection. She used to wear make-up for parties when she was at university. But that seemed so long ago – and in such a different world. Standing here in the tent, Essie's face was side-lit, accentuating her features. Her cheekbones appeared more striking, her eyes deeply set. Her sun-bleached hair looked almost white. The make-up added to the effect. The person facing her was like a stranger. Ian and Julia would barely recognise her. Whether that was a good or bad thing, she could not decide.

Essie hung back, letting Ian approach the pool. It was late in the day, but the sun was still hot on her shoulders; the mud beneath her feet felt warm. Reeds tickled her bare calves and a fly buzzed around her head. She eyed the water longingly. Her face had been washed recently – she'd returned to the tent twice during the afternoon to make sure every trace of the make-up was gone – but the rest of her was sticky with sweat.

The pool was one of a whole chain of spring-fed waterholes on the plains below Ol Doinyo Lengai. They looked like miniature versions of the vast Lake Magadi. Some were hot, or so caustic with salt that even a splash on your skin would burn. Others were tepid and brackish. A few were fresh and cold. It all depended on the source of the water.

The Lawrences called their favourite pool the Swimming Bath. It was deep and wide and fringed with soft reeds. The water was a perfect temperature, with no hint of salt. It was an ideal place for a swim – just as long as you knew how to make sure it was safe.

One of the hazards of living close to an active volcano was that carbon dioxide sometimes bubbled up from the ponds. Heavier than oxygen, the odourless, colourless gas accumulated just above water level – right where a swimmer drew their breath. As they took in the oxygen-free air, they would become confused; instead of escaping they stayed where they were and suffocated. The edges of ponds where the gas erupted frequently were strewn with bleached animal bones. Plants growing nearby were sickly yellow or dead. The Africans described such ponds as *mahali pa hewa mbaya* – places of bad air.

It was rare to detect a cloud of gas at the Swimming Bath. In five years of coming here Essie had never seen it happen. But one of the graves at the edge of the camp – simply marked with the name of William's favourite dog, Badger – proved that it was possible. Badger had decided to take a nap in a sheltered hollow not far from where Essie stood, and had never moved again.

Essie watched Ian flick open the top of a silver cigarette lighter, producing a small blue-yellow flame. Bending down, he moved the lighter across the surface of the pool. Essie followed the action, wondering if this would be the day that the tiny light would dwindle and die. But as usual it burned steady and bright.

Ian snapped shut the lighter and tossed it back onto his towel. Even that small movement seemed to contain more energy than usual. Essie knew he was happy with all that had been achieved today. It was he who had suggested they go for a swim, rather than just wash at the camp.

Coming here to the Swimming Bath gave her and Ian some precious time on their own. Julia preferred to visit a small spring closer to the camp if she wanted a dip. Essie didn't know if she kept her distance in order to give her son and his wife some privacy, or if she felt uncomfortable being at close quarters when they were all half-undressed. It had been different back when there were other Europeans at the camp, two years ago. Julia had happily joined the groups of visitors and volunteers that came here. But ever since the three Lawrences had found themselves alone, aside from the African staff, every dynamic between them had become more intense.

Ian removed his watch, laying it carefully on his towel. It was a Rolex that had belonged to his father – a gift from the manufacturers in recognition of the achievements at Magadi Gorge. The face was cracked, the time hard to read, but the heirloom was still Ian's most precious possession.

Ian adjusted his swimming trunks and then plunged into the pool, sending waves lapping to the edge, ruffling the reeds. He sighed with pleasure as he floated on his back. His body was part brown, part white, the boundaries marked by his work clothes: an open-necked shirt, shorts and long socks. Essie watched him for a moment, then waded in to join him.

'I wonder how the Leakeys are doing,' Ian said happily. It was a standing joke. Residents of Olduvai Camp relied for water on a single muddy spring shared with a colony of hippos. Their laundry was stained red-brown and personal washing was limited to sponge baths. The boundless supply of fresh water was the one luxury the Lawrences enjoyed that those at the Leakeys' camp envied.

'Poor things,' Essie said. 'It can't have been easy, scrubbing up for a visit from Mr Marlow.' She laughed as she pushed herself away from the edge, ducking underwater, her hair streaming out behind her. She surfaced near Ian, wiping the water from her face.

The two stood shoulder-deep in the blue-green pool. Ian put his hands on Essie's hips, running them down over the edge of her costume onto her thighs. Then he pulled her closer, cradling her breasts against his chest. Their legs entwined, skin gliding over skin, cloaked in water that felt like silk. Essie looked into his eyes as he slid his hands between her legs. A shiver of desire ran through her. She wished they could go straight back to the camp and disappear into the tent, without questions being asked. It was a safe time of the month for her. They wouldn't have to be too careful.

Ian kissed her gently. She tasted salty sweat, still lingering on his mouth. After a brief time he pulled away, scanning their surroundings. Essie followed his gaze. The only living beings in view were waterbirds skulking in the reeds, but she knew as well as he did that at any time a human shape could emerge without warning from the background. The Maasai didn't really accept the boundaries of the Archaeological Reserve – herders often trespassed here. It was important that the Lawrences, as the people in charge of Magadi, protected their reputation. In African society public displays of affection were not acceptable. Kissing was thought completely bizarre.

'Come on,' Ian said. 'Let's swim. We have to get back for supper on time.' He smiled. 'I told Baraka we were celebrating. He's going to use the last of the Christmas hamper.'

Essie looked at him in surprise. They always kept some imported treats to celebrate the end of the Long Dry – and that was still many months away. The cook would disapprove of the break with tradition; he had been working for the Lawrences even longer than Kefa. Essie pictured him taking down the tins that were displayed on the top shelf of the bookcase in the Dining Tent. If he really opened them all tonight, they'd be having smoked fillets of herring for entrée followed by a main course of Virginia ham and asparagus. Afterwards there would be plum pudding. Assuming the description on the tin was accurate, it would be laced with brandy and dotted with plump cherries. If the Maasai women had brought fresh eggs and milk today, there would be custard too. The meal would be a welcome change from boiled rice and bean stew. But even as Essie's mouth was watering, she felt uneasy again. An African proverb came to her – *Don't make the cradle skin before the baby is born* – the local version of not counting chickens before they hatch. It was out of character for Ian not to be more cautious. He was a scientist, after all; trained to take things step by step. And he was so used to disappointment now that he normally didn't believe in anything until the proof was in front of him.

It just showed, Essie thought, as she breaststroked across the pool, that when you wanted something badly enough, your judgement could not be trusted.

TWO

A hot wind blew, stirring the dust and bending the yellow grass that bordered the steep gully. It was well past midday now, and too hot to be out walking, let alone climbing. A strand of loose hair stuck to Essie's face. She wiped it away, smearing gritty sweat.

From behind her came the sound of Tommy's hooves scrabbling on loose gravel. She usually let him come with her to the work sites and today of all days she didn't want him causing trouble back at the camp. She glanced over her shoulder to check his progress. He bleated anxiously, his eyes fixed on her as if afraid she might disappear.

'Come on,' she said encouragingly. 'There's a good boy.'

Behind the gazelle came Simon, her African assistant. He was climbing nimbly, binoculars swinging from his neck. A quiver spiked with arrows was slung across his back, looking out of place next to his khaki shirt. He kept peering up over the sides of the gully, on the lookout for movement in the bushes. Rudie and Meg were off hunting as well. Essie had seen the dogs streaking away into the distance, noses to the ground. How they ever stalked prey unnoticed, with such startling spotted coats, she never understood. With their lean bodies and long legs, they looked like some strange form of leopard. At least the distinctive dogs were well known in the area and wouldn't be mistaken for something wild.

Today, both Simon and the dogs would probably be out of luck. Ian would be disappointed; he was hoping to have some small game animal on hand so that he could show the visitors when they came tomorrow how stone tools could cut hide and flesh while human teeth were useless. With the coming of the dry season, though, most of the grazing animals and the predators that followed them had moved north. Many of the birds had become scarce too. The land had a quiet, abandoned feeling. The heat, shimmering in the air, seemed to vibrate in the emptiness.

Reaching the top of the gully, Essie climbed out onto flatter ground. As she stood up, she shaded her eyes with her hand. The place they called the 'flint factory' was visible now: a scattering of darker stones and, further on, the rocky outcrop from where they'd all been mined. After waiting for Tommy to catch up, Essie set off towards it.

With each step she studied the ground, her gaze moving steadily from side to side. The Long Rains had ended a few weeks ago, which meant this was the best time for a chance discovery. Streams of water running between the steep banks of the *korongos* sometimes exposed very old fossils. Even with all the digging that money could buy, and the best-trained workers, the truth was that many of the world's important discoveries had been found by accident. It was a frustration to researchers as it was impossible to plan and budget on the basis of luck.

Essie had to remind herself to blink, resting her eyes. It was hard not to stare for too long, when you knew that one more moment of looking could change everything. She imagined finding something important – right now. Nothing as outlandish as a whole skeleton;

her dream had to be practical. When millions of years were involved, or even tens of thousands, the most likely remains were those of the toughest part of the body: the skull. Essie pictured herself picking up a fragment of a cranium, or a piece of an eye socket or brow ridge. Something that gave solid clues to what the whole head would have been like. She'd mark the spot with a cairn, then wrap up the treasure and slip it into her pocket. Tomorrow, while Frank Marlow was at the Steps, she'd casually bring it out. The fantasy ran on. Frank would be so impressed that he'd take out his chequebook, then and there. Everyone would know that it had been Essie's find that had saved Magadi. This gully where she now stood would be named after her: *Essie Lawrence Korongo*. All the results of the work that would ensue here – every fossil and artefact that was found – would bear her initials . . .

Reaching the scattered flint, Essie let go of her daydream. She glanced across the sharp flakes and stone tools that lay among naturally broken pebbles. Here and there she could see lumps of uncut flint that would be perfect for her knapping demonstration. But she walked past them towards the outcrop. There she pulled a small pick from her pocket, balancing its weight in her hand. She preferred to mine her own stones. There would be nothing wrong with her collecting the ones lying here on the surface; the flint factory had already been thoroughly documented. William had published two papers about it. But Essie still felt uneasy taking anything from the site. The nodules of flint had been chipped from the surrounding sediments with stone tools more than one-and-a-half million years ago. She couldn't forget that this work had been done by creatures who were almost like her. She kept visualising them, with their hands more ape than human, but their eyes more human than ape. Picking up their flints felt like stealing. Ian would shake his head at such an idea. Essie could picture his tolerant smile – one that would make her feel much younger than him, even though their age gap was only a little over ten years. Julia would just give her daughter-in-law a blank look, as if such an idea were beyond comprehension.

It didn't take Essie long to gather a good collection of flints. The nodules were like large heavy potatoes coated in earth, giving no hint of the fine-grained grey stone concealed inside. Tommy ambled up to her as she stashed them away in her bag. She was eager to get back to camp now that her mission was accomplished. Hopefully, some of the frenzy of activity had died down – after all, they still had half of tomorrow to finalise the preparations. There could even be time for another afternoon swim. Essie felt a wave of pleasure when she pictured herself and Ian immersed, again, in the pool – the intimacy of their bodies meeting underwater.

Shouldering her bag, Essie was about to turn back to the gully when she noticed Tommy suddenly freeze. At the same moment, she felt an odd sense that she was being watched. A prickle of fear ran up her spine. Glancing behind her, she saw that Simon was still out of sight, presumably stalking game. The dogs were not around either. Her pulse quickened as she looked about her. She remembered what Simon had taught her.

You never see the leopard that kills you.

She grasped Tommy's collar and pulled him close. Her hand moved to her prospecting pick, even though she knew it would be of little possible use.

Loose stones and a scattering of earth fell down the cliff face in front of her.

Slowly she raised her eyes.

Never run from a predator.

Bare dusty feet were planted on the rocky ledge above. The lean body of a man stood over her. A tall bow rose behind his head, curving against the sky. His skin, leathery with age, was so dark it was almost pure black. He wore a baboon pelt, complete with tail and limbs, fashioned into a crude waistcoat. For a second, Essie saw the man and the fur as one: a human with a long tail and an extra pair of hairy arms. He carried a dead gazelle slung over his shoulder. Essie glanced from its two spiralled horns, pointing downwards, to the glazed eyes crusted with flies.

The tribesman looked from Tommy to Essie, and back. His eyes narrowed. Essie's hand tightened on Tommy's blue collar.

'*Nyama huyu ni mali yangu*,' she said firmly. This animal belongs to me.

The man's attention shifted again to her. His dark eyes were faintly clouded, yet his focus was intense. He studied her as if he'd never seen anything like her before.

Essie gave him a nervous smile, observing him as he continued to stare at her. She could tell he was not a Bantu villager far from home or a Maasai herdsman wandering, for some reason, without his cows. He was very different to any of the Africans she'd met at Magadi. Aside from the baboon pelt, he wore a rawhide loincloth. Around his neck were strings of dried seeds. There was no sign that he had any connection with the modern world. Essie scanned the old man's face, noting the broad nose, the high cheekbones. He was short but had a well-developed upper body. He could have come straight from an anthropological textbook about East Africa's only surviving tribe of hunter-gatherers. The Hadza.

In her five years at Magadi, Essie had never encountered a single member of this tribe, even though she knew groups of them moved around the area. They had a reputation for being invisible until they chose to be seen. The hunters were usually just shadows glimpsed in the bush. The women and children, out collecting plants, seeds and fruit, were rarely seen at all. Anthropologists were always keen to make contact with them. But the Hadza could not be lured by gifts. They had no interest in European possessions. There was nothing they wanted, except to be left alone – which made this hunter's keen interest in Essie strange and unsettling.

'*Hujambo kaka.*' Hello, my brother. Essie offered the belated greeting, trying to sound relaxed. The Hadza had their own language, but she hoped this man might at least know a bit of Swahili.

The hunter didn't answer. Now he was looking at Tommy again. It was as if he recognised something about the connection between the woman and her pet – and whatever he saw was of more than idle interest to him. In spite of his age he looked fit and strong. Essie glanced over her shoulder uneasily, to see if Simon had appeared. She didn't like to shout for him. If there was reason for her to be afraid, it would only make her look weak. If not, she'd seem hysterical and rude.

In the gully below, nothing moved. Tommy pressed up against her, sheltering behind her legs. When Essie turned back to the rock ledge, she saw that a second hunter was approaching. He leapt from boulder to boulder as easily as if he were running across an open field. In one hand he held a large hare, his fingers wrapped around its neck. The long furry legs swung from side to side.

Very soon, he too was staring down at Essie. He had ritual scars – a single short slash on each of his cheeks. Instead of a baboon pelt, he wore the spotted coat of a serval cat. He was taller than his companion, and much younger, but his skin was the same deep black.

28

There was silence, broken only by the hum of crickets in the bushes. Then the two men began talking in low voices. Essie listened to the distinctive sounds of their language – the tongue-clicking she'd read about. It gave the impression they were talking in a secret code.

Their voices rose as they began arguing. Whatever issue was at stake clearly concerned Essie. They never took their eyes from her. She felt like an animal caught in the crosshairs of a riflescope.

Eventually the men seemed to reach a consensus. The older one waved his arm towards Essie, then looked away to the east, beyond the flint factory. It was clear they wanted her to follow them.

Essie shook her head firmly but the men's gestures were only repeated. Speaking in Swahili, in case the second hunter might know the language, she explained that she could not come with them. She had to return to her home. She had lots of hard work to do. Her husband was waiting for her.

The older hunter spoke directly to Essie. She didn't need to understand his words; the urgency was obvious. She wondered if there had been an accident. If so, there wouldn't be much she could do to help. She didn't have a first-aid kit with her – not even the bandages and antiseptic she usually took to a work site. There was just a collecting bag, her tools, a notebook and a bottle of water.

'*Pole*,' she said. I am sorry. Then she backed away, dragging Tommy by his collar. The man holding the hare put his free hand on the ground, preparing to swing himself down after her.

Essie froze, unsure what to do. At that moment she heard the sound of boots crunching over dry earth, lower down in the *korongo*. Exhaling with relief, she turned to see Simon striding up towards her, the Dalmatians at his heels. Even at a distance Essie could see the ridge of raised hairs on Rudie's back. He and Meg both had their heads up, sniffing the air.

The Hadza men seemed as glad to see Simon as she was. They watched his approach with a studied stillness that somehow conveyed intense impatience. When Simon came near, the older hunter began calling out in the Hadza tongue. Simon ignored him, speaking instead to Essie.

'Are you all right? What is happening?' He used English, as he always did with Essie. The young man was ambitious and knew that a good grasp of the language was the key to promotion.

'I don't know. They want me to go with them. It seems urgent.' Essie checked her watch. It was now almost midafternoon. 'I said we had to get back. But they don't understand Swahili.'

Simon nodded, as if this was no surprise to him. 'They are *Hadza pori*,' he stated. Wild Hadza.

The hunters continued to talk to him – first one, then the other. Their stubborn insistence gave way to what appeared to be distress. Essie looked at Simon. A frown marked his brow. Slowly it came to her that he was listening to the hunters – and making sense of their words.

Simon glanced at Essie, then lowered his gaze. For a moment he seemed torn. Then he replied in the Hadza language, speaking quietly, as if ashamed of his own words. The clicking joined naturally with the unusual vowels. Essie listened in surprise. It sounded like a skill that would be almost impossible to learn, if you hadn't been born to it.

It dawned on her, then, why Simon had always seemed to be a loner, over at the workers' camp. It wasn't because he spent his spare time reading textbooks instead of sitting at the fireside with the others. Or because he flaunted his fashionable tastes by choosing not to go barefoot around the camp after removing his work boots, instead changing into a pair of blue winklepickers he'd bought in Arusha. The truth was that Simon was isolated because he was a Hadza. The hunter-gatherers might be of academic interest to Europeans, but to other Africans they were primitive. It occurred to Essie that his tribal background was also the reason why Simon had ended up being her assistant. Her work held less status than that of Ian and Julia. She and her assistant were well matched: a newcomer and an outsider; both second-class.

Simon began arguing with the hunters, raising his voice indignantly. He turned to Essie. 'They won't tell me why we must go with them. Yet they insist.'

'Tell them to come back with us. Ian will help them.'

Simon shook his head. 'They are only interested in you.' He sounded as mystified as Essie.

'Where do they want to take me?'

'*Pango ya picha*,' Simon replied.

'The cave of pictures . . .' Essie frowned. Why would they want her to go there? She knew the place well. The cave study was the project that had brought her to Magadi in the first place. She'd once spent weeks at a time at the shelter, tracing the rock art with crayon on cellophane, and taking photographs.

'They have made a camp there,' Simon added.

Essie shared a look with him. Most people thought the Hadza were the descendants of the very people who'd made the cave paintings thousands of years ago. It was extraordinary to think that now, in the twentieth century, the tribespeople were there again, in that same cave – still living the same lifestyle. Normally, Essie would jump at the chance to see such a scene. Any researcher would. But she didn't like not knowing why she – in particular – was wanted there.

She whistled for the dogs. Julia had trained them well. They bounded to her side. Essie rested her hand on Rudie's head. As he picked up her anxiety, a low growl buzzed in his throat. Essie registered the men's long hunting knives, sheathed at their waists, and the quivers full of arrows. The weapons definitely looked daunting, but she didn't imagine the hunters would really use them against her and Simon, or even their pets. In Tanzania, Europeans – as anyone fair-skinned was called – were almost always treated with respect. And unlike the Barabaig and some of the Maasai, the Hadza didn't have a reputation for being aggressive. Essie decided she would simply ask Simon to say firmly but politely that she was going home.

As if reading her mind, the old man suddenly knelt down, moving his face closer to hers. She could see the tracery of fine lines on his skin and a dusting of ash blending with the grey in his hair. He began talking to her in a low voice. The words – unintelligible, yet potent – were like a spell.

'He is asking you with his whole heart.' Simon's words came to her from behind.

Essie felt herself drawn to the hunter, caught up in his emotion. She nodded slowly. Scooping Tommy into her arms, she hoisted him up towards the younger hunter, who quickly tucked the dead hare into his leather belt in order to free both hands. Then she raised one arm to the other man, waiting to be helped onto the ledge. A rough-skinned palm closed over her hand. She was lifted easily, as if she weighed nothing. The hunter's limbs were all muscle and bone, with barely a layer of flesh, just sinew and veins. As the man hauled her up beside him, Essie breathed his smell of wood smoke and tobacco.

'Nandamara,' the older man said, pointing at himself. He gestured to his companion. 'Dafi.'

Essie told them her name in response. They both repeated it, stretching out the first syllable the way all the other Africans did.

Barely waiting for Simon to join them, the two Hadza marched her off in the direction of the cave. Essie eyed the distance anxiously. She told herself that if Ian were here, he'd have made the same decision. Whatever it was that the Hadza wanted, he would deal with as best he could. Meanwhile, he'd be planning to make the most of every moment of this encounter. He'd be filling his notebook, using Simon to ask questions as he documented these unique people who were seen as a link between the present and prehistory – the living and the long, long dead.

The walk to the cave was easy, covering ground that was mostly flat. There was a path made by game heading to the plains to drink. Nandamara led the way followed by Simon, Essie, Tommy and the dogs. Dafi walked behind, presumably to make sure no one decided to stop or change course. Before long, another rocky outcrop came into view. Essie felt a strong sense of recognition: she knew the cave was at its base. She hadn't been here for at least a year but every detail of the location was marked in her memory. When she'd been doing the cave project, she was new to Magadi. She wanted to get a grasp of the area around the Gorge as quickly as possible, though she knew she'd never match Ian and Julia's intimate knowledge of the place. Instead of blindly following Simon, she'd stopped at regular intervals to refer to the geological survey map, comparing the terrain to the contour lines.

Now, as she walked, she was reminded of all the times she'd arrived here in the fresh air of early morning, eager to begin work. She could almost feel the waxy crayon in her hand and the rungs of the ladder pressing into the soles of her feet; she could smell the dew-damp earth. She knew every one of the paintings as intimately as if she'd been the one who'd ground up the ochre and clay and created the pictures with a chewed-stick brush. She could have drawn the main image from memory – the group of strange tall figures dancing with long sticks. The heads were made up of radiating lines that were thought to be elaborate hats or wigs. There was one small child in among the dancers, looking vulnerable surrounded by the towering legs and sticks. Essie had had to carve a fine point on her crayon to capture the miniature shape.

It occurred to Essie, then, that the purpose of her being taken to the cave might have something to do with her work on the site. She knew researchers often ran into problems with local people, even ones whose connection with an area was so old it was lost in time. If there was some issue with the Hadza, then it was wise of Essie to have agreed to come. It was her project; her responsibility. But when she thought of the older hunter's face, the look in his eyes, she felt there must be something more personal at stake.

As they neared the outcrop, Dafi ran ahead. Peering past Nandamara's shoulder, as they rounded a thicket of bushes, Essie saw the rock shelter. Some of the paintings were visible from here. Smoke curled up over the lip of the roof in a wispy grey cloud. There was a broad rock platform, like a stage, in front of the cave entrance.

At first, the figures gathered there blended with the ochre and brown hues of the stone. But as Essie came nearer, the details of clothes, bodies, bows and animal skins emerged. It was easy to imagine these Hadza were the descendants of the artists whose paintings, in similar tones, formed the backdrop to this scene. The group of people was not large – maybe twenty to thirty. Whatever the hunter had hurried on to tell them, it had grabbed their attention. Every eye was fixed on the arrival of the two strangers. Essie might have been viewing a frieze, with people captured unmoving in the midst of their activities. She saw a hunter's hand poised over the shaft of an arrow, binding a feather into place. An old man squatting on skinny legs, a pipe in his hand. A woman on her knees beside a grinding stone, a wreath of red and yellow bead necklaces hanging between her breasts. Children, naked but for leather thongs around their waists, were gazing at Essie with wide eyes. One of them, a boy, was daubed with white clay, his eye sockets forming dark holes in his face. He held a child-sized bow in his hand.

As Essie reached the Hadza she smiled a greeting. The only movement her arrival provoked came from a yellow-eyed dog that took a few steps towards her. Its upper lip curled back, exposing sharp teeth. Dafi made a noise in his throat and the dog dropped to its haunches. Essie checked for Rudie. He was right behind her, standing on full alert. Meg was next to him, hovering protectively over Tommy.

Essie scanned the far side of the platform, still looking for some clue as to why she was here. A young woman sat at the edge of the group, breastfeeding her baby. Not far away, another woman suckled a toddler. The little boy held his mother's breast as he fed, his chubby fingers pressing into the soft flesh. Nearby, Essie caught sight of a teenage boy with a hand that had been badly burned. The skin had contracted while healing, curving the fingers into a claw. Aside from him, though, Essie thought everyone looked healthy and well fed. There was no sign that anything was wrong.

Essie turned around, seeking the man who'd summoned her so urgently. He was already leading the way through the middle of the group, beckoning her across to where the young woman was feeding her baby. When he bent down, Essie thought he was going to pick up the child but instead he gathered up a bundle of soft hide edged with grey fur – a piece of a baboon pelt.

As he carried it towards Essie she saw a tiny hand reach out, dark brown fingers unfurling to form a star. There was a glimpse of tight-curled hair. The fur wrap fell partly open, revealing more of the baby. It was a girl, long-limbed and round-bellied. She was naked but for a string of white beads around her neck. Her dark skin was smooth and perfect; shiny with some kind of oil. The closed eyelids were fringed with thick lashes.

Nandamara looked down at the baby as he spoke.

'This is the child of my daughter,' Simon translated. 'As you see, she is too young to have a name.'

Nandamara offered the baby to Essie to hold. She smiled politely but shook her head. The man's action took her by surprise. During her years of working at the Gorge she'd met plenty of Maasai mothers, and they never passed their babies over to Europeans. They probably knew the gesture would be rejected. Aside from the Mission doctors and nurses, Europeans were always wary of dirt and disease when it came to cuddling babies. Essie felt the same way. And the truth was, even back in England she normally avoided holding babies – they looked too fragile; too easy to drop. She kept her arms by her sides. But Nandamara pushed the fur-wrapped bundle against her chest. Her hands came up automatically to prevent it falling.

Essie held the baby stiffly, away from her body. In the transfer, the fur had all but dropped away, leaving the bare bottom exposed. Essie pulled the covering back into place. She didn't want to have to walk home doused in urine, or worse; Julia would be the first to notice the smell. She looked to Nandamara, waiting to at last find out why she was actually here.

The hunter spoke to Simon again, but kept his gaze locked on Essie's face. Simon's voice faltered as he translated.

'My daughter did not survive the day of this baby's birth. Her blood came out of her, like a stream. Within a short time, her life was gone.'

Nandamara was silent for a moment, pressing one hand over his eyes.

Essie bit her lip. It was hard to watch an old man fighting tears. 'I am very sorry.'

Nandamara pointed at the woman feeding the other baby. 'Giga has kept her alive since that time. Two moons have come and gone. But now her own child is becoming hungry. It is the same with the other mothers. The dry season is here. There are hardly any berries for us to eat; all the big animals are leaving. We have to move north. Every day we will be walking.' He gestured at the baby. 'She will surely die.'

Essie stared at him. 'What do you mean?'

'The mothers must put their own babies first.'

As she tried to absorb the grim logic of these words, Essie looked questioningly at Simon.

He nodded slowly. 'If two babies become thin, then they are both in danger. It is a hard situation for people like these wild Hadza.' He turned to Nandamara. 'This man loves his granddaughter. They have tried their best.'

Essie looked down at the baby nestled against her chest. The child stirred, making little sucking movements with her pursed lips. There was a dribble of milk in the corner of her mouth.

Essie shifted her gaze back to Nandamara. He was holding a discussion with Simon now. They seemed to be communicating easily. She wondered if the two had ever met before, or if they were relatives. She had no idea how the Hadza groupings worked. She also knew very little about Simon's home or family. He avoided discussing such topics – focusing instead on what he hoped to make of himself in the new United Republic of Tanzania. Eventually, Nandamara stopped talking. He turned to Essie. She seized the moment to offer the baby back, but the man stepped away.

Essie felt a spike of alarm. She sensed she was being drawn into a situation she would find hard to control. 'Here, take her.'

Simon cleared his throat. 'He wants you to look after her.'

Essie's mouth opened but she didn't speak – the suggestion was too outlandish.

'They know you can.' Simon looked towards Tommy, who was now stripping leaves from a bush at the edge of the platform. 'You are the mother of this animal.'

Essie stared blankly at the gazelle. Slowly she grasped the meaning of Nandamara's words. Someone in this group must have seen her feeding Tommy at one of the digging sites. From the beginning she'd taken the baby gazelle with her to the *korongos* each day. Originally it was to prove to Julia that his presence wasn't affecting her ability to work. Then she found she enjoyed having Tommy trailing after her. The sight of an animal being bottle-fed had caused great interest among the Maasai. They would edge close, watching Tommy suck on the teat. They found the scene endlessly amusing. Whichever Hadza hunter had witnessed the spectacle would have shared his tale of the madness of Europeans when he returned to the camp. And today, when Nandamara had chanced on Essie and Tommy at the flint factory, he had remembered it.

Essie scanned the watching faces. Even the children were motionless, waiting for her reaction. The woman, Giga, who had been feeding two babies, looked up at her. With one arm she made a gesture that seemed to confirm what Simon had said: that she'd done what she could. She had no more to offer. Essie understood now why Nandamara and Dafi had refused to tell her the reason why she had to accompany them. They knew that here, with the baby in her arms, and this young foster mother looking on, it would be difficult for her to refuse to help. She felt a sharp anger – directed both at herself and Simon. How had they let this happen?

'Look, I want to help,' she said finally. 'But this is a baby. You can't just give her away.'

'That is not the plan,' Simon explained. 'These Hadza will return with the Short Rains. Then you will give her back to them. At that time there will be plenty of food around. Giga will be able to feed her again.'

'But that's in . . . October. Four months!'

Nandamara continued speaking, waving his hands to underline his words. Essie didn't even want to know what he was saying. She turned to Simon. 'You'll have to make him understand. It's a crazy idea. These people don't even know me.'

'They just want to save the child.'

Essie thought quickly. 'There must be another way . . .' As soon as she'd spoken, she regretted it. She'd opened herself to dialogue about the problem. Now she was involved.

'Where is the father?' she asked – but she was just playing for time. What difference did it make?

Nandamara shrugged. 'Far away.'

Essie looked down at the ground. A beetle walked between her boots, leaving a trail of tiny prints in the soft earth. The baby could not stay at Magadi Camp – that was obvious.

'There's a place in Arusha that would take her. An orphanage. Ian could contact the Mission.' As Essie said her husband's name she felt a surge of apprehension. She felt sure he'd be handling this situation differently.

Simon didn't give an interpretation straightaway. Essie assumed he was struggling to find the right words to describe an orphanage. A big house where children from different tribes were all living together, cared for by white women, until they could be given to strangers, never to be seen again?

However it was that Simon eventually managed to describe the institution, a wave of shock spread through the crowd. Giga reached towards Nandamara, her face torn with concern. The old man responded to Simon with a look of outrage and a stream of vehement words.

When Simon translated, he spoke firmly and clearly. 'The child must not be taken away, even for one moment. You have to look after her at your camp, like you did that animal baby. She must stay here in this place.' He pointed in the direction of Ol Doinyo Lengai. The volcano was known by the Maasai as the Mountain of God. The dwelling place of Lengai. The peak was clear of cloud today; a thick tendril of dark smoke reached into the blue sky. It was like proof that the mountain was alive, a presence looking over them. 'You have to promise not to let her go.'

Essie could understand their fears. Arusha was far away. The Hadza had probably never seen a city, but they must have watched vehicles disappearing into the distance, or a plane passing over and vanishing beyond the horizon. No wonder they didn't like the idea. And if Essie were honest, she had reservations too. Could she – or anyone – guarantee that the baby would be handed back when the Hadza returned? That nothing could go wrong? She had to accept their concerns.

She must have nodded to herself, while she was thinking. She didn't even realise she'd done it until a smile broke across Nandamara's face. It was like a beam of light that travelled from face to face around the wider group. Dafi, the young hunter, began to sing, his body moving in time to his words. The clicks in his speech were a percussion instrument following the rhythm of his dance.

Soon all the Hadza were on their feet, joining in. Only the skinny old man remained kneeling, coughing as he drew on his pipe. The people surrounded Essie and the baby. The men stood barely eye to eye with her; the women were shorter. In their midst she felt even taller than she really was. Over their shoulders, she could see the dancing figures in the paintings. They seemed to mirror one another, as if past and present were one.

As the singing wrapped around her, Essie felt herself being caught up in their world. The baby, nestling against her, was at home in her arms. Breathing in her milky smell, she experienced a strange pull of emotion as if some deep part of her memory was being awakened.

She bent her head, letting the beat of the song flow through her. The land, the trees, the watching birds, all seemed a part of it. She felt like a swimmer poised on the edge of a diving board, ready to fall.

A lock of hair that had escaped from her rough ponytail fell forward. The straight, blonde strand came to rest on the baby's black curls. The contrast – as extreme as that between noon and midnight – pulled Essie back to reality. She looked up, with a sense of rising panic. What did she think she was doing? She had to put a stop to the madness.

But as she stared around her, she saw that it was too late. A transaction had taken place. The baby was in her care. The fact that Essie had never meant to agree to the deal was of no interest to anyone.

THREE

Essie stood motionless while Nandamara tied a leather sling across her shoulders. When it was in place he settled the baby inside, still wrapped in the fur. She remained deeply asleep, her body resting limply against Essie's hip. Giga hovered nearby; as soon as the old man stepped back she began talking, an urgent tone in her voice.

'The baby has just been fed.' Simon passed on the translation. 'So she will now have a long sleep. This time should be used for the journey.'

Giga waited for Essie to nod, before continuing. She explained that because there had been two infants for her to care for, this one was not used to being suckled constantly. But that did not mean she could just be left alone. Between feeds her grandfather always carried her around if he was in the camp. When he went hunting he gave her to one of the older children. Sometimes the baby was placed on the ground to sleep, if someone was right beside her. When she awoke, she was picked up straightaway.

'That is what you must do,' Giga instructed.

Essie nodded again, even though she couldn't see how such a scenario could possibly be continued at the camp. With salaries for workers under pressure, they could hardly hire a nanny to carry the baby around, and everyone else would be too busy. The baby would have to adjust to some new ways.

'She is always happy,' Giga added. 'Everyone loves her.' She smiled encouragingly.

Essie saw the same look replicated by all the other Hadza. It crossed her mind that no one would be likely to say if they were handing her a difficult baby. Back in England, Essie had heard women talking about croup, colic, teething pain . . . There was so much that could go wrong. And babies were such hard work. Essie's mother had made that clear enough. She'd said it was the reason she'd only had one. Essie felt panic breaking over her again. She turned to Simon.

'I don't know how to look after her. You have to tell them – I'm not a mother.'

When Simon conveyed her words there were exclamations of surprise, quickly followed by looks of frank pity. A man said something, which was met with obvious widespread agreement.

'What did he say?' Essie asked.

Simon looked awkward. 'He suggests that you get another husband. It's what they would do.' He shook his head. 'I told you, they are wild Hadza.'

Essie let out a brief, shocked laugh. 'They don't understand. It's something we've chosen – not to have a family.'

'I cannot translate that,' Simon said. 'It is too complicated.'

Essie sighed. 'It doesn't matter, anyway. Just explain to them . . .' She turned to address Giga and Nandamara directly. 'I don't know how to care for a baby.'

Giga must have picked up her meaning without needing Simon's help. She pointed at Tommy, as if feeding an orphaned animal were the same as caring for a small human. Essie remembered how she'd struggled, at first, to get Tommy to feed, and the satisfaction she'd felt as she watched the creature grow healthy and strong. For a moment, Essie was swept up in Giga's confidence. Then she remembered how desperate the situation was for this baby. Essie offered the only chance for her survival. These people were clinging to a lifeline and were not about to ask if it was sound and strong.

As Essie stood in front of Giga, paralysed by shock and indecision, she could feel the warmth of the little body resting against hers. Glancing down, she saw a fly settle on the edge of the sling and begin creeping down inside. She swatted it away, then left her hand there, on guard against its return.

She became aware that a pair of teenage girls had edged close to her. They were both naked but for a slip of leather wrapped low over their hips. Their half-formed breasts were adorned with strings of beads. They studied Essie intently, taking in every detail – from her blonde hair right down to her feet. One reached out to pick at a bootlace. The other leaned forward to examine Essie's watch. A vast gulf, in almost every aspect of life, separated these Hadza girls from Essie. Yet the fact that the baby – probably a relative of theirs – had been put in Essie's care formed a connection that drew them together. The usual boundaries that would have kept them apart melted away. The potency of the moment seemed to be felt by everyone. There was complete stillness in the air, as if the normal rhythms of life had been suspended to let this interlude linger.

Then Giga broke the quiet. 'You must go, while she sleeps,' she urged. Bending to peer into the sling, she made a gentle cooing sound like a birdsong. As she stepped away, her lips were pressed together. She nestled her own baby's head into the crook of her neck as if seeking comfort. Nandamara's face was impassive as he took his final look at his granddaughter, but there was a faint shimmer in his cloudy eyes.

Essie said her farewell in Swahili, wanting to show that she was not a complete outsider in this land. Simon translated, turning her words into the Hadza blend of throaty vowels and clicks.

'*Kwaheri. Tutaonana.*' Goodbye. We will see one another again.

A murmur of agreement rose from the Hadza. Essie automatically added the phrase most Africans used to complete their leave-taking, regardless of whether they were Muslims, Christians or followers of older beliefs: '*Mungu akipenda.*' If God wills it.

Simon didn't translate immediately. He seemed to be hunting for the correct words. When he finally spoke, he was looking at the mountain. He talked, then, for so long that Essie wondered what he was saying. She began to wish she hadn't mentioned God. Her father – a Darwinian and an evolutionist – had raised her as an atheist. Simon was struggling to convey something she didn't even believe in.

When the speech was over, Nandamara backed off a little and stood looking down at the ground. Simon picked up the bag of flints. Sensing that it was time to move, the dogs appeared at Essie's side. They both sniffed cautiously, their snouts level with the sling. Essie gave them a warning stare in case they mistook the baby for some kind of prey. Rudie must have been scrapping with one of the Hadza hounds; his left ear was torn, blood staining the white background to his smudgy black spots. Meg was trying to lick the red away, but the other dog kept moving around. Tommy skipped over, still chewing a mouthful of leaves. Essie nodded to Simon. They were ready to depart.

As Essie walked away, she kept her gaze fixed ahead. But she could feel the watchful eyes of the Hadza trained on her back – it was like a cord stretching behind her. She wasn't sure if she felt relieved by the lengthening distance, or afraid.

The journey back to the camp was mostly downhill. Essie picked her way cautiously over patches of loose gravel. Though Nandamara had knotted the sling with great care, she was afraid to trust it; she kept one arm over the small body that swung gently at her side.

As she stepped from rock to rock or bent over to steady herself with her free hand, she tried to avoid jolting the sleeping child. The last thing she needed was for her to wake up too soon and want to be fed. Essie remembered one Christmas when her father had held a party for his colleagues. Her mother was sick, so Essie was allowed to stay up and pass round bowls of crisps and nuts in her place. She'd walked into the kitchen to find one of the professors' wives holding a screaming newborn with one hand while struggling to prepare a bottle of milk formula with the other.

Essie had looked at the distressed baby in alarm. The little face was red, lips quivering. The cries were so constant there was barely time for breathing. 'What's wrong?'

The mother had given a weary smile. 'Nothing. He's just hungry.'

The frantic sound had made Essie anxious. She felt an impulse to press her hand over the gaping mouth. She just hoped her mother couldn't hear the disturbance from her bedroom. The noise had gone on and on, until the bottle was ready at last and the grasping mouth latched onto the rubber teat.

Now, as Essie hurried in the direction of Magadi Camp, she felt as if she had a time bomb on her hands. And her fear of the baby waking up wasn't all that weighed on her mind. She dreaded to think how she was going to face her husband and mother-in-law.

One thing was clear: she would have to pretend that she was up to the task she'd taken on. The golden rule at Magadi – the starting point for each proposed project – was 'Don't bite off more than you can chew'. If you carried out an excavation, you had to be able to document it, fully and correctly. Once an area was disturbed it could never be studied properly again.

While Essie worked her way across a field of pebble scree, she added up everything she knew about babies. It didn't amount to much. She hadn't grown up seeing little cousins being cared for – she had no relatives in England. Back in Tasmania they never saw her father's family, who were on the mainland. Essie's mother Lorna came from a big clan who lived in the north-east of the island, nearly a day's journey from Hobart. Essie remembered holiday visits to her grandmother's cottage by the sea. Some impressions were quite clear in her mind – falling asleep on a blanket by a smoky campfire; the voices of the adults, chatting and laughing, a comfort in the darkness; swimming in the clear blue sea with kids whose names she barely knew. But she was little herself; she'd had no interest in anyone younger. In her new life in Cambridge she'd gravitated to other single children. They understood the adult world she lived in and were more likely to share her interests. Aside from the episode at the Christmas party, Essie's exposure to babies was limited to walking through parks and playgrounds or watching television.

There was only one recent encounter with the topic that came to Essie's mind. A journalist from the *Guardian* had travelled to Magadi to do a story on the Steps, focusing on a new footprint that had been uncovered since the initial discovery. She had originally been sent to Tanzania to research a story about a baby formula company that was targeting African mothers with a poster campaign. In an after-supper conversation she'd told everyone how babies were dying from malnutrition and stomach infections because people living in huts didn't have the facilities to wash and sterilise bottles, or money to buy enough formula. The manufacturer didn't care, apparently, as long as the market grew. While the young reporter talked passionately, Essie had watched the men trying not to link the issue with the woman's own breasts. Her deep cleavage was revealed at the open neck of her shirt. An archaeologist from Harvard had abruptly changed the subject, talking to Ian about an article in a journal. Julia had joined in eagerly. She seemed as put off by the topic as the men. It was hard to imagine her as the mother of little children, let alone babies. In that way, she reminded Essie of her own mother. The idea of having to turn to her for advice was daunting to say the least.

With nothing else to go on, Essie found herself clinging to Giga's belief that Tommy's care could be used as a model. She pictured the high shelf in the storeroom where she'd put his bottles when he no longer needed them. There had been two of them – clear glass, with brown rubber teats. The Ranger at Serengeti had sent them from his veterinary store after Essie radioed him for advice. Until they'd arrived she'd fed the gazelle using an over-sized eyedropper that was part of the equipment in the Work Hut. It had been slow and messy. She just hoped the two bottles had not gone astray.

She planned her entry to the camp. She'd go via the storeroom, then straight to Baraka in the kitchen. She'd explain how to boil the bottles for three minutes – the same amount of time it took to kill germs in drinking water. Then she'd prepare some powdered milk, diluting it to half the normal strength as she'd been advised to do with Tommy early on. Tonight, she'd have to radio St Joseph's Mission in Arusha and get proper advice on how to proceed. Maybe it would be better to use fresh milk from the Maasai, boiled and cooled. Watered down, perhaps. The nurses at the orphanage would know.

Then, there was the matter of nappies. It had always been a mystery to Essie that Maasai babies had bare bottoms, yet their mothers never smelled of urine or walked around wearing stained cloths. There hadn't been time to discuss this issue with Giga at the cave; for now, Essie had made do with ensuring the sling was lined with the piece of baboon pelt. At the camp she'd have to find old towels or sheets that could be torn up. Even that simple requirement would not be easy to meet; the linen cupboard was in need of restocking, and spare beds had been made up to impress the important visitors.

Essie closed her eyes. Words shot through her mind like arrows.

Frank Marlow.

Sundowners.

Research grant.

Her heart began to beat faster. She imagined how Ian and Julia would react to her arriving home with a baby – their shock and disbelief giving way to outrage. What had possessed Essie to make such a rash promise that would affect others as much as herself? She knew children weren't allowed at the camp. The only ones ever seen here were offspring of the Maasai women delivering milk. The workers never broke the rule by inviting their wives to visit. They understood that Magadi Research Camp was not a playground. It was a place of serious work.

If Essie had brought home a baby who was sick, in order to arrange transport to Arusha, it would have been acceptable. Rescues had occurred before. Taking care of an orphan until it could be relocated to the Mission would come into the same category. But this situation was so different, even leaving the bad timing aside. The Lawrences would be sympathetic to the predicament of the Hadza family, but Essie felt sure they'd have insisted on a different solution – one that didn't involve a little baby coming to live at the camp.

Essie jerked to a halt and turned around. Simon slid to a standstill behind her.

'We have to go back,' she stated. 'I can't do this.'

Simon looked at the little dark-haired head peeping from the top of the sling. He said nothing. Essie knew he was caught squarely between her and the people at the cave. He knew why Essie had to look after their baby. And he knew why she could not.

While they stood there, a rhythmic flapping sound came from above. Essie looked up to see a marabou stork circling overhead. Even in flight the massive bird looked ugly, with its hunched shoulders and drooping throat. But this was nothing, Essie knew, compared to how it would appear close-up. Marabous were like creatures from a nightmare with their bare, scabby faces, matted feathers and jabbing beaks often stained with dried blood. They were the biggest land birds in the world – some were the size of a child. Being scavengers as well as hunters, they were equally at home picking through rubbish or stalking prey.

Without warning the bird swooped down, as if it had detected the presence of a small, defenceless creature. Essie bent over, shielding the baby. Only last year she'd witnessed an attack on a young flamingo as it learned to feed on the shoreline of the lake. The marabou had swung the bird like a rag doll into the air, snapping its neck, then swallowing it in several bites. According to Ian, the predators also raided the hatcheries in the middle of the lake, sampling gangly chicks like party snacks.

Straightening up, Essie eyed the stork as it flapped away. She felt a flash of anger, alongside the usual disgust. If her hands were free, she'd have grabbed a rock to hurl at it.

'If it comes back, shoot it down,' she instructed Simon, pointing her chin towards his bow.

The man looked at her in confusion. The stork didn't pose any real danger to an adult holding a baby. Seeing herself through his eyes, Essie was surprised at her reaction as well. She normally prided herself on being logical, methodical and steady.

As the marabou approached again, riding the breeze like an aircraft, Simon snatched an arrow from the quiver on his back. In one motion he lodged the feathered end against the bowstring and drew it back. Picking up the threat, the bird veered sharply away.

As if sensing the tension, the baby stirred. Essie froze, holding her breath, willing her to not wake up. When all was still again, Essie risked walking on. She kept a hand hovering over the baby's head. The appearance of the stork proved that dangers could be lurking. She looked extra carefully for snakes, and listened out for insects — killer bees, wasps — even though they were rarely so far from bushland. She was glad that Simon was behind her, watching her back.

Soon, they were close to the camp. The plains, dotted with blue circles of water, were spread out below them. And there was the landing strip with its newly weeded gravel . . . Essie's step faltered as a gleam of metal snared her gaze. A plane.

Simon drew up next to her. 'I heard the engine before, when we were at the cave. I thought it was someone flying over the mountain.'

'It can't be the Marlows.'

'It is the wrong day for them to arrive,' Simon agreed.

Narrowing her eyes, Essie peered closer. It was not one of the zebra-striped Dorniers that belonged to the Lodge. Nor was it the battered Cessna that made deliveries to Olduvai piloted by an ex-mercenary who'd fought in the Congo; the fuselage of Erik's ageing aircraft was pitted with bullet holes and one wing was dented. The aircraft parked on the strip had a smooth rosy sheen. It had sleek modern lines and sat low on its wheels. Essie had never seen anything like it before. She lifted her hand to her mouth as a sinking certainty spread through her.

'It has to be them.' Her voice was barely audible. 'Who else could it be?'

The silk dress stuck to Essie's damp skin as she pulled it down over her head. A quick wash with a sponge had smeared the dirt rather than erasing it; the raw smell of untanned animal hide clung to her. As she leaned towards the mirror to apply some lipstick, her hands were shaky with haste; the line ran beyond her lips and she had to wipe it away as soon as it was done. From over in the Dining Tent she could hear snippets of light conversation. There was a rich, deep male voice that she guessed belonged to Frank Marlow. It dominated the interchange, but Essie also picked up Ian and Julia's familiar cadences. Mrs Marlow seemed to be remaining silent. You'd hardly know there was another person there, except that Essie had glimpsed four figures through the gauze window of the tent, while creeping past it en route to the kitchen. A glamorous-looking woman had been lounging in a deck chair, head tipped back as she drew on a cigarette. She wore a striking turquoise dress with a skirt made of fabric so fine that it fluttered in the light breeze. As Essie had hurried on, she just had enough time to register Ian in his linen suit, Julia in her cream lace dress and a large-framed man wearing a white dinner jacket and black bow tie.

Essie tuned her ears towards the kitchen. It was a wooden structure but the walls were thin. She could hear Baraka moving around in there. His usual clattering of pans and utensils was toned right down; he was humming quietly too. He had taken in his stride Essie's sudden appearance just before, thrusting bottles and teats at him, amid a torrent of instructions. He'd told her that the Bwana had received a radio call just a few hours ago. The special visitors had decided to come a day early.

'Why?' Essie asked.

Baraka shrugged. Africans tended not to take plans as seriously as Europeans. Every arrangement was considered provisional, which meant people had to be adaptable. He'd helped untie the sling, smiling as the sleeping baby was revealed. Then he'd handed her to Simon, who was sitting on a chair in the corner. Essie noticed he'd taken the precaution of laying a folded cloth over his lap.

'If she wakes?' Simon queried.

'Feed her,' Essie said. 'No, come and get me.' Her thoughts were in turmoil. 'I don't know!'

'Go and sit with them.' Baraka spoke calmly. 'They have been to the digging site. Now they are looking at some of the special things. You have arrived at the right moment. The demonstration is next.'

Simon had handed Essie the bag of stones. Now, as she stood in her tent hastily applying mascara, the chunks of flint were spread out on the dressing table nearby, ready for her to select the ones that would make the best mother stones.

Essie stood back from the mirror, adjusting the position of her dress so that the V-shaped neckline didn't plunge so low. Perhaps the amount of cleavage it revealed was the reason her mother had never actually worn the dress after bringing it home. Essie smoothed down her hair. She noticed how her honey-brown skin complemented the orange of the gown. Her eyes were big and shiny. She didn't look too bad; somehow she'd expected that the enormity of what had just happened to her would show on her face. Perhaps the situation was so extreme that all expression had disappeared.

Slipping on her party shoes, she hurried outside. The high heels wobbled in the soft earth. Like the dress, they had never been worn since her arrival in Africa. Walking around in them here at Magadi was impractical, but Essie could hardly pair her cocktail gown with work boots.

She focused on keeping her feet moving. If she stopped, she feared she might turn around and rush back to the safe haven of her bedroom. The challenge of acting as if everything was normal felt completely beyond her.

Drawing near to the Dining Tent, she paused in a spot where she could not easily be seen, yet could peer in through the open front. Ian, Julia and the two visitors were sitting around the table. Kefa was standing nearby, a white tea towel folded neatly over his arm. Frank Marlow and his wife had their backs to Essie. The 'typical day's find' tray was in front of Ian. He held one of the items in his hand. Essie didn't have to listen to know what he would be saying.

This might look like an ordinary fragment of bone. But it's not. See this groove? That's where an animal has chewed it. From that small detail we know for sure that . . .

Mr Marlow was leaning forward eagerly. As Essie watched, he turned away from the display to look at his wife. His face was alight with enthusiasm. In the gap between their chairs, Essie saw him reach for her hand, obviously seeking a moment of shared excitement. But as his fingers folded over hers, they were abruptly shaken off. The man's hand reached again. This time his wife literally slapped it aside. Before Essie had time to absorb her surprise, Ian stood up. As he saw her there, mixed emotions flitted over his face. Then he found a smile.

'Essie! At last.' Beneath his genial tone was an edge of frustration. 'We were wondering what had happened to you.'

Essie walked into the tent. 'I'm sorry. I was held up. It's a long story.' She smiled brightly. 'Hello, everyone.'

Frank rose to his feet as Ian began the introductions. Even being preoccupied, Essie was struck by how handsome her husband was in his linen suit. 'Frank, this is my wife, Essie. Essie – Frank Marlow.'

'How do you do?' Essie greeted the visitor. He looked like a rich man. It wasn't just his well-cut jacket or the bow tie. There was something about the style of his streaky grey-blond hair, the big square teeth that were too white, and the evenly tanned skin that was the result of lying in the sun rather than being outside working in it.

Frank strode up and took her hand in his, shaking it warmly. 'It's a pleasure to meet you, Mrs Lawrence.' When his gaze met hers, it was unwavering, confident.

'Call me Essie, please.'

Ian turned to Mrs Marlow. 'Diana, this is my wife, Essie. Essie – Diana.'

Diana regarded Essie impassively; her beautiful face might have been a cardboard cut-out. Essie took a step towards the far side of the table, then stopped and smiled awkwardly. She could never work out how to greet other women. It was easy for the men; they always shook hands. Women tended to hover uncertainly, until one took the initiative by either offering their hand or holding it still.

Diana waved her cigarette. 'Hi.' She looked Essie up and down. Her gaze lingered on the orange dress. Essie was glad it was of good quality, with a name on its label that even she had recognised when she'd bothered to check. She took the opportunity to study Diana back. From what Ian had said, she must be in her mid-forties, but she appeared younger. She had fair, flawless skin. Her long dark hair was teased into a mound on top and curled up at the ends. A sleek section at the front had been brushed across her forehead. Dark eyes sat below brows that were like the wings of a tiny black bird. Her contrasting features – light skin, dark hair – were set off perfectly by her turquoise dress. Even Essie, who hadn't been shopping on a high street for five years, could tell that the gown was very modern. The bodice was gathered into a strap that fitted close around Diana's neck like a choker. It reminded Essie of Tommy's collar – only this one was crusted with seed pearls and silk embroidery. The design drew attention to Diana's bare shoulders. The effect was more suggestive and daring, for some reason, than if half of her breasts had been exposed.

Diana drew on her cigarette as she finished her own appraisal, carefully shaping her mouth to avoid puckering her lips. Then she looked down at the ground, revealing eyelids shadowed with turquoise.

Essie didn't think she'd ever seen such a beautiful woman in the flesh. She had to make herself turn away in order to greet her mother-in-law. Julia was sitting upright in her chair. In front of her was a plaster model of a skull reconstructed from fossil fragments she and William had found in their early years here. It represented one of the most important Australopithecine finds yet made by anyone. No doubt Ian had been talking about the fact that evidence of these early precursors of humans – the ones who had emerged from the forests when the grasslands formed – had only ever been discovered in Africa. This was why the Lawrences, as well as the Leakeys, believed this continent was where the human family had originated, even though this flew in the face of the more popular view that Europe or Asia – where the Neanderthals eventually evolved, with their impressive sophistication – was our first home. It occurred to Essie that Ian's perspective might have particular appeal to Marlow. As a Canadian he might be drawn to the idea that somewhere remote from the regions usually seen as the heart of civilisation could be the place where our story began.

Julia's work-roughened fingers draped down over the yellowed cranium, resting on the protruding brow ridges. Essie thought she looked surprisingly comfortable in her cream lace dress, considering she probably hadn't been out of her work clothes for decades. The gown still fitted her well. She'd pinned up her thinning hair, which made her look younger. If the image of her were blurred, she'd look as she did in her photo with the Queen. However, in the strong light that angled into the tent, her upper arms sagged and her neck was creased. She must have been tapping her foot against the table leg – a sign of contained impatience that she often displayed. Normally, Ian would have found it intolerable, but right now he was distracted by his role as host.

Essie could tell that her husband was trying hard to appear relaxed. Her late return home had come on top of the early arrival of the Marlows, and he hated surprises of any kind. She wondered what explanation – if any – had been given for the visitors' change of plan. Perhaps the couple needed to cut short their holiday. Essie could imagine that someone like Frank Marlow might have to deal with business crises whenever they came up.

Ian was smiling at his guests. 'Now we can have our knapping demonstration,' he said.

'Ah yes, the Professor's daughter!' Frank turned to Essie. 'You know I've met your father?' Without waiting for a reaction, he went on. 'I flew from Toronto just to see his collection. I was amazed to learn how he just wandered around Tasmania picking stone tools up off the ground by the hundreds.' He nodded in the direction of the excavations. 'Not like here. All that digging.' He whistled through his teeth. 'I'm going to take a trip to Tasmania this fall. I want to see what I can find myself.' He shook his head. 'It's a terrible shame what happened to those people. What a lost opportunity for research.' He turned to his wife. 'The British managed to kill off every last one of them. And it took less than seventy-five years. There's not a single full-blood Tasmanian Aborigine left.'

Essie glanced at Kefa, who was still lingering nearby. She hoped he was not listening in. Any discussion about colonialism had to be handled delicately in Africa. Various European powers had exploited the continent mercilessly. The British, however, had treated the people of Tanganyika – now the United Republic of Tanzania – benignly, on the whole. Hearing the shameful story of how they'd behaved on the other side of the world would not be helpful. Essie swapped a look with Ian, unsure where the conversation might be headed.

'Let's get on with the demonstration,' Ian suggested.

'Good idea,' Essie responded. Leaving aside the need to change the subject, she was keen to get on with the knapping. Once the task was over, perhaps she could plead a headache and avoid going down to the Steps. It would be ideal to have some time at the camp without the others. She felt reassured by Baraka's calm response to the arrival of a baby in his kitchen. At his age, the man had probably fathered plenty of offspring. He must have learned a thing or two, watching his wife. Perhaps he could be encouraged to take charge.

Essie looked across at Diana, wondering how she'd react if Essie absented herself, especially since she'd been late turning up. Mrs Marlow was watching her husband as he rubbed his hands in anticipation of the demonstration. To Essie's surprise, a fond smile curved her lips. The expression didn't fit with the interchange that had occurred between the two earlier. Diana had definitely been annoyed. This smile had to be a fake. What could have gone wrong between them? Maybe Diana was upset that the celebration had been brought forward, presumably to the wrong date. But Essie sensed there was something more seriously amiss. Whatever was really going on, though, Essie's presence at the sundowners wasn't vital. In fact, it should really have been just the Marlows down there, toasting their marriage – though how romantic the event was going to be, in spite of the setting, now seemed questionable.

Essie put on a leather work apron and led the others outside. In front of the tent was a clearing with a fireplace in the middle, bordered by bushes and clumps of sisal; it had the feeling of a stage. There was a creak of canvas as the others took their places on some camp chairs. In the area where she planned to do the knapping, Essie laid down a piece of sacking ready to catch the chips of unwanted flint. If anyone was researching this area in a time to come, she didn't want her work to be mistaken for something ancient. She sat on a solid stool, resting the mother stone on her knee. Grasping it in one hand, she held the egg-shaped hammer stone in the other. The familiar feeling of flint pressing into her skin was reassuring. She'd done this task hundreds of times before.

She looked up at Ian, who gave her an encouraging smile. He appeared much more relaxed, now that everything was proceeding according to plan. She let him do the commentary, while she concentrated on her technique. She struck the mother stone lightly to check her position, then hit it hard, making sure she aimed for a spot beyond the stone. She watched with relief as a perfect flake fell from the core.

'It's all about the line of impact,' Ian explained. 'What you want is a glancing blow with a follow-through.'

Essie began making secondary strikes, forming an edge. She was creating an Acheulean hand axe. It was a sophisticated tool, associated with our most recent ancestor, *Homo erectus*. Frustratingly, not one example of this advanced technology had yet been located in Africa, even though plenty had been dug up in places like China, Indonesia and across Europe. It was as if the earth was playing a trick: while Australopithecine remains had only been found here in Africa, *Homo erectus* fossils, along with the Acheulean tools, had only been found in Europe and Asia. Nowhere had both bits of the puzzle been discovered in the same region – the proof of our beginnings as ape-people, and then of the *erectus* stage, which was just before we became our modern selves, *Homo sapiens*. It might have made more sense for Essie to create a tool similar to what was found here at Magadi, but the idea was to inspire Frank Marlow to fund the research that might solve the stubborn mystery.

As the stone artefact slowly took shape, Ian threw out relevant nuggets of information. Leaving his objectives aside, Essie was glad of the excuse to make an Acheulean tool. The axe was satisfyingly big, filling her hand. It would be worked on both sides, the whole surface faceted. When it was done it would be like a huge jewel made from stone.

Essie heard Ian's tone change as he shifted his focus to Diana. He knew it would be wise to draw her in, too.

'Some two million years ago, it is the invention of stone tools that now changes the world.' Ian sounded as if he were parroting someone else. Essie had heard him do this before, using the present tense to speak about the past; she wondered if she was listening to the voice of William Lawrence, who'd died five years before she came here. 'Hominids can fight harder now, even though their fighting teeth – the incisors – have become smaller. They can cut through animal hide to reach the flesh, and break bones to eat marrow.'

Diana must not have looked very interested; Ian went back to addressing Frank. Essie barely took in his words, giving all her attention to the curves of flint that sheered off the core as the hammer stone struck, then fell to the ground like petals.

As the axe took shape, Frank whistled softly.

'It's even harder than it looks,' Ian said. 'Takes years of practice, and you need a natural flair as well.'

Essie could hear the pride in his voice. Looking up, she gave him a smile. For a moment she was back in England, the cold flagstones of the university courtyard seeping up through the soles of her shoes. She was showing off her skills in a demonstration arranged by her father in honour of a visit by Ian Lawrence. Some of Essie's university friends were gathered too, keen to make the most of the chance to meet the famous archaeologist from East Africa.

Arthur and Ian had stood together, talking, while Essie worked. She knew they'd been instantly drawn to one another. It made sense: while being admired in academic circles, they were also outsiders. Arthur was an Australian who'd once worked at the tiny and obscure University of Tasmania; Ian had been born in Africa, as had his father before him. They were both far removed, by breeding and life experience, from the upper-class English world of Cambridge. The two men had shared jokes about Tasmania and Tanzania being thought, by many people, to be one and the same place.

Watching the demonstration, Ian had been impressed by Essie's skills.

'I think I'll take her back to Africa with me,' he'd said to Arthur. He was joking, of course, but Essie savoured his words, replaying them in her head.

'Sorry, but I can't spare her,' Arthur had responded. Whether he was being humorous too was unclear – but Essie could tell he was pleased.

She had bent her head over the chunk of white chert in her lap, absorbing the moment when Ian Lawrence – a man who everyone admired, even her father – had chosen to make her the centre of his attention.

Now, perched on her stool outside the Dining Tent, in the barren surroundings of Magadi, Essie felt the cooling air that blew in as the afternoon drew to a close. It seemed a long time ago that she'd been sitting at the breakfast table, planning her day down to the last detail, never suspecting what was actually about to take place.

Pausing in her work, she looked across to the Marlows to check how her performance was being received. Frank was leaning forward, getting the best view. Julia mimicked his posture, as if this spectacle was equally new and exciting to her. But Diana was showing no interest at all. Instead, her gaze swung steadily from Ian to Essie and back. She might have been assessing some item she was thinking of making hers – except that such an idea made no sense. Lowering her eyes, Essie grasped the mother stone tightly and prepared to make another strike.

Small flakes and chips speckled Essie's apron as she worked. Beyond the rough canvas she caught glimpses of orange silk. Her high heels, planted apart as she balanced herself, were dulled with dust. When she stood up, she knew her dress would stick to her sweaty body. She might have been made up of two people that were impossible to connect, and yet equally real.

Essie began tackling the sequence of mini-strikes that would harden the edges of the axe. It was a crucial stage. Making a mistake now could ruin all that she'd done. Ian was continuing his commentary, dropping familiar phrases that Essie could have recited for him. Then his voice cut off.

Essie looked up to see Tommy trotting into the circle. His head was lowered; he was thinking of practising his butting technique. Diana shrank back in her chair as though she were being confronted by a dangerous carnivore, not a young gazelle.

'It's all right,' Essie said quickly. 'He's tame.' Diana didn't show any sign of relaxing; perhaps she was concerned about the cloud-like fabric of her dress.

'What is it – some kind of deer?' Frank asked. He stretched out one hand towards the animal, perhaps wanting to prove he had a different response to his wife.

'A Thomson's gazelle,' Ian said. 'A juvenile male.'

'He's called Tommy,' Essie added, reaching to grasp her pet's collar. As she said the name she wished she'd come up with something a bit more imaginative.

'You've got quite a menagerie here,' Frank commented. 'With all those dogs, as well . . .'

Essie wondered if he'd seen the collection of animals that lived at Olduvai. There were four or five mongrel hounds, as well as the pedigreed Dalmatians whose offspring Meg and Rudie were. In addition there was a serval cat, hyrax, mongoose and an African crow with one wing. The Leakeys probably had the good sense to keep them all out of sight during the philanthropist's visit.

'My wife has a tender heart,' Ian explained. His indulgent smile betrayed no hint of the annoyance Essie knew he felt. 'She rescued Tommy as a baby.' He gestured towards the nearby tree where the dogs were resting. 'That lot actually earn their keep. There are leopards in this area, you know.'

Diana looked around her. 'Here?'

Ian shook his head. 'No. I meant in the *korongos*.'

Essie stood up, still holding on to Tommy. 'I'll put him away. I'm sorry. I can't have closed his pen properly.'

'I'll deal with him,' Julia said.

'No, no – I'll do it,' Essie insisted. His pen was too near the kitchen. Julia might decide to check in with Baraka on her return. 'I've finished anyway.' Essie handed the axe to Frank with a smile.

He turned it over, testing the edge against the side of his thumb before nodding his head admiringly. 'Beautiful.'

Essie felt her face heat up. The way his eyes engaged hers, she wasn't certain he was referring to the stone.

'Keep it,' Ian said. 'A reminder of your visit.'

Frank slipped the artefact into his jacket pocket. He looked away, towards the plains. The sun was a round ball of gold floating in a pale green sky, not far above the horizon.

Ian followed his gaze. 'It's about time to make a move.'

'I'll tell Daudi to drive the Land Rover round,' Essie offered. She was about to lead Tommy away when Diana got to her feet.

'Can you show me to the bathroom? I need to freshen up.'

'Ah – sure,' Essie said. 'Of course. Follow me.'

She and Julia had planned for this possibility. The *cho* tent had been perfumed with burning frankincense. An extra layer of earth had been piled into the long-drop hole to conceal its contents. There was nothing to be done about the elephant jawbone that stood in for a toilet seat. They could only hope that the Marlows would be intrigued by it, rather than put off. In the bathing tent next door, a near-new hand towel had been laid out and there were two pitchers of water standing next to the enamel basin.

Essie led the way around the side of the tent. 'I hope your shoes won't be damaged.' Diana was wearing white snakeskin sandals. They were as modern as her dress, with block-shaped high heels. They were still shiny and clean. If she'd worn them to the digging sites earlier, she must have remained in the vehicle.

'It doesn't matter.' Diana shrugged. 'Frank bought them for me. I don't like wearing snake. He should know that.'

Essie couldn't think of anything to say. The remark seemed both disloyal and ungracious. The two women walked together in silence for a while. Tommy tore at a bunch of leaves as they passed a bush growing by the path.

'Frank said you've been working here with your husband for years.'

Essie nodded. 'I came in 1965.'

'And there's just the three of you? Don't you get tired of each other's company?'

'There are the local workers, too,' Essie explained. 'But we do spend a lot of time together. Ian and me. And Julia.'

'God. How can you live with your mother-in-law?'

Essie laughed softly, feeling guilty. 'I know. I have my moments . . .'

Diana laughed too, but then looked thoughtful again. 'She's famous, though – isn't she?'

'She and William discovered the Steps together. Then there are the Australopithecine remains. You saw the model of the skull. They also found parts of a *Homo habilis* cranium. He's like a slightly more developed Australopithecine. The first to make stone tools.' Essie smiled understandingly; she guessed Diana would be struggling to make sense of what she was saying. For one thing, the Latin names were hard to remember. When Essie had first learned about Australopithecines, it had taken her a while to shake off the idea that they were somehow linked to Australia.

'So you and Ian are the next generation husband-and-wife team,' Diana said.

Essie felt a wave of pleasure at these words, but said nothing. She was grateful Diana didn't seem to know that since Essie's arrival at Magadi nothing important had been found. Not yet.

'Then there's your father, the Professor,' Diana continued. 'He's well known for his collection. Don't tell me your mother was famous as well?'

The idea was so foreign Essie took some time to reply. 'No, she's . . .'

She's no one. 'She's dead.'

'I'm so sorry.' Diana's tone didn't change to match her words of sympathy. 'So you landed on your feet here with the Lawrences. You must be happy.'

In the moment of silence that followed, Essie pictured her life. It was like a tapestry hung on a wall – colourful, complex, complete. 'Oh, yes. I'm very happy. It's a dream come true for me.'

'What are you, exactly? I mean, what do people like you get called?'

'In general terms, we're archaeologists. But we're researching the process of hominisation – the evolution of primates into modern humans. So we're actually paleoanthropologists. We're paleontologists, too, when we're working with fossils.' She smiled again. 'It's confusing. The fields of expertise overlap.'

'I can't even imagine what it would be like to be so . . . interested . . . in your work. It sounds like you never stop.' Diana wrinkled her nose.

'We do work hard,' Essie confirmed. 'There's so much we want to do.'

Diana turned suddenly, to face Essie front on. 'I hope you know how lucky you are – having a husband you can share everything with. A man that everyone respects so much.'

'I am lucky,' Essie agreed. In spite of her complicated relationship with Julia, the isolation of the camp, and the fact of being cut off from all her connections in England, she knew that in her marriage to Ian she possessed something most people only dreamed of. Yet Diana's life must be enviable, too – in a very different way. Essie looked from the salon-perfect hairdo to the extraordinary dress. 'But so are you.'

'Lucky?' Lifting one hand, Diana studied her red-polished nails. 'Frank is a nice man,' she said slowly. 'But he can't keep to one woman. Won't even try.'

She looked back at Essie, her arched brows raised as if she'd asked a question. Essie had no idea how to respond. She knew lots of women had the ability to fall into instant intimacy – sharing troubles and advice with strangers – but she'd never found it easy. And after being at Magadi for the last five years, she felt even more inadequate.

'I didn't marry Frank for his money, you know,' Diana added. 'I've got wealth of my own. I was a Sherman.'

Essie eyed her blankly.

'Sherman Hotels,' Diana prompted. 'They're right across America.'

Essie had never heard of the family or their empire. She smiled vaguely. 'So, which part of America are you from?' The question seemed a good way to steer the conversation away from Mrs Marlow's revelations about her husband.

'Well, I was born and bred in Massachusetts,' Diana replied. 'But I haven't been back there for years. I'm more or less Canadian now. I've lived there so long. Anyway, the point is, I chose Frank for who he was, not what he owned. I fell madly in love with him. I didn't see what I was getting myself into . . .' She let out a bitter laugh. 'You know why we had to come here on the wrong day? There's a film crew staying at the Lodge. We've been invited to go and watch them shooting tomorrow. Frank's very keen. Needless to say, there's an actress involved.'

By now they were nearing the small tents at the edge of the camp. 'Ah – here we are.' Essie spoke lightly, as if Diana had not just shared things that were deeply private. 'The one on the left is the lavatory. You wash your hands next door.'

'Thank you,' Diana said. But instead of keeping on walking, she stood still, gazing about her. 'I like it here at your camp. It's so simple. Everything in its place, and nothing extra.'

Essie thought of all the things that were actually not in their place, because they'd been used up or worn out. She knew what Julia would be expecting of her, in this moment when she was alone with Diana Marlow. Rich men could often be influenced by their wives. Essie should be finding a way to bring up the topic of research funds. But she couldn't afford to lose any more time if she was going to visit the kitchen before delivering her message to Daudi. She pointed back the way they had come.

'Just rejoin the others afterwards.'

Dragging Tommy behind her, she strode away. When she reached his pen she shoved him inside and closed the door. She found a couple of large rocks nearby to lodge against it. With her flimsy shoes she was unable to kick them into place, so she had to bend over, her skirt draping the ground. She'd just finished the job when she heard a noise. Turning her head, she identified the call of a waterbird. It came again – high and plaintive. Her stomach tightened. It was too loud, too close. As she spun in the direction of the kitchen, the crying continued, winding up like a siren. Kicking off her shoes, she ran towards it, as if the sound was a physical presence that she could somehow stop in its tracks.

FOUR

Essie took two steps into the kitchen, then jerked to a halt. The baby was flailing in Simon's arms, head flung back, screaming. Close-up, it was hard to believe that so much noise could be fuelled by such small lungs. Baraka was holding a bottle, the teat waving from side to side as he followed the movement of her mouth. Her face and neck were shiny with spilt milk.

'She woke quietly.' Simon raised his voice over the noise. 'When we tried to feed her, she became angry.'

With a look of relief, he pushed the baby towards Essie. A damp towel fell to the ground between them as the weight was transferred to her arms.

Essie held the naked baby against her body, gripping tight, in fear of dropping her. Between screams, there were brief silences while the baby caught her breath. But then the cries erupted again. Essie tried to make calming noises but couldn't even hear them herself. She could feel panic building, adding to the tension in the small space.

'Has she drunk any milk at all?' Essie asked Baraka.

He shook his head.

Closing her eyes for a few seconds, Essie tried to gather herself. She shifted the baby to rest her head against her breast, as Giga had done. But the baby just arched her body away. She was caught up, Essie understood, in a maelstrom of hunger, and perhaps fear of strangers as well. She would never drink until she calmed down. Dimly, Essie remembered how she'd struggled to get Tommy to feed at first. She'd had to wrap him tightly in a large towel to contain his legs, then hold his head still while she dripped milk into his mouth. When he had swallowed enough of it, he finally grasped the function of the bottle.

Hanging from a nail on the wall was an old Maasai *shuka* – a thin blanket that Baraka used on cool nights when he sat outside by the fire. Essie gestured for him to spread out the red and purple plaid cloth on the table. He faltered. It would be a breach of Julia's hygiene rules, as Essie well knew. The table was meant for food, nothing else. Even food that wasn't yet ready to be cooked – still clad in fur, feathers or dusted with earth – was forbidden. But Baraka didn't object as Simon took over, flinging the blanket onto the scrubbed wooden planks.

The men stood back, watching, as if Essie would know what to do simply because she was a woman, or perhaps a European – she wasn't sure. Regardless, it gave her an odd sense of confidence. She wrapped the baby briskly, remembering how she'd once handled her dolls. When she was finished, the little body was suddenly still, perhaps purely from surprise. In the quiet, Essie murmured soothingly. She held the swaddled shape against her chest. A bubble of pride formed inside her. She threw a look of triumph at the two men. Then the baby lifted her head and began crying again.

Essie loosened the blanket a little, in case it was too tight. One arm escaped and began batting her face. Fingers brushed the soft skin of her chest where it was exposed by the low-cut dress. As if recognising the sensation, the baby became still again. Essie leaned forward, exposing more of the round swell of her breast. The hand came to rest there – a little black star pressed against creamy skin that had rarely seen the sun. Wide, shiny eyes stared up at her. The contrast between light and dark was repeated there, the near-black irises surrounded by purest white. As Essie smiled down at the baby she noticed silver tear-tracks running back into the fuzz of her hair.

Without being asked, Simon brought a chair and placed it behind her. Slowly, Essie lowered herself onto the seat. Baraka handed her the bottle. She stayed bent over, so as not to dislodge the fingers that were now clutching her breast. Carefully she nudged the teat at the pursed lips.

Essie wondered, suddenly, if she should have questioned Baraka about whether he'd sterilised the bottle and made up the powdered milk half-strength. Had everything been done correctly? Was the milk warm? But she didn't want to jeopardise the fragile peace. She glanced across to the man. His brow was furrowed with tension as he willed the baby to drink.

'She needs to taste the milk,' Essie said. With Tommy, she'd squeezed the teat for him, until he learned what to do.

As if reading her mind, Baraka squatted beside her. Essie felt awkward having him right there, with her dress pulled aside like this. She reminded herself that to a Maasai man, breasts were no different to other parts of the body. Their purpose was feeding the young and there was no need for them to be hidden away like a secret. As Baraka bent close, Essie picked up the smells of his cooking – yeast, cornmeal, honey. He squeezed the teat carefully. A dribble of milk came out, but the baby turned her head away, letting it run onto her cheek. Essie stroked the back of her hand.

'Come on, little girl. You know you're hungry.' Essie fell into the singsong voice she used with Tommy. The way of speaking had felt natural to her from the beginning, even though it irritated Julia and Ian. It was like a language she'd always known.

As Baraka persevered, the baby's tongue began trying to lap like a kitten. Then her lips closed over the teat. Essie held her breath. But after only a few seconds, the baby spat it out and began crying again.

Essie threw Baraka a desperate look; she didn't know what to try next.

Baraka squeezed the teat again, dripping milk into the wide-open mouth. After a brief splutter, the baby swallowed. She looked surprised, but then parted her lips, ready for more.

'Let her drink this way for now,' Baraka said. 'She cannot learn everything in one moment.'

The baby gradually settled into a rhythm, swallowing the milk as it pooled on her tongue. She closed her eyes as if the task needed all the concentration she could muster. Essie looked up, sharing a smile with the others. It was a slow process, but the baby was being fed.

There was a scrape of timber as the door opened. Essie's jaw clenched as she saw Julia standing there. Her long dress made her seem tall, regal. Her eyes were wide with shock. Essie imagined how the scene must appear to her: her daughter-in-law inexplicably bottle-feeding a baby; her dress askew, the skirt stained with milk; Baraka at her side and Simon hovering nearby.

Julia turned to Baraka. 'Whose is that? Where's the mother?' Her tone was low and calm – this was what happened on the rare occasions when Julia was emotional. The effect was much more daunting than a raised voice.

The cook looked at the baby, saying nothing.

'I brought her here,' Essie confessed. She was surprised at the tone of her own voice; she didn't sound as apologetic as she'd intended. 'She's a Hadza. The people asked me to.'

'Hadza!' Julia moved closer. Essie saw her eyes travelling over the baby's head, noting the shape of the skull, the jut of the jaw. 'You can't really see it. Maybe she's too young. What's the matter? Why is she here?'

'Her mother died. There's no one who can feed her.'

Essie decided to lay out all the facts, quickly and simply. She kept her eyes on the ground as she spoke. When she reached the part about her promise to care for the baby until the rainy season, and not to send her away from Magadi, she had to force herself to keep talking. Finally, she was finished. She waited numbly for Julia to react. Since nothing was said, she looked up.

Diana was standing on the threshold, looking over Julia's shoulder. Her gaze darted from Essie to the baby and back. The sculpted eyebrows were arched with interest.

Questions burned in Julia's eyes, but she just stared at Essie in silence. Diana eased past her, crossing the small kitchen to stand next to the chair. She bent over from the waist, flat-backed and elegant, like a ballerina. A cloud of strong perfume came with her. Like the lipstick, it must have been freshly reapplied. Essie had a flash memory of being in Harrods, spraying fragrances in long rows up both of her arms, while she waited for an interminable shopping excursion to be over.

Diana clicked her tongue as she peered curiously into the blanket. 'Poor little thing. What did you say happened to her mom?'

'She died in childbirth.'

Diana whistled through her teeth. 'My God, I can't imagine what it would be like, having a baby out here in the bush. It's bad enough in a top-class hospital.' She gave a faint shrug of her bare shoulders. 'Well, so I've been told.' Leaning closer, she studied the baby. 'What's her name?'

Essie eyed Diana uncertainly. She didn't want the baby disturbed by voices. On the other hand, the visitor's interest was welcome. Perhaps the presence of the rescued baby could somehow be turned into an asset – after all, she was a member of a rare tribe. Frank might well be intrigued. Essie considered extending the conversation by telling Mrs Marlow that the infant didn't actually have a name yet. She could show off her knowledge of local customs by explaining that parents sometimes felt it wise to hold off choosing one until the youngster was old enough to have a good chance of surviving. In other cases, the delay was more a matter of the family wanting to find out what would suit the child's personality. Before Essie had a chance to speak, however, she felt a sudden warmth, accompanied by wetness, reaching through Baraka's thin blanket. Diana stepped back as a splash of urine landed on the toe of her shoe.

Julia took a deep breath, her chest rising visibly. Then she approached Diana, a thin smile on her lips. 'The others are waiting for us. The sun sets quickly here in Africa.' She addressed Simon in an undertone. 'Get some towels from the guest tents. There will be safety pins in the first-aid kit.'

She turned to Baraka. 'Make sure you've got boiled water.' Baraka was already on his knees, mopping the floor with a grey rag worn to threads. He kept his head down.

Diana remained at Essie's side, gazing intently at the baby. She seemed reluctant to leave.

'I can hear the Land Rover,' Julia said firmly. 'Let's go.'

*

76

The white-topped peak of the volcano stood out against the clear sky, the outline crisp and craggy as an iceberg. The cloud of smoke and steam that had hovered around the summit all day was gone. Essie had no idea why. The life of the volcano was powered from deep inside the earth and followed no rules but its own. It was a frustration to the volcanologists who came here to monitor its activity. They could measure, record, describe, but they could neither predict nor exert control.

Essie walked along a narrow track that led away from the camp. It was surrounded on both sides by bushes, giving it a sense of secrecy. The leather sling held the baby against her chest. She had her arms wrapped over the sleeping child. With each step, the limp weight moved as she moved, like part of her own body. The bundle was more bulky now, with a makeshift nappy in place. When Essie had put it on, back at the camp, she'd had only a vague idea how to fold the towel correctly. The cloth was rectangular instead of square, which hadn't made the task any easier. Baraka and Simon had apparently never seen a nappy before, so they were no help. And the whole process had had to be carried out with minimum disturbance to the baby. After another episode of screaming – her face contorted, hands closed into fists – she had eventually consumed a whole bottle of milk and then fallen into a deep sleep. Essie smoothed the lumpy nappy through the thin leather. At least now, held in the sling, it wasn't able to fall off.

The hem of the silk dress lapped softly around Essie's ankles as she took each stride. She'd have preferred to change into practical clothes, but when she'd tried handing the baby to Baraka, there was a cry of protest, so she'd set off as she was. The long skirt would keep mosquitoes off her ankles, at least. To protect her upper body she'd draped a colourful cotton *kitenge*, lent by Simon, around her shoulders and over the baby's head. Down at the Steps, she guessed, Daudi would have offered the guests the use of the Lawrences' last bottle of imported insect repellent.

The path came to a more open area. Reaching a small *korongo*, Essie looked down its length towards the plains below. She could see the Marlows' aircraft – a splash of colour against the ochre earth of the strip. Now that the light didn't bounce from the metal so brightly, she saw that the plane was painted a pinky red – almost as if it had been chosen to match the coming sunset.

Continuing along the track, Essie veered to the right. Ahead of her now was the distinctive landmark the Lawrences called the Tower. An area of higher land had been eroded from all sides until only a square pillar of stone remained. The technical term was an erosion stack, but the name didn't suit the place. The Tower was like something from a mythic tale the way it stood overlooking the plains. You could picture a medieval castle built on the top, or perhaps a prison, like the one in the highlands of Ethiopia that Ian had told her about. Accessible only by ladders and ropes, it had once housed three hundred princes – only one of whom would ever leave by becoming the next king.

It was a long time since Essie had taken a walk to look at the Tower close-up – with no work being done in this sector, there was no reason to. But now, as she approached the landmark along the track, she scarcely gave it a second glance. She kept her eyes on the ground, wary of tripping. Carrying a baby made the path seem more dangerous than it was.

Soon she was skirting the base of the Tower. Resting her hand on the crumbly stone, she stopped for a few moments; she was carrying extra weight, and it was on her front instead of her back. Lifting aside the soft-worn *kitenge,* she peered at the baby. She was slumped down, her face hidden. Essie felt a stab of alarm. She was so still. Essie plunged her hand into the sling, breathing out with relief as the baby stirred.

Only a little further on, she got her first glimpse of the Steps, down below her. The Land Rover came into view first, parked a short distance from the edge of the site. Daudi was standing beside it, upright, like a soldier on parade. Ian and Julia must have told him what was expected; normally their driver sat on the spare wheel mounted on the bonnet when he had to wait around.

Not far from there was the rocky cairn topped with a brass plaque that commemorated William's achievements. A line of stones stretched away from it, forming the boundary of the exca- vated site. Essie could see part of the field of fossilised mud that had been exposed. The grey stone, stripped of layers of sediment built up over millennia, stood out from the surrounding land with its ochre gravel, sparse grass and bushes. Some of the footprints were visible from here. They'd been left by the three sets of feet – big, middle-sized and small, as if they belonged in a fairy story. The spaces between the indents were smooth, with no marks left by knuckles – a clear sign that they had been made by hominids, not apes. The prints looked almost more impressive viewed from up here than at close quarters. Even now, with her mind on other things, Essie was struck by the sight of them.

To see the rest of the site, Essie had to edge out towards a steep drop. She crouched down, using one hand to steady herself, while holding the baby with the other. Soon, more of the vista was revealed. When she was safely settled, she raised her binoculars to her eyes. She saw a table draped with a white cloth. A couple of platters of food sat there, along with an ornate silver ice bucket, the neck of a champagne bottle angling out from its scalloped lip.

At the end of the table stood the waiter from the Lodge, as upright as Daudi, wearing a long white *kanzu* and a red fez on his head.

And there, within the boundary of the site, were Ian, Julia and the Marlows. They held champagne glasses in their hands. The toasts must already have been done, and Ian must have finished his talk about the place, because the four were spread out, studying the footprints. With their heads down, taking slow steps, they looked like a small family of birds scouring the ground for food. Beside the pale suits of the men and Julia's cream dress, the turquoise splash of Diana's gown stood out. Essie was reminded of a peacock in the drab company of peahens. The metaphor was faulty, though. In the bird kingdom males were the ones that strutted and preened to attract, or keep, a mate. Diana was the result of an evolutionary path that had headed in the opposite direction.

Essie pictured herself moving among the figures below, her orange dress adding a second streak of colour. She imagined the tingle of cold champagne on her tongue. The tang of lemon squeezed over smoked salmon. Russian caviar, dark and salty, staining her lips. But that wasn't why she'd come here – to see what she was missing out on. She wanted to know what was happening. Back at the camp she'd paced nervously, wondering if Ian and Julia had managed to smooth over the disruption she had caused. Before long she'd set off with the baby towards the track, pausing only to grab binoculars from her tent. Now, leaning closer, she frowned tensely. Did Ian and Julia look relaxed? Were the Marlows enjoying themselves?

While Essie was seeking clues, she saw Frank approach Diana. Slipping his hand around her waist, he leaned to touch her head with his. Essie thought Diana was standing stiffly, as if she didn't want to be there. But perhaps Essie was being influenced by Diana's statement about her husband's unfaithfulness. While Essie was still studying her, Diana ducked away. She wandered over to stand with Ian. She waved one hand, taking in the scene around her, smiling. Then she cocked her head, perhaps asking a question. Soon, the two were laughing together, Diana tipping back her head, showing off her swanlike neck. She must have lost her balance, her high-heeled sandals wobbling on the rough ground, because she steadied herself by touching Ian's arm, just briefly.

Essie swung the binoculars towards Julia. She was guiding Frank across to the plaque. They appeared to be deep in conversation, too. It occurred to Essie that she and Ian might have planned to separate the Marlows, taking one each. It all seemed to be going well. Everyone was happy.

When Essie looked back to Ian and Diana, they were at the far corner of the site, where the last of the footprints could be seen. Squatting down, Ian had placed his hand in the indent. When he took it away, Diana mirrored his action. Essie guessed he'd been inviting the visitor to connect with the ancient ancestors who'd walked right here, so long ago. Or he might have been pointing out to Diana that standing upright was the defining characteristic of humans. The development had led to enormous evolutionary change. With their hands free, the Australopithecines were now free to carry food or simple weapons or tools, or to hold the hand of a child. It was equally possible that Ian was explaining to his guest how William had brought a forensic footprint expert from America to verify the discovery. Whatever line he was taking, Diana was listening very intently. Her head was bent close to Ian's. Where Essie and Ian were opposites, blonde and dark, the two bending over the footprint were like a matching pair.

Essie turned away, heading back to the Tower. She now felt left out, abandoned, up here alone – even though it was the outcome of her own actions. In the shade that stretched in front of the rock, she lowered herself to the ground. Cross-legged, she rested her back against the upright shaft of stone. The movement disturbed the baby, who wriggled in the sling, making a mewing sound. Essie stroked her back gently through the soft hide. Thoughts and emotions tumbled inside her but she focused on the rhythmic movements of her hand. The baby soon settled again, but Essie continued patting her. She was comforting herself, she realised, as much as the baby.

Sunset was not far off. From the western horizon, hidden behind the Tower, shafts of light reached over the plains and bathed the slopes of the volcano. Before long it would be time for the Marlows to fly back to Serengeti, and for everyone else to return to the camp. Essie lingered, hanging on to the interlude of calm. The storm would come soon enough. She watched as the lava on the peak became tinged with blue. The sky behind it was awash with orange and pink. Thin green streaks of cloud looked like seaweed drifting in a gentle sea.

FIVE

There was the occasional clink of cutlery as Ian, Julia and Essie consumed the food that had been left behind by the Marlows. The champagne was flat and the crackers under the caviar and cream cheese were now soft, but they all ate steadily. There was plenty to choose from. Devils on horseback and mini sausage rolls; slices of terrine topped with gelatine; cheese spiked onto cocktail sticks along with tiny pickled onions dyed red and green. The luxurious spread made a mockery of the tinned Christmas treats that had seemed so special the night before.

The scene was lit by lanterns that had been set up by Kefa as the darkness closed in. In the middle of the table was the centre-piece of the feast. The chef at Serengeti Lodge had created a pastry model of the Steps site. Stuffed eggs with yolks piped into yellow swirls marked the rock boundary and a tall club sandwich represented William's plaque. Three pairs of footprints had been cut out of the dough. Gherkin rounds, olives and pieces of pine-apple were strewn across the miniature field. Someone had eaten one of the stuffed eggs, leaving a break in the line, and in the trans-fer from the Lodge's porcelain platter to a wooden board from Baraka's kitchen the club sandwich had acquired a lean, but other than that the model still looked impressive.

Talking was limited to comments on the food or wine – remarks about tastes long forgotten, or unusual combinations of ingredients. The words had a hollow ring. Disappointment floated in the air like a dark cloud. Essie had been given the brief report that no generous offer had been made by Frank Marlow. All that remained for her to discover was if there was any hope at all.

The issue of the Hadza baby was yet to be addressed. Julia had simply refused to discuss the matter until after they'd eaten. It felt like an attempt on her part to exert some kind of control over a day where almost nothing had gone to plan. When they did talk, Essie knew the tone would be cool and restrained. It would be easier, in a way, if shock and outrage were expressed, but that wasn't how the Lawrences operated. Sometimes Essie had the feeling that when Julia and Ian were together they actually competed with one another to be extra calm and civilised. The tension around the table now made it hard for her to eat, but she forced herself to comply.

In stark contrast to the mood in the Dining Tent, there was singing, laughter and the throb of drums coming from the workers' camp. Frank Marlow had arranged for the Lodge to send food for the Africans so they too could share in the special occasion. This had sparked a celebration that Essie knew would have eclipsed anything evoked by the Marlows' wedding anniversary. People would be dancing and telling stories for hours. They seemed to possess the gift of being able to enjoy life in the moment, unfettered by thoughts or worries about the future.

Essie wondered where Baraka was – whether he'd remained in the kitchen with the baby or taken her out with him to the fireside. Essie had given her another bottle of milk and then changed her nappy, having relocated, along with a supply of towels and washcloths, from the kitchen to one of the guest tents. Then she'd left the baby in Baraka's care. Since she'd not heard from him, she assumed all must be well. She had no idea how long a baby of this age usually stayed awake, or how they spent their time. But Baraka had seemed unfazed as he'd tied on the sling and settled her on his hip. With her head up, the baby was able to see out. Her eyes had been wide and shiny as she'd gazed solemnly around her. The baby would have hampered Baraka's movements had it been necessary for him to prepare a meal. Essie was acutely aware that the reprieve given by the Marlows' leftovers was only for tonight; the next day the cook would be working hard from dawn until dark.

Essie picked up her champagne. The glass was a sturdy tumbler with a chip in the rim, a far cry from the cut crystal she'd seen through her binoculars earlier. She watched the lamplight glow through the golden liquid. A few bubbles straggled to the surface. There was a small fly floating there. Fishing it out with her finger, she rubbed it off onto her dress, adding a black mark to the milk stains and the smudges of ochre earth she'd picked up at the Tower. She took a long gulp of the tepid wine, then put down her glass and looked up.

'What exactly did Frank Marlow say?'

Ian finished a mouthful, swallowed hard, then shook his head. 'Nothing.'

The single word conveyed a deep well of despair.

Julia stabbed an olive with a cocktail fork. 'He seemed impressed by what we've done. But he showed no interest in our plans for new work. I'm sure he knew we wanted to ask him for a grant. He avoided the whole topic.'

'Flamingos,' Ian said bitterly. 'He kept talking about flamingos. He's funding some work on them – at our lake!'

Essie looked down at her plate. No one could know if her presence at the Steps would have made any difference to how the occasion might have unfolded, but she felt guilty anyway. And she didn't need the others to tell her that the financial problems that were now not going to be solved by the Marlow Trust would be exacerbated by the presence of a baby. Precious supplies of powdered milk would be used up. Nappies would have to be washed, requiring both laundry soap and labour. Who knew what other expenses there might be? Essie turned from Ian to Julia and back, eyeing the scraps on their plates. Surely enough food had now been eaten. She tried to think of the best way to begin the conversation about the baby.

'What would you have said to the Hadza?' she asked finally. 'In my place?'

Julia sighed, her lips pursed. 'There are always lots of Africans with lots of big problems. You can't help them all. Even if we thought it was practical – for one second – for us to have a baby here, where would it end? We'd be flooded with demands for help. You know that.'

Essie gazed at a sliver of smoked salmon that was curling at the edges as it dried out. She remembered how after she'd adopted Tommy, the Maasai herd boys kept arriving at the camp trying to sell her baby animals they'd captured. Essie had said no to them from the start, hoping to send a clear message. But the offers kept on coming; she didn't like to think how many deaths had resulted from Tommy's rescue. Nothing was as simple as it seemed.

'You should have insisted they come to see us,' Julia said. 'They took advantage of you.'

Essie nodded. She wished she had done exactly that. Then she wouldn't have felt personally responsible for the outcome. She was just glad the others didn't know that she'd not even made a deliberate decision about the baby. She'd just nodded her head at the wrong moment, and then been caught up in a current that pulled her along. Julia would have handled it so differently. Essie had seen how strict she was in her dealings with the Maasai. She ran a weekly clinic for them as part of an agreement made back when the Archaeological Reserve was established. The herdsmen had to keep their cattle out of the area to avoid damaging potentially precious sites; in return Julia attended to minor injuries and illnesses. Whenever the deal was broken, she kept her medicine cabinet shut. And while the Lawrences helped with emergencies as best they could, she was never persuaded to feel accountable when people who needed hospital care had no way to get it.

Ian leaned towards Essie, placing his hand on her arm. 'No one blames you for being emotional about a baby. And you haven't been in Africa long. But the fact is, we can't afford any distractions. Our only hope now is to find something important enough to get more government funds. We have to watch every shilling.' Ian raked his fingers back through his hair. Essie could see the fear in his face. 'If we don't succeed, we really will have to close down.'

Julia lifted her head. Her eyes were hard splinters of light.

Ian stared around the room looking like a hunted animal searching for an escape. Seeing him like this – when he was usually so confident and in control – made Essie feel as if she was standing on the edge of a cliff. She wanted to scramble away from the edge but couldn't see how to do it.

'I can't just take her back.'

'You might not be able to find them if you did,' Julia pointed out. 'They've got what they wanted.'

Essie closed her eyes. She felt suddenly exhausted. It had been only this morning that she'd set off to the flint factory to pick out some stones. She could barely take in what had happened since then. One thing she knew for sure. She couldn't be responsible for a baby for the whole of this crucial dry season. She had to be free to work hard alongside Julia and Ian to try to save Magadi. She remembered Diana saying how lucky she was, how others would envy her life. She didn't want to lose what she had.

Essie glanced up at Ian. If she showed how much she needed him to take charge, perhaps he might rise to the occasion. It had happened before. She leaned towards him. 'What can we do?'

She waited for him to bend his head, resting his chin in his hand. This was what he always did when he was thinking hard. The workers all knew not to interrupt him with questions or suggestions. They just squatted on their heels, out in the *korongos*, awaiting his instructions.

Ian started pushing a pickled onion around his plate with his fork. As the quiet lengthened, Essie turned to Julia. She was watching Ian, too. She always let him take the lead, as William had evidently done when he was alive. From what Essie gathered, the Lawrences' marriage had been typical of their era. And William's status as a man had been further enhanced by professional fame and a personal charisma that people still mentioned. Though times had changed (in England, if not here) Julia expected Ian to take his father's place. It was as if – with her husband's death – ultimate authority had to be passed to the next generation.

Finally, Julia broke the silence. Her tone was brisk. 'I know what I would do. Give the baby to the Maasai. Pay one of the women to nurse her.' Ian and Essie both turned to her. Their focus seemed to urge her on. 'She'd be better off with them. The life would be more like what she's going back to.'

Ian put down his fork. 'That's true. It makes much better sense than having her here.' He looked at Essie. 'You could visit her. Check she's okay. I don't think the Hadza could expect more than that.'

Essie ran through the conversation at the Painted Cave. The people feared their baby being sent out of the area, but the Maasai village – the *manyatta* – was nearby. Although the cattle-herders were normally semi-nomadic, the tribe in this area didn't move around much. In fact, their substantial huts and thorn barricades hadn't been relocated for many years. 'It sounds like a good solution.'

'We'll ask Baraka to find someone,' Julia said.

Essie smiled with relief. They could trust Baraka to choose a suitable foster mother. Caring. Kind. A woman who would carry the Hadza baby on her back all day and sleep with her at night.

'I'll get him now.' Julia left the table, picking up one of the kerosene lanterns to light her way.

When she was alone with Ian, Essie reached across the table, touching his hand. 'I'm sorry.' She wasn't sure exactly what she was apologising about – whether it was the baby, or the disappointment of Frank Marlow's silence, or all the other let-downs the Lawrences had suffered over recent times. Perhaps it was just everything.

Ian gave her a wan smile. He looked tired, too. Essie wished they could retreat to their tent. The place had always been a haven for them – earlier on, when there were frequent visitors in the camp, and in these last few years when Julia's undiluted company made them feel like a threesome rather than a couple. The canvas walls formed a barrier to the world outside, and the mosquito net around their bed created an intimate inner sanctum.

It didn't take long for Julia to return. Baraka appeared beside her at the entrance to the tent, sharing the light of the single lantern. Essie's eyes went straight to the bulging sling that was resting at his side. She thought of the baby, sleeping innocently, while her fate was being discussed. She could just see the top of her head emerging from the wrapping of fur.

Baraka scanned the table. 'Do you need more food?'

'That's not why we've called you,' Julia said.

The cook looked around for some other source of concern.

Ian cleared his throat. Then he began to lay out the plan they had in mind for the Hadza baby. He ran one sentence into the next, leaving no room for any questions or comments. Though Ian spoke in Swahili, Baraka seemed to be having trouble following. A deep line appeared between his eyebrows. He kept looking at Essie, even though Ian was the one addressing him.

When Ian was finished, he poured himself some more champagne as if preparing to celebrate finding a solution to at least one of the Lawrences' problems.

'You want a Maasai woman to become the mother of this Hadza baby?' Baraka asked him.

'She has to breastfeed her,' Julia said. 'Bottles aren't an option in the *manyatta*. There must be someone ready to wean a toddler. We can provide the food for them.'

'It's only for a little while,' Essie said firmly. 'They have to give her back when the rains come.'

Baraka began shaking his head before she'd even finished. 'They will not consider it.'

'Why ever not?' Julia demanded. 'We will pay – money or cattle, whatever they prefer.'

Ian nodded, lending authority to the offer. Essie guessed he knew that the price negotiated would not be too high for his bank account to meet.

'It is not a matter of payment.' Baraka spoke carefully as though his words were like pieces of fruit to be turned over before being selected. 'It is rare for a mother to take another woman's baby to her breast. She will do it for one of her own tribe, of course. And it will happen when Maasai have been fighting and they want to make peace. A mother from each tribe is chosen. The women swap their babies. The mothers' milk binds the agreement. They bring up the children as their own.' He looked down into the sling. 'This baby has nothing to do with us. She is not a Maasai.'

There was silence as the meaning of his words was digested.

'Couldn't you at least ask?' Julia said.

It took Essie a moment to identify the emotion on Baraka's face: it was not confusion but embarrassment. He hung his head, speaking to the floor. 'It would be an insult.'

Ian threw an olive pip onto his plate. 'Bloody Maasai . . . You think the Hadza are beneath you! Like everyone else you ever meet.'

Essie looked at her husband in surprise. It was true the Maasai were famous for having a superior attitude to other tribes, but Ian wouldn't normally state the fact openly like this. It showed just how annoyed and frustrated he was.

'The Hadza are not like everyone else,' Baraka said firmly. He must have decided to be blunt, too. His frank gaze swept between Ian, Julia and Essie as he continued. 'These people have no cattle. Not even goats or donkeys. They have no *manyattas*. No spears, no cooking pots. They are nothing. They don't even believe in God.'

As he finished his speech, Baraka drew himself up to his full height, pushing out his chest. In spite of his grey hair, it was easy to picture him as a spear-wielding warrior daubed in ochre paint. In the pause that followed, Essie noticed the drumming in the camp had increased in tempo.

'Then maybe someone in the village would do it,' Julia persisted. The settlement was further away than the *manyatta*, but not impossibly distant.

Baraka shook his head. 'The Warangi look down on them, too. All the farming people do – the Wagogo, the Wachaga. Why would they not? The Hadza cannot grow crops. They feed like animals in the bush. And the others who have cattle – the Sukuma, the Barabaig – despise them as much as we Maasai do.' He glanced down at the baby. 'No one will take this child.'

Essie stared at him. 'But you've been looking after her.' She felt a flush of outrage. 'You like her!'

Baraka gazed at her in silence. He seemed to be searching for an answer to give himself as well as her. Finally, he spread his hands. 'She is a baby. Someone must help her.'

'This is a Tanzanian baby,' Julia said. 'A Tanzanian should look after her.'

Baraka gave her a knowing look, indicating this new tack was not going to draw him in. Essie felt for the old cook; he was not accustomed to arguing with these people he'd served for most of his life. The implications of her decision to follow the Hadza hunters seemed to be spreading like tentacles that kept catching more prey.

Pulling the sling around so that the baby was in front of him, Baraka bent over, causing the opening to gape. Carefully he lifted the sleeping baby out. His hands were under her arms, fingers supporting her head. She was like a floppy doll, limbs dangling down. Her trunk seemed to lengthen, becoming impossibly thin; the bulky towel that stood in for a nappy hung precariously from her narrow hips. Baraka took her over to Essie, hovering by the chair until her weight was transferred. At the moment when he removed his hands, the baby opened her eyes. She stared around her, before fixing her gaze on Baraka. As he backed away, her mouth began to quiver. Then she whimpered as if in pain.

Essie jiggled the baby in her arms as she'd seen mothers do. She looked pleadingly at Baraka – but he just slipped the sling over his head and passed it to her. The whimper turned into a wail. Essie stared helplessly. The baby couldn't be hungry yet. The nappy didn't feel wet. The distress seemed to be caused by Baraka handing her over. There must be something familiar about his smell, his manner with her – perhaps it was the touch of an experienced father. But the baby had been content, earlier, in Essie's care. That was why babies were so difficult to manage, Essie realised. They made no sense.

As the crying continued Ian stood up, but then seemed unsure what to do. He began pacing. Essie turned to Julia; she was a mother, after all. Julia was rolling a cigarette. Her fingers were clumsy. The tobacco fell to the floor.

Essie tried holding the baby close, but she wriggled and screamed even more loudly. Tears ran down her cheeks. Essie turned back to Ian. He was watching Julia, frowning with concern. His mother had abandoned the cigarette rolling; her hands were gripping the edge of the table, her knuckles white.

Essie met Baraka's gaze. He nodded almost imperceptibly towards the entrance of the tent. Pushing back her chair with her legs, Essie stood up. Throwing another look at Ian and Julia, she carried the baby outside.

Almost as soon as Essie left the tent the baby became still. It was as if the sudden darkness had distracted her. Or perhaps the night air playing over her skin soothed her. The cries became less frantic, and gradually died away. Then there were just brief silent sobs that made her chest heave. She seemed to be listening – perhaps waiting to see what the change of place would bring. Tipping back her head, she looked up into the sky. Essie followed her gaze. The last shadows of dusk had gone; the stars were bright pinpricks in a field of black. The moon was full and round with just a wisp of cloud travelling over its blue-patterned face. Essie lifted the baby against her shoulder. She could feel the strong neck craning to keep the sky in view. Essie rubbed the baby's back, feeling the nubs of her spine, the splay of her shoulder blades. The little body began to relax, the head falling forward. A soft, warm cheek came to rest against Essie's shoulder, printing tears onto her bare skin.

Essie tiptoed across the bedroom floor. On her side of the bed was a makeshift cot. The baby was sleeping there, almost hidden behind the draped mosquito net. Ian had brought a wooden box over from the Work Hut and added a couple of cushions to make a mattress. He'd set it down in reach of where Essie slept. The baby had not stirred as she was gently lowered inside. She was deep in slumber. Essie had fed her again, in the peace and quiet of the guest tent, while Ian and Julia were still at the dining table. This time Essie had tried slipping her finger into the baby's mouth, along with the dribbled milk. When she began sucking, Essie brought in the teat. After a few more tentative sucks, the baby seemed to make the connection with the familiar sensation of breastfeeding. Before long she had drained the whole bottle.

Rudie was stretched out in his place at the foot of the bed. His sprawled body formed a monotoned pattern in the moonlight that shone in through the gauze window. As Essie approached he lifted one ear, his eyes remaining shut.

Ian took off his suit, dropping his crumpled jacket and trousers onto a chair. After removing his shirt and tie he stretched his neck, rolling his head, undoing the constriction of the formal clothes. Then he lifted up the net and sat on the bed. As Essie kicked off her shoes she was aware of him watching her intently. She tried to read his expression as she reached behind her to unzip her dress.

'Stop. Leave it on,' Ian said.

Essie paused, eyeing him in surprise. Then she walked towards him. Without her shoes the skirt was too long so she lifted it to avoid tripping. When she reached the bed Ian drew her against him, nuzzling his face into her breasts. He slid the straps over her shoulders. Undoing the zip, he eased down the bodice. Essie's worn-out bra looked tatty beside the orange silk. She undid the clasp, letting it drop. Her skin glowed golden in the lantern light.

'You look beautiful.'

Essie smiled. She hadn't known what to expect of her husband when they finally made it to bed – a cool, punishing quiet, perhaps; or an exhausted few words then a turned back. Instead Ian pulled her down onto the bed. He ran his hands over her hips, the silk making his touch smooth and sensual. Then he lifted the skirt and moved on top of her. Their sweat-damp skin clung together. Ian sighed with pleasure. As Essie tilted back her head, he kissed her neck hungrily. Closing her eyes, she willed the tingling warmth to spring to life, travelling through her blood, setting her on fire. But nothing happened. She felt cut off from her body. She knew why. It was because of the baby being right there beside her. Her attention was focused on wondering if she was going to wake up, and what might happen then.

'Are we safe?' Ian whispered.

Essie nodded. He always asked, even if sometimes he must have known where she was in her cycle. She didn't mind. It gave her a sense of power, knowing that she was the one protecting them both from something they did not want. As if evoked by this thought, a tiny murmur came from the cot. Essie caught her breath, waiting for more.

Ian's head was above hers, his face turned to one side, as he pushed inside her. He moved quickly, almost roughly – as if he could drive out all the fears and worries that had come between them. His breath shortened, then he reared up, gasping. In a sudden movement he pulled out of her.

'I'm sorry,' he muttered.

'It's okay,' Essie responded. 'I'm too tired anyway.'

As he collapsed back onto her she felt the slick wetness on her belly. Usually, when she said it was safe, he risked staying inside her. It wasn't hard to guess why he'd been extra careful tonight.

Essie stroked the back of Ian's head, running her fingers through his hair. After a short while, he rolled off her. He kissed her cheek. 'Will she wake up, do you think?'

'I don't know,' Essie replied. She didn't bother to pass on what the Hadza had told her. *She is a good baby*. It sounded ridiculous to her now – too simple to mean anything.

Ian mumbled a few words, then turned over. Within moments he was asleep.

Essie was wide-awake. She pulled the sheet up over her body and lay there listening to the sounds inside the tent. There were two sets of breathing: the light flutter, barely audible, coming from the baby; and Ian's slow, deep rasp. Now and then Rudie stirred before settling down with a sigh. From outside came the usual noises of the African night. In the distance was the rising whine of a hyena. Close-up, the racket of insects clicking and buzzing. Cries of night herons beginning their waking hours. From the workers' camp came soft voices and the clank of lanterns being carried around. The drums had fallen silent.

Tommy was still shut up in his pen; Essie hadn't wanted to risk him causing any problems today. Now she pictured him guiltily, knowing he'd be sulking in the corner. When she let him out in the morning he would turn his face away from her.

As she gazed into the shadows she tried not to think about what had happened during this long day, but it was hard to hold it all at bay. She soon found herself drawn back to the Hadza cave. She was surrounded once more by the curious eyes of the tribespeople. She saw their nearly bare bodies, lean and fit. She felt the desperate gaze of Nandamara, the grandfather. And Giga's wistful look as they said goodbye . . .

Abruptly Essie switched her thoughts away from them. She focused instead on the backdrop to the Hadza camp – the Painted Cave. Stroke by stroke, she conjured the pictures in her mind. Over the generations new paintings had been superimposed over earlier ones. Her task as a researcher had been to isolate the layers in a way that a camera never could. As she'd done her drawings – taping her paper onto the rock surface, using a soft crayon so she didn't press too hard against the precious artwork – she'd experienced a sense of satisfaction that went beyond Ian's academic objectives. She felt she was making it possible for all the different people and animals to become themselves again. Separate, whole, free.

Now, beginning at the far end of the cave wall, Essie recited in her head the individual titles she'd given them – rolling them out, one by one.

Family of stick dancers.

Tall woman with hat or wig.

Hunter with arm tassels and penis.

Reclining man with lenticular shape – maybe a rattle.

Child with warthog.

Crisscross lines. Bones?

Circle of dots.

Crouching dog.

Long-necked bird. (Flamingo.)

Volcano . . .

As she drifted into sleep, the image of the mountain lingered – hovering above her like a beckoning dream.

SIX

Essie was drawn out of her sleep by the frantic buzzing of a fly trying to escape through the gauze window of the tent. As soon as she opened her eyes she knew the light was wrong. Bedroom furnishings that should have been draped in pre-dawn gloom were clear-edged; surfaces were bright. The door was unzipped, rolled up. Daylight streamed in.

She frowned, confused. Ian always woke her up. It was a daily ritual. He would shake her shoulder, then wish her good morning in the formal manner of the Lawrences. As he climbed out of the bed Essie would lie still for a while, listening to him getting dressed – the rustle of fabric, his footsteps on the wooden flooring, first the pad of socked feet, then the solid thud of work boots. There had been a time when she could hear fresh energy in his movements. But that had been at least two years ago. Now she sensed only weariness, as if he were exhausted already by the challenges of the coming day. Sometimes she picked up a brittle impatience, too, in the way he shoved his shirt into his trousers and tightened his belt. If a bootlace was tangled, he swore under his breath. Perhaps the problems he faced felt more acute, piling up in front of him, than they did after he'd been awake for a while. Or maybe it was just that there was no one but his wife watching on.

By the time Ian was in the company of others he'd have adopted a businesslike manner that was sometimes almost cheery. But by then Essie was already drawn into his hopeless mood. Any joy sparked by the chorus of songbirds in the trees outside was dulled. Even the colours of the dawn sky, glimpsed through the window, seemed muted. Essie had to drag herself from the bed. If she was too slow, Ian hurried her along before he left the tent. Sometimes he reminded her of the need to be washed and dressed before Kefa appeared with her *chai*.

Turning over, Essie stared at the bare pillow beside her – at the rounded hollow where Ian's head had been. She felt a flicker of anxiety. Why had he not woken her? Glancing around, she could see that Rudie had disappeared as well. Where the dog had lain last night there was just a speckle of stray hairs.

Suddenly, Essie was fully awake. Rolling over, she looked down at the box beside her. The sight of an African baby lying there jolted through her like an electric shock. The infant was fast asleep. The towel that had served as a light blanket had been thrown off. She lay so still that Essie fastened her gaze on the bare chest until she saw that it was rising and falling evenly. The rounded arms were flung out to the sides, with hands opened showing pink palms, the fingers half-curled. Her legs were bent at the knees, crab-like, due to the bulky nappy. Very gently, Essie touched one of the feet. The tiny toes, lined up in a row like pieces of corn on the cob, were warm. She was used to sleeping outside, Essie reminded herself. And the dry season brought heat, not cool. Nevertheless, Essie felt an impulse to cover her. She looked so vulnerable, lying there. But there was a risk of disturbing her by pulling up the towel. She had to be hungry after sleeping for so many hours; it would be wise to have a clean nappy and a bottle on hand before she woke. Essie eyed the peaceful face – the eyelids sealed shut, the bow lips slightly parted. The baby must have needed this rest.

Essie peered around her. The room was a mess. Ian's suit and shirt from yesterday were still draped over the chair. Essie's orange dress, which she had eventually replaced with a nightgown before falling asleep, lay in a heap on the bedside table. Her work clothes were where she'd dropped them when she'd rushed in to get changed for the Marlows. Essie knew she should be up, putting the room straight and getting herself and the baby organised. Ian and Julia would be at work by now, and Essie had to join them as soon as possible. She had to show that she could still meet her commitments. And she needed to talk to them. Together they'd have to work out what to do about this baby.

But for a moment longer, Essie stayed where she was, gazing down over the side of the bed. She took in the whole image of the baby, lying there in her makeshift cot. The cushions Ian had used as a mattress had red velvet covers. The corners were worn bare but the rest of the pile was still thick. Essie was reminded of a display in a museum – the baby a precious relic laid out in a soft-lined case.

The wooden crate was rough, though; it had originally contained tins of fuel. The Lawrences re-used the boxes for storing fossils and artefacts. The containers were strong enough to be sent all the way to places like the British Museum or Edinburgh University. On the bare wooden sides a set of numbers and letters were painted in black; they indicated exactly where, when and by whom the items inside had been collected. This particular box must have been sent away and later returned. Next to the numbers were the words *National Museum, Dar es Salaam*. They'd been crossed out and *RETURN TO SENDER* painted in bright red.

On the other side of the box would be another name and address: *Ian Lawrence, Magadi Gorge*.

Essie's gaze snagged on the words in red. They seemed to be speaking to her – the message short and straight. Simple.

Except that the contents of this box could not be sent back. It would be a death sentence. For better or worse, for at least four months, this Hadza baby was part of Essie's world.

As if in response to these thoughts, the black-lashed eyes sprang open. The baby stared around, taking in her surroundings. She fixed her eyes on Essie, wide and fearful. Her lips began to tremble, then they turned down at the corners.

'You poor girl.' Essie imagined what it must be like for a baby to wake up and find herself in such an alien setting. Without even thinking, Essie scooped her up into her arms, hugging her close, speaking soothingly. The little hand grabbed a bunch of her hair and clung on as if it were a lifeline. 'It's all right.'

Essie patted the baby's back. The muscles relaxed for a few seconds, but then stiffened. Essie could feel the lungs filling with air, ready for the first wail. She jumped out of bed. Crossing the room, she located her dressing-gown. She managed to shove her free arm into a sleeve while grasping the baby with the other. She hitched the second sleeve over her shoulder. The garment had once been pretty, fresh, summery – one of her mother's purchases for a holiday abroad that had never been taken. It looked very shabby now; Tommy had torn the sleeve with his budding horns and the fabric was faded from constant washing during the period when she'd had to get up in the night to feed the newborn gazelle. Normally she only wore the gown inside the bedroom tent. Whether it was better than nothing, right now she wasn't certain.

Without even sandals on her feet, Essie half ran towards the kitchen, holding the baby against her shoulder, steadying her head. Not watching the ground, she trod on a sharp stone, but didn't pause. The camp had a deserted feel. Most of the workers would have gone to the digging site with Ian and Julia, leaving only the domestic staff. But Essie counted at least three sets of eyes staring at her in shock. She knew how she must look. Her hair in a tangle around her shoulders. A ragged dressing-gown half put on. A nightdress flapping around her knees, baring way too much leg. Mascara smeared around her eyes. Essie didn't have time to care. All she wanted was to grab the bottle of milk that she knew was waiting ready in the fridge, and then head for the seclusion of the guest tent where her supply of towels and washing cloths was laid out. The baboon pelt – surely comforting in its familiarity – was there, too.

Baraka must have heard the baby crying or watched Essie approach through cracks in the timbered walls of his kitchen. As she reached the door, he opened it, letting out the aroma of porridge, honey and fresh bread. He handed her the bottle. Essie grabbed the offering like a baton in a relay race without breaking her stride. As she limped away she could feel Baraka's eyes following her. She tried to read the expression she'd seen on his face. He'd definitely looked uncomfortable. Was he dismayed by the state she was in? Concerned about the welfare of the baby – even though she was a Hadza? Or was it something else altogether?

In the guest tent Essie sat down in a camping chair, but then moved to the bed when she realised the baby barely fitted between the two wooden arms. The baby had stopped crying, as if she'd learned already that the proximity of a bottle was a comforting sign. Settling her on her lap, Essie found that the nappy was wet through. She didn't bother wasting a towel protecting her dressing-gown; it would just have to join the growing pile of laundry that was waiting to be done.

As she aimed the bottle towards the baby's mouth, already open, Essie felt the chill coming off the glass. It should have been heated a little or at least brought up to air temperature. But that didn't seem to matter. Within seconds the baby was feeding hungrily. Essie felt a twinge of pity for her. The infant had spent her life sharing another baby's mother. She was only a couple of months old, yet had already learned to take what she could get and be glad of it.

As the sucking and gulping fell into a contented rhythm, Essie breathed easily again. She noticed the little fist was still closed around a lock of her hair.

'*Hodi?*'

She looked up as someone – she thought she recognised Simon's voice – announced his presence outside. Everyone at Magadi, including the Europeans, followed the African protocol for arriving at someone's dwelling. You couldn't knock at a canvas door, after all, any more than you could on the empty hole that formed the entrance of a mud hut.

Essie stood up, moving to the chair, taking the chance to shake her nightdress loose so it wasn't bunched up around her thighs.

'*Karibu,*' she called. Come close. You are welcome.

Her assistant appeared in the doorway. He was smartly dressed as always. He kept his eyes politely lowered until Essie spoke.

'Good morning, Simon. How did you awake?' Essie had switched to English but found herself still using the traditional phrases.

'I woke in peace,' Simon replied. 'And you?'

'Peace also.'

'And this baby?'

'She slept very well. I think she was tired.'

They both watched the baby in silence. She had one hand on the bottle as if trying to hold it in place.

'She is learning very quickly,' Simon commented. Essie saw a softening in his eyes. Then he gathered himself. 'Bwana Lawrence has left a note.'

Essie saw the piece of yellow field-pad paper in his hand. It was not unusual for her husband to prepare written instructions for her. It was part of his scientific approach to life. If he was going to delegate, he needed to know that a task would be carried out correctly. Knowledge was only valuable when based on a solid process. His notes were formal in tone, with no closing 'love' or kisses. Essie was a co-worker where this kind of communication was concerned, not a wife. Ian took professionalism even further where his parents were concerned, only ever naming them Julia and William, as if they were always colleagues first and family second. When Essie initially arrived at Magadi she had found this odd, but she'd come to like the sense of equality it conveyed.

'Show me.' Essie managed a small smile, even though she felt uneasy about what kind of instructions she might be about to read. Today was not an ordinary day.

Simon unfolded the paper and held it up, angled to catch the best light.

Essie scanned the letter, picking up the key phrases.

Radio contact with St Joseph's Orphanage . . . absolute guarantee the baby will not be removed from their care . . . after a night's sleep I know you will agree that this is the best way to proceed . . . welfare of the baby . . .

Her eyes widened as she read the final lines.

Mission plane booked . . . arrive early afternoon . . . nurse on board . . .

Essie sat motionless as the meaning sank in. Then she looked up. She could tell from Simon's expression that he knew the contents of the note.

He cleared his throat. 'Bwana said to let you know they are returning for lunch.'

Essie's jaw tightened as she imagined Julia and Ian discussing the baby over their breakfast, reaching a decision and taking action – all without involving her. At lunchtime they would present a united front, making it impossible for Essie to take part in any real debate. And anyway, by noon the pilot might already be at the airport in Arusha, preparing to fly to Magadi.

As she tried to decide how to respond, she gazed around the guest tent. It was as messy as the bedroom. Even with no possessions, the presence of this baby – who'd been at Magadi for less than twenty-four hours – seemed to fill the place. The baboon pelt, a bright *kitenge*, and Baraka's faded Maasai blanket were strewn across the double bed. An enamel bowl of water sat on the floor, a wet cloth abandoned on the mat nearby. There was a tin of powdered milk from the store that had not yet made it to the kitchen. Essie couldn't help noticing the dwindling pile of threadbare towels. By lunchtime she might be on the last clean nappy. Presumably the nurse from the orphanage would bring some with her – proper square ones, correctly folded. Essie pictured a woman in a white uniform, a watch pinned onto her chest. She had a stern look on her face. Perhaps she carried with her the faint smell of disinfectant. Her hair was swept up into a sensible bun. No draping locks for a little hand to cling to. The thought of giving the baby to such a person made Essie's breath catch in her throat.

'I haven't agreed to the plan.' Her voice sounded surprisingly firm.

Simon stared at her in confusion. 'But the Bwana and Mrs Lawrence have made their decision.'

Essie looked past him, out through the doorway where a flock of birds on the wing speckled the rectangle of blue sky. She was shocked by how bluntly Simon's words expressed his understanding of her status. She knew this could be based on views he may have adopted over the years about the position of women, especially a wife who had not borne children. The Hadza were known to believe in equality between the sexes, but such a stance would be rare among the Africans with whom Simon now spent his time. On the other hand, it was just as likely he had drawn his own conclusions about Essie's standing from what he'd observed of the Europeans at Magadi. Essie tried to see the situation through his eyes. It was obvious that both Ian and Julia had authority here because of their professional achievements. After William's death, Ian had taken over as Head of Research because he was a man. Julia had special status because she was Ian's mother, and an elder. That left Essie answerable to them both. Why should she expect to have any power now? Why should the question of what would happen to the Hadza baby be treated any differently to all the other decisions that were made here?

Essie looked up at Simon. 'I promised not to send her away.'

'Yes,' Simon agreed. Then he spread his hands. 'But what can you do?'

As Essie hunted for an answer, a gurgling sound came from the bottle, air mixing with the milk. Quickly she tilted the bottle up further. As the milk filled the teat the baby gulped deeply again. She might have been drinking this way for all her short life.

In the quiet Essie heard a cricket chirping outside. Her nostrils picked up a sharp ammonia smell drifting over from the old fuel drum in the corner where the used nappies were stored. They urgently needed to be washed. Essie knew none of the staff would agree to do this work. The Maasai women would be no help either. They wouldn't even be able to make sense of a soiled nappy when with their own babies they simply relied on the ever-absorbent, all-forgiving earth. Essie recalled seeing some Maasai staring in disbelief when they saw Ian blow his nose into one of his handkerchiefs then fold the cloth and put it away in his pocket as if saving the contents for some later use. The women would probably think nappies served some inexplicable – presumably superstitious – purpose as well.

The fact was, Essie would have to deal with the washing herself. The process would have to be kept separate from the other camp laundry. The nappies might have to be boiled over a fire. It sounded like a disgusting business. And where in Essie's day would such a task fit? How would she maintain her work output? The baby was – as Giga had promised – easily contented. But that didn't mean that taking care of her wouldn't use up a great deal of time.

Essie breathed out slowly, trying to think more clearly. Perhaps Ian and Julia had made the right decision. Julia, after all, knew what it was like to have a baby at the camp. The Lawrences had spent some of their children's early years here, before the world of Magadi had been disrupted, first by the tragedy that had befallen Ian's brother, and then by the war. It occurred to Essie that maybe, in not consulting her, Ian was just doing what he thought every good husband should. Trying to protect his wife from her own weakness.

The baby finished drinking and let her hand drop from the bottle. Essie looked down at her, but only for a moment. The wide trusting eyes made her indecision feel treacherous. She stared blankly across the room. She remembered how the baby's grand-father, Nandamara, had pleaded for help. She saw the depths of love and fear in his hazy old eyes, opposites twined together, like an impossible blend of light and dark that did not blur into grey. How could she contemplate letting him down? But then another thought came to her, with a stroke of clarity. Perhaps she needed to protect Nandamara from his own weakness, just as Ian intended to protect her. If the Hadza tribesman really understood the world of Europeans, he wouldn't be afraid to let his grand-daughter go away to Arusha. He'd welcome the chance for her to be placed in the expert care of St Joseph's.

Essie turned towards Simon. 'Ask Kefa to bring a kettle of hot water and a laundry tub. I also need soap and another towel if he can find one.'

'You going to wash this baby.' Simon's words were somewhere between a statement and a question.

Essie avoided his gaze. 'I want her to make a good impression.'

Kneeling on the mat next to the tub, Essie tested the water with the tender skin on the underside of her forearm.

'That feels about right,' she told Simon, who was holding a steaming kettle. 'Warm but not too hot.'

On the floor beside her the baby was kicking her legs, clearly glad to be free of the nappy. Her hands moved in time with her feet, as if connected by invisible strings. Essie shared a smile with Simon – she looked like a little beetle lying on its back. She still wore the string of beads. Essie hadn't liked to remove it – perhaps Nandamara's daughter had put it there, in the short time she had shared with her baby before she died. Anyway, the ends of the strand were knotted tightly – clearly not intended to be untied until the necklace became too small.

The baby gave off the smell of fresh urine, like the sodden towel Essie had tossed into the tin. Apart from that, she was pretty clean – with each nappy change Essie had wiped her bottom with a wet cloth. On closer examination, though, there was a faintly dusty look to her skin. There were also smears of something oily on one leg. Giga obviously hadn't given her a proper bath recently. Perhaps this was because there were no pools of water near the Painted Cave. It was also quite possible that the Hadza simply didn't see the need for constant washing.

Regardless of what suited them, Essie was determined for this baby to be as spotless as possible. She couldn't forget Baraka saying that the Hadza were despised by everyone. She hated to think that the baby might be shunned by the African staff at St Joseph's. Perhaps they wouldn't pick her up if she cried. They might not want to carry her around. The Europeans would not neglect her, but they might see her as a curiosity. The baby might be made into a talking point: a specimen of a rare breed put on display, like an exotic animal in a zoo.

This made Essie feel even more uneasy. She knew the anthropologists who'd come to Magadi over the years were interested in the Hadza because they saw them as being the most primitive people alive who still had intact traditional societies. They compared them only with the Khoisan in South Africa, who shared the unique manner of talking using click consonants. Essie felt their fascination herself; she knew Ian and Julia did, too. But it could lead into dangerous territory. There had been researchers, over time, who supported the idea that Africa was the likely birthplace of

humanity but believed that black people had remained primitive –
their development stalled – while others had evolved into
superior races. Not surprisingly this kind of thinking – the field
of eugenics – had fallen out of favour after the horrors of the
Holocaust. But Essie was all too aware that preoccupation with
the physical characteristics of different peoples lingered in the
field of anthropology. In museums and universities across the world
academics still studied human skulls and other bones, many of
which had been stolen from graves or mortuaries. The remains
came from places as far afield as Namibia and Java; and, of course,
Tasmania, which was seen as the home of possibly the most
isolated humans ever to have lived. Brain cavities were filled with
gunshot, the contents weighed for comparison with other samples.
Bones were measured. Researchers looked for links between
anatomy and the other things that defined people – technology,
culture, belief systems, art.

It wasn't all about science. In the minds of some researchers –
and ordinary travellers as well – there was a romantic reverence
for the noble savage: a belief that something desirable, that had
become lost in the modern world, could be seen in tribes like the
Hadza. But even this approach risked a negative outcome. Humans
could still become specimens, rather than being real individuals.

As all these thoughts ran through Essie's mind, she began to
wonder if there was some way the baby's status as a Hadza could
be concealed. Perhaps they could say she was just an African baby,
her origins unknown. Or they could give her a misleading tribal
name. But even if the Lawrences were prepared to be dishonest,
it was doubtful the ploy would work.

Essie grasped the infant under the arms, fingers extended
behind her neck to support the weight of the head. She lifted her

up until the legs were dangling, then lowered her into the water. As the warmth lapped her skin, the baby opened her eyes wide in surprise. Her dark irises, starkly outlined by white, stood out in the soft light of the tent.

'Isn't that nice?' Essie murmured encouragingly.

Uncertainty travelled from the eyes to the lips, which began to pucker. As the emotion spread, the little hands grasped at the air. Essie glanced across to Simon.

He said something in Hadza, soft clicks accompanying gentle vowels. The baby turned towards the sound. She relaxed in Essie's hands, her limbs drifting in the water. Then she began to kick her legs, just as she'd been doing on the floor. As splashes flew, spattering her face, she looked shocked. Then she smiled, her tongue pushing forward, pink between her dark lips. She kicked again, and then lay completely still, absorbing the effect. A chuckle rose from her throat. Essie looked up at Simon. The sound seemed oddly adult and surprisingly loud. The cycle continued, one action triggering the next – kick, splash, pause, chuckle. Soon Essie and Simon were laughing too.

'Isn't she a bit young to be showing off?' Essie grinned, water dripping from her hair.

'African children grow up quickly,' Simon stated.

Essie nodded. She'd seen Maasai offspring running around when they looked barely old enough to stand up. Very small boys drove goats all day by themselves.

Eventually the bath began to cool. Essie rubbed soap over the baby's skin, lathering away all traces of dirt. It wasn't easy to keep track of the soap; it was just a sliver. The Lawrences ordered supplies of blue-and-white marbled soap from a factory up on Lake Tanganyika. It came in substantial slabs that you broke into hunks, but it was a long time since a fresh bar had been seen at Magadi. The fragment Essie was using had lost its perfume, letting the unpleasant smell of lye come through. The aroma would cling to the baby's skin, but at least it would indicate that she was clean.

As a last task, Essie carefully submerged the back of the baby's head, then scooped water up until all the hair was wet. She rubbed her hands through the downy fuzz to clean the scalp. As she did so she felt the shape of the skull beneath the skin. The posterior fontanel was almost completely closed up; the anterior fontanel, located nearer the forehead, was still coming together – it wouldn't be fully fused until the little girl was about two. The slight dip, and the softness in the area of the open fontanel, made the baby seem frighteningly vulnerable; there was nothing but a thin covering of hair, skin and flesh to shield her brain.

Essie couldn't help picturing how the skull would look, with fine cracks marking the plates, and ragged holes where they were yet to be joined up. Most archaeologists studied anatomy, but Essie had paid particular attention to the subject; at university she'd even joined the trainee doctors in their classes. To carry out fieldwork, researchers needed a sound knowledge of the human body (and of animals, birds, fish, insects – even molluscs, for that matter). They required a grasp of botany as well. How else would they be able to identify a shard of fossilised bone, or the imprint on rock of a particular lichen? Additional advice from specialists was often sought; that was one of the reasons – along with storage, preservation and display – that fossils were sent away from Magadi. But the researcher in the field had to make the first judgement about what was unearthed. Essie had honed her knowledge over the years. If she ever had the good fortune to come across a career-making fossil, she wanted to recognise it straightaway.

Essie carried the baby across to the bed and laid her on a towel. She stood still, looking down at the miniature limbs, torso, head, feet and hands. Knowledge could be used to the wrong end, as the Nazis showed. But that didn't mean facts about Hadza physiology might not still be valuable. Medical research, for one, benefitted from such information. She was tempted to take measurements of key bones and the cranial circumference. And to make notes on the presence or absence, at this early age, of the receding forehead, the rounded jawbone, and other known hallmarks of these unique people. Fate had delivered her a rare opportunity to examine a Hadza infant. There might even be enough data to write up a short paper.

As Essie stood there, gazing down, the legs began kicking again. A look of puzzlement crossed the baby's face.

'The water's gone,' Essie said. She raised her eyebrows as though she, too, was surprised at its disappearance. 'All gone. Bye-bye.' She glanced across to Simon, hoping he hadn't heard her talking in a silly singsong voice. Luckily, he seemed preoccupied retying his bootlaces.

Carefully she dabbed the baby with the towel, making sure every fold of skin was dry. The infant eyed her solemnly. Essie found herself captured by the stare. It was so intense and focused it drew her own gaze like a magnet. Essie couldn't remember her attention being so completely caught like this – unless it was when she'd first fallen in love with Ian. The baby was so young, yet Essie sensed that she knew, somehow, that her situation was precarious – that she needed to connect with someone bigger, stronger, for her own survival. It occurred to Essie that perhaps the baby had known this feeling all her life. Giga had done her best, but her first allegiance had always been to her own child. At some deep level this baby understood that the person who was meant to be there, especially for her, was absent.

The thought brought a pang to Essie's heart. She understood what it was like to feel vulnerable to the world. How your own skin felt too thin to cover your flesh. How you wanted to press your back to the wall so no air could move behind it. She remembered how she used to hug her own body, skinny arms wrapped across her child's chest, as if she could keep herself safe. She remembered the ache she felt when she saw mothers kissing their children goodbye at the school gate, while her father dropped her off with a wave. And how, after she got home, she often stood in the hallway staring in the direction of the guest bedroom.

She saw herself there now – waiting all alone, passing the time watching dust motes dance in the air. From the kitchen came the burbling sound of the radio. Her clothes smelled of the supper prepared by her father: baked beans and fried eggs. No matter where she stood, or where she looked, all her attention was focused on the guest room down the hall where Lorna now slept. Every nerve was like an antenna, pointed in its direction. The room was a vortex, drawing in all the warmth and comfort of the whole house, sealing it away behind a closed door.

Her father emerged from the kitchen, letting blue fluorescent light into the dimness.

'Don't bother your mother. She's having a bad day.' Behind his weariness was a sharp flint of resentment.

Essie kicked the wooden wainscot with the heel of her scuffed school shoe. 'I want to play with her.'

Play. That was the only word she felt she could use. What she really wanted was to get into bed with her mother, pulling the sheet over their heads so that the air was heavy with the smell of their bodies and breath. She wanted to feel her mother's skin and bury her face in the tangled mess of her hair.

Her father sighed, cupping her bony shoulder with his heavy hand. 'She wants to play with you, too. It won't always be like this.'

Essie heard the hopeless tone in his voice.

It would always be like this . . .

Wrapping the towel over the baby, Essie lifted her up, holding her against her chest. The cloth moulded itself around the narrow shoulders, the curved spine. Essie rested her cheek on the baby's head. Skin to skin, she picked up a faint throb, coming through the soft fontanel. Her lips parted in wonder as she realised what it was. The steady pulse of the baby's beating heart.

The old Land Rover rattled as it bumped across the trackless ground. It was rarely used these days and was difficult to start. Essie hoped it would at least keep running until she was well out of sight of the camp.

Grasping the sun-cracked steering wheel, she leaned forward, searching the terrain to find the smoothest path. On the seat beside her lay the baby in her fossil-crate cot. Now and then, Essie had to steady the box with one hand. The baby seemed to enjoy the jolting motion; as soon as Essie had begun driving, she'd fallen asleep. Tommy was sitting awkwardly in the footwell, his nose jammed against the side of the crate. He seemed to prefer being squashed in there to being relegated to the back.

In the rear-vision mirror Essie watched the camp dwindle in the distance. She could still see Simon standing outside the Dining Tent. Even from here she could detect tension in his upright posture. He'd agreed with Essie's decision to be absent when lunch-time came. He would probably have preferred to leave along with her, except he feared Ian might see him as her accomplice and dismiss him from his job.

Reaching a copse of scrubby trees, Essie swung the Land Rover to the right, then drove on until she was safely hidden. Turning off the engine, she climbed out, slowly and quietly, leaving the sleeping baby inside, the door open.

Tommy skipped around the clearing, stretching his legs. He'd stopped sulking about being locked up in his pen and now just wanted to play. Lowering his head, he butted Essie in the thigh. She pushed him away distractedly. Her stomach heaved, unsettled by hunger as well as tension. Before leaving, she'd focused on preparing two bottles for the baby and had forgotten any breakfast for herself.

She sat down on a low boulder, resting her head in her hands. When she thought back over the last hour, it was like viewing a horror film. She didn't want to watch what came next but couldn't look away.

She saw herself in the radio room, holding the microphone to her mouth, putting through her call. Someone at St Joseph's had answered, speaking English with an African accent. The transmission had been patchy, so Essie had kept her statement simple.

'This is Magadi Camp. There is no need for anyone to come today. The baby is staying here. Over.'

The African woman repeated the message back.

'Please let the pilot know,' Essie added. 'Cancel the flight. Thank you.'

After having her words relayed again, Essie ended the call. She felt guilty about leaving what sounded like a casual message, while being well aware that the missionaries in charge at St Joseph's would be confused at the very least, and most likely annoyed – even alarmed – at the change of plan.

Essie went over to the Dining Tent next and found the yellow notepad Ian had left there. The top sheet still bore the imprint of the words he'd written to her this morning. She paused in front of the blank paper, gazing across the table at a smear of blue-black caviar that Kefa must have missed. When she picked up a pen and began to write, she was conscious of Simon watching her. She kept the communication brief – every letter of every word took all her courage to complete.

> *The plane is cancelled.*
> *I am keeping the baby.*
> *Just until the rains.*
> *I can't break the promise I made.*
> *I'm sorry.*

Essie propped the note up against the saltshaker. She quailed at the prospect of it being read. Even with the apology at the end, the message sounded bold, almost rebellious. But it was too late for second thoughts now.

She got ready to leave, grabbing the last of the clean towels, the sling and the *kitenge* cloth. Baraka had already prepared a bottle of milk for her to take, presumably on Simon's request. As he handed it to her, he gave a faint shake of his head.

'*Ukicheka mkwe-mkwe,*' he warned, '*utapata uchafu katika jicho lako.*' If you laugh at your mother-in-law, you will get dirt in your eye.

Baraka's words stayed with Essie as she headed for the parking area at the rear of the camp, with Simon at her side carrying the baby in her makeshift cot. Baraka liked to quote traditional sayings that suited a situation. Had he chosen this one because he thought Julia's displeasure would be greater than Ian's? Or was it more that Essie would have fewer cards in her hand when it came to appeasing her? Ian loved Essie, after all. Julia's relationship with her daughter-in-law was always much more complicated.

When Ian and Essie had decided to marry, Julia indicated that she was glad her son had found someone who shared his passion for the research at Magadi. Essie had already proved that she knew how to work hard and do without luxuries. Julia, evidently, had been chosen by William to meet the same criteria, when he'd left Africa as a young white Tanganyikan in order to do his degree in England. Essie's mother-in-law took time to teach her all the things she needed to know in order to operate in this remote location. But beyond this, Julia was largely indifferent to Essie, expressing little emotion towards her – unless you counted the undercurrent of criticism that was always there, waiting to rise to the surface. At first, Essie had been hurt by Julia's attitude. But she now understood that this was just how Ian's mother was. She was uncompromising – as tough on herself as she was on others. And she didn't like to share her feelings. Even with Ian, she was reserved. It was impossible to picture her having cuddled him or his younger brother as babies. Essie felt sure she'd never talked to either of them in a silly voice, or licked her finger in order to wipe dried food from their faces, as Essie had watched other mothers do. Julia would never have been seen running her fingers absently through her boys' hair when they were little, as if their bodies were an extension of her own.

If Julia had once had a soft, motherly side, it was well buried now. After supper last night, when Essie had brought the sleeping baby back into the Dining Tent, the woman had barely looked up from lighting her cigarette. Ian had met Essie's gaze over the little dark head cradled against her chest, even offering a small smile. He had moved around quietly, finding the fossil crate and then the cushions to use as a mattress. All the while, Julia had remained seated, her hand moving in a steady motion to her lips and back to the ashtray, peering through the smoke with narrowed eyes.

Now, in her hiding place among the trees, Essie rubbed her hands over her face, kneading her knotted brow. She glanced at her watch. It would soon be lunchtime. Her note would be read, first by Ian, then Julia. Essie hadn't decided how long she would stay away from the camp. Part of her wished she need never go back – that she could just remain here forever, letting the hum of insects in the midday heat fill her head. She didn't want to face the questions that arose from what she'd just done. She had no answers, no plans . . .

She looked around to check on Tommy, who'd given up trying to attract her attention and wandered off to graze. She located him on the far side of the clearing. He was standing very still, his nose lifted into the air. His tail flicked from side to side, which meant he was either excited or afraid. As Essie straightened up, instantly focused, she saw what appeared to be a piece of the bushy undergrowth separating from its surroundings. Fragments of patchy shadow joined together, forming a solid upright shape.

Essie rose to her feet as a man walked noiselessly towards her. He looked almost the same as the hunters who'd found her the day before, except that in place of a baboon pelt he wore a garment made of small grey skins stitched together. He had the body of an athlete. On his bare buttocks, the outline of the gluteus maximus – the muscle that had evolved to allow humans to walk upright – became visible as he moved. Slung over one sculpted shoulder was the hind leg and haunch of a zebra. The perfect black-and-white stripes on the hide, and the neat shape of the hoof, made a harsh contrast with the bloodied mess where the limb had been hacked from the carcass.

A stream of Hadza click-talking came from the man's lips. It was a gentle sound, like the running of water over pebbles. Essie offered a cautious smile. The hunter's gaze was trained on the leather sling, which Essie had put on ready for when the baby awoke. He frowned questioningly – he obviously knew about the baby. Essie pointed to the Land Rover, where the fossil crate could be seen resting on the seat.

The man put down his bow and shrugged off a quiver of arrows, before laying the hunk of zebra meat on top of a sturdy bush. Then he strode across to the vehicle. Essie hurried after him. She had a sudden fear that Nandamara had had second thoughts about their plan. He'd sent the hunter to reclaim his granddaughter. That made no sense though; Essie was the only one who could feed her. And anyway, this encounter had surely only happened by chance. But even as Essie told herself this, she had to admit that the way the Hadza had appeared right here, just now, seemed almost eerie. It was as if the hunter-gatherers were so closely connected with their surroundings that they were an omnipotent presence in the land – all-seeing and all-knowing – with eyes everywhere.

Essie's body tensed as the hunter reached into the crate. While she was still trying to decide if she had the right to intervene, he carefully lifted the baby. She stirred but didn't wake. The Hadza studied the nappy, hanging loosely around her hips, before shaking it gently off, as if it was something that had stuck to her by accident. Then he settled her in the crook of one sinewy arm.

Essie relaxed a little – he had the casual confidence of someone who knew exactly what he was doing. She noticed the fine coat of dust on his skin, contrasting with the pure black of the newly washed baby. She hoped the hunter hadn't noticed the off-putting smell of the lye. She hated the thought that he might report the observation back to Giga.

The hunter strolled over to the boulder where Essie had been and sat down. Essie perched on another, smaller, rock right beside him. Tommy stood next to her, eyeing the hunter warily. Essie put a comforting hand on his collar, then took it away in case the Hadza thought she suspected he might be a threat to her pet. Looking at the man now, it was hard to imagine him hunting anything; he gazed down at the baby with such tender eyes.

Essie found it frustrating, not having Simon here to translate. She couldn't enquire if everyone else was still camped at the cave, and if so, when they expected to begin their journey to another area. She had to accept being silent. The hunter seemed relaxed; he began to hum quietly. Clearly, he was in no hurry to go on with his day. Perhaps now that he had meat to take back to camp his goals were accomplished. Gradually, Essie absorbed his mood. There was nothing for her to do right now, either. She was just killing time.

She eyed the dismembered piece of zebra. She wondered idly if the Hadza had an explanation for the black-and-white stripes. Their evolutionary purpose was hard to see, since zebras lived on the savannah, where the striking markings made the animal stand out instead of providing camouflage. The only explanation Essie had heard of was that tsetse flies, whose stinging bites were a torment to any kind of mammal, had been shown to dislike landing on the striped coats. Tsetse flies evidently made use of light and dark when seeking food and water, and they found the contrasting pattern disorientating. This hunter would probably not be interested in this fact, Essie guessed, even if she had some way to communicate it. He was just carrying home his supper.

From down on the plains came the peeping of waterbirds. Essie followed the direction of the sound, then turned back to scan the branches of nearby trees, where yellow weavers chattered as they swung from their pendulous nests. She shifted her attention to the hunter, still holding the baby. A long gash on the man's forearm caught her eye. It looked as if a large claw had been dragged through his flesh. The wound was old and well healed. His feet had obviously never been anything other than bare; the skin was thick and grey.

The baby stirred again, opening her eyes. The hunter talked soothingly to her, until she sighed and went back to sleep. Essie felt a twinge of envy, knowing how familiar the touch and smell of the Hadza man must be.

Tommy sat down, tucking his legs beneath him, resting his head on Essie's knee. A lizard waddled slowly across the clearing, pausing to flick out a long purple tongue, snatching a small cricket. The baby was deeply asleep, her arm draping down over the hunter's scarred forearm. Essie leaned closer to swish a fly away from her. Meeting the hunter's gaze, she smiled.

He looked at her thoughtfully, his head tilted to one side. Then he used his free arm to gesture in the direction of the Painted Cave. He mimed the act of someone drawing, then pointed at Essie.

She nodded, confirming her link with the place. She assumed the Hadza man had either seen her at work tracing the cave art or heard about it. She wondered what he made of the activity, but his face showed no emotion. Instead, he swung his arm away towards the distant gleam of the lake and the lower foothills of the volcano. Once again, he mimed someone drawing.

Essie was puzzled. There were no significant caves over there – let alone ones that contained rock paintings. The area had been well surveyed. A German missionary named Wolfgang Stein had once lived down near the lake. He'd settled there before the First World War and stayed on for nearly twenty years, leaving only just prior to the arrival of the Lawrences. His stone house was still standing. Stein's goal had presumably been to convert the local people to Christianity. He was also an amateur archaeologist – the kind that destroyed important evidence by using poor methods, at the very same time as they were making valuable discoveries. He was the one who'd first recorded the existence of the Painted Cave, and the flint factory as well. He'd made maps of the foothills of Ol Doinyo Lengai – the documents were in a missionary society archive in Berlin, but there were copies at Magadi. The Lawrences had made use of them during their own assessment of the area. It had been while Julia was working over there that tragedy had struck – the disappearance of Ian's little brother. Large parts of the foothills had, as a result, been scoured by police and volunteer searchers. No one had mentioned a cave, as far as Essie knew.

She raised her eyebrows curiously. The Hadza repeated his mime, but it made no more sense to her than the first time. She wondered if she'd misread the hunter's meaning completely. Perhaps he had seen visitors to Magadi making paintings or sketches of the volcano. Academics, students and journalists alike seemed to feel an urge to make images of Ol Doinyo Lengai, as if the act formed a personal connection between them and the mountain. Julia disapproved of it – she didn't like the landscape being romanticised like this. Such a view clouded the eye of the researcher. Nevertheless, it had become something of a tradition.

It had all been started by one artist who'd stayed here with the Lawrences a long time ago. She'd done nothing but paint while she was at Magadi, judging by her output. A whole stack of her work was in the storeroom, in a folio tied up with ribbon. She'd left paints and a palette there as well, as if she'd planned to return one day. A couple of her paintings were still on display in the Dining Tent. They bore her simple signature in the corner: *Mirella 1955*. The works were unframed, just pinned to the canvas walls. Over the years they'd been marked with stains, spotted by fly dirt, the edges frayed. But the pictures were still eye-catching, with their vibrant colours and bold lines.

The hunter, roaming the area over the years, could well have seen Mirella – or one of the other visitors who'd followed in her footsteps – at work. He might be speculating about the purpose of the images – whether they had the same meaning to the Europeans as the cave paintings did to the Hadza.

Essie gazed helplessly at the hunter. She wished even more keenly that she'd persuaded Simon to come with her. Who could say what insights into Hadza life this hunter might have been willing to share, now that the baby had formed a bond between them? But Essie's assistant was probably standing in the Dining Tent right now, being interrogated by Ian and Julia.

With the topic of the paintings abandoned, the pair sat quietly for a while. Then the hunter pointed at the portion of zebra, while raising his eyebrows at Essie. She understood he was offering to give her the meat. She smiled warmly to show her gratitude. It was a generous offer. Even just carrying the leg and haunch around must have been hard work; and before that, there had been the hunt, the kill, the butchering. Politely she shook her head. The Lawrences might be short of meat, but they wouldn't resort to dining on zebra, any more than they'd consider eating one of the carnivores. For some reason zebras were nearly always infected with parasites. Also, in Essie's mind, there was something about the decoratively patterned coats – regardless of their function – that would make eating the animals feel wrong. She had a similar feeling about giraffes. The plain brown hides of other herbivores – goat, deer, wildebeest – whether tame or wild, made them different somehow. The distinction applied to birds, too. Essie found it easier to watch plain grouse and ducks being plucked than to see guinea fowl stripped of their black-and-white spotted plumage. Essie was aware that her prejudice made no sense at all.

The hunter repeated his offer. When Essie declined again, shaking her head to push home her meaning, he smiled, showing teeth that were strong and even but stained, perhaps from tobacco. Then he broke into laughter, shaking his head as though a wonderful joke had been made. Words flowed from his mouth. He laughed again. Essie smiled cautiously, suspecting she was the butt of the joke.

As the man's humour subsided, the sounds of the bush took over again. A crow cawed as it flew overhead. Closer at hand something rustled in the undergrowth, making Tommy tense. The disturbance was too minor to cause Essie any alarm. She patted him absently. Though she was sitting here, her attention drifted elsewhere. She couldn't help picturing what might be going on at the camp.

The hunter looked up first. Then Essie turned her head, frowning as she detected a distant hum. The Hadza gave her a knowing nod. He moved his free hand through the air in a slow smooth arc.

Essie jumped to her feet. Scanning the sky, she found the black speck of an aircraft. It was approaching quickly. She told herself that it could be a tourist joy ride. But it was right on schedule to be the plane coming for the baby. Essie stared blankly at the hunter as her mind raced. Had her message not been passed on? Had it been ignored? Or countermanded somehow? But by whom?

The plane passed overhead, a bright yellow shape against the sky. Essie didn't recognise the aircraft, but it was possible St Joseph's Mission had chartered one she hadn't seen before. She just hoped the Land Rover, parked in the shade for the sake of the baby, could not be seen from above. With her khaki clothes she wouldn't attract any attention. And the hunter in his grey skins and tawny leather, his black skin the same tone as shadow, would be completely invisible.

She waited to see the aircraft veer off in the direction of the volcano. But it only came lower, homing in on the Magadi landing strip. To control her anxiety, Essie paced in circles, avoiding the quizzical gaze of the hunter. Then she stood still, letting out a long breath. Whatever was going on, there was nothing she could do about it.

Crossing the clearing, she found another stone that would make a better seat – bigger, with a smoother surface on top. She rolled it back to the spot where she'd been before. Then she sat down to wait. With or without the company of the Hadza hunter, she would be here for some time – until the yellow plane was safely back in the air, returning to wherever it had come from.

SEVEN

Essie tried to close the Land Rover door quietly, hoping to postpone the moment when her return to camp was noticed. The baby was settled in the sling, content after gulping down her bottle. She had no idea, Essie thought grimly, of the tense scene they were about to enter.

She trailed towards the Dining Tent, Tommy nudging her calves from behind, frustrated by the slow progress. Essie tried to think of the occasion when she'd seen the Lawrences at their angriest. Running a camp, they had to be tough with staff, though they were usually also calm and fair. But one confrontation stood out in her memory. It was with a young Maasai worker who'd stolen a fossil and sold it to a Serengeti tourist. Julia and Ian had acted as a team, taking turns to interrogate him. Their outrage had grown as the culprit showed no remorse. Essie replayed the interchange in her head. It helped contain her own anxiety. Whatever was going to unfold now, it could surely not be as bad as that event. Words had been flung back and forth so rapidly that Essie had struggled to follow the Swahili.

'You accuse me of stealing!' the Maasai had said.

'You were caught in the act,' responded Ian.

'And yet you are the ones who are thieves.'

As soon as he'd spoken, the young man bit his lip as if regretting his words.

'What are you saying?' Julia's tone was icy.

She and Ian were both sitting down and their employee towered over them. He wore his work trousers but had replaced his shirt with a red and purple *shuka*. The sections of his body that were revealed – the bare shoulders, arms and one side of his torso – might have been modelled on a Greek statue; a perfect example of a male human. Yet he still reminded Essie of a boy standing in front of a headmaster. It took him some time to gather his nerve, but when he continued, his voice was bold.

'The bones that you collect belong to us.'

There was a dense quiet. From over in the kitchen Essie could hear Baraka shooing Tommy out of his way.

Ian took a deep breath. 'They have nothing to do with you! You Maasai migrated from the north, from the Nile valley. You've only been here for a few hundred years.'

The worker leaned forward. 'How long have you been here?'

Julia and Ian exchanged glances. What felt like a considerable time to the Lawrences – two generations – could hardly be held up as an answer here.

Raising his voice, the Maasai continued. 'How many boxes of bones have you sent away to another country so that rich white people can have their feasts?'

Ian frowned. 'Feasts?' He rephrased the Swahili. 'Big meals with visitors?'

The young man nodded.

'No one eats the bones,' Ian said impatiently. 'They study them.'

The Maasai shrugged his shoulders. 'The main point is that they pay you a lot of money.'

Julia let out a laugh that sounded like a cough.

'They do,' he insisted. 'When you find special bones, you are rich. Now you have none, you are poor.' He spread his hands. 'You eat the food of peasants. No one comes to pay you their respects. All your special things are broken. It is time for you to go away.'

Julia's mouth fell open. Ian looked around as if seeking advice. Essie saw his gaze settle on the *National Geographic* magazine – his father's face. He stood up, confronting the Maasai. 'That is enough! You will not work here any more. You must leave the camp. Right this moment.'

Fury flashed in the sacked worker's eyes. He rested his hand on the hilt of his sheath knife. 'You are the ones who should go. This land belongs to Lengai. Not to you. We do not want you here.'

Essie noticed the ritual scar on his leg that proved he'd slain a lion as part of his initiation to warriorhood. She bit her lip. Suddenly Magadi Gorge felt very isolated and remote. They were three white people, out of place among dozens of Africans.

Slowly and calmly, Ian lowered himself to his chair. Earlier on, the fact that the Europeans were seated seemed to give them an advantage. Now the situation was reversed. Why Ian had made that move Essie didn't know. But it left room for the Maasai to back down with dignity. The man stepped away, turning cold eyes from Ian to Julia and back. For the first time, Essie felt glad that she wasn't truly seen as a Lawrence – that she was an onlooker in this confrontation rather than a player.

With an angry swish of his blanket cape, the worker left the tent.

As soon as he was gone, Julia had turned to Ian. 'You handled that rather well.'

Essie had watched her husband swell with the pleasure of his mother's praise.

Now, as she neared the corner of the tent, she wondered if she should try to follow the Maasai's example: pretend to be strong, undaunted by the choice she'd made. But she knew she simply wouldn't be able to do it. Writing a bold note was one thing; being face to face with Ian and Julia, her courage would surely fail.

She came to a sudden halt. From the other side of the canvas came a peal of laughter. It sounded like Julia, except it was too loud, and went on for too long. Essie was puzzled: there was no one else it could be. Unless, that is, the yellow plane had delivered a visitor here. Essie felt a thread of hope – her encounter with the others might be easier with a stranger present. They would all feel constrained by politeness.

Breathing more freely, she rounded the front corner of the tent. Then she blinked in surprise. The scene came to her in fragments. An impression of wheels with glittering spokes. White tyres. Sleek lines of a smart white pram with a black hood. A sun canopy with a fringed edge – white, lined with a rosebud print. A pink ribbon tied to a silver handle, gleaming in the sun.

With the next step she saw a chest of drawers, painted white, decorated with pink bows. Resting on top was a baby-sized wicker basket garnished with a flurry of lace. Standing next to it were three tea chests, stark lettering on their sides: *Highgrown Kenya Tea*. The open tops revealed cardboard shopping bags with glimpses of pink-and-white fabric, and several bulky packages wrapped in paper. Peeping from one tea chest was a honey-brown teddy bear with a pink satin bow around its neck.

Essie gazed at the array of baby paraphernalia. Even knowing nothing about such things, she could tell that a huge amount of money had been spent. With it all laid out here, the barren *korongos* of Magadi Gorge as a background, the scene was like something from a nonsensical dream.

Ian could be heard laughing now, too. As Essie skirted the chest of drawers, the open front of the tent came into view. He was standing up, pouring champagne into a cut crystal glass. Judging by the way he tilted it, the bottle was nearly empty. Another stood unopened nearby. A spare glass stood next to it. Essie's note had been pushed across to the far side of the table, as if forgotten. Julia sat back in her chair, smiling. There was no one else in the tent.

When Ian saw Essie there, he grinned, raising the bottle. 'You're back!'

At a loss for words, she just stared at him.

'We have a grant, Ess.' Ian almost skipped across to her. 'A huge one!' Champagne floated on his breath. He seemed about to hug her, but then looked down at the baby and stepped away. 'You won't believe it.' His gaze jumped from place to place as if he was too excited to concentrate on any one thing.

Essie's eyes widened. 'The Marlow Trust?'

'Not exactly.' He took a slip of paper from his shirt pocket and held it towards her. It was a cheque made out to Ian Lawrence. At a glance Essie saw lots of zeros. She focused on the signature, but it was just a scrawl.

'It is a personal grant from Mrs Marlow. Diana. No strings attached. We can do whatever we want.' He whistled through his teeth. 'It's more than we've ever dreamed of.'

'And she sent all this?' Essie scanned the assemblage of furniture, equipment and boxes.

'Ridiculous, I know.' Ian returned to the table and picked up his glass. 'According to the pilot, Mrs Marlow contacted the Nairobi Club via the Serengeti radio and got the manager to send his wife shopping. Apparently there's some place in town called Babyland. The woman was told to buy everything a baby needs. It was for a little girl and she had to have the best.' Ian waved at the elegant pram. It would have looked at home in a London high street. 'Obviously the circumstances were not mentioned.'

Essie imagined an eager shopkeeper bringing out his wares, making suggestions. He'd have had a coffee planter's young wife and baby in mind, or the family of a government official, still clinging to his post in Independent Tanzania, or maybe even a fortunate missionary.

'The pilot had the wrong impression, too. He congratulated me.' Ian's voice was suddenly spiked with anger. 'It was very awkward.'

'I'm really sorry,' Essie said. She knew Ian hated being embarrassed more than anything. She glanced down at the baby who was quietly taking in the action around her. When Essie looked up, she kept her gaze away from her husband. Outside the tent, she noticed that a crowd of onlookers had gathered – camp staff, field workers, even a teenage Maasai goatherd. Keeping a respectful distance away, they were whispering and pointing – no doubt finding it incomprehensible that all this equipment was for one little Hadza baby.

Julia sniffed. 'Hopefully they sent some items that are actually useful. Nappies, for example, and plastic pants.'

'I should think so,' Ian said, 'if she ordered everything.'

'You'll need a lot of formula, you know,' Julia continued, 'to last four months. At least a tin a fortnight.'

Essie's lips parted as the meaning of these words sank in. In spite of the tart tone, Julia had obviously accepted the baby was going to stay at Magadi, from now until the coming of the rains.

And she was even sharing information from her own experience. Essie felt the knot of tension begin to loosen inside her.

'What made Diana want to do all this?' She gestured at the deliveries outside, the bottles of champagne, the fancy glasses and the cheque resting on the table.

'There was a letter,' Ian answered. 'The pilot came via the Lodge to collect an envelope from Diana. The champagne was put on board, too; it was nice and cold.' He poured a third glass and gave it to Essie. 'She just said she was impressed by her visit and wants to support the work. I guess she has money of her own – there's no mention of Frank.' He looked thoughtful. 'She did show a lot of interest, down at the Steps. And who knows, maybe she was also touched by the idea of you rescuing a Hadza baby. Philanthropists can be quite irrational.' He shrugged. 'Anyway, we have the grant. That's what counts.' He smiled as he looked outside, into the distance. 'I'll go to Arusha as soon as possible. I can't wait to see the bank manager's face when I bring out that cheque!'

Julia was gazing in the opposite direction as if she could see through the back of the tent, up towards the Gorge. 'We can begin work in the *korongo* where the *Sivatherium* was found.'

Essie nodded her agreement, even though no one was looking at her. Her current project in the Work Hut involved working on the fossil remains of a dinosaur that was an ancestor of the giraffe. She was cleaning and assembling small fragments of the cranium. There were three leg bones, a tooth and half a vertebrae, too. Together the fossils were sufficient for a definitive identification. The discovery of a *giraffid* at Magadi wasn't extraordinary in itself. The importance lay in the fact that a particular stone tool had been found nearby, in the same strata. It had been used to butcher the *giraffid;* there were nicks on the leg bones consistent with the cutting edge. With the three elements taken together – the bones, the tool and the matrix in which it was located – the find was significant. Everyone at Magadi had been excited the day it was all revealed.

The tool was similar to ones made by *Homo habilis*, the hominid whose remains had been discovered a decade ago at Olduvai, drawing worldwide attention to the Leakeys. *Habilis* was more advanced than Australopithecine but still had a brain only half the size of modern humans, and short legs and long arms. He'd been given the nickname Handyman, because *Homo habilis* was the first category of hominid to actually create stone tools, rather than just make use of rocks picked up from the ground. The artefact that was sitting in the tray on Essie's work table was just a little bit more sophisticated, however, than could be expected of Handyman. This offered the tantalising possibility that somewhere in that site were the remains of an even more evolved hominid. Someone more like us. The potential of the location was the very reason excavation had not yet begun. There had not been the resources to do it properly.

Until now.

Julia turned back to Ian. 'We should think about a name for the site.'

There was a brief silence, with looks passing between the three. The naming of a *korongo* could be a contentious matter. The one where they were digging now was called Alice Jones Korongo – AJK for short. It was in honour of a primatologist who studied bonobo apes in the Congo. Her work was of interest to the Lawrences, since the great apes – so humanlike, with the absence of tails – were our closest relatives. Aside from the orangutans of Indonesia and Malaysia, they existed only in Africa. The fact added weight to the proposition that this continent was the setting in which the genus *Homo* had begun to evolve. Alice Jones had visited Magadi around the time the excavation had got underway, nearly ten years before Essie had arrived here. William had named the *korongo* after her. Julia had not approved. She didn't think Alice Jones deserved the honour. In fact, Julia must have taken a deep dislike to her. Essie had heard her description of the woman's unexpected arrival at Magadi one day, in a jeep full of bonobos rescued from poachers. With her dirty clothes, dishevelled ponytail and her cargo of what might have been wild hairy children, she looked as if she'd been in the jungle for far too long, according to Julia. The primatologist had no business turning up at Magadi just because she'd happened to meet William on a trip to Arusha. She had worse manners than the animals she studied. The Africans agreed with Julia's low opinion of Alice Jones. Some even believed she was a witch, who had given birth to animal children. They blamed her for the lack of success the Lawrences had experienced while working in AJK.

'Diana might appreciate her name being used,' Ian said.

Essie quashed a sense of disappointment. William, Ian and Julia already had sites named after them; she was the next obvious choice. But then, Diana was the one who was making it all happen.

'That would be a nice idea.' Essie smiled as she eyed her glass of champagne. Fortunately, she didn't still have an empty stomach. The Hadza hunter had produced a leather pouch bulging with yellow berries and shared them with Essie before handing back the baby and heading off into the bush with his zebra meat. Though a bit shrivelled, the berries had been sweet and fleshy.

'To us!' Essie raised her glass. It wasn't important what the new site was called; the results were what mattered. The whole digging season – the Long Dry – lay ahead of them. They'd all be working together from dawn to dark. She sipped the cool drink, savouring the sweet tingle on her tongue. As the alcohol entered her blood she felt her body relax, her spirits rise. As if on cue, the baby made a small mewing sound and stretched out her arm.

Essie put down her champagne so she could carry her outside as soon as she woke fully and started to cry. Kefa separated himself from the other onlookers and hurried over. 'Would you like me to unpack these boxes?' He looked eager to begin.

Essie nodded vaguely. She couldn't think where all the contents should go. She glanced over at Ian. Presumably he, like Julia, had accepted the baby was staying here. But that didn't mean he wanted his bedroom turned into a nursery.

'Take it all to the guest tent I've been using.' Essie stood up. 'I'll come too.' She took two steps towards the doorway, before turning back to Julia. 'How do you fold a nappy? I haven't got it right yet.' She held her breath, torn between fearing she was pushing things too far and hoping Julia might even offer to come along and help.

Julia reached across the table for Essie's note. She tore the sheet of yellow paper into a rough square and began folding it.

'You make the shape of a kite and turn up the bottom.' She handed the example to Essie, then turned to Ian, holding out her glass. 'Let's open the other bottle before it gets too warm.'

The last of the tea chests was half empty and still no nappies had been unearthed. Essie was jiggling the baby in her arms. The *kitenge* she'd wrapped around the bare bottom, after the Hadza hunter had departed, was sodden. It must have felt uncomfortable because the baby kept wriggling. She was not unhappy, though. She had her eyes on Kefa as he moved around the tent, accompanied by

Simon, who'd also come to help. The baby followed the action with as much interest as if the men had been putting on a performance just for her.

After some debate, all the nursery furniture was eventually arranged. Essie mostly let the others decide where to put everything. They all spoke in Swahili so that Kefa could follow; even after his long years with the Lawrences his knowledge of English was largely limited to topics like cleaning and serving food. Essie had to step in once or twice during the process, when there was a misunderstanding about what a particular item was for. There was one object the purpose of which none of them could guess – an inverted cone on a stick, made of galvanised steel. Kefa placed it near the door of the tent.

A change table and a plastic bath complete with rubber duck were grouped near the chest of drawers. The bed was dotted with tiny dresses and nightgowns, satin-edged blankets, plastic pants, crisp sheets and soft towels – all folded into neat piles. There were crocheted booties, tied by their laces into pairs; singlets; stockings; socks. Everything was either white or pink – though before long, Essie knew, the striking contrast between the two options would be dulled by the pervasive dust of Magadi.

The imposing pram and a matching carrycot stood by the door. A bassinet with an elaborate net was there, too; it was going to be taken into Ian and Essie's tent. Kefa and Simon had assumed Essie would sleep here in the guest tent with the baby. That was not surprising. Most African mothers shared a bed with their children. Sometimes their husbands had another hut; sometimes there was another wife, as well. Essie intended to spend her nights at Ian's side, just as she always had. There would be clear boundaries and routines where this baby was concerned. The infant would sleep next to Essie in the bassinet. When she awoke, she would be taken away to the nursery for a bottle and nappy change. The guest tent wasn't too far for Essie to walk at night, with a torch in hand and Rudie as an escort, but it was far enough away for her not to have to worry about disturbing Ian.

Essie surveyed the rest of the tent. A shag pile rug in soft pink had been unrolled on top of the sisal mat on the floor. It was half-covered in toys – a rag doll, a grey plush elephant, some rattles and the teddy with the satin bow. Along with a few picture books, Essie was relieved to see a large solid tome called *Complete Babycare*. Flipping through it, she saw lots of diagrams and tables as well as dense text; it had the reassuring look of a field manual.

The shopkeeper had sent plenty of milk formula, as Julia had hoped. While Kefa stacked the tins near the back of the tent, Simon read out one of the labels.

'Lactogen. Net weight 2 pounds. Pasteurised. Modified. Fortified.' He made the English words sound impressive. 'Added milk fat, milk sugar, vitamins.' His brow furrowed. He switched back to Swahili. 'And iron? Like an arrow?'

Essie shook her head, even though she couldn't think if there was actually a difference between the two kinds of iron. She looked across to the bedside table, which was packed with bottles, teats and lidded containers. Kefa was standing next to the collection, examining an object in his hand – a circle of pink plastic with a ring attached, holding a rubber teat. He showed it to Essie.

'It's called a dummy.' She gave the name in English; it couldn't possibly be translated.

'How does it work?'

'The baby sucks on it, instead of crying.'

'But there's no milk.' Kefa frowned. 'Is it a trick?'

'Ah – yes,' Essie said awkwardly. 'I suppose it is.'

Kefa and Simon exchanged looks. As Essie glanced away, she saw Kefa slipping the item into an empty bag on the pile of packaging.

As soon as one question had been answered, there was another, it seemed, the two men taking it in turns to ask them. Having disposed of the dummy, Kefa removed a mobile from a box. Essie explained how it had to be hung above the baby. As he held it up, she set the pieces moving, so he could see how it would catch the baby's attention. Simon joined Kefa, studying the mobile.

'A dog, a cow, a moon,' Simon said.

'Cat. Plate. Spoon,' Kefa added.

'And a guitar?' queried Simon.

'A fiddle,' Essie said.

'Why have those things been chosen?' Simon asked.

Essie eyed the hanging objects. 'They're from a nursery rhyme. A song for children.'

'Can you sing it?' Simon requested.

'It'll have to be in English,' Essie said. 'I'm not sure I remember all the words.'

She hadn't heard the rhyme since she was a child, but once she began, it started coming back to her.

'"Hey diddle diddle, the cat and the fiddle, the cow jumped over the moon".' Essie paused, oddly aware that she was listening to her mother's voice. The words weren't shaped by the English accent Lorna had eventually perfected, though; the vowels were longer, broader; the syllables merged together. They belonged in that hazy time Essie thought of as 'before' – when the family lived in the place that was no more than a speck on the underside of the globe that stood on Professor Holland's desk.

'But what about the dog?' Simon prompted.

'Oh yes. "The little dog laughed to see such fun, and the dish ran away with the spoon".'

Simon looked mystified. His lips moved as he repeated the information to himself. Then he translated it for Kefa.

The other man raised his eyebrows, his whole forehead wrinkling. 'What does it mean?'

'I don't know,' Essie replied.

'You must know. Think harder,' Simon pressed her. 'What did your grandmother tell you?'

Essie smiled. Her assistant sounded exactly like an anthropologist she'd once heard interrogating a Maasai woman. 'I have no idea what it means,' Essie insisted. 'No one does.'

Simon gave her an accusing look. 'You do not want to share your stories.'

'It's not that . . .' Essie shifted the baby from one hip to the other. Her shirt would now be wet on both sides. She glanced across at the last tea chest; surely there would be nappies in there. She couldn't wait to have a clean, dry baby, wearing plastic pants. She realised Simon was still waiting for an explanation. 'It's not really my story. It's English. And it's very old. The people who sing it to their kids don't know what it means.'

'That is not wise,' commented Kefa.

'Wait – did you say it is not your story because you are not English?' Simon sounded almost shocked.

'I am now,' Essie clarified. 'But I was born in Tasmania. A small island off the bottom of Australia.'

'I have only heard of Australia – not that other place. What language do they speak there?'

'English.'

'No, I mean the language of the mothers.'

Essie recognised Simon's version of the term 'mother tongue' – the first means of communication that a child learns. In Africa it was rare for no other languages to ever be acquired. 'We only speak English.'

Essie found it strange to be saying 'we', even though she was – technically – Tasmanian. She had become used to being thought of as a Lawrence, and while William and his father had both been born in Africa, the family was never viewed as anything but British.

Simon looked puzzled. 'Does that place have no languages of its own? Not even one?'

Essie didn't answer straightaway. She had no desire to embark on the whole history of Tasmania. It would be too complicated, especially when everything had to be told in Swahili. And there was still an urgent need to find those nappies. On the other hand, she had always encouraged her assistant to have an enquiring mind.

'The English set up a colony on the island, nearly two hundred years ago. When they arrived, people were already living there. They spoke several languages.'

Kefa moved to stand near her. 'Were there lots of tribes? Can you tell us their names?'

Essie pictured the hand-drawn maps in her father's publications. When she was little, she used to read out the melodic names that labelled different territories, stumbling over all the syllables. They sounded so mysterious to her – linked with a faraway place. 'There are the Nuenonne. Larmairene. Melukerdee. And others, too. But most people just call them all Aborigines.'

'Aborigines.' Kefa repeated the word as if trying it out on his tongue. He glanced at Simon, then turned back to Essie. 'Did they like the English being in their country?' he asked. 'Or is there fighting – even today?'

Essie eyed the men uneasily. She was very aware – as she had been when Frank Marlow had started talking about Tasmania's history – that the topic was fraught, especially here in newly independent Tanzania. The best thing, she decided, would be to keep the story simple.

'Those first people are gone now,' she said. 'They lost their land to the English.'

She knew this idea would be familiar to both men – one group moving in on another's tribal homeland and pushing them out. The consequences for the displaced were often devastating. Africans had been doing it to Africans for as long as humans had lived here; now foreign powers had joined in.

Simon was nodding slowly. 'So those Aborigines – they went away to another place?'

Essie hesitated again. She knew whatever she said could be passed around the camp, harming the image of Europeans. If they heard about it, Julia and Ian would be angry. But she couldn't just refuse to answer. She shook her head. 'No. They were killed by the English. Or they caught diseases they weren't used to. In the end, there were no full-blood Tasmanians left.'

Simon lowered his gaze as he absorbed the information. When he looked up his eyes were sharp with interest. 'What kind of people were they?'

'Dark-skinned, the same as you. They lived like the *Hadza pori*, hunting and collecting food. Moving around.'

'So they are gone . . .' There was regret in his voice. 'Have they disappeared completely? Or did some of them marry with the new people? And mix their blood?'

'That did happen,' Essie confirmed. This scenario would be well known to the Africans, too. Intermarriage with other tribes was common. Among the Hadza, it was more usual for a woman to do it than a man. If she wasn't happy being a farmer's wife housed in a village, she often just gathered up her children and returned to her old life.

'So they still kept their stories, and their songs?' Simon queried. 'They remember all the things their ancestors did?'

'I suppose so. Some of it, at least . . .'

Essie pretended to be occupied with the baby as she tried to think of a better answer – she understood why Simon was so intrigued. But the question of how much culture had or had not survived the devastation wreaked by the English wasn't something she'd heard talked about in any real detail. In Australia, anthropologists focused on the mainland, where there were Aborigines in remote areas who still lived pretty much as they always had. It was easy to gather information. If researchers had tried to carry out interviews in Tasmania, it occurred to Essie, they might not have got very far. Honesty relied on trust, which would be a rare commodity in a place where the memory of massacres was only a few generations old.

As far as the academic world was concerned, the interest in Tasmania lay in the question of what level of culture had evolved in the first place. Hunter-gatherers left behind little concrete evidence for archaeologists to collect. Research had to be based mainly on stone tools, as well as the middens that dotted the island – collections of mollusc shells, animal bones, flint shards and other domestic refuse found in occupation sites. The sum total of knowledge didn't add up to very much. This didn't mean it wasn't of great significance, though, as was proved by the status of Essie's father's research. But the concern wasn't really with the story of an island at the far end of the earth. Academics wanted to use information gleaned about the first Tasmanians to build a picture of the ancient people of Europe – illuminating the meaning of stone tools and other items that had been found there.

When she looked up, Essie saw that Simon was about to speak again – but this time she shook her head.

'No more questions, now,' she said firmly. 'We've got a lot to do here.'

She crossed to where Kefa was bending over the last tea chest. He pulled out more clothes and another mosquito net. Then Essie sighed with relief as he began removing a snowy pile of nappies. He placed them on the bed. Selecting one, he went over to the change table.

'Can you fold it for me – like this?' Essie offered Julia's scrap of yellow paper.

Kefa brushed it aside. With a few deft movements he prepared the towelling square. Then he picked out a pair of plastic pants, a tin of talcum powder and two nappy pins.

As Essie put the baby down on the change table, she looked at him in surprise. 'You've done this before.'

'When Ian was a baby the family lived in Arusha. They travelled here only for the digging season. Mrs Lawrence had an *ayah* to help her. But the little one . . .' The man's face softened into a smile. His gaze was fond and sad. 'He was very small when they came to stay all year round at Magadi. Mrs Lawrence decided not to bring the *ayah*, so she asked me to do some things for her. I folded the towels, tidied his clothes, pushed him in the pram. But she wanted to be the one to change his nappy or give him a bottle. She loved him too much. She did not like to share.'

A dense quiet fell. Essie was taken aback by this unimaginable picture of Julia. She was also confused. She didn't know if Kefa was saying that Julia's love for Robbie was too extreme, or just that she loved her baby a great deal. With the Swahili words he'd used, the meaning was unclear.

Was it possible to love a baby too much?

Was it possible to love a baby too little?

Essie unwound the wet *kitenge* and dropped it into a pink plastic nursery pail. She caught both of the little feet in one hand, lifting the lower body up. With the other hand she wiped the round buttocks clean with a wet flannel provided by Kefa. She shook some talc from the tin, sprinkling white on the black skin. She smoothed the silky powder into all the folds. Her touch must have tickled, because the baby laughed, showing her bare gums and fat pink tongue. Essie found herself laughing back at her, as if they were sharing a private joke.

Somehow, she managed to get the folded nappy into position. Lowering the baby down, she let go of her legs. Immediately the baby began kicking. Essie was conscious of the men watching on as she tried to avoid being hit in the face while she was wrapping the nappy tightly.

Simon brought the mobile across and held it above the baby. She grew still, as she stared up at it.

Essie struggled with a safety pin. Until now she'd made do with tucking in the ends of the folded cloth at the baby's waist; it was easy, but not very secure. Now, she found the towelling was surprisingly hard to penetrate with the pin. She was afraid of piercing skin as well as cloth. She pictured red blood staining the white. But the baby kept smiling and kicking, apparently unharmed.

'She likes the moon,' Simon commented. 'Because it is female.'

That was the belief held in many traditional societies, Essie knew. It had something to do with women having a monthly cycle that matched, in length if not timing, the phases of the moon.

'Why does the cow jump over the moon?' Simon mused.

Essie shrugged. She imagined how Baraka, the Maasai, was going to react to the story he would no doubt be told. He would approve of it wholeheartedly, since cows were supreme animals, far above cats and dogs, let alone inanimate objects like a fiddle or a spoon.

Kefa chose a pink dress with a white smocked yoke, offering it to Simon for approval. Essie hid a smile. She knew it wasn't usual for African men to be this interested in a baby. Maybe it was the novelty of all the gifts Diana had sent. On the other hand, Kefa had spoken so fondly about Ian's brother as a baby. And perhaps Simon had younger siblings at home, whom he missed.

Eventually, the baby was clean, dry and dressed. Essie tied on a pair of knitted booties. The black skin somehow made the white appear brighter and the pink softer.

'Doesn't she look beautiful!' Essie said.

Kefa eyed the baby critically, then nodded. 'She is a fine baby.'

Essie saw a tentative glimmer of pride in Simon's eyes.

'She needs a name,' Essie said. 'We can't just keep calling her "the baby".'

'She is very young,' Kefa responded doubtfully. Then he waved one arm, taking in the contents of the tent, focusing on the stacked tins of formula. 'But, God willing, I think she can survive.'

Essie felt a rush of anxiety. He made the situation sound so precarious. What if something happened to this baby? She thought of the box she'd opened that contained chloroquine syrup to prevent malaria, and several other medicines especially for babies. Then there was the *Complete Babycare* book. Surely Essie – at the age of twenty-eight, with a university degree – could keep one baby healthy and safe for four months?

'You could choose the name of your mother,' Simon suggested. 'Or your aunty.'

'I can't do that,' Essie said. 'She's not joining our family. I'm only taking care of her.' She didn't say that giving an innocent baby the name of her mother – one that carried with it such a weight of unhappiness – would have been like a curse. Nor did she add that her father had no sister, his mother was only ever referred to as 'Grandma', and Essie had no knowledge of any other female relatives he might have. Arthur rarely spoke of his family in Sydney. There was a rift between them; from something Essie had once overheard, she thought perhaps his parents hadn't approved of his choice of a wife. There were definitely lots of aunties back in Tasmania – Lorna's kin – but Essie could not remember their names any more than she could picture their faces. They were just a blur, lost in time. All Essie recalled of them was a sense of quiet busyness. Of soft conversation broken by bursts of laughter. They were always outside, it seemed – their presence blended with the hush of waves washing over sand. And the sound of seabirds calling on the wind . . .

'I know lots of good names,' Simon offered. 'Susan. Elizabeth. Mary. Jane.' He eyed Essie thoughtfully. 'I have never heard of anyone who has the same name as you.'

'It's short for Esther,' Essie explained. She had been named after an obscure Jewish archaeologist admired by her father. When she married Ian and became a Lawrence, Julia had tried to get her to use the full version of her name. Essie's refusal was one of the few battles with her mother-in-law that she'd managed to win.

'Esther.' Simon repeated the name, stretching out the sounds. He shook his head. 'Essie is better.'

Essie gazed around the tent, her focus returning to the question of what to call the baby. She wished she could have been discussing this with Ian. But choosing a name together was something couples did with their own babies, or babies they'd adopted – not ones on short-term loan. And anyway, Essie was the person who'd taken on this responsibility. Ian hadn't been consulted about the promise to care for the baby, so why would he want to be involved in selecting her name?

She looked back at the infant, who was waving her hands above her face, following the movement with her eyes. Essie remembered the moment she'd first seen her, almost lost inside a baboon pelt, and naked but for her string of beads.

'It should be a Hadza name,' Essie said. 'Something from her family. Did you know those people at the cave? Had you met them before?'

'Never,' Simon said firmly. 'They are wild Hadza. Where I come from, near Lake Eyasi, our children go to school. We grow our own food. We have a clinic and a church.' He was now looking at Kefa as he spoke. Essie was struck by how complex this situation was for Simon. Her field assistant prided himself on being more educated, modern and sophisticated than the other staff. Now the presence of the Hadza baby in the camp was a constant reminder of a tribal background he had tried to leave behind.

'Do you remember if Nandamara mentioned the name of her mother?' Essie asked him.

'He only called her his daughter.'

'Then Nandamara is the only name we have,' Essie said.

'But the baby is a girl,' Simon pointed out.

'I'll shorten it,' Essie said. 'It's what we call a "nickname".
Nandamara can choose the real one when the baby is returned.'
She tried some options in her head. *Nanda. Nandy. Mara.*

'I'll call her Mara.' The name had a gentle, lyrical sound. As
soon as she'd said it, Essie knew it was right.

The two men repeated the nickname, eyeing the baby as they
tested it out. They both nodded.

Essie bent over the baby, scooping her up. 'Hello, Mara.' She
murmured into the tiny ear, feeling its soft contours against her
lips. Emotion welled up inside her. She felt a sense of relief. She
had everything she needed, here in this tent. She was going to be
able to save this beautiful little girl, without creating turmoil in her
life and that of her family. And alongside relief was deep gratitude
to Diana Marlow. It wasn't just that she'd been so generous with
the nursery provisions; spending money wasn't hard if you were
wealthy. Diana had acted so quickly and decisively. She must have
made helping Essie her top priority. And as for the grant . . . With
a literal stroke of her pen Diana had changed the whole world of
Magadi. Ian and Julia were so happy they had no room to be angry
with Essie. And now that Diana had made a show of support for
the baby, no one would question the situation. It was as if the
woman who'd flown in for sundowners – dressed like a queen in
her turquoise gown and glittering jewellery – was nothing less than
an angel in disguise.

EIGHT

Essie stifled a yawn as she bent over her specimen tray. Many of the fragments of fossil laid out were tiny, and she was glad of the strong morning light coming in through the open front of the Work Hut. With a pair of tweezers she gripped one of the pieces. Carefully she flicked a paintbrush over its pitted surface to remove a few more grains of earth. On a card table beside her was a book opened at a full-page picture of the dinosaur giraffe, *Sivatherium giganteum*. The drawing showed the creature's moose-like antlers, as well as the distinctive secondary ossicones above the eyes. The shoulder muscles were huge, as they'd have to be in order to hold up the heavy head.

Now, as Essie glanced sideways at the image, her eyes lingered on the neck, which was short compared with the giraffes of today. She was reminded of one of her first lessons in evolution. At bedtime her father, despising fairy tales, liked to teach her useful things. The special storyteller's voice he used came back to her.

Once upon a time a giraffe was born with a longer-than-usual neck. All the other little giraffes teased him for being different.

Arthur went on to tell of how the situation changed when there was a terrible drought. Soon, all the giraffes were hungry.

'Long-neck' was able to eat the leaves that were out of reach of the others. They died of starvation, while he survived to become a father. His children inherited the long neck, and in turn bred with other survivors of the drought, who also shared the same advantage. The next time the rains failed and food was scarce, the ones most able to chew away at the treetops again won the battle to survive and become parents. Over millions of generations of giraffe families – with the circumstances repeating – necks grew longer and longer. At the same time the heart had to become bigger and bigger in order to pump blood all the way up the neck to the brain. It happened by the same process: chance mutations proving useful. Essie was only young, but she could already see that her father was right: the simple facts of evolution were far more extraordinary than any work of fiction.

The artist's impression of the *Sivatherium*, elaborate in its detail, suited Essie's childhood memories. It was fanciful – there was even a family of hominid hunters crouched in the background. The illustration had no value as a reference, and could even be misleading, but it helped Essie imagine the ancient *giraffid* as it had been while still alive. If Ian and Julia were around, she would never have brought the book to the Work Hut. It would have caused odd looks, perhaps even negative comments. But that wasn't going to happen today. By now, the two of them were many miles away from Magadi Gorge.

They'd left at first light. Julia had decided to accompany Ian on his trip to Arusha. She hadn't visited the place for such a long time. Essie didn't begrudge her mother-in-law the chance to see old friends, and share in the triumphant excursion to the bank, but it had been hard to watch the others prepare for the journey. It had gone on all week, with the pair discussing plans and forming strategies for making use of the new funds. During this time Essie had devoted herself to keeping the baby out of their way – anticipating Mara's every need and meeting it before any upset could occur. Essie seemed to be preparing bottles, changing nappies, jiggling toys and rocking the pram all day. She spent her nights going back and forth between the bed she shared with Ian and the guest tent. She was determined to avoid disrupting her husband's sleep. With exhaustion setting in, it wasn't easy to think about anything but the baby. Whenever Mara was sleeping, Essie longed to lie down and rest as well. But she refused to give in to the temptation. At every opportunity, she forced herself to hurry to her desk.

This morning, sitting alone here in the Work Hut, she felt she'd been abandoned by Ian and Julia. But it was her own fault, she knew. The staff were more than capable of being in charge of themselves for a few days. If Essie hadn't had a baby to care for, she could have joined the safari. The best she could do now was make good use of the time alone.

The harsh ring of a wind-up alarm shattered the quiet. Essie almost knocked over a bottle of ink as she hurried to turn it off. She checked the clock face, surprised that two hours had gone by. It felt like less than one. She stared, frustrated, at her work. She was just about to slot a fragment of the cranium into place. It was the part of the task she relished most – when pieces of the puzzle finally came together. Now it would have to wait.

She turned her ear towards the guest tent. Mara must still be sleeping peacefully, tucked up in her pram. Essie would have preferred to have her here in the Work Hut, since Nandamara had explained that the Hadza baby was used to always being around her tribe. But *Complete Babycare* said the nursery was the correct place for a baby to sleep. How else would she learn to be independent? Isolation was also the best way to ensure that sleep was not accidentally disturbed. A routine could then be established with waking, sleeping and feeding locked into a firm timeframe. It was the only way a busy mother could expect to take proper care of her home and her husband. There was no mention in the book of a professional being able to continue her work, but the same rules would obviously apply.

As Essie walked to the guest tent she felt a burst of anxiety. Had she zipped up the tent properly? Was there any chance that a snake could have slithered in? She'd left Rudie on guard outside the entrance. Her impulse had been to put him inside, right next to the pram – they were living in the African bush, after all, not an English village. But the manual said the family dog should never be left alone with the baby. They could not be trusted.

Rudie lifted his head as Essie appeared, with Tommy at her heels. The Dalmatian didn't look guilty, his mouth was not bloodstained; the tent walls behind him had not been ripped apart. Essie smiled at herself. It was the sheer helplessness of the baby that sparked such ridiculous fears. As Essie well knew, young humans were uniquely vulnerable, among all the mammals. Babies were born long before they were mature enough to take care of themselves. This was the direct result of humans having evolved such large brains. Their offspring could remain in the womb only for as long as it would still be possible for the head – which was huge, relative to the size of the body – to be pushed through the mother's pelvis. There was another issue here: the shift to walking on two legs had brought with it skeletal changes that made childbirth both agonising and dangerous. If not for these structural issues, a human pregnancy should have lasted for nearly two years, like the elephant's, rather than just nine months.

Lifting the net that draped over the sunshade, Essie peered into the pram. Mara lay on her back with her arms flung up to each side of her head. There was something deeply peaceful about the expression on her face combined with the complete abandonment conveyed by her posture. It was as if, for this time, the infant had journeyed away to another realm, leaving her body here to hold her place in the everyday world. Essie was reluctant to wake her and drag her back. But Mara had to drink one full bottle of formula, be patted until she burped, then have her nappy changed, all before mid-morning bath time.

'Hello, Mara. Time to wake up,' Essie said brightly. The baby stirred but didn't open her eyes. Essie gave her shoulder a shake, but that had little effect. The book recommended using a light flick of the finger against the cheek if necessary. Essie reached one hand into the pram, letting it hover for a moment. She watched the closed eyes for a while. There was a faint movement behind the dark lids, like secret signals from a dream. Essie drew back her hand and walked away.

It was another half an hour – two more fragments of bone had been cleaned and set in place – before Essie heard Mara wake up by herself. Her cry was sudden and loud. Rudie barked in alarm. Essie told herself to sit still – to give the baby a chance to discover that she was alone and get used to the idea. The crying continued, winding steadily up. Essie watched the clock, timing two minutes, then three. Four. Five. It felt like forever. The screams seemed to float above Magadi like the plume of smoke that rose from Ol Doinyo Lengai. When Essie could stand it no longer, she pushed back her chair, dropping the toothbrush she was using as a cleaning tool. The alarm clock tumbled off the desk, rolling away over the floor.

Baraka emerged from the kitchen to hand Essie a bottle as she passed. He gave her a questioning frown but said nothing. Essie slowed to a walk, trying to look as if she was in control. She wished she had time to explain to the man that she was following a guide written by experts. She was doing the right thing – she just wasn't very good at it yet, and nor was Mara.

By the time Essie had lifted her from the pram, the baby was sobbing so hard her whole body shook. Her hands were curled into tight fists. Essie held her against her shoulder and walked around patting her, but Mara was caught in a whirlpool of panic, and probably hunger as well. Carrying her to the change table, Essie laid her down under the mobile, but the jiggling cow and moon did nothing to calm her. Essie felt desperate. The cries seemed too loud to be made by such a small creature. Mara's panic aroused an answering emotion in Essie. The air felt stifled by it – too thick to breathe.

At a loss, Essie looked helplessly around the tent. Her eye was caught by a music box on the chest of drawers nearby; with so many items in the nursery there always seemed to be another surprise. Quickly she wound the key at the back. As she lifted the lid a miniature ballerina with a pink net skirt popped up. The doll revolved jerkily on one pointed toe, as tinny music entered the air. Essie stared at the box. The decorations on the outside were new to her, but everything else was deeply familiar – the image of the dancer reflected in a tiny mirror mounted inside the lid; the pink silk lining; the tune that was playing. Essie breathed a perfume that couldn't possibly have been lingering in the brand-new musical box. She could feel herself being caught up, every turn of the dancer winding her back into her past.

Snapping down the lid, she cut off the song and made the ballerina fold forward and disappear. Essie didn't need to have the weight of childhood memories added to this situation that was already so tense. She was about to pick Mara up, to try carrying her again, when she realised the baby had quietened. Her hands were reaching towards what had been the source of the music. As the silence lengthened, a frown crossed Mara's face. Her mouth opened as she prepared to cry again. Reluctantly Essie lifted the lid of the box, bracing herself as the tune was triggered again. But the memories that came to her were not what she was expecting. There was no rasp of irritation in the air. No dark weight of unhappiness. Instead she felt warmth, excitement.

Happy birthday, darling.

Look at her, Mummy. She's going round and round!

There was tinkling laughter, following the notes of the song.

A kiss dropping like a ray of sunshine onto skin . . .

Essie stared blankly down at Mara as she tried to tease the memory out a little further. But the fleeting power of the music evaporated like steam. Essie tried to think how old she might have been when she'd received the music box. She didn't know. Were they living in England, or was it before? It felt crucial to her to work it out – not because it mattered when she'd been given the gift, but because it signalled a time when her mother must have been happier, more normal. Behind the issue of timing was another, deeper question. What had happened to Lorna to transform her so completely? Essie remembered how, as a little girl, she'd believed she was the source of her mother's despair – it was due to something she had done, or not done, or had failed to be. Now, Essie knew that there had to be another cause:

some inherent weakness, perhaps, that meant Lorna couldn't deal with the challenges of life the way other people did; or a mental illness that just set in, and got worse, like an unstoppable cancer.

Essie gazed at the music box. There was no point now in thinking about her mother's life. The questions this would raise were ones she had finally managed to leave behind her – far away, on another continent. She focused on Mara instead, following the movements of her waving hands. The tiny fingers grasped at the air as if music was something tangible that could be caught and held. Eventually, the mechanism inside the box wound down and the music stumbled to a halt.

Essie quickly produced the bottle of formula, before Mara could become upset again. The strategy worked well. Soon the baby was sitting on Essie's lap, feeding happily. Afterwards she lay still, sucking her fingers, while Essie changed her nappy. Bath time was next. Essie was about to call out for Kefa to bring hot water when she heard someone enter the tent. She turned to see Simon standing there. His hands were clasped tensely together; he glanced back over his shoulder, then at Mara.

'Visitors are here,' he announced.

Essie eyed him uneasily. Had Nandamara and his friends come to check on how she was caring for Mara? She felt, as she had before, that the Hadza might be able to see and know everything – that they'd heard the baby screaming in fear after waking to find herself alone. But then Essie remembered how firmly Simon had replied when she'd asked him if he thought the Hadza might come and say goodbye before actually leaving the Magadi area. They would not. The farewell had taken place. What would be gained by having to go through it all again?

'The women from the *manyatta* have come,' Simon elaborated.

Essie looked in the direction of the kitchen. The cook was the one who purchased the eggs, milk or honey. 'Where's Baraka?'

Simon shook his head. 'That is not why they are here. They have come to see the baby.'

Essie nodded slowly. The news that a band of Hadza had convinced the Bwana's wife to look after their baby would have spread like wildfire. There wasn't an oversupply of excitement around Magadi so it was not surprising a few sightseers had turned up. Essie pursed her lips, recalling how Baraka had said it would be an insult for a Maasai woman to be asked to feed a Hadza baby. Had they now come to gawk at her? Essie looked down at Mara. She was smiling trustingly in the direction of Simon's voice. The little girl had no idea that the world was a place where one group of people looked down on another, and that she was a member of the wrong tribe.

'Tell them we will come,' Essie said to him. 'But they will have to wait for us to be ready. Tell Baraka to serve them tea.'

'All of them?'

Essie felt a hollow in her stomach. 'How many are there?'

'They are still arriving. Not just from the local *manyatta*, but from Engare Sero as well.'

Essie stared at him. She pictured dozens of Maasai women gathered in the open space in front of the Work Hut and Dining Tent. Listening past the squabbling weaverbirds and strains of song coming from the workers' camp, she could now detect a hum of voices. The women would have brought their children with them, Essie realised, even though many would know they were banned from the camp; Maasai mothers didn't see the company of their offspring as optional. Essie was just grateful the visit was happening now, while she was here alone. Hopefully Ian and Julia need never know that their camp had been invaded.

Essie pushed the pram along the path, jolting over the stones that always seemed to be on the path, no matter how often they were cleared away. Folds of cloth rustled around her legs with each step. Without even looking down, she could see the bright blur of her skirt – green, red, splashes of yellow. She was reminded of wearing the orange cocktail dress for the Marlows' visit. It was hard to believe that it had only been just over a week ago. And it seemed absurd that she was now getting dressed up for a second time. It was as if the first event had somehow led to this one, like a chain reaction.

Pausing near the kitchen, Essie leaned around to look at Mara. The baby grinned up at her, as if the bumping motion had been done purely for her amusement. The eye-catching fabric of Essie's gown was mirrored in Mara's miniature dress. The two garments had been packaged together – they were a 'Mother and Daughter' set, according to the label attached to the cellophane. When Essie had first seen the matching clothes, she'd rolled her eyes. The owner of Babyland was obviously an opportunist. Diana Marlow's offer of a blank cheque had been seen as a chance to unload some stock that few people would be likely to buy, especially with the population of wealthy English settlers on the decline since Independence. But for this occasion – the meeting of the Maasai women – the ensemble was perfect. Mara looked even more striking in the colourful print with its pattern of flowers and leaves than she did in pink and white. Essie wasn't so sure the bright, busy pattern suited her, but that didn't matter. Her goal was to send a message about how she viewed this Hadza baby. She wanted everyone to know that Mara deserved fine clothes; that she was accepted here, with the Lawrences. Essie hoped the statement might reflect well on Simon, too, though she was wary of social manipulation. Ian had warned her against trying to change the way Africans saw the world, in terms of their own affairs; the Lawrences weren't missionaries, after all. The Africans should only be expected to conform to the demands of scientific practice. But in this instance, the gesture of solidarity seemed a small thing Essie could do for the Hadza – and for her assistant, who'd been caught up in this delicate situation through no fault of his own.

Rounding the corner, Essie came to a halt. There must have been fifty women, plus at least as many children, all squatting in a loose circle around the central fireplace. Some of the adults wore *shukas*, creating splashes of purple, orange, red and maroon that clashed strongly, but en masse became oddly harmonious. Many women had plain cloths that blended with the burnished tones of their ochre-painted skin. Some were young, with swanlike necks and upright backs. Mothers of all ages cradled toddlers and babies. There were grandmothers, too: grey-haired, with sunken eyes and bony limbs. Everyone must have dressed up for the occasion. They all wore elaborate jewellery – earrings made of metal, shells, feathers; coloured headpieces; and the distinctive Maasai beaded discs, the size and shape of dinner plates, that circled the wearer's neck, resting on their shoulders. The overall impression was of colour and life. The impact of the group seemed to spread beyond their physical boundaries, overtaking the whole camp. It was as if a huge flock of exotic birds had inexplicably landed here, claiming the place as their own.

At the sight of Essie pushing the pram, a hush fell over the crowd. Essie tried to walk tall and gracefully, like the music box ballerina.

But her nerve failed; she suddenly felt ridiculous in the elaborate dress with the skirt that swept the ground and the generously puffed sleeves that fell to her elbows. She was reminded of how it felt to arrive at a party wearing an unusual outfit: in the seclusion of home the choice seemed viable. Then as you entered the space filled with guests, you felt so exposed you might as well have been naked.

But as the Maasai women studied her, Essie realised she'd made the right choice. The long gown added to her stature. The powerful colours lent her their strength. She was used to seeing the Maasai looking pityingly at her fair skin, blonde hair and drab clothing. She'd once even seen a worker pick up a white grub that was squirming in a shovel of earth. It had the blind, bleached look of something that lived its whole life in the dark. The man had pointed surreptitiously at Essie. That had been back when she was new here. As soon as she'd acquired a tan she'd looked healthier. But she had never been seen wearing anything but her work khakis. Now, under the eyes of these women, Essie got the feeling that she had finally presented herself in a better light.

As Essie approached, adults and children alike shuffled aside to make a pathway to the centre. They looked from her to the pram and back, and craned their necks, trying to see in under the fringed canopy.

Essie came to a halt, parking the pram next to the circle of stones. Her feet were bare, since the sturdy boots she'd had on in the guest tent would've looked ridiculous with the dress. A piece of charred firewood brushed her skirt, leaving a black smear on the hem. Bending over, she peered into the pram. Mara was waving her hands in excitement. She was wide-awake, ready to play.

As Essie lifted Mara out, there was a brief, dense quiet. All eyes were fixed on the baby. She had on some yellow booties that

Essie had found to go with the dress. The plastic pants had yellow butterflies on them. There was even a sunbonnet made from the same fabric as the dresses, with ribbons that tied under Mara's chin. Again, Essie was overtaken by doubt. Had she gone too far? Had she made Mara into a doll – her toy?

There was nothing she could do except proceed with her plan. She raised the baby up so everyone could see her. For a few tense seconds, she held her breath. Then she heard gasps of admiration spreading across the crowd. Relief fell over her. As the onlookers stared, wide-eyed and smiling, Essie pictured how she and Mara must look to them, bound together by the matching clothes. Another emotion welled up inside her then – something stronger, deeper. It was a warm rush of joy. Essie no longer looked like a researcher holding a foreign baby. She and Mara were like two parts of a pair. Mother and daughter.

It wasn't real – she knew that. Mara belonged to Nandamara and Giga. And Essie had chosen a path that would never lead her to motherhood. She was indulging a fantasy. It was irrational; probably inappropriate. But Essie didn't care. In that moment, it felt right and true.

Essie looked around for Simon. He had stepped forward, away from where he'd been loitering by the tent. He had a small smile on his face. The man would never appear tall, especially beside the Maasai whose long limbs hinted at their stature even when they were seated. But he looked strong, nimble, at home in his body. In spite of his pressed uniform and shiny, lace-up shoes, Essie could picture him in a loincloth and baboon-pelt waistcoat, a quiver of arrows across his back.

One of the older women stood up. She began to sing, invoking an echo-chorus from the others. After a short time, she was joined by more voices. From somewhere came the beat of a drum. The people formed a row and began to dance, ducking their upper bodies forward, swinging their arms. Soon, all the visitors were on their feet. Their earrings swung, bracelets jangled. The dance made sense of the plate-necklaces, which flopped up and down rhythmically. A tiny toddler who looked too young even to be walking gave an expert imitation of his mother. Several of the women had the humped shape of a camel, caused by blankets draped over babies tied onto their backs.

The dancers closed in around Essie and Mara. An energetic young woman threw a cloth over Essie's head and danced next to her, shoulders touching shoulders, the fabric forming a tent around them. Essie picked up her smell of rancid milk, sweat and cow dung, contrasting with Mara's baby powder and the starchy fragrance of the new dress. It seemed impossible that the two worlds of smell could be taken in with one breath.

The old woman was still leading the dance with her song. Some deeper voices began joining in with the chorus. Essie noticed that the gathering of Maasai was now ringed by camp staff. She found Baraka standing not far away. Like Simon, he'd lost the guarded expression that had been there when Essie appeared with the pram.

Essie leaned towards him. 'What are they singing about?'

'It is the story of a white woman with a black baby,' Baraka said. 'They have given you a special name.'

Essie waited to hear what it was. He spoke first in Maa, then translated into Swahili.

Mama Mzuri. Beautiful Mother.

Essie smiled, lifting Mara's face to meet her own. As she kissed the rounded cheek, she repeated the words, pressing them into the soft smooth skin.

NINE

The pram bumped gently over the stony plain. With its large wheels and elaborate suspension, it could have been especially designed for the conditions, even though Essie presumed most owners of Silver Cross prams confined their adventures to strolling over pavements or manicured lawns.

She brought the pram to a halt and peeped round past the fringe of the sun canopy to check if Mara was asleep yet. Seeing the closed eyes and peaceful face, Essie sighed with relief. The baby had been unsettled for most of the morning – refusing to take the bottle when it was time to feed, then crying if she was put down for her sleep. It had been the same yesterday. Essie had abandoned all hope of working on her fossil tray and given Simon the day off. She'd tried writing to her father instead, to cheer him up by sharing the good news of the grant. It was a welcome change not to have to skate around the gloomy facts of life at Magadi, yet she'd managed less than half a page.

Today Essie had not even tried to work. Perhaps anticipating this scenario, Simon had failed to turn up at the Work Hut after breakfast. She assumed he'd joined the other staff who were lingering around the camp. They were doing various maintenance tasks, in a half-hearted way; it didn't seem worthwhile to continue work at AJK while the Lawrences' plans were up in the air.

Now, though, everyone was going to have to wait a little longer than expected for Ian's new instructions. There had been an unscheduled radio call this morning. Thankfully it had come during a brief interlude of peace so Essie had been able to concentrate. Ian gave her the surprising news that Diana Marlow was in Arusha. The Serengeti holiday was over and Frank had returned to Canada, but she'd decided to stay on in Tanzania. Whereas she'd appeared bored by the Lawrences' work during her visit to Magadi, she was now showing a keen interest. Ian and Julia were having meetings with her to discuss options for research. They wouldn't be back for at least another two days.

Essie had felt a twinge of unease at this development – perhaps the grant wasn't going to be 'no strings attached' after all. And Diana's change of attitude seemed odd. But Ian sounded so buoyant that she'd expressed only her excitement. She'd been pleased, too, that he had finished the call by asking after the baby. Without a second thought Essie had told him that everything was fine. She could hardly complain of being exhausted and stressed, caring for a baby, when she was the one who'd brought the situation on herself.

As she pushed the pram along, Essie took some deep relaxing breaths. The sun was not yet too hot; a faint breeze toyed with her hair. She looked down towards the lake where the masses of flamingos created a vivid band of pink set against a backdrop of white salt flats. The sight was so spectacular that each year, when she witnessed it, Essie could hardly accept that it was real. She had the same sense of disbelief about the volcano – not the parts of it she could see, but the crater she knew was there, inside the broken tip of the summit. Ol Doinyo was a unique volcano, with lava that erupted at a relatively low temperature. The molten rock was black and silver, rather than red. Formed from a rare cocktail of calcium, carbon dioxide and salt, the flow was unusually liquid. When it burst from the crater it travelled down the slopes faster than a person could run. As the lava cooled and weathered it turned white, thus creating the impression that the holy mountain was topped with snow. Essie had never found the time to climb to the peak. People who had – volcanologists and adventurers – described the crater as a seething cauldron with fountains of lava that leapt into the air. It had to be approached with great care. Ol Doinyo Lengai was one of the few volcanoes in the world that was always active. When Essie had first arrived at Magadi, she'd been frightened by the rumbling noises that occasionally emanated from the mountain. The plumes of smoke. The earth tremors. Now, she took the fluctuating activity in her stride. As Ian liked to point out, getting used to such a dramatic backdrop was just part of living in a land that was still being formed. The ever-changing face of this world was, in fact, the very reason the Lawrences were working in the area. So many clues to primordial history had been preserved here.

In the Rift Valley, where two tectonic plates rubbed up against one another, the landmass of Africa was slowly being pulled apart. The *korongos* were like deep cuts into the planet's surface; they exposed layers of sediment in which fossils were trapped, forming a unique record of past times. For millennia this region had also been a place of constant shifting between dry and wet; desert and rainforest. These transformations had taken place over relatively short periods of time. In the area where Essie now walked, lakes had appeared and disappeared within as little as a hundred years:

grandparents would have been able to give eyewitness accounts of lost worlds to the children at their knees. In such a place all life forms had to adapt quickly or die out. This was why, according to Ian, this part of Africa had seen the emergence of some of the first hominids. Our ancestors had had to develop bigger brains in order to figure out how to adjust to the changing climate. When each crisis struck, the smartest individuals were the ones who made it through. Later on, in Europe, *Homo sapiens* would survive, while the larger, stronger Neanderthals who'd evolved alongside them died out. It was assumed by most people that this too was a matter of superior intellect. Not everyone, though. Essie had once heard a student from America propose another theory. She still remembered the way he'd spoken – his intense tone, the ardent look in his eyes.

'Yes, but what if one species looks at another,' he'd said, 'and decides they'd rather die out than become like their competitors? What if not everyone is prepared to be competitive, greedy, violent?'

He'd suggested that the Neanderthals might have retired to the fringes of society, choosing to relinquish their place in the race to become more and more human. To support his idea, he'd pointed out that Neanderthals were the first known artists. Essie had nodded as Ian delivered a blunt rebuttal, though she'd secretly admired the young man's ability to think outside the boundaries that were being observed by everyone else – and not be afraid to say what he thought.

Essie marched on, keeping up a steady pace as if she were aiming for a particular *korongo* or some other work site. It was odd to have no destination, no reason to be walking beyond the act itself. There was no hurry, she told herself, yet she found it hard to slow down. As she strode along, she scanned the area closer at hand, looking for Rudie and Meg. She knew Tommy had not strayed; he was right at her heels, his front hooves almost touching her boots. The dogs were chasing something in the distance, running with their bodies stretched out, heads low, as if drawn along by their noses. She was about to call them back when they both stopped, suddenly shifting their focus. Essie saw a figure come into view over the brow of a shallow rise. It was mainly the movement that caught her eye; the person's body, formed of muted, natural colours, merged with the landscape.

As the shape became clearer, Essie saw the stark line of a bow rising above the head. A hunter. She barely had time to speculate about the man's identity, when she recognised Simon.

He lifted his arm in a wave. When he drew near, Essie stared in surprise. His upper body was bare; his shirt was tied around his waist by the sleeves. He had an animal – or perhaps part of one – draped over his shoulders. He gave her a cheerful smile as he approached. There was a hint of a swagger in his step.

The two exchanged the usual greetings, just as if they were meeting in the Work Hut to begin their day's tasks. Simon leaned round to see Mara in the pram, acknowledging her presence as well. Essie noticed a bleary look in his eyes.

'You have been out all night?' she enquired. That would explain why he'd been absent this morning.

As if in reply, Simon swung his load down to the ground where it landed with a solid thud.

It was a substantial portion of a large species of antelope – an eland, perhaps. Essie doubted he could have stalked, killed and butchered it by himself. Perhaps he'd managed to form a connection with the Maasai from the *manyatta*. Sometimes young warriors led groups from the staff camp in a nocturnal hunt. It caused Ian great annoyance as work was disrupted; sometimes there were meat-eating parties that went on for days.

'You were with others?' Essie queried.

Simon hesitated. 'The Hadza.'

She raised her eyebrows. 'They have not left yet?'

'They are still at the cave,' he confirmed. 'There was some delay. But they will go very soon.'

Essie scanned Simon's face as questions chased through her head. How had he met up with the hunters? Had he actually been to the cave? If so, had he seen Nandamara and Giga? Had they talked about Mara? Even though she'd have liked some answers, Essie remained quiet. She knew Simon might not wish to discuss his connection with the wild Hadza – he'd been so keen to keep his distance from them. It would be best to let him tell her more when, and if, he chose to.

Essie made herself focus instead on the huge hunk of meat on the ground at his feet. Visions of a hearty stew came to her mind. Ian and Julia would return with supplies for the storeroom, but for now the shelves were still bare. Baraka had begun serving porridge for evening meals. Mara was the only person at Magadi who had everything she could possibly want.

'It was a long walk to find this animal,' Simon said. He pointed towards the country that lay beyond the Steps.

Essie wasn't surprised. Most of the herds would have set off on the migration – only stragglers were left behind. 'It was worth the effort. You have brought back lots of good meat,' she complimented him. 'Baraka will be very happy.'

Simon shook his head. 'You should not say that.' He spoke lightly, with a touch of humour.

'Why not?'

'It is not the Hadza way.'

Essie was intrigued. 'What is the Hadza way?'

'You remember you told me how that hunter offered you zebra meat and you rejected it?'

'He didn't seem to mind,' Essie said. 'He laughed at me. In fact, the more I shook my head, the more he laughed.'

Simon nodded. 'He thought you were pretending to be a Hadza, and not doing it very well.'

Essie frowned, mystified. 'What are you talking about?'

'I will show you.' Simon gestured energetically at the meat. 'Are you the one who has brought this to the camp?'

Picking up on his performance, Essie played her role. 'Yes,' she said proudly. 'It was me.'

Simon spat on the ground. 'You think I will thank you for it? It is from a skinny animal. It has died from old age.' He shook his finger at Essie. 'You are no good as a hunter.'

'But it looks like very fine meat,' Essie protested.

'It is,' Simon agreed. He abandoned his theatrical tone. 'But that is not the point. The hunter must feel humble. If he is proud, his heart becomes hard, and he is no longer gentle.'

A fly buzzed down, settling on the tawny hide. Simon flicked it away with his bare foot.

'So nobody should be proud?' Essie asked.

Simon spread his hands. 'If one person wants to be above another, they will not put the tribe first. So it must be discouraged.'

Essie thought back to the after-supper conversations that used to take place at Magadi when anthropologists were visiting. The topic of Hadza culture was often brought up. Essie had soon learned that they had created one of the few truly egalitarian societies that had ever been studied. Men and women were equal. Children were respected. They had no religious leaders to demand offerings. No kings or queens. Everything was shared freely regardless of whose labour had provided it. This wasn't a big issue because the Hadza had nature as their larder, and they only spent a few hours a day working. There was nothing to be gained by putting in extra effort because there was no tradition of storing excess food. The people had no huts, and no possessions beyond their hunting weapons, collecting bags, simple clothes, strings of beads and sleeping skins. They were completely self-sufficient.

Over coffee and whisky, academics and students alike debated the pros and cons of this way of life. The Hadza enjoyed so much spare time. They faced seasonal hunger at times but didn't suffer real famines like farmers did; when necessary they simply moved to another place where conditions were better. But their lack of possessions was off-putting, to say the least. People raised in England or America simply couldn't imagine having so few things to call their own. There were other drawbacks, too. The Hadza moved around in remote areas – in the lands that had not been taken up by settled tribes. Consequently, they usually had no access to schools or hospitals. Nandamara's daughter had given birth in the bush, and not survived. Mara was lucky not to have met the same fate.

Essie gazed into the distance while she absorbed the new information Simon had just shared with her: that the Hadza – unable to show off through possessions – could not even enjoy status earned by skills and talents. She thought of the framed photographs in the Dining Tent, and William's picture on the *National Geographic* cover. Her own father, too, had a collection of career memorabilia including museum catalogues, certificates and newspaper cuttings, as well as invitations to special occasions.

From an early age she'd sensed their purpose: it was to show that Professor Holland was successful and important, that the world recognised him. The treasures had more to do with anxiety – the need to prove himself – than celebrating good memories. Essie tried to imagine a life in which status did not exist. In one way it would be a huge relief. But at the same time, what would propel people to great achievement? The more Essie learned about the Hadza, the more paradoxes she saw. No wonder Simon found his position so complicated.

Turning back to her assistant, Essie searched his face. She couldn't really see the distinctive features of the Hadza that the experts identified, but that was probably because she knew him so well. When she spoke she made sure her words could be taken equally as a question or statement. 'You have rejected the Hadza way.'

'I know more than they do,' Simon responded. 'I have been to school. I was baptised. I am a modern Tanzanian.'

Essie suppressed a smile. He didn't look very modern right now. His skin was dusty and marked here and there with scratches. His boots, tied together with a leather thong, hung from his shoulder. He had a long cut on one forearm, oozing blood.

'You have hurt yourself,' she commented.

Simon wiped away the blood. It left a shiny smear on his arm, the colour lost on his dark skin. 'The moon was small. It was hard to see. And I had no fur jacket to protect me.' As he spoke, Simon was putting his shirt back on, and pushing his feet into his boots. 'I did not want to join the hunt,' he said.

Essie made no comment. She remembered the lively expression on his face as he'd approached. Was he trying to fool her, or himself, or them both?

'But I had to be polite,' he added. 'So I could ask about the cave.'

Essie's lips parted. She'd told Simon of her mimed communication with the hunter but had been too distracted by Mara to think of sending her assistant to see if the Hadza were still around to be questioned about a second cave. She'd never imagined he would take the task on for himself. 'What did they tell you?'

Simon gave her a satisfied look, clearly pleased with his investigation. 'There is a cave, with many paintings inside. They are very old like the ones you have studied. These Hadza people have not seen the cave themselves. Their ancestors stopped visiting there – for some reason that is no longer remembered.' Simon shrugged. 'But they know about it. They say it is on Ol Doinyo Lengai, down at the bottom.'

Essie caught her breath in excitement. Hominid remains would always be the jackpot as far as Ian and Julia were concerned, but the fresh discovery of a cave of prehistoric artwork would still be a very good way to mark Magadi's return to the world stage.

'At the bottom of the volcano?' Essie checked she'd heard correctly.

'That was what they said.'

Essie went back over the conclusions she'd drawn at the time when the Hadza hunter had mimed the act of painting and had then pointed towards the lake and the volcano. She reminded herself, again, that parts of the foothills had been searched when Robbie went missing. But the police and volunteers had their mind on other things, and in a landscape formed almost entirely from rock, an overhang or cave could easily be missed. The most likely source of information would have been the missionary, Wolfgang Stein. However, as Essie had already noted, there were no significant caves marked on his maps, let alone one containing paintings.

While she was still thinking this all through, Mara began to stir, kicking her feet and whimpering. Quickly Essie grabbed the handle of the pram and began to shake it, mimicking the movement of wheels over the gravel. She kept it up until Mara was quiet again, then she turned to Simon.

'That is a very big area. Did they say any more?'

'Only one thing,' Simon answered. 'The cave is near a tall rock that stands by itself.'

'Something like the Tower,' Essie mused. She pictured the erosion stack near the camp that captured everyone's attention. She'd not heard of any other landmarks like it. But that didn't mean there wasn't one, somewhere in the foothills. 'Do you think we could find it?'

Simon nodded. 'Of course. I hope so.'

From the typical African response – one that politely left room for whatever might eventuate – Essie couldn't tell how optimistic Simon actually was. Regardless, she was grateful for the effort he'd made. 'Ian will be very pleased to hear what you have learned.'

Simon shook his head. 'It was for you.'

Essie was taken aback – not just by his words, but his sombre tone. 'For me?'

'You like copying these ancient paintings. It makes you happy.'

Essie eyed him uncertainly. Was he saying that – more recently – she appeared to be unhappy?

'When you worked at the Painted Cave,' Simon added, 'you laughed every day.'

Essie gazed into the distance. What he said was true. But back then she was newly married and madly in love with her husband. She was living out a dream she would never have dared even to imagine. She was working with the Lawrences in Africa. Even her own father was envious of her! But she couldn't deny that a lot had changed since then. The financial issues and lack of success with work had weighed heavily on her in recent years, just as it had on Ian and Julia. Nevertheless, it was embarrassing to think that this had been so apparent to her assistant. She should have been more professional. She managed a smile. 'Let's just hope we can find it.'

'We will try,' Simon said, as if that was all they could expect of themselves.

He scratched his head, fingertips buried in his tight curls. Then he bent over his prey. Essie watched as he hefted the meat back onto his shoulders. She was touched by his concern for her happiness. It underlined, however, his attitude to the work the Lawrences were doing at Magadi. He was not personally committed to the research. To him, a position on the staff was no more than an opportunity for advancement; it was a part of his ambitious plan for his future. Essie had tried to explain to him, one day, how the Lawrences were striving to find evidence that *Homo erectus* had once lived in this region. Combined with the existence of the Australopithecine remains, it would help build the case that Africa was the place of origin for the whole human family.

'And what would that mean?' Simon had responded when she'd finished her speech.

'We would know that we are all one people.'

Simon had tilted his head questioningly. 'And this would change the way humans treat one another? Everyone would become like the *Hadza pori* and share their food? Everybody would be equal?' He'd laughed at the proposition. Essie had been about to insist that the knowledge would, indeed, have a big impact on society, but as she'd opened her mouth to speak her conviction had failed. The fact was that it was impossible to extrapolate in the way Simon proposed. Essie had been left trying to explain that the knowledge itself would have value – even if, from this vantage point in history, she was not able to say exactly what that might be.

'I shall return to the camp now,' Simon said. 'Baraka will be happy to see me.'

'I'll go on a bit further,' Essie said. 'I want Mara to stay asleep.' She glanced at her watch. If they could make it until lunchtime, there would be a chance of getting the routine back on track. 'She has been crying again today. I don't understand it. I am doing everything according to the book.'

Simon gave her a blank look.

'Timing feeds. Timing sleeps. Not making eye contact when I'm getting her ready for bed. But it's just not working.'

Simon frowned, as if her words made no sense. He bent over the pram, the hunk of antelope joining with his head to cast a strange shadow over the lacy coverlet. He murmured something so softly Essie could only hear the clicks in his words. There was a sympathetic expression on his face. He obviously pitied Mara, left in the hands of such an amateur. Essie felt a lump in her throat. She busied herself adjusting the sun canopy, keeping her head down until Simon stepped away. Then she gave him a brief, forced smile and nodded goodbye.

The old Mission house was a squat white shape surrounded by the remains of an overgrown garden. Exotic plants – strangers to the landscape – had thrived in the small spring-fed oasis. Essie hurried towards it, trying to block out the sound of Mara crying. The baby had woken up some distance back but she'd decided not to stop and feed her. She didn't want to deal with an unhappy baby out in the open or in some skimpy patch of shade. The abandoned house was boarded up – aside from a team of volcanologists who'd once spent a month there, no one had lived in the place since Stein departed forty years ago – however, there was a shady verandah running along the front.

Essie cursed herself for having ended up so far from home. While Mara slept, she'd just kept on walking, distracted by thoughts of her work, Ian, Diana Marlow – and especially the new cave. Unconsciously she'd aimed for the lake, where she would be able to take out the small binoculars she always carried in the pocket of her safari vest and scan the foothills for any sign of the landmark tower of rock. Somehow the distance had lengthened without her noticing. Now it would take well over an hour to walk back to the camp. Normally it wouldn't matter if Essie ended up worn out and thirsty. But with Mara awake and crying again, she felt suddenly vulnerable.

She approached the house from the rear, leaning on the pram as she pushed through an area of tall grass. Bougainvillea climbed up the wall, almost obscuring the back door. It was a relief to reach the pathway. A large lizard sunning itself on the paving stones flicked out a yellow tongue before waddling into the shadows.

Essie half ran down the side of the building. Mara's cries were frantic now and bouncing off the stone walls they sounded even louder. Essie couldn't wait to reach the sanctuary of the verandah.

Rounding the corner, she jerked to a halt, the pram lurching on its springs. Parked in front of her was a black jeep. She could see it was brand-new. The gleam of polished duco penetrated the coating of dust. The tyres had the crisp pattern of unworn tread.

On the door was a small pink shape – a flamingo – and the logo of the Frank Marlow Trust. As Essie stared at it, rigid with surprise, she recalled Ian's gloomy report on the visit of the Canadian philanthropist to the Steps.

All he talked about was flamingos.

Spinning round, Essie saw that the boards had been removed from the windows. There was a folding canvas chair on the verandah, an open book lying on its seat. The front door was ajar. Essie glanced back the way she'd come. The last thing she wanted was an encounter with a stranger – especially one who may well have diverted Frank Marlow's interest from the Lawrences' work. But she couldn't leave Mara crying in the pram any longer.

She lifted the baby out, smoothing down her dress and holding her against her chest. Through the fine cotton, she could feel Mara's ribs expanding as she sucked in air to fuel another wail. In the brief quiet there was the thud of footsteps. Then a man stepped onto the verandah. Essie caught an impression of messy dark hair, deep brown eyes and scruffy clothes.

For a few seconds the man was motionless, his gaze travelling from Essie and Mara to the pram and back. Then he jumped down the verandah steps in one bound and ran over to them.

'What's happened?'

Essie guessed he was picturing a scorpion bite or worse. She shook her head. 'Nothing. I don't know.' She heard the desperate edge in her voice.

The man looked around urgently, as if some solution to the situation might pop into view. He ran his fingers back through his unkempt hair, revealing the tanned face of someone who worked outdoors.

'Come inside,' he said.

Essie gestured towards her bag, stowed on a rack under the pram. He grabbed it and tucked it under his arm.

Essie bent her head over Mara's as she walked up the verandah steps. The woolly hair was damp from tears that had run back onto the silk pillow.

'I'm sorry, baby. I'm sorry,' Essie murmured. She wasn't sure what she was apologising to Mara for – failing to implement the Enforcement Parenting approach properly or upsetting her by trying to do it in the first place. Presumably the people at Babyland had included the book because they believed in it – and they should know. But the fact was, Mara had been quite contented, if unpredictable, until the regime had been started. Essie was lost in confusion.

It was a relief to step over the threshold into air that was even cooler than she expected. The walls, almost a foot thick, did a good job of keeping out the heat. She found herself in a long room, dotted with items that obviously belonged to the man outside, including half-unpacked luggage. There were, as well, two ancient armchairs, with stuffing emerging in tufts from torn velvet upholstery.

Essie sat down on one of them, rusty springs creaking under her weight. She tried to lay the writhing baby over her lap. The man came to stand beside her.

'What do you need?' He rummaged through the bag, pulling out a nappy, scattering safety pins onto the floor.

'There's a pink plastic container.'

The man glanced anxiously at Mara as he located the insulated box. He took out a bottle of milk and removed the cap.

Essie offered it to Mara but she just batted it away. Essie tried following the open mouth with the teat, having no success. The man watched helplessly for a while, then began pacing the room.

Mara screamed even more loudly. Essie would have been convinced there was something seriously wrong except that the baby had worked herself up into this state several times before. When she eventually drank her milk, she was fine. But maybe it was different this time? Perhaps an experienced mother would know she was dealing with an emergency.

When the man returned to stand next to her, Essie gave him a despairing look.

He eyed Mara for a moment, then sat down in the other chair, holding out his arms.

'Shall I try?'

Essie passed Mara over. He held her carefully, a focused expression on his face. As his fingers closed around her body, Essie wondered if it felt safer to the baby, being in such big, strong hands.

He laid her on his lap, her trunk between his legs, her head resting on his knees. Mara arched her back and kicked her feet against his abdomen. The man spoke to her in a low voice – a striking contrast to Essie's female pitch. The baby fell instantly quiet, gazing up at him, wide-eyed. Then she began crying again. Essie saw her trying to draw up her knees, like a woodlouse flipped on its back, wanting to curl into a ball. The man caught both feet in one hand, holding them still. With the other he began massaging her belly using slow, steady movements. The screams continued but he just kept on rubbing her stomach. Gradually the cries quietened, then died away. Mara's arms flopped, her hands unfurling.

Essie knelt beside the chair, nudging the teat at the baby's mouth. Mara latched onto it straightaway and began gulping the milk. Essie looked up at the man. As their eyes met, they both smiled with relief.

The man swivelled Mara around, without interrupting her feeding, until she was resting in his arms. Essie passed over the bottle, and then sat down again in the second chair. Part of her felt she should be taking the baby back – this person was a stranger, after all. But it was such a relief to let someone help her.

'How did you know what to do?' she asked.

'I saw a mother massage her baby like that once, in Thailand.' He nodded towards Mara. 'I thought she looked uncomfortable, tensed up, so it was worth trying. It seemed to work.'

Essie frowned thoughtfully. He made it sound so easy – a matter of trial and error and filling the gaps with guesswork.

The two sat quietly, watching Mara drink. There was no close-up sound except for the steady swallowing and an occasional sucking noise as she paused to let air go back into the teat. Essie took quick glances at the man, while he was focused on the baby. His weathered skin made his age hard to guess. He looked younger than Ian, though – maybe closer in age to her. His hair hadn't been cut recently; long wisps curled around his ears. Dark stubble on his chin showed he hadn't shaved for several days.

Instead of practical khakis with plenty of useful pockets, he wore casual clothes – more suited to a holidaymaker than an ornithologist in the field. His shirt, now faded almost to white, had once been brightly patterned. His shorts were sky-blue. Essie could just imagine what the Lawrences would think of him. One digging season a student had arrived at Magadi in an outfit something like this, and Julia asked if he was looking for a golf course. He hadn't lasted long at the camp.

Thinking of Julia reminded Essie that the man sitting in front of her was not welcome here at Magadi Gorge. The funds from Frank Marlow that had been used on the jeep and other expenses could have been given to the Lawrences. If Diana hadn't come to the rescue, the diversion of funds would have been disastrous. On the other hand, the stranger had been so kind and concerned.

Essie stared down at the floor, trying to sort out her conflicting emotions. The concrete had been recently mopped; a swirly pattern of dust had been left behind when the water evaporated. There was no sign of a houseboy or other staff; the man must have cleaned up the abandoned house himself. She wondered how long he was planning to stay here.

Lifting her gaze, she scanned the room. The stone walls, once painted white, were rosy with dust and tracked with brown termite trails. Only rotten threads of green-and-white checked curtains hung at the windows; pieces of new mosquito gauze had been taped over two of the openings. On a card table was a pair of binoculars, a folded map and a tube of toothpaste. There was a jar, its glass clouded with age, holding a sprig of a desert rose.

Turning to look behind her, Essie saw two stainless steel cases of the kind used for camera equipment. They were covered in airline labels, and each bore a *DO NOT X-RAY* sign. Propped in the corner of the room was an ex-army kitbag, a tartan blanket spilling from the open top. There was a patch of white paint on the canvas side covered in black writing. It looked like a name, followed by several crossed-out addresses. Craning her neck, Essie was able to pick out the largest letters.

Carl Bergmann.

It was a name that would have suited someone Nordic, as blonde as Essie – not this dark-haired man. She turned back to face her companion. Since she now knew his name it seemed the right time to share her own.

'I'm Essie Lawrence. From Magadi Research Camp.'

'Carl Bergmann,' he responded. Unable to shake hands, he just nodded. 'I know your family, of course.'

'I'm married to Ian,' Essie said, in case he was mistaking her for a real Lawrence. She found she wanted to add more, to show that she was not just a wife. 'I am a paleoanthropologist as well.'

Carl didn't react – he was busy juggling the bottle while adjusting Mara's position in his arms. Essie wondered if he was married, too, and a father. He'd been as rattled as she was when Mara was screaming, but now he looked quite relaxed as he fed her. Perhaps the Thai mother wasn't his only source of information about handling babies. If he did have a family, Essie felt sorry for them – they'd been left behind somewhere while he did his work. This scenario was common among professionals, Essie knew. It was precisely the life that she and Ian had rejected. She decided not to pursue the topic of her role at Magadi, in case it became awkward. It had happened before. Some visitors to the research base, who had spouses back at home, seemed to be confronted by watching a husband-and-wife team at work, as if it raised questions about the choices they had made for themselves.

'What are you going to be doing here?' Essie enquired instead. Ian would be keen to know, when he got home. He'd also be interested in whether Carl Bergmann had approached Frank Marlow, or vice versa – either way, though, the newcomer was trespassing on the Lawrences' territory. 'You're an ornithologist, I'm guessing.'

Carl shook his head. 'Not really. I'm a photographer. I do some ethnographic work – that's why I was in Thailand that time. But I specialise in birds.'

Essie tried to place his accent. It sounded like a blend of different tongues that she couldn't identify. 'You missed seeing the flamingos arriving.'

He nodded regretfully. 'The funding only just came through. I got here as soon as I could. The aim is to document the breeding. The government is talking about building a soda factory on the lake here, like the one in Kenya. It would be a disaster for the species. That's why I wrote to Frank Marlow about it. Someone has to get shots of the nesting. It's hard to protect something that no one has ever seen.'

Essie wasn't sure how to respond. She assumed the photographer already knew just how difficult it was going to be for him to succeed with his plan. Lake Magadi was the only place in the world where the lesser flamingos nested, and they chose the location – out of all the soda lakes in the East African Rift Valley – for one very good reason. In the dry season a lot of the water evaporated, leaving an island of mud in the middle. It was surrounded by what remained of the lake: water so concentrated with salt it was like acid. In effect, it formed a moat around the breeding grounds. Beyond it lay a wide expanse of hard, dried salt. Flamingos had evolved thick skin on their legs, so they were able to wade in the water, but hyenas, jackals and other predators could not. The only threat on the island came from marabou storks and vultures that swooped in from the air. With the difficulties of crossing the saltpan, and then the corrosive water, no human had ever, yet, been able to view the nests and chicks except from a plane.

The Maasai didn't even believe the birds came from eggs. Each year, they saw them emerge from the shimmering heat haze of the lake in vast throngs. The parents synchronised their breeding so the baby birds were all the same age and were able to be marched together across the saltpan like some massive kindergarten group, shepherded by a few adult guardians. Safety in numbers was their key to survival. Due to the grey-white colour of the juvenile feathers, the Maasai believed Lengai had formed the birds from salt. No one yet had been able to prove to them that they were wrong. The last ornithologist to try had been flown to hospital with serious burns on his legs where water had leaked over the top of his gumboots.

Essie found herself peering down at Carl Bergmann's bare feet. Where most people had a white sock mark, his were the even brown of someone who spent lots of time with no shoes on. Even if the man didn't go anywhere near the lake, he was risking other dangers. Essie looked up, eyeing him doubtfully.

'Do you live here in Africa?'

'Sometimes. It just depends where I'm working.' He smiled. 'I'm a nomad – like the flamingos.'

Essie nodded. So he didn't have a family, then. He was one of those professionals who lived only for their work. It was a status she understood and respected.

Carl was smiling down at Mara now – she'd finished her bottle and was pulling off one of her booties. His eyes creased at the corners, and a line formed down both his cheeks. He was lean, Essie noticed, as well as being tall.

'What's her name?' Carl asked.

'Mara. After her grandfather.'

Essie guessed he thought the baby was adopted – that the Lawrences had visited an orphanage and picked out a child to fill the gap left by their inability to conceive. 'I'm looking after her,' she explained. 'Just for the dry season. She belongs to a tribe of Hadza. Her mother died giving birth to her.'

Bergmann raised his eyebrows as he absorbed her words. Essie waited for him to ask the predictable questions and raise the obvious concerns. Instead he just touched Mara's hand. 'How old is she?'

'About two months.'

'She is so beautiful.' He sighed, settling back in his chair. It was as if the need to talk was now finished – and this was the final truth.

Essie relaxed in her own chair. She was silent as well. From the lake came a dulled blur of honking, peeping and singing – the sound of the multitudes of flamingos. Overhead the tin roof creaked in the heat. The whole situation felt unreal – the house, the man, the Hadza baby, the pram parked outside. And all this was on the back of the inexplicable turnaround in the fortunes of the Lawrences. After years of a predictable existence at Magadi, one unexpected event now seemed to follow another like a chain reaction. It was as if the world had been tilted from its axis, and now anything could happen.

TEN

Two-dozen white squares patterned the tufted grasses that surrounded the washing pool. Essie surveyed them with a satisfaction that felt out of proportion to what they were: clean, almost-dry nappies being sterilised by the strong rays of the sun. Not far away, on a line hung between two stunted trees, was a row of little dresses, bibs, bunny rugs and plastic pants. Essie pictured the guest tent – which was now known as the 'nursery' – back at the camp. The dirty laundry buckets were all empty; previously washed nappies and clothes were folded away in the drawers; Mara's cot had been made up with fresh sheets. Everything was in order.

Essie smiled across at Kefa. He stood with his arms crossed, gazing out over the expanse of white. It had been he who had discovered that one of the staff knew the purpose of the odd galvanised tool sent by Babyland. It was a washing implement. The idea was to press the metal cone down onto an item soaking in a bucket, causing water to be forced through the fabric. Openings in the cone allowed the trapped water to escape. After a few energetic pushes, all dirt was lifted from the fabric without the need for anyone to touch it with their hands. Now that the tool was in use there were plenty of volunteers for the role of nursery launderer. It was pleasant working here by the pools compared to being in

188

the *korongos*, exposed to wind, dust and sun. A young Chagga man called Tembo, from one of the sieving teams, had been given the role. A small deep pool fed by a hot spring had been selected for his use. A stony area some distance away was perfect for disposing of contaminated water. Tembo was there now, emptying out his buckets.

'I can't think of anything else we have to do,' Essie told Kefa. She ran through a mental list, covering not just the nursery but the Work Hut, Dining Tent, the staff quarters – the whole camp. Assuming Baraka had managed to find something to serve for supper, everything was in place for Ian and Julia's imminent return.

The trip to Arusha had been extended twice. The pair had been gone for nearly two weeks now – but it felt like much longer. Essie hadn't been able to get used to their absence. She was reminded of a centipede waving its feelers constantly, searching for boundaries and obstacles that were not there. She told herself she should feel carefree and relaxed, left on her own – instead it was as if she'd been cut adrift and had lost her bearings. Essie hadn't realised how completely Ian and Julia dominated the world of Magadi – with their expectations, idiosyncrasies, shared history, even their moods. Without them, Essie was in a vacuum.

It was hardly surprising she felt this way. In the five years she had been here she'd barely been apart from them. And it was not as if she'd had a very independent life even before that. When she was at university, doing what all the other students did – going to parties and concerts, making shopping trips to London, as well as studying – she was always conscious of feeling responsible for her father. For a long period after Lorna's death he'd been ill – falling prey to every passing infection. It was as if the dark spirit that had plagued his wife for so long had leapt from her shoulder as death approached, taking possession of him instead. He wasn't able to visit digs or even give lectures. Instead he spent hours sitting at his desk – not reading or writing, just gazing out over the front garden with its narrow winding path. Essie used to watch how he raked the gravel with his eyes as if somewhere among the stones was the answer to a deep and burning question. She didn't like to think of him passing his days like this – solitary and unwell – so she made sure she considered him in all her daily plans. Arthur eventually became stronger again and returned to work, but he never regained full health. Essie's habit of being always mindful of his wellbeing lingered. With her mother's needs, through all the years of illness prior to her death, and then those of her father, the demands on Essie had been unrelenting. The truth was that she had never been a person on her own.

Of course, she was not alone now, either. There were lots of people at Magadi – Simon, Baraka, Kefa, Daudi and all the other staff. And there was Mara. The baby's presence filled every moment of Essie's day and a fair portion of the night as well. But it was still different to having Ian and Julia here.

Leaving Kefa to supervise Tembo, Essie headed back towards the camp. As she ambled along the path, she was followed by Tommy. He bleated loudly. Since Mara's arrival a plaintive note had crept into his voice, and there was often an accusing look in his eyes. Simon said it was a good thing if the gazelle felt he'd been displaced; it was time for him to grow up and return to his own kind. Essie knew her assistant was right, but she still felt guilty. She carried bread crusts around in her pocket so she could offer Tommy regular treats.

Mara was in the leather sling, swinging gently at Essie's hip as she took each step. Essie's spine curved to compensate for the extra weight. It seemed second nature to her already, as if the baby had become an extension of her own body. Glancing down, Essie saw that Mara was now wide-awake. Her eyes were fixed on Rudie, who was strolling along beside them. She had one finger hooked over her lower lip. She was calm and relaxed. Over the last few days Essie's attempt at forcing a routine had been abandoned. The baby had been allowed to wake and feed and sleep whenever and however she chose. Near the end of the afternoon, when she tended to be unsettled, Essie massaged her body like the photographer had done, before offering her a bottle. She also made sure Mara spent a lot of time outdoors; she seemed happier there than shut up inside a tent. As a result, the baby now barely cried at all.

Essie found it hard to match her with the screaming infant that had prompted the frantic rush to the Mission house. She thought back to the time she'd spent there with Carl Bergmann – how he had responded so warmly to Mara. She remembered the two of them just sitting like devotees at a temple, admiring the baby – the tiny features, so finely formed; the darkness of her skin that seemed to highlight the perfect contours of her nose, chin and brow.

The interlude had seemed timeless. But the angle of the sun, reaching in through the dusty windows, had been a reminder that the afternoon was dwindling. After Mara had finished the bottle and had her nappy changed, Carl had offered to drive Essie home. She had accepted gratefully. While she climbed into the passenger seat, lodging the baby on her lap, Carl lifted the pram onto the back of the jeep. Looking over her shoulder as they lurched away over the rough track, Essie watched the fringe on the canopy blowing in the breeze. She smiled to herself at the thought of how incongruous the sight would be, for anyone who saw them pass by.

On the way back to the camp Essie tried to work out how to avoid asking Carl to stay for a cup of tea. The rules of hospitality out here in the bush required her to offer, but she wasn't sure how the Africans would view her entertaining a man while her husband was away. They were very old-fashioned in some ways. It was a relief when Carl said he had to return to the Mission house straightaway. He had tasks to complete by nightfall.

As they stood by the jeep, shaking hands, Essie knew she was being watched. Baraka, Simon, Kefa and Daudi were all among the staff who'd come out to see the jeep arrive, and then lingered at a distance.

'Thank you so much,' she said politely.

'It was no trouble.' Carl's tone matched hers.

'Ian and Julia will be keen to meet you,' she added. 'Perhaps you could come for lunch one Sunday?' She'd begun to think the Lawrences would change their attitude to Frank Marlow's Flamingo Project. Carl Bergmann was going to be their neighbour, after all, for at least the next couple of months. It would be churlish to maintain their animosity, especially now that their future at Magadi was secure.

'I'd like that,' Carl said. 'Just send someone over with a message.'

Essie nodded. He'd already told her the Marlow Trust had arranged access to the house and provided some of what he'd require to live there – but they'd overlooked his need for a radio.

As he said goodbye Carl rested his hand on Mara's head. In response, she began blowing bubbles at him. Then she giggled as if she'd played a joke. The formal mood was gone in an instant. Essie and Carl both laughed with her. It was impossible not to.

Essie had hugged Mara against her chest as she watched Carl drive away. When the jeep picked up speed, his hair blew back from his face and his shirt flapped against his body. Soon the vehicle was just a small black shape with a long cloud of dust stretching behind it like steam following a train. Then it was gone.

The table was set for three, each place marked with a napkin rolled neatly and tucked into a ring. Ian and Julia had solid silver rings with engraved initials. The third one, Essie's, was formed from brass wire and coloured beads – the work of a Maasai souvenir maker.

Sitting in her chair, Essie fiddled with a fork, scoring lines in the white linen. Mara was asleep in her pram, parked not far away where she could be heard if she woke. The only noise for the moment was the fluttering of a moth caught in the flue of a lamp. The urgent sound mirrored Essie's rising anxiety. She pushed out a breath through half-closed lips, trying to relax. She was looking forward to Ian and Julia's arrival – after the long separation she wanted to be reunited with her husband, and to hear all about Arusha – but at the same time she was worried about how she was going to manage Mara when there were the others to consider. Also, Essie had nothing to show for the days that had gone by. The *Sivatherium* cranium was virtually untouched. Her father's letter was nowhere near finished. Mara was generally contented now, due to Essie's new approach, but caring for her still seemed to fill the whole day. Even when there were peaceful times, like now, Essie felt too tired to concentrate. How she was going to take part in the projects that were about to commence – meeting the rigorous standards of Magadi Research Camp – was a question she couldn't even begin to tackle. Sometimes, as she collapsed in a chair, barely able to find the energy to move, she couldn't help thinking how much easier it would be to look after a baby if there was a father involved. Of course, Mara was not Ian's responsibility; Essie alone had made the promise to the Hadza. But even if Mara had been their own baby, she knew it was unlikely her husband would have taken on any of the laborious tasks. European men didn't change nappies or prepare bottles or rock babies in the night. The attitude Carl had demonstrated was, as far as Essie knew, most unusual.

She remembered how Nandamara had spoken about his grand-daughter, and the ease with which the hunter – who'd just put down a haunch of zebra – had cradled the tiny baby in his arms. She knew the Hadza were an exception to the norm, in terms of African families. Baraka and Kefa had been helpful with Mara, but they probably saw that as part of their job. From what Essie had observed of the Maasai, as well as the other tribes, men didn't have much to do with caring for babies. They left the task to the women and older children. Of course, childrearing was very different in their traditional societies. People lived in large extended families. No one was a mother on her own. And there was less work to be done. No nappies, for a start. No daily baths, or piles of clothes to launder. Even so, Essie wondered if the women wished their husbands were more involved.

The best examples of fathering, Essie knew, were to be found in non-human species – birds, in particular. It was a matter of survival. A mother trying to hatch eggs would starve to death unless her mate brought her food or took her place on the nest while she provided for herself. The young had to be cared for too. Some males even fed them from their own mouths. This shared parenting was just an outcome of evolution. Nevertheless, it seemed very civilised to Essie – thoughtful, and simply kind . . .

Essie looked up from the table as Kefa entered the tent.

'They have arrived,' he announced.

'You mean they are here – now?' She'd expected some warning. Usually one of the boys from the *manyatta* climbed a tree so they could report the first glimpse of an approaching vehicle.

Scraping back her chair, she got to her feet. 'Stay with Mara, please.'

With Tommy at her heels she strode off, ignoring the look on Kefa's face. As the houseboy he should be waiting in the car park when the Bwana arrived – but that could not be helped.

Hurrying towards the rear of the camp, Essie tidied her hair, smoothed her eyebrows and rubbed her lips together. She checked her shoulders for patches of dribbled milk.

When she reached the turning circle, Ian was already standing beside the Land Rover. As he turned towards her, Essie was amazed to see he was wearing sunglasses. He'd always despised them, saying they obscured the small details that a researcher needed to notice. The sleek black frames and lenses suited him, though. In brand-new khakis and with a fresh haircut, he looked more like a film star than an archaeologist.

Essie raised her hand in an awkward little wave. She felt almost shy, suddenly, as if she were meeting Ian Lawrence for the first time. He responded with a hasty smile. His attention was focused on the passenger side of the Land Rover. The sun glanced off the windscreen so the interior was just a blur. Essie peered past him, wondering why Julia was taking her time climbing out. Normally she was impatient to escape the confines of any vehicle; she resented wasting time on the road. A Maasai boy ran to open her door, standing to attention like a soldier.

As a figure emerged, Essie stiffened in surprise. The hair was dark and thick, not wispy and grey. The body, unfolding from the seat, was too tall. The khaki trousers were too new.

Diana Marlow stepped from the car, a smile on her red-painted lips. She was dusty and hot; she had to be tired. But she was still beautiful. Cigarette in hand, she surveyed the scene, nodding graciously, as if everyone gathered there had come especially to greet her.

Before Essie had a chance to react, a second Land Rover pulled into the car park. Essie took in the brand-new-but-dusty look that reminded her of Carl's jeep. The vehicle jerked to a halt. Essie saw Julia wrench up the handbrake. The boy approached the door, but she waved him away.

Essie glanced at Ian. The sunglasses concealed his eyes, but his posture betrayed tension. His shoulders looked rigid; his chin was held a fraction too high. He smiled at Essie again, but only briefly. He turned from Diana to his mother and back.

Julia walked past him. Her face was composed, unreadable. Essie couldn't imagine what had gone wrong. Surely she didn't mind being relegated to the second vehicle since it was obviously brand-new and comfortable. Anyway, it would have been the only option. Over such a long journey Ian would have insisted on driving the Land Rover they'd set off from Magadi in; though it was easier to manage than the one that had remained here, it was still cantankerous. And it was obvious that Mrs Marlow would want to share the ride with the Head of Research, since she was interested in the work. Probably, Essie concluded, the benefactor had interfered too much with plans for the new research during the meetings in Arusha.

As Julia approached, Essie smiled cautiously. 'I hope you had a good journey.'

'Fine, thank you.' Julia replied, her tone abrupt. She looked exhausted, every year of her age showing.

While Julia headed for the tents, Diana swept across from the Land Rover, embracing Essie in a cloud of perfume and cigarette smoke.

'I am so happy to be back!'

Essie responded with a welcoming smile, but her thoughts were racing. How long was Diana Marlow planning to stay? Where would she sleep? The conditions at the camp were very basic for someone like her. Essie was glad to have an opportunity to thank her in person for her generosity in providing everything Mara needed. But on the other hand, with all the new work to begin, and a baby to consider, there were enough complications at Magadi already. It made sense that Diana might want to return to the area, now she was funding the research. But why had Ian and Julia invited her now? Or had she invited herself? Regardless of how the plan had come into being, why had Ian not made a radio call to warn Essie about it?

Diana didn't seem to notice that Essie hadn't spoken yet. She eyed her eagerly. 'How is that baby? Did Babyland send you everything you need?'

Essie nodded. 'Mara is doing really well. And all the things you sent are perfect. Thank you so much. I can't wait to show you the nursery.'

'Good, good.' Diana glanced around distractedly. 'I really admire you for taking her on. It must be quite a burden for you.' Through pursed lips she blew a stream of smoke into the air.

'Not really,' Essie protested. She couldn't think what to add. She bent to pat Tommy. Running her hand over his sleek coat, she found a prickly burr. She picked it out carefully, rolling it between her fingers before dropping it onto the ground.

'I'm sure she's heaps of fun, too.' Diana touched Essie's fore-arm. Then she went to stand next to Ian, who was supervising the unloading of the vehicles. A pile of luggage grew on the ground. Now and then Diana called out instructions to the workers. Essie watched on, surprised and impressed. For someone unaccustomed to being in a place like Magadi, Diana Marlow seemed amazingly confident and in control.

A small photograph was propped against the bottle of Worcestershire sauce. Essie studied it as she sat in front of her untouched meal. The black-and-white tones of the print matched the content of the image: a black woman, white uniform, black pram, white baby.

'She's very experienced,' Julia was saying. 'Trained by the wife of the Regional Commissioner.'

Essie stared down at her lap where her napkin had been twisted into a mess of creases. She could just imagine what kind of training the young woman had been given, if the uniform was anything to go by.

'It's ideal,' Ian said encouragingly. 'She won't expect to be in here with us. She will live in the staff quarters. The nursery tent can be moved there.'

Ian and Julia both looked at Essie, awaiting her approval. When she said nothing, the quiet became strained. Essie noticed Ian glance warily across the table at Diana. The proposed plan for Mara's care wasn't meant to have come up now, during this first meal with their special guest. The photo of the nanny had fallen out of a folder while Julia was searching for some notes made in Arusha. Feeling a buzz of instant alarm, Essie had picked it up and asked to know who the person was. The topic then had to be addressed.

'I'm sure we would all agree,' Julia added to her speech, 'that this approach will be better for Mara. After all, she's going back to tribal life. She should be with Africans.'

Essie felt dismay spreading inside her. She thought Ian and Julia had accepted Mara's presence – they'd seemed pleased about all the things from Babyland, and their focus had shifted to the exciting options for research. Now it seemed they had a new agenda. She wasn't sure where and how it had arisen.

'I appreciate all the effort you've made,' Essie ventured. 'But it's not what I had in mind. I want to look after Mara myself.' She turned towards the pram, positioned near the doorway where it could be wheeled outside when Mara woke up. For now, the baby was deeply asleep, hidden from view by a mosquito net draped over the canopy – innocently unaware that her life for the next few months was being planned out.

As Essie waited for a response from Julia and Ian, she eyed Diana. The woman had gone out of her way to make it viable for Essie to keep the baby at the camp – perhaps she might understand, therefore, that Essie wanted to be the one to take care of her, and offer some moral support. But Diana seemed oblivious to the whole conversation. She was picking at her meal, separating rice and gravy from chunks of meat. Baraka had made a curry with a goat he'd purchased from the Maasai. The spices almost covered the strong taste of the animal, but not quite. This was obviously not the kind of food Diana was used to. Essie guessed she was preoccupied not with a disagreement over a nanny, but with how she was going to survive here at Magadi.

'It would be very unwise for you to get so involved, Essie,' Julia said firmly. 'You'll get much too fond of the baby. Also, there's your profession to consider. You have earned a place here, through years of hard work. You don't want to interrupt your career.'

'It's only for a few months.'

'But it's most of the digging season. And with new projects starting, you need to be part of the team. You can lose your place, you know.'

Essie was surprised. Julia sounded as if she was genuinely concerned for her – not just trying to secure the best outcome for the research. It was so out of character, it was unnerving.

'I was thinking that I could have someone to help me,' Essie said. 'So that I can do my work, but still look after Mara myself.'

Ian shook his head. 'We discussed it in Arusha, Julia and I. One person must be responsible for the baby, with no other duties or distractions.'

'I don't think that's how it has to be,' Essie argued.

Julia took a breath, her chest rising sharply. 'But you have no idea!' Her voice had a brittle edge. 'You don't understand that when you try and do two things at once, neither gets your full attention. And that's when —' She broke off, bending her head over her plate. 'That's when things go wrong.'

After a taut quiet she began eating, gripping her cutlery tightly, chewing steadily. Ian frowned at Essie, shaking his head just a fraction. Diana was now looking from one face to another, intrigued, like a child listening in to a conversation they wished they could understand. Essie couldn't believe Ian was allowing this confrontation to play out in front of her. But since it had begun, perhaps he needed to show he was able to manage the situation.

'Essie, you cannot do two jobs,' Ian stated. 'And we are not having Mara at the excavation sites. Next thing, the workers' wives will be visiting with their babies. It'll be a circus.' He put down his glass, slopping red wine onto the tablecloth. 'We're going to bring that nanny here. She will look after the baby while you work – and that's that.' He sat back in his chair, indicating the debate was over.

Essie eyed him mutely. He'd changed for the evening meal into a jacket and shirt she hadn't seen before; his outfit had the smart casual look that cost money to create. He appeared so confident, in control. She felt a cold sense of defeat. He'd made up his mind and nothing she said would have any effect.

'But surely, Ian,' Diana finally spoke up, 'there must be room for compromise.' She took a casual sip of her wine, as if she'd just made a comment on the weather. 'After all, Essie was the one who promised to look after the baby. Shouldn't she decide how it's done?'

Ian stiffened. Instead of replying, he took a gulp from his glass.

Essie threw Diana a grateful look. She cleared her throat. 'I am sure I can figure out a way to manage work and Mara, with some help.'

Julia put down her knife and fork. She took her napkin from her lap and placed it neatly beside her plate. She swallowed hard, her neck constricting. She looked as if she was going to speak, but her lips just quivered. Then she stood up and walked away.

Ian reached one hand towards his mother as if to hold her back, but she was beyond his reach. When she was gone, he leaned across to Essie. 'Can't you see how hard this is for her?' He talked in a low voice, as if he thought Diana might not hear.

Essie said nothing. She didn't know if he was referring to the outsider's interference, or to Mara remaining in the Lawrences' domain.

'I do apologise.' Ian turned to Diana. 'We shouldn't be discussing this now.'

'I don't mind,' Diana said. 'It's . . .' She puckered her brow, hunting for a word. 'Interesting.'

Ian forced a smile. Essie could see that he wanted to change the subject now.

'While you were away,' she began, 'I went for a walk down towards the lake. I met the photographer who is working for the Marlow Trust. He's moved into the old Mission house.' As well as diverting the conversation, she was keen to report the encounter before someone else told Ian or Julia about Carl Bergmann's appearance at the camp.

'Ah yes . . . Frank's flamingo man,' Diana said.

Essie faltered. She thought there was a sneer in Diana's voice as she said her husband's name, but she wasn't sure. 'He's keen to come over and meet everyone here.'

Ian nodded. 'We'll have him to lunch.'

Essie felt a flicker of satisfaction; she'd been right in her prediction that the Lawrences' attitude to the interloper would change. She looked across at Diana. 'Where is Frank? Is he coming back to Magadi as well?'

Diana shook her head. 'He's left Toronto already. Gone off to London or somewhere. He's got his nose out of joint because I'm getting involved here.' She let out a brief, bitter laugh. 'But it serves him damned well right.'

Ian looked taken aback, then embarrassed, by Diana talking about Frank Marlow in such a tone. Essie wondered what the man was being punished for; perhaps some new infidelity had been discovered. Regardless, the uninhibited remarks suggested Diana wouldn't be finding the confrontation between the Lawrences improper at all. Essie recalled how she'd talked so intimately about her marriage, when the two of them had only just met. Perhaps it was the American way, just to say whatever was on your mind.

Ian changed the topic again. He began describing the role of photography in research. He explained how the Leakeys were able to create an international storm of interest over their discovery of the first Australopithecine remains in East Africa, purely because they happened to have a cameraman from the BBC at Olduvai when the fossil was found. As Ian talked, Essie could tell he was concerned about Julia – now and then he glanced in the direction of her tent – but he was trying to do his job as host. Essie was thinking about Julia, too. It was shocking to see her mother-in-law overcome with emotion when she was normally so calm. Essie considered going to make sure she was all right. But she knew that was the last thing Julia would want.

Ian gradually seemed to forget about his mother. His focus shifted to what he was saying. Essie watched Diana engaging with him. The visitor seemed enthralled by everything he was telling her. In one way it was not surprising; Essie still got excited about archaeology, after being involved with it for most of her life. However, it was hard to put Diana's attitude together with the languid, off-hand manner she'd displayed when she first visited with her husband. Essie knew she should be glad that Diana was so intrigued; it boded well for keeping the funding flowing. But a thread of uneasiness stirred. Diana had talked of envying Essie's life of working alongside her husband. And now Essie was about to change that dynamic – at least for a while.

Turning away from Diana and Ian, Essie stared at the collection of maps, rosters, contact sheets and other items pinned to the wall of the tent. Her attention was caught by one of Mirella's paintings. It was of the artist's favourite subject – Ol Doinyo Lengai. In this picture the volcano looked unusually imposing. The peaks rose up steeply, almost bearing down on the viewer. Essie followed the line of the pyramid down to the base. If the Hadza story were true, then somewhere there, in the foothills, was a second 'painted cave'.

She leaned round, studying the picture more closely. An idea began to form. If Essie could just find this cave somehow, she could devote herself to documenting the ancient images. Between her and Simon, they could easily look after Mara at the same time – the work would be peaceful and low-key, away from the buzz of the excavations. Essie could almost feel the crisp tracing paper under her hands; the waxy slide of the crayon. It seemed the perfect scenario.

Essie warned herself not to be too hopeful. Without further clues, locating the cave could be a long shot. But the tantalising vision lingered. She couldn't help picturing what would happen if she succeeded. She would lead Ian there, without telling him what she'd found. Just reveal it, as a surprise. A whole new collection of Neolithic paintings. It would remind him of who she was, as a researcher – and also take him back to the days when she was new here in Magadi. When she was as wide-eyed with fascination as Diana was now.

Ian and Diana continued their discussion while Kefa proudly served a steamed pudding dotted liberally with currants. He set down a jug of evaporated milk – the Magadi stand-in for cream. Baraka must have cooked the pudding hastily, using some of the newly unpacked provisions. The pudding was light and sweet. Diana seemed to enjoy it – perhaps she was hungry, since she'd barely touched her curry. When the whisky was served, Essie decided it was time to wheel the pram back to the nursery. It would be better to be ready, in there, with a bottle on hand, before Mara woke up. The evening had run less than smoothly already, without adding the disruption of a crying baby.

'Good night,' she said. 'I hope you will be comfortable enough, Diana.'

Kefa had made up a bed for her in another of the guest tents. This was just for tonight; Ian had mentioned that in Arusha Diana had purchased what he described as a canvas palace. It would be erected in the morning. Essie wasn't sure what to make of the special tent. It seemed to suggest an extended visit, even though Ian claimed nothing had yet been decided. On the other hand, someone like Diana couldn't be expected to tolerate basic facilities, even for a short time.

'I'm exhausted,' Diana said. 'I could sleep anywhere.'

Essie studied her face. She didn't look exhausted. Her eyes were bright, her smile vivacious. Ian had moved on from photography to an explanation of exactly how evolution occurred. All paleoanthropology relied on this understanding. Ian was a good teacher – Julia said he'd learned the skill from William, as well as inheriting his natural flair. Ian whistled for Meg to come and stand beside him. He liked to use the Dalmatian as a prop.

As the dog stood there obediently, Ian ran his hand over her coat.

'How did the Dalmatian get its spots?' he asked, as if beginning a fable. He reminded Essie of her father. 'There are no other dogs that look anything like them.'

'That's right,' Diana agreed. 'I can't think of any other breeds with spots.'

'Originally,' Ian continued, 'a few spots must have appeared as a mutation – these are small genetic variations between generations. They happen all the time, in every living thing. Some breeder decided to let dogs with spots mate with others who had the same mutation. Over time the dogs became more and more spotty.

It was done purely for looks. The markings served no useful purpose. In fact, the spotted coat often goes along with deafness, so in the wild it would have been a fatal disadvantage, even leaving aside being so ridiculously eye-catching.' He scratched Meg's ear. 'Poor things. They don't live long either, being large purebreds. Only about ten years.' He smiled at Diana. 'If you want a long life, you're better off being a small crossbreed. Robust health comes with greater genetic variety.'

'Well, that's good for me,' Diana stated. 'I'm a bit of everything. The Shermans are American now, but our forebears were Welsh, English, German, Flemish . . . And they're just the ones I know of.' She smiled, revealing her perfect teeth.

Ian just stared at her, as if unable to find anything relevant to say. With her spectacular beauty Diana looked like the human version of a pedigree dog. Instead she was the result of a potpourri of nationalities. She could have been one of those people whose large teeth didn't fit into their small face, or whose head was too big for their trunk. Instead, in the game of genetic roulette she was a winner. Of course, it wasn't really just a matter of luck. Diana had been born into a wealthy family; her father owned a whole chain of hotels. That fact alone increased her chances of being beautiful. Her mother had managed to attract a marriage proposal from a rich and successful man. She would most likely have had appealing features, such as facial symmetry and thick lustrous hair, which her daughter could inherit.

'Tell me more,' Diana said. She reached for another cigarette. 'Tell me everything.'

Ian smiled. 'That would keep us here all night.'

Essie stood up to go, before the conversation started again. As she got to her feet she was suddenly reluctant to leave. She wanted to hear what topic would come up next. She felt like a child having to go to bed while the adults were still up. Whatever happened next – the talking, laughing, drinking – she would miss out on. She had to force herself to cross to the pram, release the brake and wheel the baby away.

Essie lay next to Ian, her body so close to his that she could feel his warmth across the space between them. She was on her back, looking up. The lamp had been turned off and the only light came from the moon, filtered through the gauze windows. Above her the mosquito net merged with the roof of the tent, making a single zone of grey. Essie turned her head as Mara murmured in her sleep. The baby was beside the bed, installed in her fossil crate; the makeshift cot had turned out to be less intrusive in here than the elaborate bassinet.

Ian was silent, but Essie knew he was still awake. He'd finally come to bed after helping Diana settle into her quarters – Essie had heard their voices in the distance as she waited for him to appear. Now they were alone together at last, Essie wanted to return to the unfinished conversation about the baby. She wouldn't be able to sleep until the issue was resolved.

'Where did we get to?' she asked Ian. 'About Mara.'

'You're the one who has a choice to make.' Ian's voice seemed to float, disembodied, above them. He sounded weary. The time in Arusha had been stressful, Essie knew. He'd told her that Diana's enthusiasm had been inspiring but having a third person to consider had added a whole layer of complexity. Then, the journey home had been long. Essie felt a pang of guilt that he'd had to deal with conflict around the supper table. And now, she had to bring it all up again.

'I know what I want,' Essie stated. 'I want to look after Mara.'

Ian turned to her, his face a blur in the gloom. 'Then you can't be part of the excavation team.'

Essie took a breath. She knew the price she was agreeing to pay. Julia had clearly warned her. *You could lose your place.* She glanced towards the spot where Mara was sleeping. 'I understand that.'

Ian shook his head as if her decision made no sense to him. 'What on earth are you going to do all day?'

Essie smiled to herself. She'd have wondered that, too, until she began looking after a baby. The whole day just seemed to vanish. 'I want to keep working, a little. Nothing difficult; just whatever I can fit in around Mara. I could do some scouting.'

At Magadi, 'scouting' was the term used for walking through an area in a way that was systematic but fairly quick. The idea was to look for surface fossils that suggested a proper survey was worthwhile. It was really a way of allowing a chance discovery to occur. A stroke of luck. It was not described in these terms, though. The closest Ian would come to endorsing the concept of chance – otherwise known as fortune, coincidence, serendipity – was to quote Louis Pasteur, the microbiologist who'd brought the gift of immunisation to the world.

Fortune favours the prepared mind.

For the person engaged in scouting, being prepared entailed having a thorough knowledge of subjects like anatomy, geology and history. It also meant being able to hold on to an intense focus while searching – not slipping into a daydream.

'Scouting could be helpful, with new projects on the agenda,' Ian said cautiously.

Essie risked pushing on. 'I'd like to keep Simon on as my assistant.'

'Absolutely, you must,' Ian said. 'I don't want to spend my time worrying over what might happen to you out in the field.' He paused for a moment. 'But how will you manage the baby?'

'It will be fine. She's so little. I'll just carry her around.' Essie hoped she sounded more confident than she was.

'It will limit where you can get to. You'll need to choose carefully. I'll give it some thought.'

Essie's jaw tensed. She could feel the chance of making her own plans slipping away. 'Maybe leave that to me.' She tried to sound casual. 'I'll visit a few places, see what I think will work, with the baby.'

Essie didn't want to name the foothills as the focus of her interest. She wasn't aware of the exact location where Robbie had gone missing, and the chance of the cave in the Hadza story being in the same area was not great – but still, it would be best to find the rock tower without involving the other Lawrences. The last thing Essie needed right now was to upset either of them any further.

There was another reason not to reveal her plans to Ian and Julia. The survey would then become 'their project'. Essie would lose control. And the dream of surprising her husband with an amazing discovery would be lost.

The two lay in silence. Essie listened to the night sounds outside. It was surprising how loud they were, once one focused on them.

Ian let out a deep sigh. It sounded sad, but frustrated – even angry, as well.

'What's wrong?' Essie had to ask, even though she was reluctant to hear the answer. She feared that whatever problem was weighing on his mind, there was a fair chance it had been caused by her.

'It's just . . . I don't think you really understand,' Ian said. 'Having that baby here brings up things Julia and I have struggled to put behind us. That's why we'd rather she lived in the workers' camp.'

Essie nodded. At least now it was clear what had been behind Julia's emotional outburst earlier. It wasn't to do with Diana's interference. Nor was it concern for her daughter-in-law's career or personal wellbeing. She simply wanted Mara out of the way.

'I can see how it affects Julia,' Ian added. 'Every time she hears the baby crying she thinks of . . . him.'

Essie knew Ian didn't even like speaking his brother's name. The grief, though old, was still raw for both of the Lawrences.

There was a short pause. Essie heard Ian swallow. 'How could you imagine what it was like for us to lose my brother? To have him just disappear and never be found? Not to know how he died . . .'

Essie felt a wave of sympathy for him. It was unfair that he, and his mother, should be thrown back into a terrible trauma. But the past couldn't be allowed to control the present. If painful memories were being brought up by Mara's presence here, it was better they be talked about.

She reached over, touching Ian's forearm. 'Tell me,' she said simply.

In the stillness she could feel her heart beating. Then, from over near the doorway, came the sound of Rudie dreaming – a faint whimper and the twitching of paws on the mat.

'Okay. I'll try.' Ian took a long breath, the sheet tightening over his chest. 'Well, that day . . .' His voice faltered. 'That day, Julia was doing a survey over in the foothills. We were with her, my brother and I. So was her field assistant, Kisani. It must have been late afternoon when she discovered a fossil. A piece of jawbone, with two intact teeth. She knew straightaway it was important.'

Once Ian had begun his account, the words flowed freely, as if he were telling a story that had been practised over and over. Essie understood that only some of what he was saying was his own memory; gaps had been filled in with what he'd learned later on.

'Normally she would have returned the next day with William but there was a journalist back at the camp – someone big, from the *New York Times*, I think. It was in the lead-up to the war, so it was hard to get anyone to show interest in a place like Magadi. He was leaving first thing in the morning. So, of course she wanted to show him the fossil, but she had to do the proper documentation before she could disturb the site.

'I was playing with my brother. I kept hiding and waiting until he got scared because he thought I'd disappeared. Then I'd jump out at him. You probably don't understand that kind of game because you're an only child. And a girl . . .' He was quiet for a moment. Essie sensed the tension in him, making his body rigid. 'I used to torment him. I don't know why, really. Maybe I was jealous because he was the favourite.'

Essie turned to look at him. He'd spoken as if delivering an undeniable fact. 'Whose favourite?'

'William, the visitors, the Africans . . . Everyone. But especially Julia.'

'He was her baby,' Essie pointed out. She'd heard women describe the youngest in the family as their 'baby' even when the child had grown into an adult.

'That's why she couldn't bear it,' Ian said. 'If someone had to die, it should have been me.'

Essie wanted to deny his words, but knew it would make no difference – his tone was so certain. She put her hand on his shoulder, drawing light circles on his skin with her fingers.

'Julia told me to look after my brother while she and Kisani worked. We knew never to go out of sight of an adult. But I took my brother further and further away. It was part of the game. Then I decided it was time to go back, but I must have walked in the wrong direction. I panicked when I couldn't see the adults. I remember running, dragging my brother with me. And all the time I was thinking how angry Mummy was going to be with me.' Ian shook his head. 'We just got completely lost.'

'Didn't you have a dog with you?'

'No. That rule came in afterwards. Then, suddenly, I couldn't see Robbie. I turned around to make sure he was following, and he was gone. I kept looking for him, calling out his name. Then I tried to go back and get help. I was just running. I would see a rock or a tree that I thought I'd seen before. When I got to it, nothing else was familiar. I was afraid of leopards, snakes – everything. I crawled into a gap between a tree and a pile of rocks to hide. I must have fallen asleep in the end, I was so exhausted. I woke up, hearing our names being called out. Julia had driven back to camp to get help. A Maasai found me. It was nearly dark by then. He carried me on his back. I can still remember the smell of ochre in his hair, his sword bumping against my leg.

'When we found Julia she ran towards us. She was relieved to see me, but she was looking for someone else: another Maasai, carrying a second child. But there was just me. She was crying. She kept shaking me and shouting, "Where's Robbie? Where is he?" I didn't know. I just kept saying I was sorry.' Ian fell silent for a few moments, then took a long shuddery breath. 'I was frightened.

I wanted her to comfort me. But she just walked away. She didn't want to be near me, because it was my fault that he was lost.'

Essie could hear the child's faulty logic still shaping his thoughts. 'You were only a little boy,' she said. 'Julia and Kisani were the ones responsible for taking care of you both.'

She could feel Ian dragging his thoughts back to the present. He turned to her. 'Julia knows that. She can't forgive herself.' He rolled onto his side, propping himself on one elbow, looking down at Essie. In the low light, his eyes were dark hollows. 'The fact is, she was trying to do two things at once.'

Essie knew he was waiting for her to say that she now understood why she'd been asked to make a choice between work and looking after Mara. But surely the outcome of one story didn't determine how another would unfold? Mara was so little; there was no danger of her being left unobserved. Essie decided to say nothing. Instead she lifted her hand, smoothing the tight muscles of Ian's face. Eventually she felt them relax.

'I'll miss working with you in the *korongos*,' he said.

Essie felt a sense of loss, as he put it this way. In the five years they'd been a couple they had done nearly everything together. No wonder he didn't want to lose that intimacy. Essie didn't want to lose it either. She felt a thread of doubt tighten like a knot inside her.

'I'll be at the camp each day when you get home,' she said. 'And it's only a few months. Just until the rains come.'

Neither spoke for a while. A gust of wind made the tent walls ripple. Somewhere outside a piece of loose tin creaked as it flexed.

'Then you will hand her over,' Ian said. 'The Hadza will leave. And we'll go back to normal.'

The quiet suddenly felt fraught. Essie's stomach tensed.

'But you will be heartbroken.' There was an accusatory edge to Ian's voice.

'I won't,' Essie said, 'because I know she's going back to them. I'll have that in my mind, all the time.'

Even as she spoke, she knew it was not going to be easy. She already found herself thinking constantly about Mara, after caring for her for just under three weeks. It seemed impossible that the period was so short; the day Essie first met her felt so long ago already. The time had become stretched out of all proportion. Essie was reminded of how, as a paleoanthropologist, she'd had to learn to be able to conceive of time in spans of hundreds of thousands of years. Now the process was reversed. Every hour, marked out by nappy changes and bottles of formula, felt like an age. By the end of the dry season, Essie knew, it would be very hard to adjust to Mara's absence. But she was planning for it. She intended to keep a little distance between her and the baby, a defensive barrier like the moat around the nesting island in the lake. She was aware of exactly how to do this; it was a skill she'd learned from living with her own mother. She knew how to harden her heart for her own protection.

'I know what's going to happen,' Ian continued. 'Next you'll want a baby of your own.'

Essie's lips parted in shock. 'What?'

Ian sat up, hugging his knees. Essie did the same, mirroring his actions as if connected to his body by strings.

'No, I won't,' she protested.

'We agreed we wouldn't have a family,' he added, as if he'd not heard her speak.

Ian had raised the issue of children as soon as their relationship became serious. He said he was committed to being free to live and work at Magadi, and he wanted to share this life with his wife. He didn't want to have her based in Arusha for the sake of their children's education, or to resort to boarding schools.

Ian hadn't expected Essie to give an instant response. He knew the decision he was asking her to make was even bigger than accepting a proposal of marriage. But Essie had surprised him. She'd said straightaway that she had no desire to be a mother. She could picture nothing she wanted more than to stay at Magadi and work at her husband's side. Essie still felt this way today – especially now, with the exciting new prospects for their research.

She put her arm around Ian's shoulder, nuzzling her head into his chest. 'Don't worry. Mara won't change anything.' She felt quite sure as she said the words. 'I don't want to be a mother.'

Ian turned to kiss her, then lowered her back onto the bed. He rolled on top of her. Their bodies were matched shoulder to shoulder, hip to hip, right down to their toes. He let out another long sigh. Essie could feel him shedding a fear that had probably been there ever since Mara's arrival. She felt strong, being able to offer him comfort like this. But as he relaxed, his full weight pressed down. Her lungs felt crushed inside her. She struggled to take a breath.

ELEVEN

The little plastic moon danced on its string just out of reach of Mara's waving fingers. The baby was lying on the change table while Essie made final adjustments to her nappy. There was a stray edge of towelling that needed to be pushed up under the plastic pants. Essie had already discovered how any exposed piece would act as a wick, spreading wetness onto bedding, blankets and clothes, including her own.

Bending over, Essie smiled into the wide, bright eyes. 'Ready for breakfast?' It seemed odd to be talking to the Hadza baby in English – a language Mara would never speak in her lifetime, unless she followed the same path as Simon. But it felt even stranger to be silent around her. 'Let's go, then.'

Essie paused to check Mara's outfit. This was the first chance to really show off to Diana the beautiful clothes she'd so generously paid for. Essie had picked out the smartest of all the frocks – it was made from *broderie anglaise*, white with pink stitching. The plastic pants were covered in the same fabric. The dress was teamed with white crocheted booties. Set against Mara's dark eyes and skin, the overall effect was very striking.

Essie's gaze came to rest on the Hadza necklace draping the yoke of the dress. Carl had told her the beads were made from fragments of ostrich shell, painstakingly shaped and smoothed into balls. They were beautiful, with a shiny white surface that reminded Essie of clotted cream. But she tucked them away, hidden from view. The tribal decoration looked out of place beside the Babyland clothes.

With Mara on her hip and bottle in hand, Essie made her way from the nursery towards the Dining Tent. A large part of her wanted to divert to the kitchen and just get some breakfast from Baraka instead of joining the others. She couldn't forget the conversation she'd held with Ian last night – how he'd said that having a baby around was upsetting to Julia. That Mara should be kept in the workers' camp. Essie understood that the tragedy Ian and Julia had suffered was at the heart of their feelings – but it had happened such a long time ago. Mara didn't deserve to reap the consequences. And anyway, an agreement had been made between Essie and her husband last night before they went to sleep. Essie could continue to look after Mara in their part of the camp, but she would keep her away from the excavation sites. That was the deal. It would be a mistake for Essie to begin this first day by choosing to eat in the kitchen.

Start as you mean to go on.

The saying came to Essie out of the blue. It was one of the few pieces of advice she remembered being given by her mother. It had been delivered more than once. There was an ominous ring to the words, as if ignoring them could bring dire results. A second phrase often followed. Essie took a moment to reel in the memory and pin it down.

Start as you mean to go on . . .

Because you don't get a second chance.

As Essie walked on, she replayed the words in her head. Had her mother wanted to have a second chance, in her life? And what different path might she have wished to follow?

A hum of conversation broke into her thoughts as she neared the entrance to the tent. Then came the sound of Ian laughing. He must have woken up in a good mood again. Essie hadn't seen him yet today; he'd left the tent without waking her. There seemed to be an unspoken agreement that they were now running on separate schedules.

As she came into view, Ian half rose to his feet. 'Good morning, Essie.'

His gaze flicked over Mara, then fixed on his wife. Essie stiffened, creating a fractional distance between herself and the baby.

'Good morning.' Julia echoed Ian's words. Then Essie repeated them in response.

Diana smiled, as if charmed by the old-fashioned manners. Then she added her own greeting. 'Hi there.' Her eyes latched onto Mara. 'Oh my God, just look at her. She's perfect in that dress!'

Essie smiled gratefully. It was good to have an ally in the camp.

'She is so adorable!' Diana added.

'Thank you.' Essie's smile widened. It seemed natural, somehow, to accept praise on Mara's behalf. After all, it had been Essie who'd washed the baby, dressed her, fed her, sung to her . . .

Kefa pulled out a chair for Essie and poured her some tea. Holding Mara with one arm, she sipped her drink. She could almost feel the strong brew entering her blood, waking her up. Mara had disturbed her twice in the night. Both times Essie had sat bolt upright at the first whimper, ready to jump out of bed and carry her away. She didn't have to be reminded that Ian needed his sleep.

There was the clink of cups on saucers and cutlery on plates as Ian, Julia and Diana ate toast and poached eggs. A new jar of marmalade held pride of place in the middle of the table, beside a bowl brimming with fine white sugar. While Essie waited for Kefa to bring her some food, she observed Diana covertly. The woman looked a bit pale – her features stark, somehow.

'Did you sleep well enough?' Essie asked. While she was still speaking, it came to her that the reason for Diana's changed appearance was simply that she was wearing not a trace of make-up. Essie was taken by surprise. She'd expected Diana Marlow to be one of those women who enjoyed the idea of being off the beaten track in Africa but couldn't relinquish the need to be glamorous. Lots of the female students and academics who came to Magadi fitted this category. Maybe Diana had taken her cue from Essie's appearance. If that were true, Essie should be flattered. Instead, she felt oddly dismayed – as if Diana had stolen a card from her hand.

'The birds were very noisy,' Diana responded. 'And the moon was bright. Luckily, I always travel with earplugs and an eye mask. But the stretcher was rather hard, to be honest.'

'Tonight you'll be more comfortable,' Ian said. He nodded towards an area a little way beyond the other side of the Dining Tent. Peering past some bushes, Essie noticed a pile of orange canvas spread out on the ground. Standing near it was a proper wooden bed. She wondered, again, exactly how long Diana was going to be here. Ian spoke as if her plans were still evolving. Essie had a feeling he was being deliberately vague, but she hadn't yet pursued the topic with him – their conversations had been dominated by issues surrounding Mara.

As Essie was finishing her cup of tea, Kefa appeared with her eggs and toast. Her stomach growled with hunger, but she looked helplessly at the plate. She couldn't tackle it with only one hand free. She glanced across at Diana. The visitor had finished her meal but showed no sign of wanting to hold the baby – her initial enthusiasm seemed to have waned. Essie turned to Julia. Their eyes met for a few seconds. Then Julia gave Kefa a curt nod. The man took Essie's plate to the sideboard. Moments later he returned it, with the toast and egg cut up into portions.

Essie smiled apologetically at him, wondering what he thought about having to look after her like a child. This was part of what being in charge of a baby entailed, she realised. You were at a constant disadvantage compared to other adults.

She ate clumsily with her one hand, balancing Mara with the other. She was aware of the baby watching her – those wide dark eyes following the fork from plate to mouth and back as if watching a fascinating dance. Mara had already consumed a bottle of milk in the nursery; the one now standing next to Essie's plate was just a precaution. Essie wanted to ensure Mara was quiet and contented. Aside from making a good impression with her outfit, the baby had to be as unobtrusive as possible. After all, breakfast time was not just for eating. It was when the events of the day were planned.

Ian had already begun. While still sipping his tea, he was outlining the new strategies for research. They had obviously been formulated back in Arusha. Diana seemed to know a lot of the details already. Essie was amazed at how freely she took part in the discussions. She seemed happy to give her views on things she obviously knew almost nothing about. As the conversation went on, Essie waited for Ian to let the others know about her idea of doing some scouting. But he said nothing. Was it possible he'd completely forgotten the conversation? To prompt him, she asked where Simon was.

'Helping with the tent,' Ian answered.

'Which is no small task,' Julia added.

There was a sharp edge to her tone – so slight that Essie was only able to pick it up because she'd spent nearly every day for the last five years in her company. Glancing across the table, Essie saw that Julia was now sitting very upright, the tendons in her neck standing out. No doubt she was finding it difficult to accept Diana's position here. Julia would normally have put such an upstart firmly in their place – making only slight concessions for an influential journalist or academic. But she had to take a different approach to Diana Marlow. Essie felt a guilty satisfaction at seeing her mother-in-law powerless like this, for once.

Ian got out a notebook. He rolled up his sleeves as if signalling serious work was about to occur. Essie leaned forward as his left wrist was revealed. He was wearing a new watch. She couldn't see the brand – whether it was a Rolex like William's – but it looked impressive. It had to be a gift from Diana. Essie felt a twist of jealousy in the pit of her stomach. She didn't know why the present should affect her this way. The fact that it would have cost a huge amount didn't matter; Diana was obviously so wealthy the price tag was irrelevant. Essie should be glad for Ian that he had a new watch with a face that was easy to read. Why shouldn't he benefit from their benefactor's largesse? After all, Diana had been even more generous to Mara – and therefore Essie – with the gift of a whole nursery.

'Isn't that a great watch?' Diana must have been following Essie's gaze. 'It's an Oyster Perpetual. Edmund Hillary was wearing one when he climbed Everest. I bought it for Frank. He likes that kind of thing.' Her mouth thinned. 'Then I decided he didn't deserve it.'

Ian looked embarrassed. 'I had no idea. You shouldn't have . . .'

Diana shrugged. 'Yours was broken. And it was a waste, just leaving it in its box.'

Listening to these words, and their tone, Essie decided there was something naïve, almost childlike, about Diana. If she wanted to do something, she just did it. It was probably the result of growing up as an heiress, then marrying into even more wealth. The woman had never lived in the real world.

As if to shift attention from the watch, Ian tapped his pencil on his notebook. He began talking about the new excavations. The work was going to be centred on the *korongo* where Essie had found the *giraffid* fossil and the promising stone tool. Ian was already referring to the site as DMK. Diana Marlow Korongo. This, too, must have been decided in Arusha. Essie felt a glimmer of resentment every time Ian uttered the initials. The name was not a surprise, and the choice was not unreasonable. But as Ian and Julia both knew, it had been Essie's turn . . .

As the talking continued, Essie struggled to absorb the reality that she was not going to be involved in the work. She was out of the picture for the whole of this season. Even though it was by her own choice, she felt excluded. She shifted Mara to her other arm. As she did so she felt the warmth of a wet nappy through the plastic pants. She was about to quietly withdraw when Diana stood up. She stretched like a cat, arching her back. Then she pointed at the painting of the volcano.

'Who is Mirella?'

Ian threw a cursory look at the artwork. 'Just someone who came here a long time ago. She pinned some of her pictures up here. William liked them, so they stayed.'

'I think I recognise the style. Is she well-known?'

Julia let out a small laugh, almost a bark. 'I shouldn't think so. I don't even remember her other name.'

'Me neither,' Ian said.

'It's not in good shape,' Diana continued. 'I know a man in London who could restore it.'

'Not to bother,' Julia said. 'The thing's been there too long. They all have. They should come down.'

Ian looked shocked. The way Julia spoke made it sound as if her husband's heritage was a casual affair, rather than something that was carefully curated by staff and family alike.

'Nineteen fifty-five . . .' Diana read out the date next to the signature. 'That was fifteen years ago. I must've had half-a-dozen homes since then!' She shook her head, smiling. 'I love the way everything here just stays the same.'

'Until now,' Julia pointed out, her tone a little tart. She eyed Ian's notebook. The plans under discussion involved creating a replacement Work Hut – to be called a 'studio' – and a whole new accommodation area. Again, Essie sensed how Julia was being torn. She wanted the work to be developed, but she didn't like losing control.

Diana continued to enthuse about Magadi Camp, while also identifying a few problems she'd noticed. Essie only half heard her. She was staring at the painting. For years she'd eaten her meals in front of the picture, barely noticing it. Now the image seemed to be speaking to her. As she took in the stark lines of the volcano, she thought about the fact that the artist, enjoying William's support, had wandered freely around Magadi, not limiting herself to where archaeological work was being carried out. Mirella might well have seen a towerlike rockform in the foothills. She might even have captured its likeness.

'Please excuse me,' Essie said, getting to her feet. 'I hope you have a good day, everyone. I'll see you later on.'

No one questioned her walking away. That was one advantage of being in charge of a baby – you always had a reason to disappear.

The storeroom was shadowy and cool compared to outside. The sunlight that angled in was crisscrossed by thick wire mesh. Over in the Work Hut, which had no front wall, let alone a door, there were dozens of priceless fossils and valuable reference books. All that had ever gone missing from there was the odd toothbrush, candle or a box of matches – and that was rare. But the storeroom had always been kept locked, even when the supplies had dwindled almost to nothing. Now that the shelves were stacked with tins and jars and boxes, unpacked from the two Land Rovers, Baraka was even more protective of his key than usual. While Essie was in here, he was waiting right outside the open doorway, next to the pram. She could hear him murmuring softly to Mara, even though the baby was sound asleep.

Reaching up to the top shelf, Essie was just able to grasp the edge of the art folio. As she pulled it down, a dead moth fell in a spiralling flutter amid a cloud of dust. Essie laid the folder on the floor, choosing a spot where the light was best.

Silverfish had chewed their wandering pattern through the navy linen cover of the folio. Essie untied a ribbon. The silk fabric, stiffened by time, held on to the shape of the bow. As she opened the cover, she smelled pencil lead, wax crayon and a faint musty perfume. She began flicking through the drawings, looking for any that included the volcano, especially the lower slopes. She held in her mind the image of the Tower that was near the camp, superimposing it onto the landscapes in front of her, wishing the scene into reality. She stopped on one that looked promising. It was a charcoal sketch formed from deft, purposeful lines. There were lots of heaped rocks in the foreground. The mountain rose up in the rear. But there was no sign of anything remotely like the Tower. Essie scanned drawing after drawing but found nothing of interest.

Soon she was nearing the bottom of the pile. As she turned to a new page, her hand froze. Someone had taken a dark-red pencil and drawn over the work, covering it in jagged red lines. The next picture was defaced as well. This time the red had been used to blot out the signature. The next four artworks were ruined. The pencil lines were not a child's carefree scribbles. There was malice in the way they were dug into the page – long gouges scored across the detailed work.

Essie's mouth opened in shock. Who could have done this? It had happened a long time ago – the dust proved that. Had it occurred while the work was in here, under lock and key? Or was it before the folder had been packed away on these shelves, along with Mirella's art supplies? None of the staff would have even opened the folio if they'd come across it somewhere in the camp, let alone destroyed the work. However it had occurred, Essie guessed the damage must have been done by another visitor to Magadi – one who'd had some conflict with Mirella.

When Essie had first arrived here she'd noticed how the various people who came to assist the Lawrences competed with one another for their attention. William had already been dead for several years, but even the ownership of his memory was a source of keen competition. The rivalry was one of the reasons Essie had felt so privileged to discover that Ian Lawrence was focused only on her. Perhaps Mirella had monopolised William, taking up too much space – literally and figuratively – with her paintings. Someone had taken out their jealousy on her work. Presumably the artist had not even known about it; surely she would have thrown the ruined pictures away. If that were the case, it was quite possible that Essie was the only person, apart from the perpetrator, who was aware the damage had been done.

These musings were pointless, Essie knew – the matter wasn't her responsibility. And it was a distraction from her goal. She glanced over the next few images. One looked as if it had been screwed up, then flattened out again. Another had the signature corner torn off. The rest of the drawings were undamaged. Essie searched them for a rocky tower, a pillar of stone – or any other unusual landmark. Even the tumbled remains of one.

There was nothing.

Essie reached the end of the collection and gathered up the drawings. As she slid them back into the folio, she could still picture the dark-red lines, like angry welts whipped across the artworks. Though the attack had been done years ago she could almost feel the emotion clouding the air. She was glad to return the folio to its place on the shelf. Shoving it in next to a box of paint tubes and brushes, she pushed it as far back as possible, almost out of sight.

Outside, Baraka still stood by the pram. He was chewing on a piece of dried meat. It looked like a hunk of old leather frosted with salty sweat.

'Did you make that *biltong*?' Essie asked in Swahili. She felt she should chat with him for a while to make up for interrupting his morning schedule.

He shook his head. 'I have visited the *manyatta*.'

Essie was so used to the man being in the kitchen or around the camp that she often forgot he had a private life.

A thought came to her. 'Do you know the place called the Tower, where you can stand and look down to the Steps?'

'Of course.'

'Have you seen another one – something like it? In the hills at the bottom of the volcano?'

'The mountain belongs to God,' Baraka responded. 'Maasai do not go there.'

Essie pushed on. 'Mrs Lawrence worked in that area a long time ago. I am talking about when her child, the *mtoto wa siri*, was lost.'

Baraka frowned warily. 'Yes.'

'Her assistant was a Maasai called Kisani. And the man who found Ian was also a Maasai. So some of you have been there.'

The man looked around him as if afraid of being caught in a forbidden conversation. When he spoke it was in an undertone. 'Kisani should not have agreed to do that work. It was wrong. The mountain is holy. It is not a place for digging in the earth, removing stones. The only Maasai who trespass there are women who want to have children but have been unsuccessful. And they do not go wandering around. They just climb to the top, where they can see into the heart of Lengai, and plead for a miracle.'

Essie nodded. She knew how holy the volcano was for the Maasai. An expert had once explained they felt about it the same way people back in England did about Westminster Abbey. In fact, their emotions were even more intense. They believed Lengai actually resided in the mountain, whereas the English pictured their God installed in heaven.

Baraka lowered his voice even further as he continued. 'No one wanted to take part in the search. They had no choice. A child was missing. The Maasai are expert trackers. They were needed.' He shook his head. 'But it was very bad.' He added a final word, and then repeated it. Essie guessed he was resorting to Maa – that he found the Swahili word for 'bad'– *mbaya* – inadequate for what he wanted to express.

'Those trackers – did they come from the local *manyatta*?'

'Some of them. People came from many places, even Arusha.'

'Are these Maasai still there now?'

Baraka looked reluctant to reply. 'Why are you asking these questions? Things of past times should not be disturbed. Do you not have a baby to occupy your thoughts? You should see if Tembo is doing his washing to a high standard.'

'You are right.' Essie spoke lightly, as though the intensity of the conversation was already forgotten. She released the brake on the pram. 'I will talk to him.'

The smell of dung baking in the sun reached Essie even before the *manyatta* came into view. She heard goats bleating and the occasional lowing of a cow. A rooster called – running very late with his announcement of the day. Somewhere, a man was singing.

From the crest of a low hill, Essie saw the village spread out in front of her. There was an outer perimeter fence made from piled thornbush. Within it were several smaller enclosures where goats and donkeys were separated from the sacred cattle. At the heart of it all was the cluster of huts made from woven sticks daubed with grey mud. Surrounding the *manyatta* was a wide arc of semi-denuded land; it was tracked with red lines where cloven hooves had pressed into the sparse covering of vegetation exposing the bare earth. Everything was round: the huts, the fences, the clearing, the layout of the whole place. Essie gazed down over the pattern of circles formed within circles. It looked as if it was meant to be read from far above – the vantage point of a plane, a mountaintop, the heavens.

The *manyatta* was a long-established settlement, as far as Maasai villages went. Because the waterholes on the plains never dried up, there was some grazing to be had all the year round in this location. During the dry season – when the zebra, gazelle, wildebeests and other plains animals migrated – the cattle became thin, but they survived well enough. And no one had died inside their hut, which would have caused the village to be moved. Another reason, Essie knew, for this group of Maasai to have virtually abandoned their nomadic ways was the presence of the research camp. The Europeans provided a market for the women's produce, a source of employment for men and an opportunity to sell artefacts to visitors. The dynamics that had ruled the lives of the tribespeople for as far back as their oral histories reached had been tipped out of balance.

Moving on, Essie pushed the pram down towards the *manyatta*. It would have been easier to carry Mara over this terrain, but there was the nappy bag, the insulated bottle container and all the other accessories to be considered. Also, Essie felt that it was better for Mara to be in the pram as much as possible. It would help develop her independence.

As people caught sight of the visitors, they must have called out to others. Soon there was a crowd awaiting Essie's arrival. The bright daubs of their *shukas* – the red, purple and black plaids – stood out against the muted palette of their surroundings.

When Essie drew near she saw that some of the women looked puzzled. She realised they'd been expecting to see her and Mara in their coloured dresses. They eyed Essie's work clothes with open disappointment. When they peered into the pram they looked only slightly more approving of Mara's pink frock.

An old woman came forward. She had white, wiry hair and her face was covered with fine wrinkles that puckered around her ritual scars. Essie recognised her as one of the group that had come to the camp.

'*Karibu, Mama Mzuri,*' the woman said. Welcome to the Beautiful Mother.

Essie shook her head. 'I am not the mother of this baby.'

She knew she had made this very clear back at the camp. However, she'd then let herself be drawn into the women's dance, which had encouraged the false identity to stick. If she didn't correct the mistake, it would only be a matter of time before Ian or Julia heard the name being used.

'I am looking after her for the dry season only.' Essie spoke slowly and clearly. 'When the Short Rains come, she will return to her family.'

Her words – translated and passed from tongue to tongue – sparked murmurings. Then a younger woman walked up to Essie. She wore only a cloth tied round her waist. In her arms was a naked baby, suckling at her breast. The second breast, hanging free, was full and round. Milk leaked from the nipple, dripping onto the ground. Essie could see that the baby was a little girl, like Mara. She was longer, though – fatter. Essie felt a pang of anxiety. Was she older, then? Perhaps she was healthier. Happier . . .

The young mother bent over the pram, studying Mara closely. After a while, the sharp, curious gaze began to soften. She made a gentle clucking sound. Mara reacted by reaching out with both hands. The Maasai turned to Essie. The two women shared a smile.

'You are her mother at this moment,' the Maasai stated. Her use of Swahili was clear. 'The future is another time.'

Essie nodded in response, even though she was not sure exactly what the woman meant. On face value it sounded as if Essie was being advised to think only of the present – however, concepts of time were much more complex in the African setting than one might think. Essie had heard anthropologists struggling to understand how in many traditional societies time was viewed not as a continuum that went only one way, but as something almost organic, more like a tangled web. Things that hadn't even happened yet might have an effect on the events of here and now.

When this topic was under discussion Essie soon found herself out of her depth. People referred to Einstein's theory of relativity, which apparently stated that there is no single present time – that the distinction between past, present and future was only an illusion. They talked about the Lagrangian schema, which sounded like an impossibly complex scientific explanation for what many tribespeople seemed able – presumably instinctively – to understand with ease. Essie had never actually tried very hard to grasp the concepts. For one thing, they undermined the whole premise of archaeology, which was that the present world was the outcome of all that had gone before. Every layer of rock, every step of evolutionary progress, led on one from another. All these considerations aside, Essie wished in this moment that she could be free to live only in the present, as the young Maasai seemed to be recommending. She wouldn't have to keep walking the fine line between engaging with Mara and holding back in order to prepare them both for the future that was coming. She sometimes felt like a flower that longed to open but was forced to hold itself shut.

The people were now watching her curiously, no doubt wondering why the white woman was here. Essie had only ever come to the village with Ian. The visits were rare, and always tense, with her husband raising the issue of cattle being grazed inside the Archaeological Reserve, or some other damage being caused. On one occasion, all three of the Lawrences, along with a government official, had come to make a complaint. Some of the young men had lit a fire in an excavated Neolithic hearth. It was unclear if it had been a matter of ignorance – the fireplace was there, and they didn't see the harm in using it – or an act of deliberate, disrespectful vandalism.

Essie wasn't sure what protocol should be applied now that she'd turned up on her own. Ian's arrival always sparked instant action – whoever was most senior in the village would present himself. Essie looked towards a spindly thorn tree, wondering if she should just go and sit down in the shade.

As if on cue, a teenage girl appeared holding a battered safari chair. It must have made its way here from Magadi, or perhaps been exchanged for tribal artefacts with tourists or hunters. As the chair was set down under the tree, Essie pushed the pram across to it. She put on the brake, the simple manoeuvre prompting a flutter of interest. Then she checked on Mara. The baby was gazing contentedly up at the fringed edge of the sun canopy, kicking the air with her white-clad feet.

Essie took her place on the chair, lowering herself cautiously in case the canvas was rotten. A few onlookers wandered away, but most of the people who had gathered began settling themselves on the ground in front of her. Some squatted on their heels; others sat with their legs stretched out in front of them. The old woman who had greeted Essie remained standing. She called out something in Maa. While Essie was still waiting for a translation, she strode across to the pram and picked Mara up. Essie jumped to her feet, alarm running like an electric current through her blood. She knew the old woman wouldn't mean any harm, but she couldn't help reacting to seeing Mara in the arms of a stranger.

The old Maasai smiled, her grey gums almost as bare of teeth as those of the baby. She held Mara tenderly against her chest, where her wasted breasts formed only the slightest mound under her *shuka*. Her hands, knotted with age, supported the baby's heavy head. The gesture was obviously second nature to her.

Essie sank back into her chair. Mara was in more than expert hands. The tribeswoman had most likely given birth to a baby every couple of years from the time when she was married until she was no longer able to conceive. Her offspring would have grown into adults by now or died along the way. The grandmother probably spent her days caring for the next generation. There was a lot of hard work to be done by members of the family who were stronger than she was now.

Essie was reminded of an article written by the primatologist who'd befriended William – the one Julia disliked, who had a *korongo* named after her. It was in one of the faded old journals on display in the Dining Tent. Alice Jones had written about the function of menopause in humans. Strangely, the phenomenon occurred in virtually no other mammal, the only known exceptions being two species of whale. Even among our closest relatives – chimps, gibbons, and Alice Jones' own beloved bonobos – the females remained fertile until death. Jones believed menopause had evolved so that there would be a group of women in society who were unhampered by pregnancy and breastfeeding and able to help look after other people's children. Essie hadn't been much interested in the research when she'd read it. But after even this short time of being responsible for Mara, she saw that it made sense. What she'd known for years in theory was now starkly clear in her mind. Human young needed a spectacular amount of care. They were so helpless for so long.

The grandmother carried Mara across to Essie. Before handing her over, she glanced back at the pram with a frown. Obviously, she believed there was only one place for a baby to be, and that was in someone's arms. Essie knew there was no point in trying to explain the strategy of fostering independence. She settled Mara on her lap, smoothing the lacy dress over her legs. Without making it too obvious, she quickly checked the baby over. She imagined germs swarming over the delicate skin. She doubted that the Maasai woman would have washed her hands very recently. She might even have fleas or lice. Essie wished she could get a cloth from the pram and wipe Mara's hands and face. But even as she thought of this – how rude it would be – a different idea came to her: perhaps this encounter was a chance for the baby to build up her resistance to germs that would normally be part of her world. If that were true, Essie should be deliberately passing her around the crowd from one pair of hands to another. As was the case with so many of the decisions Essie had had to make since Mara came into her life, it was impossible to be sure what was best.

Under the gaze of dozens of pairs of eyes, Essie felt as though she and Mara were on display – a strange version of a Madonna and Child statue. Their position, raised up on the chair, only added to the impression. As she smiled self-consciously, her gaze came to rest on the young mother who'd spoken earlier. She was squatting not far away. The baby was still feeding – kneading the breast with one tiny hand as she sucked and swallowed. Essie noticed how the two bodies, virtually bare, fitted closely together, skin sealed against skin as if they were one creature. She was suddenly aware of her own posture: her rigid back and the way her feet were planted together, her knees swept primly to one side. Her khaki shirt and trousers – designed to keep her well covered and protected from the hazards of the bush – felt out of place. Mara, too, seemed overdressed with her bulky nappy and long skirt.

A small gourd was brought and offered to Essie. It was half full of milk. She took it with her free hand – she knew she had to accept some hospitality before she could begin to ask questions. There was a skin floating on the surface of the milk. At least that proved it had been boiled, and any brucellosis bacteria killed. There was a short straight hair there as well – probably from a dog. It turned in a slow spiral. Lifting the gourd to her lips, Essie swallowed cautiously, tasting rich cream tainted with charcoal.

She scanned the gathering, seeking someone who appeared to be senior. It would be a mistake to address the wrong person. She noticed a strong-looking figure standing not far away. His ochred hair was held back from his face by an elaborate beaded headpiece. A sword hung from his belt.

'Greetings, my father,' she said when she'd caught his eye. 'I am seeking information. Do you understand Swahili?'

The man inclined his head, inviting her to continue. As she spoke, the air was gripped with the stillness of intense listening. Muttered translations flew.

Essie outlined what she and Simon had learned from the Hadza about the existence of a cave at the foot of the volcano. Mindful of Baraka's words outside the storeroom, she stressed that she was hoping to find very old paintings, but that if she did, they would not be harmed. She would show respect. Nothing would be disturbed. She described how carefully she had traced the images at the Painted Cave. Several heads nodded knowingly. Essie had a sense that everything she'd done at the site years ago had been observed, reported, remembered.

The man shook his head. 'We do not know this story that you have been told. It is probably a lie. You cannot trust a Hadza.'

Essie's hands tightened around Mara. She had to force a polite expression. 'Nevertheless, I would like to investigate. Do you know if there is a tower made of rock over there, like the one near Magadi Camp?'

The man shrugged. 'We do not trespass on the home of Lengai. How would we see it?'

'What about the trackers who helped search for *mtoto wa siri*? Maybe they have seen this tower?'

There was a sudden hush. A baby's cry was soothed by a mother's crooning. A large bird flew overhead, wings beating the air. Essie chewed her lip. Perhaps she'd pushed too far in mentioning the lost boy. Africans were often superstitious. They believed the act of simply talking about someone or something could have consequences. She was about to backtrack and find a new approach when she saw a man emerge from behind a nearby dwelling. As he walked towards Essie, every eye followed him.

He was tall, like most of the Maasai, but his figure was stooped. Instead of a *shuka* he wore a plain black cloth knotted at one shoulder. Where it hung open at the side, Essie caught a glimpse of protruding ribs and a bony hip. His hair was dusted with silver.

'I am Kisani. I was Mrs Lawrence's field assistant.' The words, delivered in English, sounded more like a confession than an announcement.

Essie's lips parted. Baraka had not told her the man was still living here; perhaps he was following the code of silence about anything to do with Robbie. She wondered if Kisani had been here all along, or if he'd gone to work elsewhere and had now returned in his old age.

Essie cleared her throat. After introducing herself, she asked him if he spoke English fluently.

'Of course,' he said. 'When I worked for the Lawrences, I translated for other Maasai workers.'

Essie was glad; she had enough to think about without having to worry about making any mistakes with her Swahili.

'I hope you can tell me something,' she began. She tried not to picture how outraged Ian and Julia would be if they knew whom she was talking to. 'Do you remember the tall rock near Magadi Camp that is called the Tower?'

'Of course,' Kisani said again.

'Is there one like it, near the bottom of Ol Doinyo Lengai?'

'It is there.'

Essie's mouth fell open. The answer was so short and certain. 'Can you tell me where?'

The man's eyes narrowed as though he was focusing on a distant place. 'I saw that rock many times when we were searching for *mtoto wa siri*. We gave it a name . . .' He paused, as if scouring his memory. 'The Meeting Place.'

'Did you see a cave?' Essie held her breath.

'I did not. But there are many big rocks there. Some are broken. Some have fallen over. It is caused by Lengai.' He looked at the ground, moving his open hands to give an impression of an earthquake.

'Was there anything that looked like a cave with rocks over the entrance?'

Kisani lifted his face. 'I was searching only for one thing. A small boy.' His lower lip pushed up. His eyes blinked. Essie could see him struggling to preserve a calm façade.

'I'm sorry to ask you these things,' she said.

'It is just that you . . . remind me of her.'

Essie looked at him blankly.

'You are a young woman,' he added. 'You wear the same clothes. You speak English.' He pointed at Mara. 'You are a mother.'

At first Essie couldn't think what the man meant. Then it came to her. 'I remind you of Julia?'

Kisani didn't reply. He was gazing down at the ground. 'I will never forget how she cried. She was like an animal that has been shot by an unskilled hunter. No one could comfort her. The child she loved best was gone. Her little son.' He looked up, scanning the faces of the crowd. The people listened intently, even though only a few of them could be following his English. It was as if the power of his emotion transcended the language barrier. Or perhaps it was a story they already knew.

'I tried to help her,' Kisani continued. 'Together we searched for a long time, just Mrs Lawrence and me, after the others gave up. Bwana Lawrence and everyone at Magadi – they all returned to their work. But we walked on the mountain from sunrise until it was dark. We only stopped when the rains came.'

'Where was Ian?' Essie broke in.

'He was sent away to Arusha. His mother could not look after him. She had only one thought in her mind. She had to find her son. Even when we knew it was not possible for him to be alive any more, we searched for his body. She wanted to bury him. She wanted to know how he died. But we could not find anything. There was no piece of his shirt. No bone. Not even one hair.'

'What do you think happened?' Essie didn't want to add to Kisani's distress, but she had to know what he thought. It wasn't something she could ever ask Ian.

'On the mountain there are many places where a child could fall down and disappear. Mrs Lawrence thought he was trapped somewhere. He was hurt, hungry, scared. When we were searching she always wanted to stop and listen to hear if he was calling her.' Kisani paused, putting his hand to his ear. In the quiet, it was easy to imagine a faint cry floating on the air.

'Maybe a wild animal caught him,' Kisani continued. 'A leopard, or a lion. But they always leave some remains. And the dogs did not smell blood. It is more likely that an eagle took him away. That would leave no clue behind.'

Essie stared at him. Magadi was home to martial eagles. Some days they circled above the Gorge, beaks pointed down, powerful feet thrusting forward as they swooped on their prey. Essie had only ever seen them rise back into the air with a hare or some other small animal in their clutches.

'Robbie would have been too big,' she protested.

'An eagle can steal a dog or a goat.'

Essie pictured two sets of talons grasping a struggling child. She heard the sound of huge wings beating. What came next, after the terrifying flight, was too awful to imagine.

'It is not the worst thing,' Kisani said, as if guessing her thoughts.

Essie moistened her lips. When she spoke, it was almost a whisper. 'What is the worst thing?'

'You know the Africans who are born white?' Kisani asked.

'Albinos?'

Kisani nodded. 'They are the ones I am speaking about.'

Essie frowned. She didn't understand how this could be relevant. She'd seen some albinos once, on a visit to Arusha. In the busy marketplace Ian had pointed out a family where the father and children were white but their mother black. African albinos looked exactly like very fair Europeans – Norwegians or Swedes – but with frizzy hair and colourless eyes. Essie remembered staring at the black mother holding her white toddler – the pairing looked so incongruous. The father was partially blind and had lesions on his skin. Albinos suffered under the African sun. They were pitied and marginalised. But there was nothing frightening about them.

'Some people believe they hold great powers,' the Maasai continued.

'Albinism is simply the result of a genetic abnormality. They are just people with no pigment in their skin and hair.' Essie was grasping at facts as if they might shield her from whatever she was about to hear.

'Their bodies can be used in magic,' Kisani said. 'A finger. An arm. Ears. Tongue. The *mchawi* makes medicine from them. The *dawa* can help a miner to find gold or a fisherman to catch big fish. It can cure an illness.'

As Essie absorbed the meaning of his words she felt sick. 'People kill albinos for their body parts?'

'It is called *muti*. Medicine murder,' Kisani confirmed. 'Sometimes they just capture the person and remove what they want. Then they let them go.'

As the horror deepened – bringing up a vision of an albino bleeding from the stump of a severed limb – Essie found it hard to breathe. She knew there was a dark side to some of the tribal practices in Africa, but Europeans tended to keep well away from the topic unless it was part of the reason they were here in the country. Missionaries preached against African beliefs. Doctors and nurses fought against the practices of witchdoctors. Often, according to Ian, both groups had little understanding of the Africans' perspective. Anthropologists competed to find ways to describe and give meaning to the rituals they observed. But everyone knew that the truth was often incomprehensible to the outsider. Essie felt a shiver travel up her spine. Whatever the real meaning of what Kisani had described might be, it was unspeakably evil.

Essie was glad that the children dotted through the crowd did not speak English. She rested her cheek on Mara's head, feeling the softness of her hair. She wanted to carry the baby over to the pram – to get away from the *manyatta* and back to where she belonged. But first, she had to follow the topic to its harrowing conclusion: that a dead European – or parts of one – could be passed off as a white-skinned African.

'You are saying that Robbie could have been taken for this purpose? He was only four years old!'

'It is easier to carry away a child than an adult.'

'Who would do that? Right here, near Magadi?' Essie couldn't help glancing around her, as if she might see in the watching faces some clue to a lurking evil.

'It is not the work of Maasai,' Kisani said. 'We have different medicine. The place where this witchcraft is carried out is around the big lakes – Lake Victoria, Lake Tanganyika. But traders are everywhere.'

Essie closed her eyes. Many of the possible endings to Robbie's story were so much worse than a simple death. And no one knew which of them had occurred. No wonder the Lawrences had been so traumatised. Having never met William, Essie didn't know how he'd coped. It sounded as if he'd buried himself in his work. Ian had been young, at least; he'd have been shielded from some of the nightmare. But Julia. The mother. The small glimpse of her torment that had been shared by Kisani gave Essie a hint of what she had suffered. It was like the cut of a savage knife – forging a wound so deep that it might never be healed.

Essie could not imagine how Julia had found a way to pull through. Only a couple of years after Robbie's disappearance, the effects of the war – intensifying in East Africa as colonial powers imported their nations' conflicts – had forced the Lawrences to leave Magadi. Perhaps the distance had helped. Yet the family had returned when peace was declared. They had walked, of their own accord, back into the heart of their agony. Maybe it was impossible for them to stay away. They might have felt they would be abandoning Robbie's memory. Or maybe they believed that if they could at least make an important discovery here, their decision to live and work in Magadi – which had led to Robbie's death – had not been in vain. The price of a lost life could never be repaid, but maybe at least something could be added to the other side of the balance sheet . . .

A touch on her shoulder made Essie look up. Kisani was right at her side.

'How is the health of Mrs Lawrence?' he asked. 'I have not seen her for so many years.'

'She is well. She is happy. They have plenty of money now.'

Essie wondered if Kisani saw through her glib phrases. Only the last part of what she'd said was true. From a physical point of view, Julia was becoming thin; birdlike. Her hands were arthritic after a lifetime of overuse. Emotionally, she wasn't in very good shape either. She was brittle under pressure. When she laughed, which was rare, she seemed surprised by the sound of her own mirth. The closest thing to happiness, for her, was a day of good, hard work, and the satisfaction of seeing the camp running smoothly. It was an irony that just when funding was about to appear, making everything easier, her daughter-in-law had turned up with a baby.

'Why don't you visit Mrs Lawrence and see for yourself?' Essie suggested.

Kisani shook his head. 'She wants to forget me. When they came back after the war, I went to the camp. Workers were getting jobs. But they did not choose me.'

Essie could hear the emotion in his voice, the memory of being let down. 'That seems unfair.'

'But I understood,' he said. 'The past had to be left behind, so that something new could begin.'

Essie felt humbled by his gracious words, and the empathy behind them. Standing at her side, Kisani seemed even taller than before, as if elevated by his noble sentiments. He was silent for a time, and motionless. When he finally spoke again, he sounded worn out, as if he'd been on a long journey.

'Send me someone who knows this area and I will tell them how to find the Meeting Place. I wish you well with your work. Goodbye.'

As he walked away, Essie watched his shoulders droop. He was an ageing man again, returning to the mundane tasks of his everyday life, far removed from the drama of the past. His hands hung at his sides, limp and empty.

TWELVE

A moving pattern of pink layered on pink filled Essie's gaze. A vast population of flamingos stretched away to each side of her along the shoreline. Beyond the mass of birds lay the still blue waters of the lake. In the distance was the saltpan, a white desert shimmering in the heat. At its heart, like a strange kind of oasis, was the grey mound of the nesting island. The backdrop to the whole scene was the volcano, its peak rising up against the sky and foothills descending to the water.

Essie looked down at Mara, lodged on her hip. The baby was wide-eyed, taking in all the colour and movement. She didn't seem bothered by the racket the birds were making – the loud honking calls that blurred into an incessant cacophony. Nor did she seem to mind the heavy smell of sulphur and bird droppings. She reached towards the flamingos with outspread hands.

It was still early. Essie had left the camp straight after breakfast, before the day's planning session began. Last night, Ian had finally agreed to her proposal that she and Simon begin scouting around the location she'd suggested: the lakeshore. She'd chosen the place as it gave her an excuse to be near the foothills – though of course she hadn't mentioned that. She'd talked instead about the fact that with the water level rising and falling over the seasons, there was always the chance of finding an ancient fossil harking back to the time before the lake was formed.

Essie had been allowed to take the 'good' Magadi Land Rover – with the arrival of Diana's new one, it was no longer required by Ian and Julia. The vehicle now was parked a short distance away on the other side of some bushes. Tommy was cooped up in the back; he'd have the chance to roam later on, and for now Essie preferred not to have to keep an eye on him. Rudie had been left there as well, sitting obediently on his haunches beside the driver's door. Essie didn't want to risk him running into the acidic water or disturbing the birds. All Mara's things remained stowed in the vehicle: bottles of milk, nappies, clothes; even the sling. Essie was enjoying just holding the baby in her arms. It felt more manoeuvrable and free. She looked towards the sun, climbing up from the eastern horizon. In spite of the early hour it was already hot. She lifted Mara away from her body for a few moments to let cool air wash between them.

Her gaze returned to the lake with its swirling mass of pink. The birds were in constant motion – a collage of wings, legs, necks, feathers. Watching them was like being caught in a kaleidoscope, with images blurring and changing, then taking on new forms.

Essie had all the basic facts about flamingos at her fingertips. People who came to Magadi were always curious about them and the Lawrences had a mini-lecture they often shared. In their spiel they explained how a particular algae bloomed in the soda lake, to a greater or lesser degree, depending on the conditions. They talked about the carotenoids in the algae – the very same pigments responsible for the colour in carrots, eggs and autumn leaves. The flamingos that fed on the algae were literally dyed pink. If you cut open one of these birds it was pink all through. The yolk of a flamingo egg was pink. Even the mother bird's milk was pink . . .

Essie focused on one bird, watching how it dipped its head to the water, dragging the beak along upside down as it drew in water to strain out the algae. It walked slowly along, taking high steps, pink legs bending in acute angles. After feeding for a while, the bird paused, stretching out first one wing, then the other, before folding them both away. The movements looked so considered and so elegant, the bird might have been taking part in a dance rather than just carrying out daily activities. Essie was reminded of the music-box ballerina twirling in her pink net skirt to music from *Swan Lake*.

She moved Mara from her hip and turned her around so she had a better view. Essie wished Simon were here to tell Mara the word for 'bird' in Hadza – she imagined the soft sound formed around a throaty click. But her assistant was still on tent duty. Now that Diana's 'palace' had been erected, he was helping set up some washing facilities for her. Tomorrow he was supposed to be returning to work with Essie.

'See the pink feathers?' Essie said to Mara. Foreign words seemed better, as always, than silence. She pointed at a flamingo that was running across the muddy bank, water splashing from webbed feet. It rose into the air, legs stretched out to create a perfect streamlined shape. 'Look, it's flying!'

Essie tried to imagine what a baby might make of the spectacle. She knew that without language the ability to think was limited. Yet there were times when Mara became very still, as if she was concentrating on something, or listening intently. In those moments Essie had a sense that the baby was in touch with something very old, while being herself so young. It was a fanciful idea that Ian would scoff at. But the fact was that when Essie was alone with Mara she didn't feel she was on her own, with only an unformed human for company. It was as if the person Mara would one day become was already here.

Checking the position of the sun once more, Essie decided it was time to start work. She planned to drive as close as possible to the hills and then scan the countryside with binoculars. It would not be wise for her to go any further on her own, especially with a baby, but she could at least assess what was visible from a distance.

She picked her way around the thicket of bushes, heading for the Land Rover. As she emerged from the vegetation, she came to a halt. Someone else had arrived here. Parked next to her vehicle was an odd contraption that looked like a small boat with wheels. It was painted a pale grey that had been smudged with white to form a camouflage pattern. Essie guessed straightaway that it belonged to Carl Bergmann. Who else would be here, by the lake? As she came closer she could see the photographer beside it – crouched down by one of the wheels. Rudie was hovering nearby, wagging his tail.

Carl stood up as Essie reached him. He had on the faded, almost-white shirt she'd seen before, along with a pair of grey shorts – perhaps he was dressed to match the camouflage paintwork. His hair was even more unruly than when they last met. It looked as if the salt from the lake had crept into it, forming stiff curls.

'Good morning.' Essie regretted the greeting as soon as it left her lips. She sounded so formal, like Ian and Julia. She avoided his gaze as she stepped into the shade of a stunted thorn tree, bowing her head to avoid a low-hanging branch.

'Hello.' An easy smile spread over Carl's face. 'I knew you were here, somewhere. I saw all the baby stuff in the Land Rover.' He scratched Rudie behind one ear as he gestured towards the lake-shore. 'You came to see the flamingos?'

'Just a quick look, since I'm here.' Essie didn't want him to think she always spent her time simply wandering around. She waved in the direction of the foothills. 'I'm doing some fieldwork.'

Carl eyed her for a moment as if considering asking further questions. Instead, he bent to look at Mara. He touched her gently on the cheek. The baby smiled at him so readily, Essie wondered if she knew they'd met before.

'She looks happy today,' Carl commented.

'She's very settled now. Just eats and sleeps and looks around. She even plays with things. Yesterday she tried to put her toes in her mouth!'

Carl turned back to Mara, miming amazement. 'Clever girl.'

Watching his reaction, Essie felt a rush of pleasure; with Simon so busy, she hadn't yet been able to share the story with anyone.

'She seems bigger,' Carl said.

'She can't be. It's only a couple of weeks since you saw her.'

'Babies grow quickly.'

Essie tilted her head. 'Now, you sound like a real expert.'

'Well, I know more about birds, of course, and cameras . . .' Another smile broke across Carl's face. The lines around his eyes deepened, accentuating the dark shine of his eyes. He pointed towards the boat-with-wheels behind him. 'What do you think of my amphibious craft? I had it made in Arusha – that was one of the things that delayed me. I've named it *Gari la maji*. Car of the water.'

Essie took in the clumsy lines of the contraption. The panels were crudely welded; some bits were lashed together with rope. 'Did you design it yourself?'

'I know it's not much to look at. But I've done a trial run. I can drive over the saltpan and then get across the water. The birds don't even take much notice of me.'

'So it's all going well?' Essie asked politely. Working on his own, the photographer was probably lonely. And it was always good to show interest in another person's profession.

'Yes, so far. You can see the water level's low – the island is exposed. The conditions are perfect. I'm all set up. It's just a matter of waiting now for the birds to begin mating.'

Essie recognised the tone in Carl's voice – anticipation backed by the fear of something going wrong. Lots of researchers had superstitions that helped overcome this uncomfortable blend of emotion. Lucky charms. Rituals. She wondered if Carl was one of them. She looked into the distance towards the nesting island. The stakes were high for him. If he succeeded in his goal, this would be one of the crowning achievements of his career. He'd feel the same way Essie would, if she were able to discover a second cave of paintings . . .

'I'm looking for something.' The thought just came out as words. 'A cave – containing rock art.'

'Over this way, you mean?' Carl looked puzzled. 'I only know about the one on the other side of the Gorge. Wolfgang Stein discovered it.'

'You know about his research?' Essie was surprised. The Lawrences' publications on the Painted Cave had eclipsed the work of the missionary – unsurprisingly, since he was an amateur.

'When I heard I was going to be living in his house I decided to do a bit of research. I was in Holland at the time so I went across to the Mission headquarters in Berlin. They've got an archive there.'

'We have copies of all his published articles at Magadi. He only mentions the one cave.' Essie paused for a moment, wondering if there was anything to be lost by talking openly to Carl Bergmann. She decided to go ahead. After all, they weren't in competing fields. 'There's a Hadza story about a cave with rock art, located somewhere around the base of the volcano. I checked Stein's maps of the area and there's nothing marked. But maybe there was something else in the archive . . .'

Carl shook his head. 'Not that I saw – and I looked at a lot of documents.'

'There's a landmark near the cave,' Essie prompted. 'It's like a tower of rock. Probably an erosion stack.'

'Nothing comes to mind, I'm sorry.'

'I found a Maasai who thinks he knows where it is. So that gives me somewhere to start.' Essie frowned thoughtfully. 'It's just odd that Stein didn't make any note of it.'

'But you know there's a gap in his story?' Carl said. 'Stein suddenly stopped publishing his research.'

'He died.'

'It wasn't that,' Carl said. 'Something happened to him. The people at the archive didn't want to talk about his private life. He was a failure as a missionary, apparently. He hardly made any converts. They said he lived alone for too long and got too close to the Africans. In the end he went mad. That was how they put it.'

Essie bit her lip. *Went mad*. Two words; just one syllable each. Yet they contained a whole story. A nightmare played out over countless agonising episodes, each one leading relentlessly on to the next.

'So,' Carl concluded, 'it doesn't mean anything – the fact that he didn't write about another cave.'

Essie nodded; the new information was encouraging. But the story about Stein left her feeling uneasy. She gazed in the direction of the volcano. Shrouded in smoke haze, it seemed almost defiantly mysterious. 'I'm doing a recce today – just to see what the access is like.' She gestured to the binoculars hanging over her shoulder. 'I really should get to work.'

'Me too,' Carl said.

But neither of them moved. They just stood there, as if each were waiting for the other to take the first step. Essie could feel the sun cutting through the meagre shade, dabbing patches of heat onto her skin.

'How did you first get interested in birds?' Essie asked. It was an obvious ploy to extend the conversation: the answer wasn't likely to be short. She waited to hear a story from his childhood about rescuing fledglings or feeding swans in one of those concrete-edged lakes that were installed in public parks. Or perhaps he was the son of a famous ornithologist.

'I was commissioned to take pictures for an article about short-tailed shearwaters,' Carl said. 'That's where it all began. I filmed them in the Aleutian Islands, in Alaska. They spend half of the year there. Then I went to Tasmania to cover the breeding cycle.'

'I was born there,' Essie said. It was a surprise to hear the place mentioned in connection with something other than the flint collection, or the amusing confusion over the name being so similar to Tanzania.

'You don't have an Australian accent,' Carl commented.

'I guess I did once,' Essie said. 'But we left when I was a child.'

'But you know about the shearwaters? The Aboriginal people call them moonbirds. Or muttonbirds?'

Muttonbirds.

Essie looked down at the ground. She remembered the red-gold flicker of fire, set against cool white sand. The tickle of downy feathers in her nose, the smell of roasting fat. Her lips and fingers were slick with grease. She chewed dense dark meat that tasted faintly of fish and dropped slender bones around her bare feet.

'I've heard of them,' Essie said vaguely. She pretended to be occupied with Mara. She assumed Carl knew that people ate the species of bird that had inspired his career – the name 'mutton-bird' was a clue. But she didn't want to admit to having done it herself. It would probably lead to questions she would not be able to answer. She knew the birds weren't an everyday food. They were only a part of visits to Lorna's family on the coast. Essie didn't have to be warned not to mention eating muttonbirds to the girls at school in Hobart. They'd wrinkle up their noses, like they did the time she'd talked of her grandmother's rabbit stew. But it was more than just that. Essie knew there was something about eating muttonbirds in particular that was not quite the same as other game. There was almost a secrecy surrounding it. But why this was so, she didn't know.

There was another reason, as well, for Essie to remain silent. In her time at the camp she'd witnessed some uneasy conversations – even arguments – between zoologists who studied birds or animals that were a part of the same food chain. The wildebeest man had no love of the lion; the expert on small primates saw chimpanzees in a dim light. When it came to humans who preyed on a beloved species, the tension was even worse.

'I spent a whole year following the shearwater migration.' Carl continued his story. 'The birds travel from the Southern Ocean right up to Alaska and back. They fly low over the sea, shearing the water with the tips of their wings. That's where their name comes from. They mate for life – they only separate if they fail to produce young. Every year they return to the same island, to the very same location. For some reason coming home means a lot to them. When you see the rookery pitted with burrows, you can't imagine how they find the one that's theirs.'

As he talked Essie could see the fascination in his eyes. He hadn't lost the sense of wonder about his subject – the way he spoke of the shearwaters was fanciful, almost romantic. That was probably what made him a successful photographer. Essie was reminded of the way she used to talk about the Painted Cave when she was first working there. Once she'd persisted with describing the rock art images to a couple from Arusha – detailing picture and motif, one after another – until Ian nudged her under the table.

Carl broke off, smiling. 'You shouldn't have asked. We'll be here all day.'

She smiled back. She let her eyes play over him. She noticed where there had been a small rip in his shirt – how it had been repaired by hand. The stitches were neat, but the cotton was not the right colour. She looked away, annoyed with herself. Was she collecting notes on him as if he were some rare species?

'Well, then . . . I really should head off.' She gestured towards the lake. 'Good luck out there.'

'Thanks. Same to you,' Carl replied. 'Feel free to call in at the house any time – for a cup of tea. Or if you ever need anything.'

A look flashed between them. The invitation felt charged with meaning, even though Essie knew it was a simple courtesy. Shifting Mara back to her hip, she whistled for Rudie, then turned and walked away.

Soon, she was back in the Land Rover with Mara tucked into the carrycot, Rudie and Tommy sharing space in the rear. She swung the vehicle into a reverse curve, then drove off, scattering loose stones behind her.

Essie's jumbled thoughts matched the erratic movement of the Land Rover as it lurched along the track. She went back over what Carl had said about Wolfgang Stein. The only image she'd seen of the missionary was in an academic journal – a hazy black-and-white photograph of a dour individual in a formal coat and top hat. It was hard to imagine the man becoming 'too close' to the Africans – whatever that meant. She thought of him losing his grip on sanity, here at Magadi, far from other Europeans. She saw him roaming through the stone house, muttering to himself, hands wandering aimlessly over furniture, walls, his own body, as if seeking some purchase on reality. The black coat was replaced by a dirty shirt, trailing from grubby trousers. There was a haunted look in his red-rimmed eyes. The smell of disinfectant. Doors slamming. The tormented screams of other inmates. A nurse's footsteps falling firm, heavy, as if to tread down her own fear . . .

Essie swallowed hard. She had no reason to think Stein had been locked up in a mental hospital. In her mind, his fate was entangled with that of her mother. Nausea hollowed Essie's stomach. She saw herself sitting on a hard chair in the ward at Fulbourn Hospital. She'd come there between a hockey game and a visit to the cinema with friends; the place was a harsh intrusion from another world. In front of her lay Lorna, eyes closed, arms lying over the sheet that covered her thin body. She looked so small and frail, like a child more than a mother. Aside from the slight movement of her chest, she could have been dead.

'Mum?'

Just a flicker of an eyelid.

'It's me.'

Nothing.

Essie felt the familiar fury rising inside her. Reaching out, she touched the woman's arm. Then, taking a piece of soft flesh between her finger and thumb, she pinched, hard. The eyes sprang open. Stared.

'So you are alive!' Essie's voice was harsh with teenage sarcasm. Inside, other words were forming.

Please. Don't go. You don't have to get better. Just don't die.

Essie dragged her thoughts away from the hospital ward, focusing instead on her driving; on Mara, right beside her; on the sounds of the flamingos, which still followed her from the lake. She evoked the image of Carl Bergmann, seizing on his relaxed smile, his friendly manner. Gradually, new pictures replaced the bleak memories of Fulbourn Hospital. She replayed in her head how Carl had laughed so fondly over the story about Mara and her toes. And how he'd talked about birds mating for life, and their desire to always come home. The first time she and Carl had met he'd said he was a nomad, like the birds he photographed. Did this mean that while he moved around the world he still felt a pull back to a location he called 'home'? Was it in the place where he was born? Or somewhere else?

Home.

Essie turned the word over in her mind. She thought of the house in Cambridge where she'd lived from the age of seven, right up until she left for Africa. She could recall myriad details about 26 Edenvale Road – the pebble-dash façade, a chunk of rendering missing at one corner; the clumps of mauve crocuses that poked up their heads each spring; the crocheted pot holder she'd made in primary school that hung near the smoke-stained stove; a creaky floorboard on the second landing that she knew to avoid when returning home too late from a party. There were special memories attached to the place – birthdays, holidays, homecomings – as well as scenes from the everyday that meant little on their own but which combined to form a tapestry of family life. Whole episodes had taken place in the house that no one in the world would ever want to recall. But there were happy times as well. Regardless of the weight of good memories versus bad, though, Essie didn't expect to spend more than a holiday there, ever again. It was no longer her home. Since she'd married Ian Lawrence, Magadi Gorge was where she belonged.

As the Land Rover climbed upwards, Essie's back pressed into the seat. She gazed across the dust-scoured bonnet to the stony ground in front of her. She knew the geological make-up of all the rocks she could see. She knew that the clumps of grey-green local sisal dotting the land were called *oldupai* by the Maasai. The plant's name, recorded incorrectly as 'olduvai', had been given to the gorge where the Leakeys carried out their work. Scanning the slopes, Essie could identify the approximate age of the strata revealed by erosion – around one foot of earth represented six thousand years. (Ian liked to give a demonstration at the excavation sites, walking down the hillside – literally stepping through vast chunks of time.) Essie knew, as well, the taxonomy of most of the local plants and animals and could navigate the *korongos* without a guide.

But still, with all this knowledge, Magadi Gorge didn't really feel like home. Not the way it did to Ian and Julia. Essie couldn't imagine that either of the pair would ever leave this place. Julia would one day be buried beside her husband in the informal cemetery not far from the camp, her body protected from hyenas – or other grave robbers – by a concrete slab. Then Ian and Essie would live on here alone together, continuing their work. It was possible that they would one day be forced to leave – if there was a change of government policy about their permits, or if funds completely dried up. But both scenarios were unlikely now that Diana's funds were revitalising the research. The fact was, when Essie was Julia's age, the Lawrences would almost certainly still be here.

Essie gripped the steering wheel. The dusty air seemed to tighten her chest. She couldn't remember now exactly how she'd come to be in this position. Somehow she'd let go of any chance to travel the world, like Carl was doing, even though Tanzania was meant to have been only her first stop. She'd planned to join a dig in Jordan. Or South America. She wanted to see new places, meet new people. And now none of that would happen. She hadn't understood the far-reaching consequences of her decision to marry Ian Lawrence. Not that it would have made any difference. She had fallen in love. That was that.

Essie took in a slow breath as memories returned to her of that time when all she'd wanted, in any given moment, was to be with her husband. She had been drawn to Ian from the day they first met in Cambridge. On her arrival in Magadi that interest had quickly become a fascination. It was hardly surprising. The Head of Research was famous, handsome and a talented archaeologist. Every young woman who came to the camp competed for his attention. In the Dining Tent, or out at the digging sites, Essie used to watch his face when she didn't think he would notice – tracing the strong lines of his brow, nose and chin. If she found an excuse to stand close to where he was, she would breathe in his smell – shaving soap, boot polish, leather, dust, a hint of sweat – imagining the essence of him being captured in her lungs.

All this time later, Essie could clearly recall the wonder and amazement she'd felt when she realised that Ian Lawrence was attracted to her. He could have chosen a girlfriend from any number of willing candidates – but he wanted Essie Holland. It was as if he'd seen in her something that he wanted or needed – and he'd set out to make her his own. He made sure she sat near him at the dining table. He put her on his team in the *korongos*. He took time out of his busy schedule to teach her about the work, the place – his life.

Compared with other men she'd known, Essie felt surprisingly comfortable with Ian. Perhaps because she'd grown up in the company of her father, she recognised so many things in him – his attention to detail, his curious mind, his ability to remember everything he'd ever learned. She was struck by the way he inhabited the camp, the digging sites – the whole of Magadi Gorge – with such authority. In his presence she felt completely safe in this strange, wild land.

There was nothing to keep the two apart. Their lives were joined together so easily that the time span between Essie's arrival at the camp and their wedding day seemed collapsed into just weeks, rather than months. The wedding took place in the height of the digging season. There was a celebration at the camp – a special meal at the end of the day, with everyone still in their work clothes and Essie holding a bunch of hastily picked flowers. The event was followed by a brief trip to Arusha to do the paperwork. While they were there, Essie had the chance to make a phonecall to her father. She could tell he felt torn by her surprise news – there was a quaver in his voice, even as he offered his congratulations. But he made it clear that he supported the marriage, even though it meant Essie wouldn't be returning to live in England. Essie had to put herself – her career – first. He'd made a similar decision himself, he pointed out, when he left Australia. And if he was going to lose his daughter to another man, Ian Lawrence was the best possible choice.

Returning to a busy schedule, the couple spent their days together out in the field; afterwards, in the Work Hut, they sat side by side. As a member of the Lawrence family, Essie helped Ian and Julia host the successive waves of guests. Every time she told someone her full name she felt a thrill of pride. Ian thrived on the company of these outsiders – but even as he was giving a mini-lecture or telling a story he would seek Essie out and hold her gaze. It was as if she was the only person he could see. In those moments she had a new vision of herself – she felt precious; beautiful.

Cloistered in their tent in the evenings, Essie and Ian took turns to read aloud from the odd collection of novels left behind by visitors. When it was Essie's turn to listen, she barely focused on Ian's words. Instead, she just revelled in the sound of his voice. In the soft light she watched his eyes, burning like the blue heart of a candle flame. Sometimes the reading ceased well before the end of the chapter, the book becoming lost among tangled sheets as they made love. When Essie woke each morning and saw Ian lying beside her, she could hardly believe he belonged to her, and she to him. They were lovers, friends, colleagues – all at once. It seemed too perfect to be true.

But then, as the fortunes of Magadi took a downward turn, things began to change. Without the company of all the visitors, Ian's energy flagged. He found no satisfaction in his work; everything was just a burden. Research became a source of anxiety instead of excitement. There was no joy in his eyes any more.

The transformation crept up on Essie, so she was never taken by surprise. She simply became used to a new Ian. Now, as she thought back over what had happened, she wondered which version of her husband was the real one. Had he adopted a façade earlier on? Or was the man who'd appeared in more recent years the imposter? Of course, she understood the situation was more complex than that. As people's lives threw up challenges, different parts of them emerged. They evolved into someone new.

Ian was changing again now, Essie reminded herself. Since Diana's funds had begun flowing into Magadi, he had been brighter, happier – notwithstanding the complications of Essie having brought a baby into the camp. He was coming back to his old self. His energy had been rekindled. Inspired once again, he walked with a lighter step.

Only this time, his wife was not the one at his side.

Slowing the Land Rover to a crawl, Essie leaned down to select low ratio. As she let out the clutch, the engine whined in a deeper register. The vehicle ground its way up the hillside. She remembered what Diana had said, when they were standing between Baraka's kitchen and the *cho* tent, the day they first met.

I hope you know how lucky you are . . .

Essie let the vehicle come to a halt. Torn between conflicting emotions, she stared out over the arid landscape. After a short while, though, her eyes were drawn to the passenger seat beside her, where the carrycot was lodged between the door and the gear stick. The steady jogging had soothed Mara into a deep sleep. Her head was turned to one side. Her ear was like a shell, delicately formed; her eyelashes were a perfect black crescent above her plump cheek. No matter how often Essie looked at the baby, it was still a surprise to see how nearly every part of her was such a deep brown – almost black. The colour seemed to infuse her flawless skin. She looked so beautiful.

As if able to sense Essie's gaze, Mara stirred in her sleep. Her lips made little sucking movements as though she were dreaming of milk. Essie felt a twinge in her heart. Reaching out one finger, she stroked the soft hair. Her eyes prickled with sudden tears.

You can't have everything.

Diana leaned back in her chair, long legs stretched out in front of her. Her new boots were scuffed; red dust was ground into the leather. She eyed them with a look of satisfaction.

'I'm worn out,' she said, sighing contentedly as she picked up her glass and took a gulp of her gin and tonic.

Supper was going to be served soon, but for now the Lawrences and their guest were all sitting outside. The group was gathered around the fireplace, even though the hearth contained just a pile of cold ashes and half-burnt logs. The dry-season winds had dropped for the night; the air was still and hot. Essie held Mara in her arms. The baby was calm and contented, having been recently fed. She was chewing on her fingers, looking up at the darkening sky.

Ian smiled across at Diana. 'You did well today. It was a long one.'

'Thanks.' Diana accepted the praise with a nod. 'We certainly covered a lot.'

Ian and Julia had spent the morning showing Diana over the *korongo* where the new work was soon to begin. After lunch, they'd visited one of the established sites so she could see how the excavation process was carried out – the painstaking digging, sieving of earth and tagging of artefacts. The labour was done under the glaring eye of the sun with only old beach umbrellas for protection. Diana had offered a suggestion about how this situation could be improved. She'd also made insightful remarks about other aspects of the work. When Essie was told about the tour and how successful it had been, she'd felt a guilty pang of disappointment. If she was honest, she'd rather have been told that Diana had become bored or that the harsh conditions had proved too much for her – that the guest had retreated to her tent hours ago.

Instead Diana had been in the Work Hut sitting in front of a large piece of paper. On one side of it she'd written *LEAKEY*, on the other *LAWRENCE*. Under the left-hand title she'd listed the Leakeys' key finds. *Proconsul* came first. She'd tagged it *Ancestor of Apes (therefore maybe us)*. Next, there was *Australopithecine (Ape-man)*, then *Habilis (Toolmaker)*. Under the Lawrences she'd made another list: *The Steps. Australopithecine. Habilis.*

'Three each,' she'd said, as if describing a game of hockey.

Essie had opened her mouth to add the Painted Cave, but the Leakeys had researched another set of Neolithic paintings in another area – so it didn't change the even score.

Diana drew a line down from each side – Leakey and Lawrence – angled towards a point. There she wrote *ERECTUS – TOOLS AND BONES*.

'So that's the situation?' she'd asked Ian. 'It's a race.'

Ian had looked awkward about the rivalry being named so bluntly. 'Well, we all want to prove that there was one source, and it was here in Africa. So we're really on the same team.'

Diana had just smiled. She'd drawn an arrow connecting the Lawrences with *ERECTUS*. The strong, dark line left no room for doubt about who was going to claim the prize.

Now, sitting by the fireplace, Essie could see the piece of paper pinned on the wall behind Ian's work table. She was surprised he'd agreed to it being put up there, where everyone could see it. As if he could tell that Essie was thinking about him, Ian turned to her.

'How was your day?' The query came with a smile, but there

was a cautious note in Ian's voice. Essie's scouting project had been discussed with the others, but the focus needed to remain on the serious part of the work, where Diana Marlow would be able to see her money put to good use.

'I haven't really done anything, yet,' Essie responded. In fact, she had spent several hours surveying the foothills through her binoculars, from a series of vantage points. She'd found no sign of a tower, but the vistas of broken rock had proved hard to assess from a distance. 'Hopefully I'll have Simon back tomorrow.'

'We don't need him, do we?' Diana turned to Ian. 'To finish my camp, I mean . . .'

He shook his head. 'It should all be done by now.'

Essie peered past her husband towards the place where Diana's tent had been erected. With its multiple peaks it looked like a small mountain range made from orange canvas. A short distance away from it stood a bathing tent. There was a *cho* as well; the earth dug out from the pit was piled in a mound outside the canvas walls.

Turning back to the fireplace, Essie took a sip from her glass, steadying Mara with one arm. Behind the fizz of the tonic, she felt the burn of a large shot of gin. The tang of citrus combined with the floral fragrance of juniper rose to her nostrils. She felt the cold liquid slipping down her throat, soothing away heat and dust.

As she put down her drink, she saw that Diana was studying her, a quizzical look on her face. Essie wondered if she was still trying to get used to the odd sight of a white woman nursing a black baby. Sometimes Essie felt a sense of shock herself, when she thought about the contrast between her and Mara.

Still eyeing Essie, Diana fished a piece of lime from her drink and sucked it. 'You know that Frank went to see your father's collection?' she asked.

Essie blinked at the unexpected topic. 'Yes. He mentioned that when he was here.' She remembered how she'd wanted to ask the man more about the time he'd spent with her father.

'When we got back to the Lodge that night, he told me all about his visit,' Diana continued. 'He met some people in Cambridge who knew your parents.' She broke off, shaking her head. 'It's so sad about your mother.'

Essie's lips parted, every nerve in her body on instant alert.

'Imagine . . . destroying half of your father's life's work . . .' Diana whistled soundlessly. 'Just like that.' She snapped her fingers.

There was a tense quiet. Essie stared into the cold ashes in front of her. A whole scene came into her head – as clear and detailed as if it had happened yesterday, yet telescoped into mere seconds.

She was arriving home from an excursion with her father, cheeks tingling from a day spent out in the wind. The smell of the café where they'd stopped for fish and chips still lingered in her hair. From the kerb where the car was parked she headed for the front garden. Rusty springs creaked as she pushed open the gate.

At the top of the path she faltered. Part of her wanted to put off the moment of encountering her mother. But another part just wanted to get it over with. Lorna might be in bed, the curtains closed, the air a dense fug of spent breath. Or she could be up, having made an effort to dress, to wash some dishes. Only a week ago, Essie and Arthur had come home to find a banana cake cooling on a rack in the kitchen, and several bunches of garden flowers in the sitting room. You never knew what to expect.

Essie took two steps along the gravel path. Then she felt the sole of her boot tilt sideways. Glancing down, she saw what had caused it: a stone – much too big for a pebble; the wrong colour and shape. She caught her breath, looking further. Scattered along the path were dozens of stone tools – hand axes, scrapers, shards, mother stones, strikers . . . Some stood out clearly, marked by texture, tone and shape. Others were only just visible among the pebbles. It was anyone's guess how many more artefacts were there, no longer even visible, completely absorbed into the pathway.

From behind her she heard a gasp. Turning around, she met her father's disbelieving stare.

'We can pick them up.' Essie's voice was shrill. She began collecting the stones, shoving them into her pockets.

But she knew it was pointless. Even if they picked up every one of the artefacts, they were all mixed up now. Arthur had never defaced his tools by writing on them. He labelled the trays, the bags. Some of the pieces he'd be able to recognise, but not all of them. The rest, scattered like this, could no longer be linked with a particular location. Disconnected from their story, they had lost the best part of their meaning.

Essie watched her father's rigid face; it could have been formed from flint. She ran into the house, feet drumming down the hallway, shouting and crying at the same time.

'We. Hate. You.'

Years later, and far away in Magadi, Essie could still hear the words – her little girl's voice echoing through the house. She could see the scene that followed. The empty bottles, scattered pills. Her father's voice on the telephone.

'Yes, still breathing . . . Unconscious.'

His frantic pacing, back and forth. The waiting that seemed to go on forever. Finally, people in uniforms approaching down the path, not knowing what they were treading on. The odd mix of pity and judgement on their faces.

Then the still body of a woman dressed in Lorna's red-and-white spotted dress disappearing into the ambulance . . .

Essie rubbed her hand over her face as if memories were like dirt and could be simply erased. Then she looked up at Diana. She had no idea why the woman had brought up the topic. Perhaps she was just expressing a passing thought, on impulse, as she sometimes seemed to do. Regardless, the facts needed to be laid out.

'My mother suffered from depression,' Essie stated. 'It was a psychotic episode. She didn't know what she was doing.'

'Sounds like jealousy to me,' Diana said. 'And I know a bit about that . . .' She gave a brief, hollow laugh. 'Your father was always going away, I gather. What was she supposed to think?'

'What do you mean?' Essie asked.

'Maybe she knew he was off with some gorgeous young student. Having a fling.'

Julia stiffened, as if she'd been slapped. Ian stared in shocked silence. Essie remembered this wasn't the first time Diana had been unnervingly frank about this subject; she'd told Essie her husband was serially unfaithful only hours after they first met. But this wasn't about Frank Marlow; it was about Essie's father. She opened her mouth, ready to dispute the absurd suggestion – but Diana just kept talking.

'You have to admire her. She knew how to bite back!'

Ian cleared his throat but seemed unable to find any words. Julia's eyes were wide.

'No,' Essie spoke up again. 'It wasn't like that. My father never did anything wrong. And my mother loved his collection. She found some of the tools herself – brought them up from under the sea. In her right mind she would never have thrown them away.'

Essie tried to hold a firm tone, but even as she was speaking, doubt was sliding beneath her words like a snake. She was reminded of the defaced drawings in the storeroom – the sense of fury that was etched into the sheets of paper. It was unmistakably an act of passion. Lorna's scattering of the stones had a similar feel. But that didn't mean Diana had put her finger on the cause . . .

Essie picked up her glass, intending to take a drink. Instead she just clasped it in her hand. The suggestion of adultery was ridiculous. But she couldn't deny that there was a sense in which her mother had been betrayed. Professor Holland spent all week at the university working until late, and then on weekends he went into the field, taking his daughter along. There had been occasions when Lorna joined them, but she didn't enjoy herself. She couldn't get along with the other people who were part of the excursions – Arthur's colleagues, the students, volunteers. She got too cold, too tired. It was better for everyone if she just stayed at home. Essie remembered the sheer relief she used to feel each weekend that she and her father escaped together. It was as if the air suddenly became clear and light. Essie could breathe and smile again. She'd felt guilty, even back then. But she knew her father relied on her. He'd often said how lucky he was that his daughter shared his interests.

'Well, anyway . . .' Ian finally spoke. 'The whole thing was a tragedy – such a loss. It was just fortunate that half of the collection survived. It was on loan to the university, I believe.'

'There was a special exhibition,' Essie confirmed. She pictured the artefacts laid out on their velvet-lined trays, locked safely away behind glass. Even with so many pieces lost or disidentified, Professor Holland still possessed the biggest collection of Tasmanian stone tools in the world. His research remained seminal.

'But your mother went mad,' Diana persisted. 'She ended up in an asylum.'

Essie didn't answer straightaway. She still couldn't think why Diana was pursuing the topic – it was almost as if she didn't see that it was both personal and painful. But there was no point in denying the truth about Lorna. The story was well known in archaeology circles – just as it had been in the school playground, on the university campus, everywhere . . .

'She had a complete breakdown,' Essie said.

'Well, I'm not surprised,' Diana said, 'even if your father really was, as you say, a faithful husband. Imagine what it must have been like for her! She came from Tasmania, for godsakes. Who's even heard of the place?' Opening a packet of cigarettes, she used her lips to pull one out. The sound of her striking a match, the flare of the flame, jarred the air. 'And there she was in bloody Cambridge. I've met some of those university men. The snobbery is beyond belief.' She threw Ian a smile to show she wasn't referring to him. 'Their wives are even worse.'

Essie thought of the wardrobe stuffed with unworn clothes. The obsession with visits to the hairdresser, the beauty salon. She remembered seeing Lorna mimicking a British accent while watching television. 'She tried to fit in. But she just couldn't get things right. She . . .' Essie's voice trailed off. Julia was sending her meaningful looks. Essie knew she wanted the conversation steered in a different direction – it had moved on from its bizarre beginning, but was still far too personal for the Lawrences' tastes. Diana didn't seem to have noticed that anyone was uncomfortable, though – or perhaps she didn't care. Her eyes were sharp with curiosity.

'How did they even meet one another?' she asked.

'My mother worked for my father.'

Diana frowned. 'But she wasn't an archaeologist, was she?'

Essie shook her head. 'Dad came down from Sydney to excavate a Tasmanian Aboriginal home site for his PhD. Part of the area was submerged. He needed a diver to search the sea floor.' She paused, glancing at Julia. The look of disapproval was replaced by an encouraging nod. This part of Essie's family story was in much safer territory. In fact, Essie had quite often talked about it to visitors. Everyone wanted to know the background to Professor Holland's collection – how and where the items had been found. They were keenly interested in the Tasmanian Aborigines as well. It wasn't known for sure if the inhabitants of the island had evolved separately, having travelled originally from some other place, or if they were the same people as the mainland Aborigines. Whichever was true – and most assumed the latter – they'd become cut off there when the ice age ended and the land bridge that had connected the two landmasses was flooded. For around ten thousand years the Tasmanians had lived in isolation from all other humans. How this may have affected them was one of the things that had driven Arthur Holland's fascination with their artefacts.

'My mother's family lived near the site,' Essie explained to Diana. 'She was still at high school. It was a holiday job for her.'

'How did she know how to dive?'

'Lots of people did it around there. They speared fish, picked up crayfish, scallops, abalone. My mother was one of the best, apparently – she could hold her breath a long time. Dad said she could swim like a seal.'

An image came to Essie of a slim young woman wearing a swimsuit that clung to her body like a second skin. It was from an old photograph of Lorna. The print was dog-eared at the corners, the colours distorted by time. Essie had discovered it while helping her father collect up Lorna's possessions that were spread around the guest room once it became clear she would never return home from Fulbourn. They'd left the hoard of dresses in the wardrobe but thrown most of the other things away. It had happened during term break from school, but there was no holiday atmosphere in the house. Essie and Arthur had moved around the room in silence. They both wanted to get the job done as quickly as possible. It was like ripping off a bandaid; the pain was made worse by lingering. Essie had been emptying a bedside drawer when she'd picked out the square of card from beneath a pile of medical prescriptions. She'd brushed away a film of talcum powder with her finger, staring at what was revealed.

The picture had been taken as Lorna was wading through thigh-deep water towards the shore. Her goggles had been pushed up onto her forehead. She was smiling straight at the camera. In one hand she held up what looked like a stone axe. Though the image was frozen, there was the impression of movement. Drops of salt water flying. The thrust of the hand, raised in triumph, clasping the prize. The young woman's smile breaking across her face like the light of a clear dawn over the land.

On the back of the photograph the words *Rocky Bay* were written in blue ink. There was a date as well. Essie did the calculations. Arthur was twenty-two. Lorna was sixteen. Only two years older than her daughter was on this day when she was clearing out the guest room. Essie had gripped the picture with a rigid hand. This new vision of her mother felt like a cruel joke: a glimpse of what might have been, both revealed and snatched away at the same time. Essie had not drawn her father's attention to what she'd found. She tossed the picture into a shoebox, where it settled among dried-out lipsticks, shopping dockets and half-used packets of aspirin.

'And so . . .' Diana prompted, 'they fell in love?'

Essie nodded. 'Dad had to return to Sydney. As soon as he could, he got a position at the Tasmanian university. It took three years but he and Mum waited for each other. They got married and lived in Hobart. That's where I was born. They had to wait for me, too.' Essie smiled wryly, aware that she was parroting Arthur. This was how he talked about that era of his life: how he'd had to wait for a job, a bride, and then a daughter. 'Dad went away to fight in the war – he was conscripted. When he came back he picked up his research again. I think my parents were happy. Dad worked very long hours, though. Mum must have been lonely sometimes. Every school holidays she used to take me to her family's place on the coast. For some reason Dad didn't like it, but she still went . . .'

'Typical man,' Diana said. 'He wanted her to stay at home and look after him. Make his meals and sleep in his bed.' A cynical smile quirked her lips. 'That should have been a warning to her – about whose interests were always going to come first. Of course, she was trapped by then.' Diana waved her hand towards Essie, trailing a wisp of smoke. 'She had you.'

Essie flinched at her words, her hand tightening on the arm of her chair.

'Children can wreck your life, you know,' Diana continued. 'They tip everything out of balance.' There was a short pause. She sniffed, then wiped the back of her hand under her nose. 'When I got pregnant I decided not to go on with it. I didn't want to take the risk.'

Diana's tone was calm; her face was impassive. She might have been mentioning the weather. In the taut silence that ensued, Essie felt an impulse to look down at Mara, as if the baby lying in her lap was somehow linked with the one that had never been born.

There was a creak of canvas as Julia got to her feet. Her expression was one of ill-concealed shock. Essie couldn't guess whether she was more disturbed about what Diana had done, or the fact that she'd talked about it so freely. Both would be unimaginable to her.

Julia gestured towards the Dining Tent. 'I believe it's time to move inside.'

Ian stood up as well, scraping back his chair – clearly eager to follow his mother's lead and bring an end to the conversation. He glanced across to the kitchen as though willing Kefa to appear. He leaned to picked up his glass.

Diana followed his example. 'Oh, good! I'm starving. Lunch seems years ago.'

Ian and Julia led their guest away from the fireplace. Essie heard Diana begin to talk about some event from the day. She sounded calm and relaxed, as if what she'd said only seconds ago was already forgotten, along with the rest of the conversation. She really did seem to act like a child, Essie thought, ruled by passing emotions that were there in the moment, then gone.

Essie held Mara against her shoulder while she gathered up a muslin baby wrap that was draped over the back of her chair. She was ready to move, but she sat motionless, staring ahead. Diana's opinions about Essie's parents were misguided – but they were still unnerving. Essie couldn't stop thinking of how Lorna had transformed so completely from the happy, attractive person in the swimsuit. She'd lost her beauty, her liveliness; she'd become a shadow of a person. Nevertheless, her husband had remained true to her. Essie remembered Arthur quoting his marriage vows.

'For richer, for poorer . . . In sickness and in health . . .'

He always sounded so sad, and full of regret.

Why didn't he take her back home?

The question came to Essie so clearly, bluntly, it could have been asked by Diana. The answer was obvious. It would have been crazy for Arthur Holland to return to Tasmania. He had tenure at Cambridge University. He needed to remain in England, close to the great archaeological sites of Europe and the Middle East. He could have sacrificed his career, only to find that Lorna remained ill. No one knew the true cause of her problems. Perhaps they were genetic: inevitable, regardless of her circumstances.

More questions tumbled through Essie's head. Did Lorna try to go home for a holiday? Did she threaten to leave England for good, on her own? Surely she wanted to return to a place where she'd once been happy and well? She must have longed to be reunited with her own mother, and her siblings, cousins, aunties . . .

But, as Diana had pointed out, she was trapped. She couldn't take Essie away from her father. Her only choice would have been to leave her little girl behind on the other side of the world.

Essie stared into the dead fire. She'd been fifteen years old when her mother died. She'd already become used to living without her. It was a relief not to have to think about Fulbourn Hospital any more, or to feel guilty about the long gaps between visits. The aching emptiness that she experienced was not exactly grief – or if it was, Essie knew it was not about the mother she'd lost, but the one she'd wanted to have. The comforting remarks people made about death being a blessed release felt true. Looking back now, Essie realised how young she'd been. She was so sure of her views, so clear on what she believed about her mother, and herself. Now she wondered if she'd understood anything at all . . .

Essie drew Mara closer to her chest, resting her cheek on the baby's head. She thought of Lorna, buried in a Cambridge churchyard. In summer, English birds perched on her headstone, pecking at insects in the lichen; in winter she was covered with snow. Lorna was trapped forever in a foreign country, stranded inland, far from the sea. A cold finger of regret poked at Essie's heart. She wished she believed – like most Africans did – in the living presence of ancestor spirits. Then she could reach out to her mother and acknowledge the sacrifices she'd made. It might even be possible to imagine that the events of the future could somehow touch the past. That Essie – here, and now – could connect with Lorna. Not the sad, broken woman she had become, but the young diver smiling into the sun. The two women would be like friends who had just met. At the same time, they would know that Lorna was going to be Essie's mother. And that one day Essie, too, would hold a baby in her arms.

THIRTEEN

Essie picked her way between boulders and piled stones, following an imaginary line across the hillside. Tommy was close at her heels, his hooves scraping on rocks as he found his footing. The midday sun was hot and she'd forgotten her neck scarf, so she pulled the band from her ponytail, letting her hair fall loose around her shoulders. The small rucksack on her back bounced with each step she took. From the corner of her eye she could see the silver flash of the whistle that was tied onto one of the pockets. Ian had given it to her when she was preparing to begin the fieldwork; if she got lost, she would be able to attract attention. Not that she was alone out here. Simon was moving along a parallel trajectory not far away from her. He hadn't been in the area before but seemed to have a natural ability to read the landscape and find his bearings.

Simon was carrying Mara in her sling. He steadied her with one hand as he jumped from rock to rock. In his other hand he carried a bow and quiver – a precaution against predators. He'd taken to leaving his shirt behind in the Land Rover. Bare from the waist up, he looked more like a nomadic tribesman than a member of the Magadi research team.

He often talked to Mara as he walked – telling her stories or naming the things they could see. He and Essie had agreed it was good for her to hear the Hadza language as much as possible. It would help her learn to talk herself, when the time came. But when Essie was near enough to hear the soft, intimate tone, and the constant clicking that was so foreign to her ear, she found the sound unsettling. She felt left out of the world they shared. Not only that, she was reminded that when Mara eventually said her own first words, and then her first sentences, Essie would not be there to hear them. She had to remind herself to focus on her work, and not to think of the future. Fieldwork required a calm and steady mind.

Patience was vital to the task as well. They'd already spent more than two weeks out in the foothills, searching for the cave. It hadn't taken long to locate the Meeting Place, following instructions Kisani had given Simon. The erosion stack was easy to identify, even though the top had been broken off, leaving only a squat rectangle of stone. Essie and Simon had studied the nearby terrain carefully but found nothing of interest.

Since then, they'd been investigating the surrounding slopes, checking for clues to a hidden gully or some other place where the entrance to a cave might be concealed. Progress was slow, with little open country where it was possible to stride freely along – the foothills were a place where the sedimentary geology of the *korongos* met the volcanic rock of the slopes. Essie kept a good eye on where she was placing her feet. It would be all too easy to trip over and risk dropping the baby or to tread on a snake that was basking in the sun, warming its blood.

With each step she took, Essie was aware that this was the territory where Robbie had gone missing so many years ago. She half expected to see some sign of the lost boy: a fragment of cloth faded almost to nothing; a wisp of hair; a shoelace. She found a bottle top and the remains of a box of matches, which may have been left by one of the searchers. But that was all.

Every day the pair took a new sector and followed the same routine. They walked, then rested, then had lunch, then rested again. They took turns to carry Mara in the sling. Though she was still only small, it was tiring for one person to carry her all day. Not only that, it was a good opportunity to prevent Mara becoming too dependent on Essie.

There had been times when Essie had noticed a wary look in the baby's eyes, or an anxious expression on her face. It often went with a soft cry. Her hands would grip whatever she could reach, and then cling on tightly. In those moments Essie wondered what was going through Mara's mind. Was it possible that, at some deep level, she remembered everything that had happened to her? The loss of the mother who had carried her, whose voice she would have heard from inside the womb. Then the loss of Giga, who had breastfed her for the first portion of her life. Giga's touch, smell, voice must have become familiar. What had Mara thought and felt when she found herself alone with Essie? Did she see that the face looking down at her was the wrong colour? That the voice, the smell, and the long, straight hair – the same tone as the odd skin – were all foreign, too?

When the rains came Mara would be around six months old, assuming the seasons followed their normal schedule. By then, Essie would have looked after her for far longer than anyone else. Then she, too, would disappear from the baby's life. If Mara spent time with Simon each day, she would at least learn to feel safe with more than one person. And being with a man would help her reconnect with her grandfather, and other Hadza men too. Simon had confirmed for Essie how in their traditional life everyone, male and female, helped care for children. Women spent more time with the little ones, since it was easy to include them in food-gathering trips and impractical for them to be taken on a hunt with the men. But overall, the young were raised by the whole community. Although there was always a special bond between parent and child, it was said that once toddlers were weaned it was nearly impossible for an observer to tell which of them had been born to which mother and father.

Such a society was hard for Essie to truly imagine. It was all the more reason why this time when Mara could be close to Simon was so valuable. He was a model for who she would become. Being away from the bustle of the camp had other advantages for Mara as well. It offered an interlude of peace and calm before the upheaval that was to come.

Meanwhile, Mara obviously enjoyed spending her days looking out at the passing scenery. She was more relaxed and contented riding in the sling than she was when propped up in the pram or even sitting on Essie's knee. She woke and slept seamlessly as if comforted by the rhythm of footsteps. She'd been at Magadi just over six weeks now – though it felt like so much longer. She'd grown taller and put on weight. Essie didn't need the nursery scales or the growth chart to tell her this: Mara's arms and legs were rounder and she'd outgrown the smallest of her clothes. These last few days the baby had also begun to gnaw at her fists. According to *Complete Babycare*, this was the first sign of teething. At three-and-a-half months old, the timing was right. Baraka had provided a piece of *biltong* for her to chew on. He claimed the salt in the dried meat was beneficial, too, in the unrelenting heat of the dry season – counteracting what was lost in sweat.

The instant Mara became restless, the person carrying her came to a halt. They quickly released her from the sling and held her in a seated position so she could urinate onto the ground. Simon had suggested they not bother with nappies out here in the bush, and instead follow the example of African mothers. There were occasional accidents but this didn't matter much – the baby was naked, but for her string of bird-shell beads, so there were no clothes to be changed. If Essie's shirt or the sling had to be washed, there were still some small pools – remnants of the rainy reason – to be found in the hills. Anything that got wet dried quickly in the hot sun. With no nappies to consider, Essie only had to concentrate on what Mara needed to drink – the bottles of formula, and the extra boiled water to maintain good hydration. It was so much easier than being back at the camp.

For the first hours of each day spent on the mountainside, Essie found that her mind constantly wandered. As she stepped from stone to stone, arms out to help her balance, she'd catch herself thinking of Carl Bergmann, guessing at where he might be: down at the lakeside taking photographs, or back at the Mission house, perhaps, checking his camera equipment. She imagined him working on the *Gari la maji* – sun glinting off tools laid out on the ground, a sheen of sweat on his brow, his cheek marked with engine oil. She wondered if he was lonely, all on his own. He appeared self-sufficient, but he seemed to like company as well . . . Essie would also picture what was going on back at Magadi Camp. The place was now buzzing with activity. Flights were arriving every morning delivering more equipment, more staff, more supplies. Ian and Diana virtually ran from one task to another as they set their ambitious plans in motion. Excavations were already taking place at four new sites, with more projects about to begin. Team leaders and managers had been employed, but Ian still liked to keep a close eye on everything. Meanwhile, Diana had made it clear she wanted to actually take part in some practical fieldwork. To Essie's surprise she seemed genuinely committed to the hard labour that this entailed. Each day she returned home with telltale marks of dust on her clothes from lying on the ground, picking at the earth with a trowel and toothbrush. Julia was busy, too, though her pace was slower. She was engaged in training new staff to meet the high standards that the Lawrences expected.

As time passed, Essie felt increasingly dislocated from them all. When she returned home she felt left out. Enquiries about her day, or about Mara, were fleeting. It was understandable – the work was the focus, and Essie was not involved. She found herself constantly torn between different emotions. On the one hand, she was more determined than ever to find the new cave site; it would be the thing that would draw her back into the centre of activity again. At the same time, though, she wasn't looking forward to having to juggle Mara's needs with the demands of new research – the very idea made her feel anxious.

All these thoughts and concerns, intercut with memories and imaginings, clamoured for space in Essie's head as she walked the foothills. But as each day wore on, morning reaching towards noon, she found their pull became less insistent. It was as if the steady rhythm of her step drummed them out, just as it lulled Mara to sleep and then shook her gently awake.

By the time the sun sank into midafternoon, Essie's mind was settled and calm. Then her senses turned outwards to the world around her. She noticed how the sun bounced, iridescent, off the sheered facets of stone shards. How brown-and-yellow butterflies hovered in flocks, the myriad tiny wings beating like panicked hearts. She passed desert rose plants with their stumpy succulent trunks. At the ends of the leafless branches were clusters of five-petalled flowers. They made bright splashes of flamingo pink.

These things that Essie could see were only the beginning. The visual field was a mesh laid over what she could smell, hear and feel – the green scent of a crushed plant, the whining buzz of a cricket, the rub of the rucksack straps against her shoulders.

Sometimes she had the sense that there was no boundary between herself and the world around her. The realisation was tinged with fear – as if she might actually dissolve and disappear. But mostly it filled her with a sense of peace and timelessness. She forgot why they were here, walking in the shadow of Ol Doinyo Lengai. The search for the cave drifted into the periphery of her attention, as if the goal of the mission were less important than the long journey towards it.

At the end of each workday, it became part of Essie and Simon's routine to call in at the Mission house. It offered a cool haven after the hours spent outside, and Carl was always pleased to see them. His own workday was shorter than it should have been. So far, he'd seen no sign of courting behaviour among the flamingos – for some reason they were delaying initiating the elaborate rituals. He had made plenty of successful visits to the breeding island in the *Gari la maji* and taken photographs of the birds gathered there. But the goal of Frank Marlow's Flamingo Project was to document the sequence of breeding – from courting adults to fledgling chicks. And so far, Carl had been unable to make a start.

'They'll begin any day now,' he kept saying. He sounded optimistic but Essie knew how frustrating it must be for him, being ready to work, but forced to wait.

They often sat out on the verandah sipping cups of tea, looking across the banks of reeds towards the lake – the expanse of silver water surrounded by the wide arc of the saltpan. Rising up behind it was the mountain, the upper slopes anointed with white lava, a drift of white smoke emerging from the summit. The whole scene was like a fantasy – a world in which snow and ice had been transformed into heat and salt.

Carl would carry one of Stein's chairs outside for Essie to use. As she sat on the seat with its lumpy stuffing and torn upholstery – feeding Mara or rocking her to sleep – she would listen to the two men talk. They covered topics of all kinds, Simon occasionally having to ask for Essie's help with an English word. They always came back to the wild animals, birds and plants of the East African Rift Valley. Simon's tribe came from further south, beyond Serengeti, but the flora and fauna were much the same as here.

Simon told them how the honeyguide bird, *Tik'iliko*, helped Hadza hunters find trees where there were hives, in return for a feed of honeycomb enriched by bee larvae. It was a deal that worked for them both: the hunters couldn't see the nests from the ground, and the honeyguide couldn't break them open. Simon enacted how bird and hunter whistled back and forth to one another as they traversed the bush together, the bird in the air, the man on the ground.

Simon shared the techniques of tracking and stalking – unchanged from the time before humans first began farming, ten thousand years ago. He invited Carl to discover how hard it was to fully draw back the long bow that he carried. Essie saw the effort that it took – the straining muscles in Carl's shoulders and arms. An arrow on its own was not enough to bring down larger prey, Simon explained. The sap of the desert rose was boiled down to make a poison that was lethal and had no known antidote. Daubed on an arrowhead, it could cause a giraffe, eland or zebra to collapse – but not an elephant.

He described how the Hadza men left their tribes for the major hunting expeditions. The events were always scheduled during the time of the full moon. This meant that the hunters would return laden with meat and be rewarded with sexual favours, at the very time when their women would be most fertile. The Hadza all bled at the same time, Simon claimed, during the time of the 'dark moon'.

Essie knew what Simon was referring to: menstrual synchronicity. Among scientists, it was a contentious topic. Some believed pheromones interacted so that the cycles of women who lived together gradually became aligned. Other researchers said this was nothing but a myth. Essie remembered when a Swiss student had carried out a survey of female students and volunteers living in Magadi Camp. She'd claimed that by the end of the digging season they were all menstruating together. Ian didn't believe in menstrual synchronicity. Neither did Julia. Essie avoided becoming involved in the debate, even though she had ticked the box on the survey that ended up showing that she was bleeding at the same time as the other women who took part. Ian knew Essie was menstruating then too, of course; for reasons of contraception they both had to track her periods. But he made it clear he wasn't convinced the research was sound. He pointed out that the topic would have been discussed between the participants; perhaps clues to who was where in their cycle had been inadvertently conveyed. Maybe there was even collusion in order to create a result – it wouldn't be the first time such a thing had happened. Ian's male colleagues shared his skepticism – they seemed confronted by the idea of females having some secret power. For a while there had been tension in the camp, as the women (excluding Julia) had sided against the men. But the controversy had drifted into the background when a new academic arrived, with a focus on the latest carbon-dating techniques.

While Simon talked, Carl listened intently. He didn't take notes like most people would, given the rare chance to talk to someone who knew so much. Essie followed his example even though she knew that precious details might be lost if she tried to recall it all later.

About a week ago, Essie had been sitting with Mara, drinking tea as usual, when Simon started describing to Carl the different methods for butchering particular birds and animals. He explained how each part of the body – hide, fur, bone and flesh – was used for food or medicine. Essie was struck by the fact that Carl was not disturbed by the discussion, even though the photographer's work involved capturing on film the beauty and grace of some of the same creatures, or ones like them. She could have risked telling him, she now realised, about how she had sat around a fireside as a little girl eating muttonbirds – or shearwaters, as he called them. There was the other name, too, that he'd mentioned. Moonbirds.

Moonbirds . . .

As Essie shaped the word with her tongue, images rose up in her mind. Not just the memories of taste, smell or the greasy shine on her fingers. She saw herself walking over a ground pitted with holes, her small feet bare and grey with dirt . . .

She was kneeling in the tussock grass, eyeing one of the small burrows. Holding her breath, she forced herself to reach in – wanting to be brave like the older kids. Knuckles brushed the earth, her heart hammering. If it was cold down there, she'd been warned, she had to pull out quickly. There could be a snake in residence, not a chick. She swallowed on a tense throat. She couldn't tell how warm or cool it felt. The earth was smooth, crumbly. There was no jabbing beak, no brush of furry feathers . . . A shaky smile touched her lips. The burrow was empty – no snake; but no chick, either. Relief washed through her. She wouldn't have to yank the bird out of the hole, then shake the body to snap the neck. But onlookers had seen her do her best. She'd tried. She'd proved she was brave enough for that – but only just . . .

As the edges of the memory turned to a haze she let out a slow breath. It was as if Simon's descriptions of his experiences had called up something from her past that she didn't know she'd retained. She imagined what Simon would think if she were to share the memory now – how it would sit with his picture of her as a European. She kept it to herself, though. The Lawrences always made a point of holding themselves apart from the local people. It would not be wise, as Ian's wife, for Essie to undermine this carefully preserved status. She let the conversation flow on around her.

As they came to know one another better, Carl began to draw out Simon's personal story. Being an outsider to Magadi Camp, and not the man's employer, he was freer to ask frank questions. Essie learned that Simon's Hadza name was Onwas. He'd adopted a new one to enrol in school and used it ever since. He couldn't conceal his origins from other Africans – they always understood who belonged to which tribe – but having an English name made it clear that he saw himself as part of the modern world. Before coming to work at Magadi, he'd been a farmhand for a number of years. His goal had always been to strive hard and secure a good future for himself.

One day, when the sun had been especially hot, Essie decided they should seek the shelter of the Mission house a bit earlier than usual. That meant there was time for a longer conversation. While they drank their tea on the verandah, Simon talked about the pressures that had been faced by the Hadza. He recounted how his parents, along with many of their relatives, had been influenced by the British Administration to give up their nomadic way of life. There was a scheme to teach the Hadza to settle down and grow cotton. Houses were built for their use, along with schools and clinics. But the projects failed. Simon wanted to study, so he stayed. But many of the people returned to the bush.

'They didn't want to pay the hut tax,' Simon explained. 'The Hadza have never owed payments to others. But the main problem was that they didn't like farming. It took up too much time. And it wasn't fun.'

As he said this, Simon eyed his bow and arrows, which were leaning up against the front wall of the house. Essie remembered encountering him after his night out with Mara's relatives, when he'd tried to conceal how much he'd enjoyed the shared hunting expedition. She wondered if he would describe working for the Lawrences as 'fun' – or if that lifestyle requirement only applied to *Hadza pori* – the wild Hadza.

'Five years ago,' Simon went on, 'some groups of Hadza were forced into lorries and driven to Yaeda Chini. Armed police came, too.'

'This was done by the Tanzanian government?' Carl enquired.

Simon nodded. 'They wanted to change the Hadza, too.'

'What happened at Yaeda Chini?' Essie asked the question tentatively; anything involving an armed escort wasn't likely to end well.

'People became ill. The diet was very poor compared with what they were used to. They caught diseases they'd never had before. And they became bored. They drank too much alcohol. Smoked marijuana all day. And there was something else that happened . . .'

Simon had to pause, struggling to find the right words. 'Sadness overcame them. It reached into their hearts and dragged them down. They gave up dancing, playing gambling games. They gave up the wish to be alive.'

Essie felt the words fall, leaden, into the air. She thought of Lorna, dropped into a world where there was no sparkling sea to dive into, no family bonfires on the beach. Only cooking, cleaning, shopping, dressing up to meet strangers, knowing all the time that she wouldn't manage to look right, sound right . . .

'The Hadza who survived ran away, back to the bush,' Simon said. 'They are still there.'

'That's good, then?' Essie queried.

The tense look remained on the man's face. Simon gestured at Mara, who was asleep in Essie's arms. Her arms draped down, one fist shiny-wet from being in her mouth. 'Her mother might have survived in a hospital. And Hadza children should go to school. One day they might have no choice but to change the way they live. Land has been turned into game reserves and farms. We are not allowed to hunt there.' Simon frowned, deep lines marking his face. 'We have to find a way to adapt to the present but hold on to what we need from our past.' He shook his head. 'I don't know how it will turn out.'

Essie hugged Mara against her chest, wrapping her arms around her as if she could somehow protect her from such a complex world. The threats to the Hadza way of life that Simon had described only added to a whole tapestry of anxieties that already hung in the back of Essie's mind. There were so many ordinary, everyday dangers that Mara was going to face as well. And all the decisions about her future lay in the hands of her family, her tribe. Essie would not be in charge.

She comforted herself with the thought that there were still things she could do. Send money to Nandamara. Medicines. Clothes. Schoolbooks. She could make regular visits to wherever the Hadza were. Charter planes to track them down if necessary . . .

But these were just fantasies, Essie knew. In Hadza society people didn't have any use for money. They didn't acquire possessions. They didn't even store food. They didn't have a place they called 'home'. Everywhere was home. It was such a radically different way of living that Essie found it impossible to grasp. What she did understand was that she could contribute nothing to it. Essie had to trust that Giga would breastfeed Mara until she was old enough to be weaned onto powdered baobab pod, liquid honey and chewed-up meat. She had to believe Nandamara, along with the rest of the family, would keep his granddaughter safe and happy.

Essie's role would be to let Mara go, completely. If she didn't, the child would not belong anywhere. The Hadza people were in danger of being caught between two worlds – but Mara would be in an even more difficult position. She'd be caught between two families as well. Essie could not be tempted to live in the half-light of waiting and hoping that she and Mara would meet up again. The Hadza would return to camp in the Painted Cave now and then, as they always had. It might even turn out to be an annual event, but Simon had said the Hadza didn't normally move in such a planned way. When the tribe did manage to visit, Essie might get to see Mara. It would be reassuring to know that she was safe, healthy, happy. But at the same time it would be agonising, surely, for Essie to watch the little girl's life unfolding without her. And what kind of existence would Essie have? She could drive herself mad. She remembered the absent look on Lorna's face, year after year. Essie had assumed her mother was lost in her illness. Perhaps she was just living elsewhere – abandoning those who were with her, in the here and now.

It was one thing for Essie to tell herself all this, but another to accept what it would mean. When she thought of returning Mara to the Hadza, heart-searing visions crowded her head. She pictured the moment when she would have to pass the baby over to Nandamara, or Giga, and then walk away empty-handed. She saw Mara crying, reaching out for her – afraid of these people who were now strangers to her. Essie couldn't imagine returning to the camp, packing up the nursery and giving all Mara's things away . . .

As a sense of panic descended, mad visions came to her. She thought of escaping with Mara – just climbing into the Land Rover and driving off towards the horizon. She saw herself living some-where in a distant corner of the country, just her and the baby. But there was no substance to the idea – Essie knew that. What kind of life would Mara have as the daughter – illegally acquired – of a white woman? The pair would attract interest wherever they went. Essie would soon be arrested. Who could say what would happen to Mara then? There was Ian to think of, as well. Essie's marriage. Her work. Anyway, the Hadza baby had her own loving family who were waiting to take her back. Mara belonged with them.

Essie's thoughts circled endlessly, going over well-trod ground – and leading her always back to the same place: that future time when Mara would no longer be a part of her life. Rational arguments were no help to her now. Emotions built up inside her like a head of steam that had no way to escape. Her heart pounded, and her throat clammed up as if she was trying to swal-low something much too big to go down.

Essie closed her eyes. Julia had warned her, just a few days ago, that she was becoming too attached to Mara. They were sitting at the breakfast table, waiting for Ian and Diana to join them. Essie had been playing a peekaboo game with the baby.

'You can't imagine what it will be like to lose her,' Julia had stated. 'You think you can – but you can't. Losing a child is not like anything else.' As she continued, her matter-of-fact manner disintegrated. Her voice became taut, her cheeks flushed. 'You will always be wondering, worrying . . . Is she safe? Is she sick or hurt? Is she calling my name? You will lie awake at night, trying to stop your thoughts. But nothing will help you. Nothing . . .'

Julia's voice cracked, and she stood up suddenly, tipping over her chair. Before Essie had a chance to respond, she had walked away.

Now, sitting in her chair on the verandah, Essie rested her cheek on Mara's head, feeling the hard curve of her skull beneath the soft hair. She drew in the baby's smell. Milk. Talcum powder. The subtle fragrance of the nursery soap, and the hint of wood smoke that seemed to infuse everything here, as if fire was a part of the air that all Africans breathed.

The words of the Maasai woman came to her. '*Wewe ni mama yake katika wakati huu.*' You are her mother at this moment.

This moment is all you have.

Essie picked up Mara's hand, turned it over and kissed the damp palm. She held it there, over her mouth, the little fingers pressed against her lips. She barely heard Simon and Carl talking together. She just breathed in Mara's smell. She imagined it filling her lungs, entering her blood, and travelling all the way to her heart.

FOURTEEN

The pool was a large circle set into a bed of pale rock, its edges fringed with reeds. It came into view some way off, as Essie rounded a heap of boulders. She stared in surprise. The other waterholes she'd seen up here were little more than large, deep puddles; this one was almost as big as the Swimming Bath down on the plains.

Essie hurried towards it. The pool had to be spring-fed, she realised – a part of the underground anatomy of the volcano. That meant that it could actually be hot or cold or somewhere in between. She hoped it was cool, so she could splash refreshing water on her sweaty face. The air was stifling. Tommy bleated as he trailed after her; Rudie could be heard panting from an open mouth.

As she came closer to the pool, Essie's step faltered. Ranged along one side were half-a-dozen tall stones, each about the height of a child. They were like featureless statues: a sculptor's blanks. They looked as if they could have been placed there deliberately, the way they were grouped, rather than dropped randomly by a flow of debris during an eruption or tumbled down the slopes by an earthquake.

Essie eyed the stones as she walked on. They were probably lava monoliths. One was taller than the others. Its position, relative to the slopes behind it, invited the eye to travel up to the volcano.

Essie was reminded of Neolithic sites in Europe – not of the scale of Stonehenge; more like the Devil's Arrows in Yorkshire. They were created for use in rituals connected with the sun, the stars, the moon – the changing seasons of life and death. But these stones, here at Magadi, could not have been transported and erected by humans – there was no precedent for this kind of large-scale activity in East Africa, let alone in this remote spot. Yet even while she knew all this, Essie couldn't help imagining that the distinctive stones, along with the surprising existence of the pool, were the outcome of something more than chance.

Looking back up towards the hillside boulders, Essie saw Simon approaching, holding Mara on his hip. A short way behind him was Carl. He'd taken time off from his own work today to join them in the foothills. The plan had arisen casually – Essie wasn't even sure exactly how it had happened. She told herself Ian would approve, though. After she'd informed him about her first visit to the Mission house, he'd said it was good to have a connection with Frank Marlow's flamingo man. That way, the Lawrences could call on his services when they needed a professional photographer. It could prove very useful. Ian had not yet met Carl Bergmann himself. He'd been too busy to issue an invitation to lunch at the camp. When the occasion did come around, Essie had a secret hope that Carl would pick up Mara, as he often did, and cuddle her against his chest. Then Ian would see how this other man enjoyed and admired the Hadza baby, instead of just treating her as an unwanted disruption to his world.

Essie watched the men as they came nearer – noting the moment when each one set eyes on the pool. She felt an odd pride that she had discovered the place first. While they walked down to join her, she moved closer to the water. She checked the reeds for signs of yellowing, but they looked healthy – green and supple. She noticed a dragonfly skimming the surface. Below the waterline tiny shrimps swam amid lacy strands of algae. There was nothing to suggest any leakage of carbon dioxide, *hewa mbaya*. Essie wanted to be extra cautious, though, with Mara being nearby. Shrugging off her rucksack, she felt in the side pocket for her matches. Then she knelt down among the reeds. As the blue-black head of the match ignited, a tiny flame flared. Essie moved her hand slowly over the surface of the water. The flame burned brightly, unwavering in the still air.

She got to her feet as Simon and Carl arrived at the water's edge. The three stood there, gazing at the pool. The small sounds they could hear – birds, insects, the squelch of their boots on the flattened reeds – seemed to intensify a pervasive quiet that no one was willing to break. Essie eyed Simon, wondering if he saw this as a sacred place – perhaps one where they should not linger. If he were a Maasai, she felt sure he would have this view. But then, if that were the case, he wouldn't have been here on the holy mountain in the first place.

Simon placed Mara on a cloth spread out in the shade of an overhanging rock right beside the pool. When she was happily occupied with trying to reach a leaf hanging from a nearby bush, he pulled off his boots and socks. Then, turning his back to Essie, he dropped his shorts and waded naked into the water. The pool quickly became deep, his body disappearing to his thighs.

Essie lowered her gaze. Peering through her lashes, she saw Carl pause for a few seconds, then follow Simon's example. She glimpsed the white of his skin, where it lay beyond the reach of the sun. She heard the slap of tiny waves against the sides of the pool as he launched himself in.

She turned to watch Mara while she weighed up her options. She could take off her boots and have a paddle. Or she could remove her trousers, too. On the other hand, stripping right down to her bra and pants would be no different to wearing a bikini. When she looked back the men were waist-deep in the water. They'd both been fully immersed; water dripped from their hair. Sun gleamed on their upper bodies – silver on black, and gold on white.

Essie took off her shirt and trousers quickly in case she lost her nerve. The air brushed her skin as she moved. She looked down at her bra. The lace was tatty. The elastic in the straps had perished, frilling the edges. Her underpants were baggy. She glanced at the others. They were not looking at her – she couldn't tell if they were being discreet or if their attention was drawn elsewhere, perhaps by the watchful presence of the grouped stones.

Wincing on tender feet, Essie picked her way through the reeds, mud oozing between her toes. Just as she reached the water, she paused. The idea of keeping parts of herself covered suddenly seemed like a false modesty – one that added too much significance to her body. Hadza and Maasai women alike attached no special meaning to their breasts. If they covered them with cloths, it was for practical reasons. Only the genitals were considered private. And even from the point of view of people back in Britain, nudity was not such a big thing. It was 1970, after all – not the fifties. On a summer holiday in Wales, Essie had been skinny-dipping with friends; at a music festival she'd attended, a small but noticeable portion of the women went topless. The Lawrences' obsession with protocol didn't apply up here on the mountain. There would be no goat herders or hunters turning up. Simon and Carl were the only people around. And they were both naked.

Reaching behind her, Essie unclipped her bra, then she removed her underpants. She tried to look nonchalant as she tossed the garments onto a rock. Her hair was already hanging loose, covering her neck against the sun. She quickly pulled it forward to hide her nipples.

She was ankle-deep in the water when she heard Mara crying. It was a half-hearted grumble that she knew well. It meant the baby could see that both she and Simon were right nearby, but that was not enough; she wanted to be held.

Crossing to where she lay, Essie picked her up. As she cradled Mara against her chest, she sensed the baby's instant awareness, matching her own, that something was different: bare skin was touching bare skin, the contact unbroken by clothes.

Mara buried her face against Essie's breast, moving her open hands over her skin like someone feeling their way in the dark. Essie closed her eyes as a tingle travelled up her spine. She felt the faint whisper of Mara's breath. She knew Simon and Carl were not far away – probably watching on. But in the moment she felt as if she and the baby were all alone together in their own private world.

Careful not to slip, she picked her way back through the reeds to the edge of the pool. Soon she and Mara were both half immersed in the water. Essie kept her feet planted apart, pressed into the fine gravel that layered the floor of the pool. She grasped the baby firmly under her arms. Particles of algae in the water made her skin slippery; Essie had a vision of the little body sliding from her grasp, sinking out of sight under the water. As if reading her thoughts, Mara arched her back, turning panicked eyes upwards.

'It's all right,' Essie murmured. 'I've got you.'

She repeated the phrase, needing to convince herself as much as Mara that her grip was secure. She watched the tension gradually fade from Mara's face, her arms and legs relaxing muscle by muscle. Eventually she was limp, floating weightless in Essie's arms. The baby became very still, then, as if her attention was directed inwards. After a few moments she suddenly began kicking her feet and splashing the water with her hands. A wide grin broke over her face. She'd just decided, Essie realised, that the pool was one enormous bathtub.

Carl and Simon waded over, drawn by the spectacle; the three adults stood around Mara, smiling at her expression of sheer joy. Essie watched her relishing the freedom of movement. The touch of sleek baby skin against her own was like a miracle. When she looked down through the water, tea-stained with tannin, the contrast between their two skin tones was lessened. It was as if the boundaries between adult and child, white and black, were soothed away.

Simon held Mara for a while so that Essie could bathe. She ducked underwater, rinsing the sweat from her hair, cooling her scalp. She swam below the surface – timing how long she could remain there, wondering whether, like Lorna, she might be good at holding her breath. Her lungs seemed to swell with the effort of waiting. She burst up through the water, gasping at the air, pushing back the hair from her face.

Carl met her gaze. She could see that he was taking in the image of her. Tangled hair around her shoulders, draping her breasts. Water running down her face. She smiled, blinking with wet lashes. 'It's so beautiful.'

He smiled back at her. She could tell that he understood how she felt. That everything, in this moment, was perfect. And it was all that mattered. The future, with all its worries, felt distant – as if it might never even arrive.

*

A stream of rusty water ran into the sink, catching a small spider and washing it away. Essie rinsed a cup and dried it with a tea towel, then added it to two others set out on a tray. Glancing through the dusty window she could see Simon sitting in a chair, his head bent over a pile of photographs. Next to him Mara was in Carl's arms, her fingers exploring the shape and feel of his watch. As Essie observed him, a shiver ran through her body. She could hardly believe she'd just been swimming naked in a pool – and not just in the presence of a fellow recipient of research funding, but a staff member as well. It was out of character for her to be so impulsive. She couldn't bring herself to regret her decision, though.

Snapshots of the scene played over and over in her head, bringing a faint smile to her face. As she looked out towards Simon, Carl and Mara, she was aware that the time at the pool had created a new sense of intimacy between the four of them. They were like an odd little family, gathered here at the Mission house.

Essie carried the tray outside, loaded with cups of tea. Simon was still poring over the photographs. When she'd left to boil the kettle, Carl had been explaining to him exactly how the content of a single instant could be recorded by the click of a button and then reproduced on paper. As she reached them and set down the tray, Carl held up his camera.

'I'm wondering if you'd like me to take some photos of Mara,' he said. 'Not for my folio. For you.' He nodded at the baby. 'And maybe for her, one day.'

One day . . . Essie stared at him, the words reverberating in her head. She could barely imagine the future he was alluding to: a time when there was an older Mara, who spoke in Hadza and had a proper tribal name. Essie hoped Carl was right – that the girl might want to see the pictures. It would mean that Nandamara and Giga had kept alive the story of this early part of her life – the months she'd spent with her white-skinned, stand-in mother.

'Thank you,' Essie said. 'I'd love you to do that.' Putting aside what Mara might one day make of her baby photos, she knew she would treasure them herself in the future – when they were all that she had left.

'I'll print them up when I get to a dark room and post them back to you.' As Carl spoke he removed the lens cap from his camera and began checking the aperture, making adjustments. Small sounds punctuated the quiet. He held the camera poised in front of Mara and took the first shot. Then he wound the film on, before focusing again. Mara followed him with her eyes as he took another picture, then another. The sequence was fluid, like a slow dance – a magic ritual that would capture the present and hold it still, for the rest of time.

Carl was about to put the camera down, but then Essie held out her hand. 'Let me do some.' She wanted to take her own pictures of Mara, but also some of the two men as well.

Carl's camera was bigger than the one Essie was used to, but not difficult to operate. She took a series of shots, then put it down and took Mara back into her arms. As she watched Carl pouring out cups of tea, she visualised the images she'd caught on film. There was Mara gazing solemnly into the lens, the whites of her eyes standing out against the blackness of skin and iris. Her chubby hands reaching for Carl's light meter. The close-up of her feet with the rows of toes, like peas lined up in a pod. Then there was the one of Simon and Carl, with Mara held between them.

But the picture Essie most wanted to see when it was printed had been taken by Carl. It was of her and Mara. Essie remembered the moment when the shutter had clicked. Mara was lying in her arms, smiling up into her face. With one hand she was touching Essie's lips. With the other, she'd grabbed a thick strand of blonde hair. She clutched it tightly in her fist, as if she planned never to let it go.

As they sipped their tea, Simon's attention turned back to the collection of prints that was spread over the table. He sorted through the images.

'But which place is your true home?' he asked Carl. Essie guessed he was picking up the conversation the two had been having while she was inside.

'They all are,' Carl replied. He turned to Essie. 'I was telling Simon that my parents live in France, but my father is half Swedish and half German. My mother is American. When I was a kid I went to international schools in the Middle East as well as Vienna – Dad worked in the mining industry. So I've got friends and relatives all over the world.' He grinned. 'Lots of places to call home.'

'But which is the land you care about most?' Simon persisted.

Essie eyed Carl, keen to hear his answer. He shuffled through the photographs again, pulling out one of a sweeping vista of snowy mountains.

'My uncle lives here – in the Austrian Alps. I've been visiting him there ever since I was a kid. It's one of the most beautiful places I've ever seen.'

Simon whistled admiringly through his teeth. Essie could see why he'd be impressed by the many layers of peaks lined up behind one another; it would be an extraordinary sight to someone accustomed only to seeing single mountains rising from the plains – Kilimanjaro, Meru, or the volcanoes of the Rift Valley, including Ol Doinyo Lengai.

'I love the deserts of New Mexico, too,' Carl continued. 'I visit my cousin there when I get the chance. But some of my favourite places in the world I've discovered through my work.' He found another print and held it up. 'This one, for example – in Tasmania.'

Essie's lips parted as she gazed at the black-and-white image in his hands. She took in the mounds of tussock grass pushing up between granite boulders, and the bare earth pocked with small dark holes. Without even deciding to, she reached out to grasp the print, bringing it closer. In the background of the picture, near the crest of a grassy slope, there was a man. At first glance it appeared as if he was wearing a huge furry cloak. But on further examination Essie saw that he had a long stick resting over his shoulders. Hanging from it were lots of identical birds – at least a dozen – tied on by their feet. Their bodies were mounds of fluffy feathers; wingtips and beaks pointed down. There was another man following behind, carrying a similar load. The two collections of birds, lined up in their neat rows, made a bold pattern against the sky.

'I've seen that . . .' Essie's voice was soft, almost a murmur to herself. If someone had asked her, she wouldn't have been able to evoke the scene: the photograph had to be mirroring something stored too deeply in her memory.

Carl looked at Essie. 'You've seen the muttonbirding?'

Essie nodded. She couldn't find any words.

Simon leaned over to look at the picture. 'These men are good hunters. Do they use a bow and arrow?'

Carl shook his head. 'Those birds are chicks, pulled out from the burrows.'

Simon frowned. 'They are very big.'

'They have to be fattened up ready for long-distance flying.'

'Do they taste good?'

'I like them,' Carl said. 'But lots of people don't.'

Simon studied the picture intently. When he looked up his expression cleared as if he'd just solved a puzzle. 'These hunters are the descendants of those first black people!'

Carl nodded. 'Yes, they are. So were most of the folk I met at the rookery.'

Simon pointed to the faces of the men. 'But their skin is white.'

'They can look very different from one another,' Essie explained. 'Some are a lot more like their ancestors.'

She was going on what she'd learned from Arthur. When he was collecting his stone tools – back when he first met Lorna – he'd taken every opportunity to seek out local people known to have Aboriginal heritage, in case they knew of possible research sites. When colleagues or students asked – as they sometimes did, while viewing his collection – he would describe them. He liked to say that while many had curly hair and dark olive skin, others were as blonde and blue-eyed as his own daughter.

Carl turned to Essie. 'Who was it that took you muttonbirding?'

'Well, it was . . . something to do with my mother's family.'

'Was she part Aboriginal, then?' Carl asked. He used the past tense because Essie had already told him Lorna was dead – not the details; just that one bare fact.

Essie didn't answer straightaway. It was an ordinary, simple question, yet it made her heartbeat quicken. Then her reply came in a rush.

'No, she wasn't. I know that, because I remember when someone once asked her. I was still in primary school. We were at a garden fete and we met a man from the university. He was wearing a navy blazer with gold buttons – I remember him clearly. He knew about my father's collection of Tasmanian stone tools.' Essie paused, glancing up at Simon and Carl. 'It's what Dad is famous for, in academic circles. Anyway, the man asked if Mum was a Tasmanian. When she said yes, he asked if she had black blood in her veins. He might have been joking, but no one laughed. Mum didn't say anything. She just stood there. Dad was the one who replied. And he said no. Definitely not.'

As she talked Essie kept staring at the picture; she couldn't take her eyes away.

'And your mother never said anything different to you, when you were on your own?' asked Carl. He was choosing his words carefully, Essie could tell – not wanting to be too inquisitive.

'No. Mum really didn't speak about Tasmania, or her family, at all. She said we were in England now, and it was important to live in the present . . .' Essie was talking to herself, she realised, as much as the others. 'But if she did have Aboriginal blood, somewhere in her family, I can see why she wouldn't have told anyone – including me. She had enough trouble trying to fit in, without making things any more difficult. The English are very big on breeding, especially in a place like Cambridge . . .' She smiled grimly. 'I don't think Dad would have wanted it to get out, either.'

'It is a matter of shame?' Simon looked intrigued. 'The Hadza are despised by the other tribes – the Maasai, Kikuyu, Wagogo. They do not admire anything we do. Is it the same with these other people?' He pointed again at the men in the photograph.

'It's hard to explain,' Essie said. Her head was a blur of mismatched thoughts.

'Your father probably knows the truth,' Carl said. 'You could ask him. If it were me, I'd be really keen to know.' His eyes were bright with interest. 'I'd want to go and find my relatives. Spend time with them.'

There was a brief quiet, broken only by the racket of the

flamingos, travelling across from the lake. Essie shook her head slowly. 'I don't want to ask him.'

'Why not?' Simon demanded. There was a note of outrage in his voice. Essie could tell he felt a sense of kinship with those faraway people in the muttonbird rookery; it was making him unusually bold.

'I don't believe he would tell me the truth.' Essie bit her lip, shocked by the reality of what she'd just said. She handed back the picture. 'Anyway, my mother was right about living in the present. There's no point in looking back.'

Simon raised his eyebrows. 'But every day you are busy with discovering the past!'

Essie looked at him in silence; she could think of nothing to say in response. She crossed to Carl and bent to pick up the baby. Mara stirred, letting out a mumble of protest. Essie lifted her against her shoulder, patting her back. She walked a little way off and stood gazing out beyond the boundaries of what had once been Wolfgang Stein's garden. Her eyes settled on a huge desert rose, its spreading branches dotted with pink blooms. As she absorbed the vivid colour, standing out against the backdrop of bare earth and stone, another scene came into her mind.

She saw pale rocks patterned with orange lichen – so brightly coloured it looked as if the stone had been daubed with paint. The boulders bordered a beach formed from pure white sand. Turquoise sea washed in over it, breaking on the shore. Essie could feel the water swirling around her feet. White foam settled on her skin. From overhead came the cry of seabirds. They hovered against the crystal-blue sky, suspended like marionette puppets in the wind.

She felt a shiver of cold. Strong currents pulled at her little girl's legs.

There was someone with her. A figure bobbing in the surf – diving like a seal, then rising to break the surface. A hand sweeping hair back from a sun-tanned face. A smile, a wave.

The picture was clear for a few moments, but then began to fade. As Essie tried to catch it, the memory seeped away like water between stones. Then it was gone.

She turned back towards the house. Gesturing at the sun, she called across to the others.

'It's getting late. We should go back.'

A pillar of thick smoke rose into the air. It seemed to be coming from in front of the Dining Tent. Essie watched it as she pushed the pram across from the parking area. She wasn't alarmed; she guessed Ian must have asked Baraka to prepare an old-fashioned safari meal for Diana to experience. It was a tradition here at Magadi; visitors liked to imagine they were in a scene from a Hemingway novel, or Karen Blixen's *Out of Africa*. It was a bit early to have started a cooking fire, though – the sun was still well above the horizon. Baraka must have wanted to make sure there were plenty of glowing coals to rake over his damper. As these thoughts ran through Essie's mind, she focused on the smell of smoke, the sight of it rising against the sky. She wanted to forget the unsettling conversation at the Mission house – to wrap it up in her mind like a cocoon of spun silk, the contents hidden away.

As she neared the tent, she ran her fingers through her hair. Normally she tied it back so it would dry smooth and tidy. Today she'd left it loose and the ends had turned curly. Almost certainly, no one else would notice, but Essie knew it was a telltale clue that her workday had not followed its usual course. She leaned over the pram, peering through the draped mosquito netting to check on Mara. The baby was sometimes unhappy at this time of the day – not hungry or tired, but grizzly. When this happened, Essie tried to keep her away from Ian, Julia and Diana. They didn't like the intrusion on their peace and quiet. Ian would look at Essie in frustration, as if she was deliberately allowing Mara to misbehave. Now, though, the baby was sound asleep. It had been a big day. Essie watched Mara's face – wondering if memories of the time at the pool lingered with her, perhaps even finding their way into her dreams.

Essie rounded the clump of bushes next to the Dining Tent. Julia was sitting out by the fireplace holding a long stick. Something large and flat was lying in front of her, flames licking around its edges. Essie caught her breath as she recognised the vibrant colours of the Ol Doinyo sunset, melting in the heat. And the signature in the corner of the canvas, about to be consumed: *Mirella*.

It was too late for Essie to change course. She pushed the pram over to one of the chairs and sat down, pretending everything was normal. Julia ignored her tentative greeting; she was poking the painting further into the fire. The woman's hair was dishevelled – almost as if she, too, had been swimming. Her bun had half fallen out; loose grey strands hung around her face. Her cheek was smudged with ash and there was a burn on her trouser leg. She was staring grimly into the fire.

Essie looked around for Ian or Diana. Or even Kefa. But no one was in view. She watched as Julia stabbed the painting with her stick. A blue flame leapt through a jagged hole.

'What are you doing?' Essie asked carefully. It was a rhetorical question – the answer was being played out in front of her. But it was all she could think of to say. She noticed a crystal tumbler at Julia's feet, and an empty whisky bottle lying on its side nearby.

Julia didn't answer. She just pushed the canvas further into the flames. A portion of another painting was revealed, lying underneath it. And there was something else there, too. Essie recognised the distinctive black-and-yellow borders of a *National Geographic* magazine. Her jaw dropped. It was the one with William's photograph on the front. Only fragments of his face remained – an eye, a cheek, one thick brow and just the wristband of the famous Rolex.

Essie stared in astonishment. Could Julia have brought the magazine out here by mistake, and somehow it had ended up in the fire?

'What are you doing?' she asked again.

The air was full of the crackle of flaming cloth and the fragrant smell of burning oil paints. Julia was nodding to herself as if listening to an inner voice. Eventually she looked up at Essie.

'Monogamy is not normal among mammals, you know. It's a huge disadvantage in evolutionary terms.' Her tone was conversational; she might have been embarking on an impromptu after-supper lecture – except that this particular topic was not exactly in her field. 'Swapping partners is good for the gene pool. Number one: it increases diversity, raising the chances of useful mutations, thus enabling evolution. Number two . . .' She was counting the points off on her fingers. 'It increases the rate of offspring survival. The passing on of genes, as we know, is the whole purpose of life. That is why so many traditional societies allow people to have multiple partners.' Julia smiled brightly. 'As, of course, do we.'

Essie pressed her lips together. She had been in this position too many times before: dealing with someone whose behaviour made no sense.

'Where is Ian?' she asked.

Julia nodded in the direction of the Palace. 'Having a meeting.'

Essie turned towards the orange tent. Through one of the plastic windows she could see the outline of two figures. Ian and Diana were standing close together, almost touching at the hips. Essie looked across to her mother-in-law. Julia's eyebrows were raised, her head tilted suggestively to one side. Essie's lips parted. Was Julia suggesting that something inappropriate was going on between her son and Diana?

Essie pushed away a lock of hair that hung over her eyes, her finger snagging on a tangled curl. For an instant, she was caught up in the insinuation. Then she shook her head. She, of all people, should understand that Ian and Diana were working as a team at the moment – and that jealousy would be a misplaced emotion. She was, herself, making regular visits to the home of Carl Bergmann. (She hadn't mentioned this fact to Ian or Julia, but told herself they'd approve. After all, Ian had said he was glad of the potentially useful connection with the photographer.) Essie was working alone with Simon, too, for that matter.

She looked back to the tent. It was very possible that the reason Ian was over there now with Diana was that he didn't want the visitor to see the spectacle Julia was making of herself. Having a mother who behaved bizarrely was part of Essie's family story – not his. Still, Essie felt a sense of unease. From the very beginning – when Frank had arranged sundowners at the Steps – Diana Marlow had gravitated towards Ian. She'd even told Essie how lucky she was to be married to a man like him. But there was nothing unusual about women paying attention to Ian Lawrence. Essie knew that Julia would have been used to seeing William at the centre of attention, too. Ian had inherited his role from his father. Apparently he'd also adopted one of William's most effective mannerisms – the one where he looked down at the ground or the tabletop as he talked; when he was about to deliver his major point he suddenly lifted his eyes, fixing his audience with an intense gaze. The effect was mesmerising. Onlookers felt deeply privileged to be present. The Lawrence men knew how to be perfect hosts, as well as effective teachers. Julia's husband would have fended off the advances of admiring women, just as Ian had done in the days when the camp was awash with visitors. Ian and William were the patriarchs of Magadi. All the academics, students, volunteers – whether male or female – were like their children. Nothing more.

Except that Julia was, right now, burning Mirella's paintings. Essie recalled the ruined drawings in the storeroom – the suppressed rage suggested by the deep lines scored in the paper. Then, there was the primatologist, Alice Jones. Julia's resentment of her was clear. Perhaps it was nothing to do with the naming of the *korongo*, or the dirty orphan bonobos, or the woeful manners. Maybe both of these women had had affairs with William . . .

Essie stared into the fire. Julia had always spoken with such admiration of her husband. When she brushed the dust off the memorial plaque down at the Steps, she wore such a tender look on her face. Julia must have loved William. Presumably he had loved her. Perhaps a deal had been struck between them – but one that only part of Julia had truly been able to accept. Essie reined in her speculation. She was only guessing at the truth . . .

She turned her thoughts back to her own husband, and Diana. She checked the orange tent once more. As she watched, the two figures moved back from the window, disappearing into the shadows.

'I'm sure they'll be over soon,' Essie said. 'They have to eat.'

Julia just looked at her. 'A man has his needs. They have to be met. We know that.' She let out a short, mirthless laugh. Then she shook her head. 'It used to be different. Before we lost Robbie. I know it was my fault. But I couldn't help it.' Her voice was strained, half strangled in her throat. 'I had nothing to give, to anyone. I was hardly alive.' A moan escaped her lips. 'I didn't survive. They said I would, but I didn't.'

Essie cast desperate glances around her. Whether the whisky was playing a part in all this or not, she didn't want to be the one to deal with Julia's distress. On the other hand, she wasn't keen to just walk into the Palace, interrupting Diana and Ian. She turned instead towards the kitchen. The cook had known the Lawrences for decades – he might know how to respond . . .

'I'm going to find Baraka.' She spoke in a low, steady voice as if she were a nurse from Fulbourn, or one of the well-trained nannies described in *Complete Babycare*.

After checking that Mara was still asleep, and that the net was correctly draped to keep out insects, Essie hurried over to the kitchen. Inside, the air was misty with steam rising from two pots bubbling on the stove. A knife lay on a large chopping board. Potato starch, drying into smears of white, covered the blade. Baraka must have been here only a short time ago, cutting up vegetables, but now the place was empty.

Essie rushed to the staff camp, interrupting an argument between two workers in order to ask where she could find the cook. She waited impatiently for an answer. Someone was sent off to talk to someone else. Eventually she learned that Baraka was 'searching for bush medicine' – a euphemism for using the lavatory.

Back in the kitchen, Essie surveyed the shelves. If nothing else, providing Julia with some food to go with the alcohol seemed a good idea. She grabbed a box of water crackers. Beside it was a tin of smoked mussels – probably part of Baraka's plan for *hors d'oeuvres*. She took a banana from a long stalk trailing from a hook on the wall.

Balancing all the items on a plate, Essie walked back towards the fireplace. Ahead, the plume rising from the fire had thickened. The large painting must be fully alight. As the oil paints burned, the smoke turned pink, green, yellow. Clouds of colour rose and dispersed, as if the spirit of the artwork was being released into the air.

Reaching the fireplace, Essie saw that Julia's chair was vacant. She felt a wash of relief. Putting down the food, she crossed to the pram. As she lifted the net, she froze in alarm. Mara was not there.

Essie spun round, searching for Julia. She had to have taken the baby – even though she'd never come close to picking her up before and had avoided even being near her. Essie strode into the Dining Tent, scanning the vacant space. Then she jogged across to the Work Hut. Her heart pounded. She told herself not to be alarmed. Julia had drunk too much whisky. The alcohol had caused pent-up emotions to spin out of control. But that didn't mean she'd suddenly transformed into someone dangerous. Yet in just a few seconds – less than a minute – a myriad frightening scenarios raced through Essie's mind.

Then she saw the silhouette of a tall, still figure standing at the edge of the camp. Julia was staring into the lowering sun, her face half turned against the glare. She held Mara in her arms.

Essie moved slowly up to her as if approaching a wild animal. When she was close, she leaned around to see her face. Julia was gazing down at the baby. One finger, knobbly with arthritis, touched her plump cheek. Mara stirred, then started whimpering. Julia lifted her to her chest, jogging her gently. Mara must have sensed that she was in the arms of a stranger. She began wailing. It was her fearful cry – the one that sounded like the keening of a bird.

'Shshsh. It's all right. Don't cry.' There was a pleading note in Julia's voice. 'Don't cry. Don't cry. Don't cry.'

Julia repeated the words as if chanting a spell. Gradually, Mara quietened. But when Julia turned to Essie, her own eyes were brimming with tears. Her expression was bleak. She was like a prisoner who has long given up hope of release.

'She woke up,' Julia said. She handed over the baby, expertly supporting the heavy head with her fingers, and gathering in the arms and legs. The gestures looked automatic, as if her hands still remembered their old skills. When Mara was settled in Essie's arms, Julia turned and walked away.

Essie stared into the fire while she held the bottle for Mara to drink. The sunset painting was burned almost to ash. Baraka had removed the whisky bottle and glass. At the same time he'd retrieved the singed spine, which was virtually all that remained of the precious magazine. He had maintained an impassive expression while doing this – if he knew any more than Essie about the meaning of what had happened here, he gave nothing away.

He'd returned to the kitchen now. Essie was trying to decide whether to go to Julia's tent herself and check that she was there, or to summon Ian from the Palace to do it. Either way, she had to finish feeding Mara first; the screams of a hungry baby would only strain tensions even further.

The bottle was almost empty when Essie looked up to see Ian approaching. He smoothed back his hair with one hand as he walked. When he reached the fireside he stood still, his eyes widening as he took in the bits of burned canvas; the unusual smell; the fragments of the *National Geographic*. He glanced back over his shoulder. Essie guessed he was trying to work out how to conceal from Diana that something inexplicable had occurred. But it was too late. The woman was already approaching. When she reached the fireside she poked at the ashes with the toe of her boot.

Ian turned to Essie. 'What's going on?' he demanded. He looked from her to Mara as if he thought the answer to his question could somehow be linked with the Hadza baby.

'Julia burned Mirella's paintings. And the magazine with William on the cover.'

As she spoke, Essie watched Ian's expression. The date on the paintings was 1955. That meant he would have been twenty-four when Mirella was here at Magadi. He'd finished his degree and returned home. It was quite possible he'd known there was something going on between the artist and his father. Yet Ian liked to portray a picture of his parents as having a perfect marriage. It was the image held by the public: William and Julia Lawrence were the golden couple of archaeology; they'd survived a terrible tragedy, and yet, supporting one another, they had continued their important work. If Ian had known for years that his father was unfaithful, and that the betrayal was a source of anguish for his mother, then he had kept the facts well hidden.

But as Essie scanned Ian's face she could see that he was confused – and then, as his thoughts raced on, deeply shocked. He screwed up his eyes as if tasting a bitter brew. She saw him reject the idea of his father's infidelity, spitting it out like something bad.

'Julia said the paintings should be taken down. She's tired of them.' Ian turned to Diana. 'That's what she said, the other night . . .'

Diana lit a cigarette, narrowing her gaze as she blew out a stream of smoke. 'She didn't think much of the painter, either.'

There was a dense quiet, heightened by raucous laughter over in the staff camp.

'I think you should go to Julia's tent.' Essie gave Ian a meaningful look. 'She's . . . not herself.'

In his eyes she saw a flicker of what looked like fear. It only showed for a second, then he was ushering Diana to a seat. 'She's been working too hard. Overdoing it. She probably just wants to be left alone. I'll send Baraka over with some supper.'

Ian, Diana and Essie ate their own meal quickly, with barely any conversation. The smell of burning paint floated like a pall in the air. Mara must have picked up on the mood of the adults. She'd been placed on her baboon pelt with some toys but wouldn't settle. Ian kept throwing irritated looks in her direction. Before long, Essie decided to leave the table.

It was only later in the evening, when Ian joined her in their tent, that it became clear where her husband's emotions had led him. He said nothing at first – just sat on the end of the bed untying his shoelaces. Then he drew in a breath, letting it out with a loud sigh.

'I went to see Julia, but she was asleep.' He turned to face Essie. 'It's your fault, you know – that she's upset.'

Essie's eyes widened with outrage as she took in his words. She'd put on her nightdress, but had been sitting up, waiting for the report on Julia. Now, her hands gripped her knees. Her lips were drawn tight.

'This is about *your* family – *your* parents,' she burst out. 'Don't try and blame me.' Essie swallowed, shocked by her own reaction. But she couldn't stop. It was as if all the words she'd bitten back – ever since she'd first arrived here – had mounted up inside her and were now erupting. 'And it's not just about Mirella, by the way. It's Robbie. You both act as if he never existed. No one even mentions his name. Having Mara here brings up the past – I understand that. But Robbie disappeared a long time ago. It's time to face up to what happened.'

Ian's hand froze, halfway through removing his shoe. 'We have dealt with the death of my brother. Maybe not in the way others would. But it has worked for us.'

Essie just looked at him. Anything she said would be a mistake, she was sure. But still, she couldn't stop. 'No, it hasn't. Not for Julia, anyway. It's all catching up with her. Can't you see that?'

Tiny muscles flinched around Ian's clenched jaw. 'We were fine. We were short of funds for a while – but aside from that, everything was good. Until you brought that baby here.'

He pointed across at Mara, who was tucked up in her cot. The jab of his finger underlined his cold words. He made the word 'baby' sound like a curse. Essie followed his gaze. Mara's face was lit from the side by a hurricane lantern hanging nearby. Essie took in the rounded contours of her cheeks, the curve of her forehead. She looked so innocent, trusting.

Suddenly Essie was on her feet, sweeping her into her arms. Without another word she strode towards the door. She headed for the nursery, Rudie trailing after her. The moon had yet to rise and she was careful not to stumble in the dark. As she picked her away along the path, she listened for footsteps behind her. Surely Ian would realise he'd been unfair and come after her? But she heard nothing except the usual night noises, accompanied by the faint burble of a transistor radio, travelling all the way over from the Palace on the still night air.

In the nursery she settled Mara in the bassinet. She placed a teddy, a rag doll and the grey plush elephant in there too – ranged around the baby's head so that she'd see them watching over her when she woke in the morning. After rocking her back to sleep, Essie climbed into the guest bed. She lay awake, listening again. Maybe Ian would still come. If he did, she decided, she'd refuse to return to their tent; he could join her here, in this room that was a testament to Mara's place in her life.

An hour passed, maybe two. The double bed felt wide and empty. Essie pictured Mara not far away – the baby's body a small island of warmth. Finally, she got up and moved her into the bed. Mara barely stirred as she was laid down, set a bit apart in case Essie rolled over.

Reaching across, Essie gently stroked the little hand that rested in the space between them. With her thumb she drew small circles on the wrinkled palm, round and round and round. Eventually she lulled herself to sleep.

FIFTEEN

Essie opened her eyes, staring into the shadowy gloom. It was still night-time. She rolled automatically towards the side of the bed, ready to attend to Mara before Ian was woken. For a few seconds she was confused: in the meagre moonlight she could see only a patch of sisal matting where the fossil-crate cot should be. Then she remembered – she was not in her own bedroom. She turned to the other half of the mattress. Mara was lying there, a dark shape against the white sheets. She was deeply asleep, arms thrown up beside her head, snuffling a little as she breathed. Whatever had caused Essie to wake, it had not been her.

A breeze blew in through the gauze window, stirring the mobile above the change table. Essie could just pick out the shapes of the moon and the cow. As she watched them turning slowly on their strings, the events of the evening came back to her. Suddenly she was wide-awake. The smouldering remains of the anger that had driven her to move in here last night flared up again. It didn't take long, though – as she replayed the sequence of events – for outrage to ebb away into regret. She wished she'd just let Ian's words flow past her. In the morning, she would have to repair the situation – apologise for overreacting. Ian would be polite, but deliberately cool. Essie would fall into her role of being talkative and bright, trying to fill the loaded quiet. She would be on tenterhooks from the moment she arrived at the Dining Tent until she got the chance to escape to the foothills.

It was a pattern she knew well. She rarely challenged Ian on anything – she only even contemplated it when she was certain she had a good case, and then she rehearsed her speech beforehand, just to make sure. Yet anything she said that could be construed as criticism led inevitably to conflict – and she always ended up feeling that she was the one who'd been unreasonable, unfair, unfeeling . . . However serious the original issue had been, the distress of the argument seemed much worse.

Essie tried to fall back to sleep. She worked on relaxing her body and banishing thoughts from her head. But as she lay still she noticed a strange whistling sound. It was elusive: when she focused on it, the noise blended with the foreground buzz of insects and the croaking of frogs over in the camp waterhole. She lifted her head, listening intently.

The sound became louder. Then it was joined by something else – a rhythmic thrumming in the air. Throwing back the sheet, she parted the net and climbed out of bed. Quietly, so as not to disturb Mara, she unzipped the tent door. Rudie followed her outside, his snout raised to sniff the air.

She looked up into the night sky. In the soft light of a half moon, thousands of flamingos were on the wing. They formed a wide ribbon, clustered together as if following a busy highway across the skies. Coming from the direction of the lake, they streamed over Magadi Gorge before wheeling away to the north. Though Essie had seen this mass migration happening before, it still seemed too extraordinary to be real.

The birds flew low, almost hugging the horizon. The pattern of dark shapes was set against the slate-grey backdrop of a clear sky streaked with wispy cloud. The birds' bodies formed straight lines from their heads to the ends of their feet. Wings flapped with a slow, steady beat. In the half dark the pink plumage had turned grey; the deeper reds were almost black.

Aside from the strange sounds that must have woken Essie – whispering into her subconscious – the birds were unnervingly quiet. This was normal, she knew. Often, on the night the flamingos arrived at Magadi, no one in the camp happened to wake up and witness the event. The word would go around some time the following morning. *Ndege wamekuja!* The birds have come! It was the same story when they departed. As she strained her ears into the night Essie remembered that Carl had once told her about the soft whistling noises she could hear. He named them 'night calls'. Passed from one bird to another, they were intended to keep the flocks together and share warnings of danger. Even knowing all this, though, Essie couldn't shake the sense that the flamingos were stealing away from Magadi in secret. They hadn't even waited, as they always did, to travel by the light of a full moon.

Essie wondered if Carl was awake, watching the birds fly away. She could imagine the disappointment falling over him like a heavy fog. Whatever the reason for the mass exodus, it had one clear meaning for him: the Flamingo Project was now over, before it had even begun.

As Essie stood there gazing up, a tiny shape drifted down towards her. She followed the path of a downy feather, turning in slow spirals. It landed not far from where she stood – a curl of pink, resting on the stony ground.

*

The headlights were long fingers of yellow, feeling their way over the terrain. Essie leaned forward, watching the track. On the seat beside her, Mara lay in the carrycot staring up through the windscreen. She was wide-eyed and alert as if even at this young age she felt the taste of an unexpected adventure. Rudie was in the rear of the Land Rover, his head resting over the back of Essie's seat. Sitting beside him was Tommy. He'd woken up as Essie was creeping past his enclosure. He'd made so much noise butting his head against the gate that she'd had to run back and get him. Now, as she drove, she looked across to the horizon. There was a hint of light there that did not belong to the moon. She had lost time being delayed by Tommy, as well as preparing bottles for Mara; sunrise was not far away.

Soon, the residents of Magadi Camp would begin to stir. She pictured Diana in a silky nightgown, lying in the wide soft bed shrouded with lace-edged mosquito nets. She saw Julia in her narrow cot, lying straight and still, eyes closed against the memory of the previous evening. In the staff camp the Africans would be leaving their army stretchers, heading to the pools for a wash. Last of all, Essie thought of Ian – waking up alone in their bed. His first concern would be how he was going to explain that his wife had spent the night in the nursery; there were no secrets in the camp. He could use the excuse of an unsettled baby. However, it would not be long before someone let him know that Essie, Mara, the dog and the gazelle were all absent from the camp, and that one of the Land Rovers was gone. Then the note Essie had scrawled and left in the nursery would be handed to him.

I've gone for a drive.

The brief message was all Essie could think of as she'd hurried to leave. She knew it made no sense: nobody at Magadi went driving – wasting fuel – for fun. Ian would conclude that she was still angry and had decided to punish him by disappearing. He'd be surprised – and very annoyed. Her absence at breakfast would be impossible to explain casually away. And he already had Julia to deal with, plus a guest to think of as well.

Essie steered into the space in front of the Mission house and brought the Land Rover to a halt. Then she sat still, her fingers grasping the ignition key. Tension brewed inside her. She could not imagine how she was going to explain, later on, why she had come here. It would mean admitting that her connection with the photographer had gone way beyond what had been asked of her. She'd have to confess that she and Carl Bergmann had become friends. She feared that when she did this, Ian would somehow be able to see inside her. He'd know about the swim in the waterhole. He'd know how, in Carl's presence, Essie found herself observing all the small details of the man's face, his body, the way he spoke. What Ian wouldn't see, perhaps, was the way Carl helped Essie with Mara. How he shared her enjoyment of the baby. How his conversations, ranging beyond the topic of his work, caught her interest. Essie would honestly be able to say that this trip was the first time she'd deliberately visited Carl without being in the company of Simon – but that was not going to prevent Ian being shocked, jealous, angry.

Essie pushed aside thoughts of Ian as she climbed out of the Land Rover. She paused to breathe in the marshy smell of the lake. Flamingos were still passing overhead but the flocks were smaller, forming a threadbare swathe of dusky pink. After picking up Mara, she held the rear door open for Tommy and Rudie to jump out. Then she headed for the path that led down the side of the house.

Soon she was crunching her way over the gravel, treading carefully in the gloom. She turned her focus to what she was going to say to Carl. She hadn't come here just to make sure he knew the birds were leaving – after all, he couldn't do anything to stop them. She wanted to offer him comfort and support as he faced the bad news for his project. When she'd been back at the camp watching the birds fly overhead, it had seemed obvious – urgent – that she should head to the Mission house. But now she doubted herself. She and Carl had only met a short time ago, yet she'd rushed to his side like a lifelong friend.

Glancing up at a window she saw a glimmer of lantern light – Carl must already have been woken by the birds. She walked on, rounding the rear corner of the building. Then she came to a halt. In front of her was the boxy shape of the jeep. Peering into the dimness she could see that its open back was loaded with gear. The vehicle had been packed hastily. Large and small containers were jumbled together, and loose objects just tossed in. A few clothes that looked as if they'd been grabbed from the washing line were lying on top. Essie turned towards the verandah. Light spilled from the open back door. The silver camera cases were visible, standing in a line in the hallway.

Essie stared mutely as the meaning of the scene sank in. She'd realised that the birds' disappearance meant Carl's work here was now done. But she'd assumed he would spend some time packing, winding up the project. The *Gari la maji* was still down at the lake, after all, and hides were dotted around the shore. Carl was meant to have been here for at least another month or longer. Collapsed into a few moments, Essie revisited some of the times they'd shared. Then, she thought of all the things they still had plans to do. Simon was going to guide them to a place called the Shifting Sands that the Hadza hunters knew. The strange dunes that moved from place to place were formed from black sand containing magnetic particles. If you threw a handful into the air, the grains formed into clumps before falling to the ground . . .

Carl walked outside. He was wearing his usual faded shorts and shirt, his feet bare. His dress didn't convey a mood of relaxation now, though; it just matched the tired look on his face. He stood near the verandah steps looking up at the sky. His lips were parted, as if he still couldn't believe what he was seeing. Essie approached him, scuffing the gravel with her boots to announce her presence.

Carl turned to her, his eyes widening with surprise. Then he smiled. 'Essie! You're here!' He took a step towards her.

As Essie smiled back, she glanced up at the birds passing overhead. She knew she should be saying something about them flying away – but that was no longer in the forefront of her mind. Instead she gestured at the jeep, and then the boxes in the hallway. 'You're leaving.' Her throat clamped on the words, tangling the sounds.

'I have to follow the birds,' Carl said. 'They might still breed, somewhere else.'

Essie nodded silently. Of course – it made sense. There could still be a chance to salvage the Flamingo Project. 'You're going now – straightaway?'

'I've got to get over to Serengeti and use the radio. I'll get better transmission there. I need to speak to people up north, across the border. When I know where the birds have settled, I'll drive straight there. I won't be coming back here first.' Regret was evident in Carl's voice, and in the way he stood with his hands hanging helplessly at his sides.

A look travelled across the space between them. It seemed to thicken in the air like the dust of the Shifting Sands. Essie could barely breathe. In that instant she saw herself swinging her legs up into Carl's jeep, settling back into the seat. She heard the roar of the engine, racing across the plains. She wasn't thinking about Ian, or Julia, or the camp. She wasn't even thinking about Mara, and the return of Nandamara. It was a vision freed from the constraints of reality. Anything was possible.

Then she felt the familiar nudge of Tommy's bony head against her knee. The interruption was enough to break the spell. Essie walked on, up the steps to the verandah.

'Thank you for coming.' Carl said. 'I was going to stop at the camp and say goodbye.' He looked almost shy for a second. 'I was thinking of you, during the night. I wanted you to be awake too – and know what was going on . . .' He smiled wryly at his own words. What difference could it make, whether Essie knew or not?

But it did, Essie understood. It would have made him feel less alone.

Carl gestured at the sky, which still held only a hint of the coming dawn. 'There's time for a cup of tea.'

'Thanks,' Essie said. 'I'd love one.'

The exchange was so ordinary that it released the tension. Carl put out his arms to take Mara. Essie watched him look fondly into the baby's face, his head pulled back, chin tucked into his neck. 'What about you, little one? Are you coming inside?'

Essie followed him along the hall. She saw more equipment ready to be loaded into the jeep. In the sitting room a jam jar of fresh flowers still stood on the windowsill. They'd wilt and fade there, she thought, with no one to see it happen.

When they reached the kitchen, Essie took Mara back from Carl. As he fossicked in a box for a teapot and mugs, she looked around the room. There, in the corner, was the kerosene fridge where the baby's bottles had sometimes been stored. Beside it was the gas camping stove where only a few days ago Carl had made Scottish griddle cakes, following a secret recipe from his grandmother. There were the two chairs, and the little table.

'But what about all this stuff?' she asked, as if domestic items might somehow be able to stand in the way of the departure.

'The Marlow Trust can send someone to deal with it, and collect the *Gari*. I don't have the time.'

'What will Frank think?' Essie asked. She'd almost forgotten about him being the financial backer of Carl's work – over at the camp, Diana's husband was never mentioned; her old life now seemed completely irrelevant.

'He's involved in some new venture in the Amazon. I doubt he's lying awake worrying about my project.' Carl was quiet for a moment. 'I'm sorry it has to be so rushed – saying goodbye.'

'I understand . . .' Essie's voice petered out. She knew Carl had no choice but to leave. But she wanted to shout a protest.

You're my friend. I need you.

We need you . . .

She took a breath, getting a grip on herself. She nodded in the direction of the lake. 'What happened? Why did they just leave?'

'I don't know,' Carl replied. 'There was one year I heard about when they came here and then flew off. The rains ended late and the level of the lake was too high. The island was flooded. They nested on the shoreline of another soda lake over in Kenya, just for that one season. But what's just happened tonight is completely different. The birds were settled in here. You saw – the conditions were perfect.'

Essie heard the frustration in his voice, backed by a fascination with something that made no sense.

'When I was in Berlin,' Carl continued, 'I read an entry in Stein's journal. He collected ethnographic information from the Maasai. They told him that flamingos always know when the volcano is going to erupt. Lengai gives them a warning. They fly away.'

'Could it be true?' Essie asked. She knew it was not uncommon for traditional beliefs to be grounded in facts that were supported by scientific evidence. Uneducated people interpreted natural occurrences in their own way. Their conclusions might involve magical thinking but they originated from firsthand observation, which was the basic tool of the scientist. The quest for traditional knowledge such as what Stein had recorded – information that might spur modern research – was one of the reasons the Hadza were of such interest to Europeans. They were seen as primitive on the one hand, but a repository of unique understandings on the other.

'It is a known phenomenon,' Carl confirmed. 'Zookeepers, farmers, amateur birdwatchers – they've all collected evidence of it. So have plenty of researchers. It's to do with birds and animals – even insects – being able to pick up sonic signals. And changes in air pressure and magnetic fields. They can detect the P waves that precede the main events – whether eruptions or earthquakes. They use the same senses that help them navigate. When there is a disturbance, birds can start behaving erratically – even crashing into trees. Animals will flee from an area under threat. Pets escape from backyards and go missing. Snakes leave their burrows for open ground. Ants even evacuate from their mounds.'

Essie thought of the changing faces of the volcano – how plumes of smoke came and went, and wisps of steam spilled from different locations. She had become so used to watching the fluctuating activity, it was hard to imagine that one day it would actually build into an eruption. She accepted Ian and Julia's reassurances that even if it did, there would be no danger to the Lawrences or their staff, or the people in the *manyatta*. Since records began there had been eight eruptions. The last event had been sixteen years ago. Ian had just returned to Magadi after finishing his degree in England. His parents hadn't even evacuated the camp. Ol Doinyo looked close, its pyramid shape dominating the horizon – but really, it was quite a long way away from the Archaeological Reserve. The area would only be threatened if there were heavy rains at the same time as a powerful eruption. Then there could be a deluge of ash and debris, washing down the slopes. But even if that happened, the most likely place to be engulfed was the Steps. As a precaution against this, plaster casts had been made of the footprints and transported to the museum in Dar es Salaam. Fortunately, in 1954 there had been no anxiety about the Steps site. The eruption had been during the dry season – the same time of year as it was now.

Essie shifted her thoughts to the lake. She didn't see how it could be affected by the volcano. Lava would have to flow from the summit all the way past the foothills to the shoreline.

'How could an eruption harm the flamingos?' she asked Carl.

'There could be temperature fluctuations that would result in less algae,' he replied. 'There's a period when the chicks are very vulnerable. They've left the island to feed along the shore but can't yet fly. They need to develop fast.' He looked thoughtful, one hand rubbing absently at his chin. 'There might be other reasons, too. Disturbances that we aren't even aware of.'

Carl fell quiet. He stared at the kettle, steaming on the stove. After a time, he turned back to Essie. 'This predictive behaviour we're talking about – it happens over hours, or days at the most. But it looks to me as if these flamingos decided not to breed weeks ago – when they didn't begin courting. If they're leaving now, because of an impending eruption, the volcanic activity should already have begun.' He raked his hands through his hair, then left them poised on the back of his head. 'There has to be another reason.' His tone still conveyed frustration and disappointment, but there was intrigue as well. 'I have no idea what it could be.'

As she listened, Essie became aware of Mara squirming in her arms. She realised she was holding on to her too tightly. She forced herself to relax. Taking a seat on one of the chairs, she focused on watching Carl as he set out the mugs, turned off the stove and opened the canister of tea.

'No milk, I'm afraid,' he said. 'I packed up my supplies to drop off at the *manyatta*. The kids will have fun with it all.' He grinned at Essie. 'Weird white man food.'

Essie smiled back, nodding. She could picture just how the adults would pretend to view the items – tinned fish, dried vegetables, powdered milk, mustard – with disdain, and yet be unable to conceal their interest.

'I'll ask about the birds while I'm there,' Carl added. 'See what they think.'

Essie felt another pang of loss; if he did learn something from the Maasai, she would never know about it, unless she enquired at the *manyatta* herself. From this point onwards, her and Carl's paths would diverge. Who could say where their journeys would lead them; whether they would ever meet up again.

Carl pulled up the second chair and sat down. For a while they were both quiet. Then he stirred the teapot and began to pour.

'So, after the *manyatta* – what then? How will you know where to go?' Essie asked him.

'I'll put out a radio bulletin. People will call in with reports. Tens of thousands of birds can hardly go unnoticed! I'll find them soon enough. Then I just have to wait and see if they decide it's still worth trying to breed.'

'What if they don't?'

He pressed his lips together. Essie watched him struggle with the loss that he might face – and then find a way to move on. 'I'll have to look around for another commission.' He smiled suddenly. 'Or take a holiday, maybe. Somewhere new, where I've never been before.'

'Where would you go? If you could just choose?' Essie asked.

'I've always wanted to go to Kashmir and see the saffron flowering, and float around the lake in a houseboat.'

Essie felt a stir of excitement, almost as if the trip he described was one that could include her. 'What else?'

'I want to see the glaciers in Iceland.'

'How about sailing in a *dhow* on the Nile?' Essie suggested. It was a game, drawing them both in.

'Why not off the Swahili coast? That's closer. Let's say somewhere near Mombasa?'

The sharing of destinations and experiences flowed back and forth. Then suddenly, Essie had nothing more to say. The reality of what the coming months would bring broke over her like an icy wave. She would remain here, at Magadi. She'd be working with Simon, and taking care of Mara. The dry season would stretch out ahead of her – but not for long enough. Too soon, it would be time to start making practical preparations for Nandamara's return. The first step was to gradually withdraw some of the luxuries to which the baby had become accustomed. Simon had pointed out that Mara would have to get used to sleeping on hard ground, with the other members of her family. She could not expect to have an array of toys, or to be wrapped in soft, freshly laundered blankets. Essie was dreading witnessing the signs of discomfort, the looks of confusion, perhaps even fear. She would have to be cruel in order to be kind, and Mara would have no idea what was going on.

Essie stared down at the floor. When she spoke, it was in a half whisper. 'I wish you could still be here – when they come to take her.'

These were the wrong words, she knew. It wasn't a matter of the Hadza taking Mara away. It was up to Essie to give her back – freely, gladly – to her family, where she belonged. But even now, after less than two months of them being together, Essie found the prospect so hard to accommodate that it felt like an outcome that surely had to be wrong.

Looking up, she saw that Carl's eyes were screwed up in the corners, as if he could feel her pain. She waited for him to reassure her that she'd find a way to survive the separation. Or to suggest that she focus on how good it would be for the Hadza baby to be back in her own tribe. But he said nothing. He just stood up and crossed the space between them, kneeling at Essie's side. He wrapped his arms around her shoulders, bringing her and Mara together into his embrace.

Tears brimmed in Essie's eyes, then overflowed. Carl wiped them away, drawing his thumb across her cheeks.

When, eventually, they moved apart, he rested his hand on Mara's head. 'Look at her, Essie. You saved her. Whatever else happens in your whole life, this will be one real thing that you did.'

Essie grasped his words like a lifeline.

One real thing . . .

When she finally spoke, her voice was fragile, like fine porcelain that could easily be shattered. 'Can you send me the photographs?'

'I'll print them up as soon as I can. I'll put them on a plane. I promise.' Getting to his feet, Carl went over to where his camera was resting on top of its travel bag. 'Let me take one more.'

He whistled for Rudie and clicked his fingers to draw Tommy's attention. Essie stood up, holding Mara. When they were all grouped together he placed the camera on the window ledge. As the timer buzzed, he hurried across to Essie. His arm rested lightly over her shoulder. The adults' faces were side by side. Mara's head was between their chins. Tommy had pushed his nose in; Rudie was licking his ear. The baby was giggling, her eyes turned towards the odd sound that she could hear. Essie and Carl were laughing with her. The buzzing wound to a halt and the shutter clicked – freezing them together in time, within a single frame.

Carl put the camera back in its place. Then he tore open a Kodak box and wrote something down on the flattened piece of cardboard. As he handed it to Essie, she glimpsed the name and address of his agent.

'You can always find me,' he said.

He tucked the note into the pocket of her shirt and buttoned down the flap. Over his shoulder she could see the patch of sky framed by the window. An apricot glow was creeping into the grey. The horizon was now a stark black line edged with brimming light; it was the instant just before dawn. When she looked back, meeting

Carl's gaze, he nodded. They both knew: the time had come to say goodbye.

Outside, they stood by the Land Rover. A dense silence seemed to close in around them – as though the air was choked by all the unspoken words that would have made up the conversations that would now never take place. They didn't linger. A spell was being woven around them; it had to be broken before it became too strong.

As they held one another's gaze, Essie saw the first rays of light fall over Carl's face, touching his skin with gold. The sun reached out to her and Mara as well. In that moment the three were brought together as one – wrapped in the warmth of a newborn sun.

SIXTEEN

Essie drove away from the Mission house, heading towards the plains. The route was very familiar to her now. She knew in advance where to slow down or where to speed up to keep traction over soft ground. She knew the place where the track wound between two tall anthills, and where it came close to a pile of boulders. It didn't take long for her to reach the chain of pools. Her gaze skimmed over the Swimming Bath, where she and Ian had last swum together the night before the Marlows had first arrived here, a day early – the night before Mara came into Essie's life. She barely noticed how the early sun turned the water into circles of gold, or how the yellow weaverbirds in the nearby trees dipped and fluttered busily with all the energy of a new day. Instead, she felt the pull of the place she'd left behind. Her thoughts were like a long line stretched out behind her, refusing to let go.

She pictured Carl preparing to leave, his boots making a hollow thud on the floorboards as he took a final walk through the house, picking up the last of his possessions. Very soon he'd be setting out along this same track – but instead of turning off to the camp he'd drive straight on towards Serengeti. The thought of him disappearing into the dust, leaving Magadi behind, brought an ache to Essie's heart. She could hardly imagine how she – and

Simon and Mara – were going to manage without him. Yet, only weeks ago they had not even met. It was as if the proximity to Ol Doinyo Lengai – the repository of so many stories and beliefs – had distorted all perspective. Under the watchful eye of the volcano, time had been played out on a scale that was nothing to do with days or weeks, let alone months and years. It was the only explanation for the fact that Essie felt as if she'd known Carl Bergmann for ages.

The pain of the parting was cloaked with shock; Essie was still struggling to absorb the reality that he was leaving, with no plan to return. As she steered the Land Rover along the track she could feel the presence of his note in her pocket, as if the scrap of cardboard were something alive, giving out its own warmth.

You can always find me.

Carl's words circled in her head. They were comforting as well as tantalising, like the shared fantasy about travelling to exotic places. But in reality, the name and address of a photographic agent were of no use to Essie. The Lawrences' lifestyle didn't involve touring the world, looking up old friends. And there wasn't much point in writing letters to someone you would probably not see again. It was possible that the Flamingo Project would be resurrected, and Carl would have a reason to return to Magadi next season, or in some other year to come. But Essie didn't want to spend her time living in hope of an encounter that might never occur. She just had to let Carl go, accepting that their paths had come together for a while, and would now veer apart. As she bumped along the track, she spoke firmly to herself, quashing a stubborn hope that there might be some other future. When the time came to turn off towards the camp, she marked the moment to herself – there was the fork in the road, with the two paths leading in different directions. All she had to do was stick to her route and not falter. Very soon she'd be back where she belonged.

By the time the Land Rover reached the parking area, Mara had woken up again. Essie knew there would now be a short time of peace before the baby realised she was hungry. Then the round of feeding, changing, bathing and playing would begin again. But first, Essie would have to face Ian. Not only did she need to repair the rift caused by her sleeping in the nursery, she had to explain why she'd left the camp during the night. When she thought of how she'd even begin the conversation, her stomach twisted in alarm. On the drive back, she shouldn't have been thinking about Carl, she should have been hunting for the right words to say to her husband.

Kefa was standing near the place where Essie usually parked. A smudge of blue at his feet caught her eye as she pulled up beside him. She recognised Simon's precious winklepicker shoes. She guessed the houseboy had won them through gambling – that was the usual story behind possessions changing hands between the workers.

Kefa nodded politely as Essie climbed out of her vehicle.

'Were you waiting for me?' Essie asked.

He gave an equivocal shrug. 'I saw you coming near.'

The morning greetings were exchanged. As she spoke Essie couldn't help looking down at the suede shoes. She guessed Simon bitterly regretted wagering with them. Perhaps he'd been drinking at the time.

'Simon has made me a gift,' Kefa said, as if reading her thoughts.

'That was kind of him,' Essie said.

Kefa looked mystified. 'He said he had no use for them any more.'

While Essie was still processing his words, the man pointed to the Dining Tent. 'The Bwana is expecting you.'

Essie nodded. 'I'll go to him.' She was aware of Mara fidgeting beside her. She looked towards the staff camp. 'Where is Simon?'

'He is waiting to begin work.' Kefa glanced at the sun, drawing attention to the time.

Essie gathered herself. 'Please take Mara to him. Ask him to feed and bathe her.' She ignored Kefa's raised eyebrows – it was none of his business what tasks she assigned to her assistant. Simon was as capable as Essie, these days, of taking care of Mara, and Essie didn't want to be juggling a hungry baby alongside dealing with Ian.

As she handed Mara over, she felt the baby tense. Kefa was not a stranger to her, but she wanted to stay with Essie. Her lips turned down and her hands reached out, clutching the air.

'It's all right,' Essie said soothingly. 'I'm coming back.'

Recently, Mara had begun objecting when she was handed over to anyone except Simon. Sometimes she could be distracted with a toy or a song. Other times she ended up screaming, as if in fear for her life. Essie tried to let the process play out, resisting the temptation to reclaim her. She knew that would only make Mara feel more anxious – it endorsed the idea that she'd been placed in unsafe hands. But often Essie relented. She would be swept away by an impulse to feel the weight of the baby in her arms. She wanted to hug her close. This had more to do with her emotions, she knew, than with Mara's. Each parting – even the act of relinquishing Mara to sleep – felt like a rehearsal for the final goodbye. She wanted to put it off for another time.

Kefa eyed Essie uncertainly as Mara squirmed in his arms, making urgent whimpers.

'Give her to me.' Essie held out her hands. 'Go and get Simon. Hurry back.'

As Kefa marched away, Essie stroked Mara's hair. She felt the little body relax against her. An unneeded tear clung to the dark crescent of the baby's eyelashes. As Essie watched it roll down the soft, curved cheek a feeling of deep gratification swept through her. It seemed like proof that Mara trusted her, perhaps even loved her. Essie had agonised over whether or not it was best to encourage the baby to bond with her. She knew Julia was right – it would make the parting more difficult. But Essie had come to the conclusion that love was a language Mara needed to learn. Being familiar with the emotion – and all the subtle means of giving love and receiving it – would matter much more to her in the long term than hearing Hadza spoken or acquiring other skills. When Mara rejoined Nandamara, Giga and the rest of her family, everything she'd learned to feel towards Essie could be transferred to them. Such a scenario wasn't discussed in *Complete Babycare*, but Essie didn't need any expert advice. It was a truth she understood instinctively. She could hear its voice inside her head – just as a baby bird knows to peck the tip of a parent's beak until food is regurgitated, and a dog knows to bury food, creating a secret hoard in case of future hunger.

Essie approached the Dining Tent cautiously. Breakfast had been served and cleared away; a fresh tablecloth had been spread. Ian was the only person in there. He was reading a journal, a pencil in hand. Essie couldn't decide if the absence of other people – her mother-in-law and their guest – was a good thing or not. She and Ian would be able to speak freely. But she wasn't sure where the interaction might lead.

'Good morning,' Essie said tentatively. As she sat down she saw her note lying on the table. Viewed in the light of day, what she'd written had a flippant tone. *I've gone for a drive.*

'I'm sorry.' The apology came out automatically.

Ian lifted his gaze, jutting his clean-shaven chin. 'Where on earth have you been?'

'It was because of the birds,' Essie began. 'I just woke up and —'

'Birds?' Ian broke in, frowning incredulously.

'They left in the night. I knew Carl would be upset. He won't be able to do his work now.'

Ian looked confused. Then his eyes narrowed. 'You went to see Carl Bergmann, by yourself, in the middle of the night?'

Essie bit her lip. She knew, suddenly, it was crazy how she'd let herself become involved with Carl – how she and Simon had kept on making visits to the Mission house, accepting cups of tea, staying for long conversations. Then, there was the day Carl had joined their field trip, and they'd all swum in the pool. Somehow she had pretended to herself that Ian would approve . . .

'You drove over there to comfort him?' A look came over Ian's face – shock, outrage. 'What's been going on between you?'

'Nothing,' Essie said. 'We're friends.'

'And what does that mean?'

Essie felt a wave of anger. 'You spend all your time with Diana. I don't ask what you're up to.'

There was a brief pause. 'That's different. I have to look after her. She's our benefactor.'

Essie pointed at the new Rolex on Ian's wrist. 'She's given you presents. You've taken up wearing sunglasses, like she does.'

The words sounded petulant and childish. But she knew Ian wouldn't have been too pleased if she'd been the one receiving gifts from a member of the opposite sex.

'She's just a generous person,' Ian said. 'Look at all the things she gave you for the nursery.'

Essie had to nod. Diana had been very kind. Her gesture had made it possible for Mara's needs to be met – even if many of the luxuries had proved unnecessary in the end. Yet, as she eyed her husband mutely, a new thought came to her. Maybe there had been a purpose behind Diana's generosity. Maybe she'd wanted Essie to be preoccupied with a baby so she could step into her place. The truth was that Essie still didn't know what to make of Diana – whether she was genuinely interested in the Lawrences' work, or if she had a more personal agenda in being at Magadi. Perhaps she wanted to punish Frank for his many misdemeanours by joining a new family. It had even occurred to Essie that Diana wanted to beat him at his own game and have an affair of her own. In the past Essie would have felt confident that Ian's professionalism would protect him from such a ploy. But since the revelations about William and Mirella, she wasn't so sure. Sometimes she thought she detected a sinister undercurrent in Diana's actions. She had the idea that Ian, Julia, herself – and even Mara – were like a collection of dolls that were part of some game Diana was playing. One day, she'd get bored with them all and just walk away, leaving a chaotic mess of mismatched clothes, plastic shoes and other doll's accessories behind her.

Ian closed his journal and pushed it aside. 'At least Diana's interested in the work. You aren't any more. Nothing matters to you these days except that baby.'

Essie took a breath as a thought flashed into her head. 'You're jealous of her!'

'Of course I'm not.' He looked at Essie as if he hardly recognised her. Then he sighed. 'Essie, you don't have to do this.'

He gave her a pleading look. She felt like a child who had stepped out of line and should know better. But even as she felt this, her anger flared again.

'What are you talking about? What am I doing?'

'You're escalating the situation. You know what my concerns are. Having a baby here has changed you. I'm not blaming you, but it's a fact. And because you're so taken up with her, of course I turn to someone else for . . . company.' Ian looked down at the tablecloth; he spoke in a hushed voice. 'You and I haven't touched one another for ages. You're always tired. And last night you walked out on me.'

'It was because of the way you spoke about Mara. It made me angry.'

Ian didn't react straightaway. Then his eyes widened, an idea dawning across his face. 'And this photographer. I suppose he was keen on the baby?'

'Yes. He loves Mara.'

A breath burst from Ian's lips. 'I bet he does.'

'What is that supposed to mean?'

'He was trying to impress you. A man like him isn't interested in a baby.'

'You don't know anything about Carl.'

'No, I don't. And I don't need to.'

In the silence that followed Essie saw him dismiss Carl as any kind of threat. She knew she should feel relieved, yet part of her was outraged at the arrogance underpinning his conclusion.

'What concerns me,' Ian went on, 'is that right now I feel I don't know anything about you – my own wife. You would never have behaved like this in the past.'

Essie gave no response. He was right. She *had* changed. But surely that was part of being alive? There was a quote Ian liked to use while discussing evolution: the words of the Greek philosopher Heraclitus. *Change is the only constant.* Why had they ever thought that the truths they understood to be part of their work would not also apply to themselves?

'I just know where this will end up,' Ian said. 'You'll want a different life. A family. A house. You'll want me to get a job in Cambridge. All those ordinary things.'

Essie shook her head. She'd love the chance to return to Cambridge to visit her father. Aside from her desire to see him, there were new questions she wanted to raise with him now. It would probably be pointless to ask him about Lorna's family, as Carl had suggested, but Arthur might be prepared to tell her more about her illness; their marriage; why she'd been so unhappy. The idea of moving back to England, though, was far from Essie's mind. On the other hand, if she was honest, she didn't see how she was going to slot back into her old life here at Magadi after Mara was gone. As Essie sat here now, all she really wanted to do was get away from the camp – back to the austere beauty and deep peacefulness of the foothills.

'Tell me the truth.' Ian leaned forward in his chair, fixing Essie with a penetrating gaze. 'Have you begun to think about what it would be like to have your own baby?'

Essie froze. It was a question she hardly dared ask herself.

Of course I have.

A thousand times . . .

While she was deciding what to say, Kefa appeared with a tray of tea. Ian waved him brusquely away.

'It is not what we agreed,' he continued. 'When we got married you knew what you were taking on. The work. My commitment to my mother. To Magadi.'

'But a marriage isn't a business deal,' Essie objected. 'It can't just go on and on like clockwork. A relationship has to evolve over time.' Essie listened to herself in amazement. She and Ian had never spoken so directly and openly before. They hadn't needed to.

'My parents were always the same,' Ian stated. 'They just got on with things.'

'Let's not use them as an example. Your father was an adulterer.' Essie held her breath: the words, said aloud, felt like sacrilege.

Ian pressed his lips together. He wanted to repudiate the accusation, Essie could see – but his own mother had made the claim. 'Maybe it was Julia's fault that he had an affair. A wife can drive her husband towards another woman.'

Essie remembered Julia's crazed outburst by the fireside. *A man's needs must be met.* She swallowed on a tight throat. The implication was clear. By devoting herself to Mara, Essie was pushing Ian towards Diana.

'So you're attracted to her?' Essie winced at her own words. They sounded like a cliché – part of a conversation that had already been overused by others.

Ian shifted in his chair. 'She's a beautiful woman. That's obvious.'

'Are you . . .?' She couldn't bring herself to ask the question: *Are you falling in love with her?*

'She's not my type,' Ian stated.

Essie looked down at her lap. Surely he should be reassuring her – telling her she was silly to even think he could be lured away from his wife? On the other hand, she knew the answer he'd given her was the truth. Diana was not Ian's type at all. Essie had seen how disconcerted he was by her unpredictable ways – that odd, childish streak. And how embarrassing he found her overt extravagance and unconventional manners. At the same time, though,

Essie knew he admired Diana's drive; the way she'd adapted to the conditions at Magadi, and her apparent interest in his research. It must be confusing for him. Perhaps it was this very destabilisation that was dangerous. Essie looked across at the orange tent. It stood out like a warning beacon. 'When is she leaving?'

Ian hesitated for a few seconds. 'She's not planning to, at the moment. She wants to make a new life for herself. Work hard. Achieve something.'

Essie stared at him. He'd admitted he was attracted to Diana; now he was saying that she was going to be an ongoing part of their world. 'Tell her to go. Send her away.'

'Don't be ridiculous. You know I can't do that.'

He gestured at the pin board behind him. Among the lists of things to do was an updated budget; on the bottom line was a very long number. Essie knew Diana could easily withdraw funding if she chose, and then everything would grind to a halt.

'But would you want to send her away?' Essie persisted. 'If you could?'

There was a long silence. Ian seemed to be struggling with himself. He had always been open with Essie, but she didn't know whether discovering the truth about William's unfaithfulness would undermine his honest ways, or further entrench them. The new image of his admired father could pull him either way.

Finally, Ian shook his head. 'No. I want her here.'

Essie felt sick. In this moment, the five years they'd spent together felt like a day, and the edifice of their marriage as flimsy as a filmset façade. They'd worked side by side, sharing every-thing – yet she wondered how well they really knew one another. For that matter, how well did each of them know themselves? Questions and uncertainties swirled around her until she felt as if she was drowning. She wanted to reach out to Ian, grasping his hand for safety. But as she leaned towards him, he stood up. He took his sunglasses from his pocket, flicking open the arms. As he put them on, Essie glimpsed herself reflected in the shiny lenses: her pale face, dark eyes. Then the image was whisked away. He was gone.

Wind blew across the hillside scouring the sunbaked landscape, adding stinging dust to the sweaty heat. Rudie's tongue lolled from his open jaw as he jumped from stone to stone. Essie drew a muslin scarf up to cover Mara's head. The wind tugged at it, but she held it firmly in place. She wasn't afraid of Mara getting sunburnt – the Hadza had such black skin, even by African standards. It was the result of living constantly outdoors; over countless generations they evolved to have increased melanin for protection against the harsh rays of the tropical sun. This didn't mean Mara would be impervious to heatstroke, though. When it was this hot, Hadza tribespeople would seek shelter under a shady tree or rocky overhang. Essie glanced up at the sun. It would soon be time for her and Simon to do the same.

She looked ahead to where the man was striding along, a rucksack bouncing on his back. He was turning his head from side to side as he searched the ground. She felt a wave of appreciation for the way Simon kept on working so diligently, even though after all their scouting they'd only found a few interesting stone tools and a possible Upper Paleolithic home site. There was no sign of a cave. He didn't seem to be held hostage by the idea of reaching a goal. He was as happy to play with Mara in the shade or make a length of twine from the fibres of wild sisal as he was to survey the hillsides. It was hard to match this person with the ambitious young man who'd been hired as her assistant. Essie wondered, now, what Simon really thought of the way everything at Magadi was focused on a schedule, a plan, a process. She wondered, as well, what he thought of her husband with his strict, uncompromising ways. She knew Simon might be aware of the tension between her and Ian – he'd arrived at the Dining Tent with Mara only moments after the end of their fraught interaction earlier. He'd made no reference to it, though; neither had Essie. The two were friends as well as colleagues now, after the weeks of working so closely together, sharing the care of Mara, and spending time with Carl. But their connection existed in a bubble out here away from the camp; neither of them seemed to want anything from outside to intrude.

As Essie walked on, she focused on the sound of her footsteps, drumming a slow beat. She was finding it hard today to concentrate on the details of her surroundings. After the confrontation with Ian she felt empty and lost. She almost hoped not to stumble on anything of interest – a piece of flint, dislocated from its source, or a fragment of fossilised bone. She could barely be bothered with the procedure of marking the location on the map, bagging the sample, writing up her notes. When the present felt so insecure, it was hard to be interested in a time that was long past.

Only gradually, as she trailed after Simon, did she become aware that something was missing: the sound of Tommy's hooves clattering on the rocks, or skittering over the gravel behind her. She looked around, but there was no sign of him.

'Simon?' she called out. 'Can you see Tommy?'

He turned back. 'I thought he was following you.'

Essie frowned. It was unlike the gazelle to become separated from her. If he got tired, he normally bleated loudly until she slowed down. She scanned the area, looking for the patch of tan hair, the fast-flicking tail. Nothing.

'Tommy! Tommy!' she called again, across the windswept hill-side. Her voice seemed to disappear, swallowed by rock crevices and bushes.

She started back the way they'd come, beckoning for Simon to do the same. When he joined her, she eyed him in alarm. Had Tommy's little hoof become trapped between two rocks? Had he been snatched by some predator, unseen by her or Simon, or even Rudie? A leopard, or a bird of prey . . . Essie stared from the sky to the trees and back, her heart thudding in her chest.

'Tommy!' she shouted urgently. 'Here, Tommy. Good boy. Come here.' Images flashed through her mind: the gazelle as a little baby, tottering on clumsy legs, guzzling hungrily on his bottle. His eyes, so big and dark, fixed on hers. She told herself to be calm. Tommy had only been missing for a short time – but she felt an irrational fear that she would never see him again.

'Shshsh!' Simon raised one hand, signalling to her. Then he turned his head, listening.

Essie could detect nothing unusual, but Simon suddenly began striding back along the trajectory they had taken. 'He is here. I can hear him.'

'Where?' Essie demanded. 'Where is he?' She wished she had the Hadza's keen hearing.

Some distance away she saw Simon drop to his knees. He shouted back to her. 'He has fallen. Now he is stuck.'

Essie hurried towards him. She peered ahead, but there was no sign of the familiar tawny shape. When she was closer she saw that Simon was leaning down into a crevice. She could hear Tommy's protest now – hoarse and thin. Only the gazelle's hind legs, tail and rump were visible. The head and shoulders were hidden from view. It was not just the wind that had caused her not to hear him; his cries were muffled by the earth.

On his knees, Simon was picking out stones and throwing them behind him. Rudie came to stand at his elbow as if considering how to join in.

'Is he hurt?'

'I do not think so.'

Essie crouched down, holding Mara steady in the sling. It didn't take long for Tommy to be freed. Simon lifted him from the hole. As the animal caught sight of his rescuers he started bleating more loudly. He sounded annoyed rather than in pain. Essie smiled with relief.

'You silly thing,' she murmured to the gazelle. 'You should look where you're walking.' She stroked his head, running her fingers over the whorls of hair on his forehead and the nubs of his emerging horns. Tommy stretched his spine and shook his legs, one at a time, as if to make sure they still worked properly. Then he began licking the dust from his coat.

Essie peered into the hole where he'd been caught. There were two large stones close together – he was lucky not to have broken a bone as he slipped down between them. She got to her feet – a little awkwardly, managing the weight of the baby. As she did so, a pebble dislodged by her boots rolled into the crevice. Seconds later she heard a sound, so faint that it almost didn't exist. It was the stone falling, bouncing off another stone, then falling again – into nothing.

Simon tensed, eyeing Essie. Crouching over the crevice, he began removing more stones.

'Be careful,' she warned. 'Don't fall through.'

After hefting out a large chunk of sandstone, Simon bent down, leaning further into the hole. His arm disappeared to the shoulder. Twisting his neck, he looked back at Essie. 'The air is cold.'

Essie's lips parted as the meaning of his words sank in. In order to hold its own temperature, the space he'd reached into must be big. They could be standing on the rooftop of an underground cave.

Extracting his arm from the hole, skin chalky with dust, Simon scrambled to his feet. Then he turned to scan the surrounding terrain. He pointed to a mound of sedimentary rock nearby, its ochre tones set against the lacy texture of an old lava flow. On its own, it would not have caught their attention – but now Essie saw that it could well be the remains of an erosion stack. It might once have stood tall, a prominent landmark like the Tower at Magadi. That there had been a similar rock formation at the Meeting Place was just a coincidence.

Essie glanced down into the sling, checking on Mara. When she looked up, she could see Simon already jumping from rock to rock; Rudie was following on his tail, sniffing the ground. They were aiming down the slope – if there was an access to the floor of the cave, this was where it would be.

She took a piece of twine from her pocket and tied it to Tommy's collar so she could keep him close. Then she set off over the scree. She moved cautiously – the knowledge that she was responsible for Mara's safety made her want to test each foothold before shifting her weight. In the heat, she thought longingly of the cool, underground air that Simon had reported. She rubbed her hand across her brow, feeling the grit in her sweat. Then she brushed aside a windblown strand of hair that had stuck to her lips. As she glanced up to check where she was headed, something caught her eye. Squinting into the glare, she identified the remains of a dead tree – a stunted trunk, bleached to a silvery grey. It must have been a tough specimen, to survive for years in this barren field of stone. Essie wondered what had caused it to die. A change of local climate, perhaps; disease; an earthquake . . . Then an image came to her of limp, yellowed plants collapsed onto the ground around the edges of a pool – victims of *hewa mbaya*: the fatal miasma of carbon dioxide, released from deep underground.

Essie approached the tree, stopping a short distance away. It was just a skeleton, the leaves and fine branches long turned to dust. Close up, she saw the desiccated remnants of a bush that had once been growing in its shade. Her gaze fastened onto a few streaks of green nearby – living plants, reaching up between the stones. If there had been gas emissions here, they were not happening now.

To the right of the tree was a pile of earth and rubble. Looking up, Essie could see its source: an overhang of eroded sandstone had collapsed. She skirted the base of the heap. As she stepped around a large boulder, she came to a sudden halt. It took a moment for her to process what she could see: a ragged black hole, like a giant inkblot on the side of the hill.

Essie trained her gaze closer. The opening in the rock was wide at its base, tapering to a point just above her head: the shape of a crooked pyramid. Even from this distance she got a glimpse of a shadowy interior. Her stomach leapt with excitement. It was definitely the entrance to a cave or tunnel – how big or deep she could not tell.

She called out to Simon – yelling again and again, until an answering cry travelled back on the wind. She didn't move any closer. Even if there had been no baby to think of, she knew to be cautious. The cave could be the lair of a leopard, or some other wild animal; without Rudie here to pick up the scent, there was no way for her to know.

She sat down on one of the boulders to wait. She moved Mara around to rest on her lap but kept her in the sling in case it was necessary to make a quick move. Essie felt uneasy, being on her own with the baby. Normally, she and Simon stayed in eyesight of one another, with Rudie ranging over the distance between them. The hope of finding a cave had spurred them to forget their rules. Essie couldn't help thinking of Julia, years ago also caught up in the anticipation of a new discovery – and paying a terrible price.

But even as these thoughts ran through her head, Essie's gaze kept being drawn back to the opening in the rock. She wanted to walk straight in and see what lay beyond the pyramid arch. Logic told her that it was probably just a small dank space containing nothing of any interest. Rat-ridden. Spidery. Dark. And yet, the dream of finding a cave full of prehistoric paintings rose enticingly before her. She unclipped her torch from her belt and clicked it on, off, on – the sound mimicking her impatience. In her mind, she could almost see the pictures she was about to discover – as detailed as the ones she'd already studied in the Painted Cave. Perhaps even more beautiful. And with a significance that no one had yet even imagined. Essie would surely be the first European ever to see them. The opening was hidden behind the rubble of the overhang. And assuming the tree that had caught her eye was already dead at the time, it would have been a warning to Stein, or the people in the search party, to move through the area as quickly as possible or risk exposure to dangerous gas.

A butterfly flitted past, hovering in the air, then settling on Essie's hand. Mara watched, entranced, as the wings opened and closed, displaying a pattern of brown, red and green. She gurgled with delight, looking up at Essie to share the experience. It was a good hour since she'd had a bottle of milk, but she was not hungry or thirsty. Essie could tell this, now, at a glance. She was attuned to the baby in a way that reminded her of Simon's sensitivity to the land. It was as if words, unspoken, passed constantly back and forth between them.

After what seemed like a long time, Simon arrived at a run, out of breath. Rudie was at his heels. His eyes went straight to the gap in the rock.

'It might be nothing,' Essie said. 'I haven't looked.'

She saw Simon taking in the dead tree and bush, a frown marking his brow.

'There are healthy plants growing now,' Essie said. 'But we should still check.'

Simon eyed Mara as he nodded. Swinging the rucksack to the ground, he felt inside the pocket for the matches. Then he slipped his hunting knife from its sheath.

From her place by the boulders Essie watched him approach the opening and pause to strike a match. As the flame flared he leaned inside. There was a tense wait. Then Simon looked back over his shoulder with a smile. Peering past him, she glimpsed the little flame burning brightly in the velvety gloom.

Essie and Simon hung back, letting Rudie scout ahead. They were in a tunnel, rather than a cave – a continuation of the arched entrance. They pointed their torches after the dog, watching for his responses. The Dalmatian's coat was short and smooth, which meant raised hackles could be seen straightaway. So far, nothing had alarmed him.

Essie looked down at Mara. In the meagre light the whites of her eyes stood out. She was very still, gazing around her. Essie was about to murmur some reassuring words, but then realised the baby looked intrigued more than anxious. To Mara, this was just another place into which Essie and Simon had brought her. As long as she was held close, by one of them, she felt safe.

Following behind Simon, Essie crunched over patches of gravel, picking a path between scattered chunks of stone. She glimpsed fossils lodged in the walls – dark shapes in the sediments – but decided to leave closer examination for later. Tommy walked right behind her, his muzzle nudging her leg. His presence reminded Essie how bizarre her work practice had become these last weeks. She was on a quest to discover an important archaeological site – while carrying a baby in a sling at her side and towing a small animal on a leash.

Suddenly, she saw that Simon had disappeared. Alarm flashed through her. Then she realised he had turned a corner. Moments later she was behind him again. Only a few feet further on, the tunnel widened.

Essie stood still. The air was immediately cooler. She could feel the vast empty space around her; it was as if she had some extra sense that went beyond sight and hearing. She swung her torch in a circle. A tapestry of colour was revealed – a sweep of reds and yellows; smudges of white; black lines; daubs of brown.

She caught her breath as she recognised the shape of an antelope, complete with horns and hooves. Beside it was a hunter holding a spear.

Then a bird with a long neck.

A tall figure with round circles for breasts . . .

They were similar to the paintings Essie had studied in the Painted Cave – surely created by people of the same era.

Essie's eyes were dazzled, suddenly, as Simon turned towards her. When he aimed his light away to the side, she could see his face. They stared at one another.

'We found it.' Essie spoke in a hushed tone, unwilling to break the deep quiet of the place.

Simon smiled, his teeth white in the shadows. 'Those Hadza were telling the truth.'

For a long time, neither of them spoke. The twin beams of their torches roamed in long arcs over the walls, crossing one another, then moving apart. The paintings were revealed one by one, looming out of the blackness. Essie studied an image of a porcupine. She could feel the thrust of the sharp spikes, the gentleness of the curved snout. It was a beautiful piece of work.

Essie looked back the way they had come. Barely any light filtered in via the tunnel. Before the collapse of the overhang there would have been a little more – nevertheless, the cave would have been virtually dark. The paintings must have been created and then observed by the glow of burning branches – by Neolithic times humans had long been masters of fire. But still, there would only have been a limited view. She turned to Simon.

'Why go to the effort of painting all these pictures inside a dark cave?'

'They had their own torches, made from fire.' Simon's thoughts had obviously been following her own. 'The Hadza still do this.'

'But you can't see them properly.'

'You *can*,' Simon argued. 'Only you must look slowly. It is better.'

Essie returned to the porcupine. The torch beam was like a spotlight, bringing different parts of the animal into focus. It was true, what Simon had said: the images, held within darkness, had a special potency.

'In that moment when you can see, and yet not see,' Simon continued, 'new things can be understood. That is why we like the dark.'

Essie turned his words over in her mind. She was reminded of how, at Magadi Camp, battling the night was a constant preoccupation. Memories of electric light enjoyed in other places haunted everyone's minds. No matter how many lamps were lit, there never seemed to be enough. Simon had spent the early part of his life in a Hadza tribe, where there was only the moon and stars, and sometimes firelight, to illuminate the night. No wonder he saw this place of permanent darkness differently.

'It is like the *epeme*,' Simon added.

Essie nodded. 'The night dances . . .'

She knew a little about the Hadza ceremony: it was an important ritual that took place at least two or three times a month. It was held only on moonless nights. The meaning of the event was an enduring puzzle to anthropologists. It seemed to have nothing to do with the usual preoccupations of traditional peoples. The Hadza didn't believe in an afterlife that had to be earned or a god who had to be appeased; being nomads, their fortunes were not tied to one place – they weren't held captive, in their lives, by the threat of flood or drought. They weren't so plagued by fear. There was some other agenda at stake in the *epeme*, and no one knew what it was.

'During the *epeme* we see only by the light of the stars,' Simon continued. 'Even the glow of a single smoking pipe is too bright. We are divided into two. Women and little children on one side; older boys and initiated men on the other. Between us there must be a rock or some thick bushes to keep us apart. There is a dancer – just one man at first. He wears bells on his right ankle. He has a cape to hide his body, just in case someone is able to see. He calls out names. He talks, sings, whistles in the darkness. The women call back.' Simon shook his head. 'It is too hard to describe . . .'

There was a long silence. In the dry cave there was no dripping water to break the quiet, or even the scuttle of an insect.

When Simon spoke again his tone was light, almost casual. 'When Mara returns to her family, she will attend the *epeme*.'

Essie braced for the emotions that always went with picturing the future – the wave of jealousy; the terror of letting go and trusting others with Mara's care. The ache of abandonment. And the irrational sense that somehow, once Essie couldn't see her any more, Mara would cease to exist . . .

But this time, the pain didn't come. Instead, all Essie could feel was the rightness of Mara being with her own people, taking part in their traditions.

'Can you tell me the meaning of the *epeme*?' she asked. 'I want to know what she will learn.' She had the idea that this might be her only chance to find out. Here, in the secrecy of the cave, Simon seemed able to speak with a freedom he might not find again.

'It brings everyone together. We repair all the problems that have come up since the last *epeme*. Things to do with children, old people. Arguments between lovers, hunters. We put everything back as it should be.'

Essie smiled. She'd been picturing some weighty, solemn purpose. But what Simon described just sounded simple and practical – as straightforward as housework.

She moved along one of the walls. Her torch played over another collection of paintings. She made notes in her head.

A crouched figure, male, with erect penis.

Strange prostrate form, or a pattern of sticks. Bones?

A pyramid with lines radiating from the apex. Ol Doinyo Lengai – spitting fire.

She imagined the challenge of tracing the works by lamplight. The huge scale of the investigation. There would be months and months of work.

'You can be happy now.' Simon's voice floated across to her, as if he was reading her thoughts.

Essie stared into nothing. The words seemed to bounce around inside her, not finding a place to settle. Somehow, the elation she knew she should feel was elusive. She wasn't thinking of how pleased and excited Ian would be when she told him what she'd discovered. Or how the new project was going to bring the two of them back together. In fact, when she pictured the person she most wanted to share the news with, it wasn't even the face of her husband that came to mind.

Essie swung her torch beam, checking on Mara, then Tommy. She located Rudie – he was nosing the ground as he trotted towards the rear of the cave. There must have been a niche or tunnel there, because she lost sight of him. Essie whistled him back. When he didn't reappear she headed after him. She wasn't sure if a dog could get lost in an underground maze, or if they would always be able to follow their own scent back the way they had come.

Essie found herself in another tunnel. From somewhere ahead she could hear the sound Rudie made when he was checking a scent: the repeated exhalations, as if he needed to clear his nose before taking in a new smell. Next he let out a short sharp bark. He sounded surprised, more than aggressive or fearful.

'Simon . . .' Essie's voice was thin, as if filtered through shadows. She tightened her arm over Mara, and waited for him to reach her side.

Together they edged their way along. This tunnel was short — more like a doorway in a very thick wall.

Now they were standing in a second cave. A finger of light reached down from above, painting a vague circle of white on the ground. Rudie was pushing his snout into a pile of debris. He lifted his head, an object in his mouth.

Essie stepped closer, aiming her torch. Shock tore through her like a bolt of electricity. She was looking at a small canvas sandshoe. Yellow laces, wet with saliva, draped from the dog's jaw.

She stared, frozen. 'Oh my God . . .'

Rudie dropped his prize, backing away into the shadows. As Simon reached her side, Essie squatted to pick it up. In the beam of his torch she turned the shoe over in her hand. The rubber sole was well worn, the edges ragged. Essie's heart clenched at the thought of the thousands of little footsteps that had worn the tread smooth. Folding back the blue canvas tongue, she saw something marked in biro. Three letters, faded almost to nothing, but still legible.

IAN.

A lump formed in Essie's throat. They were hand-me-down shoes, from a big brother.

Simon's torch moved away from the shoe, searching the space behind Rudie. A blur of colour was revealed — not the muted, natural tones of ochre or kaolin, but bright red and turquoise. Essie took in the remains of a checked shirt. A pair of sky-blue trousers.

Essie covered her mouth with her hand. She felt her legs weaken.

'*Mtoto wa siri.*' Simon's voice floated in the stillness. The hidden child.

The little boy's skin, mummified in the arid cave, was stretched taut over his skull, like calf-hide on a drum. Fair, wispy hair framed his face. In the low light Robbie could almost have been alive – just sleeping.

Essie struggled to breathe; her chest heaved but the air seemed too thin. She forced herself to go nearer. She had to see every detail. Pushing the sandshoe into her pocket, she dropped Tommy's leash and grasped Mara against her hip. Then she bent over the dead child.

There were pieces of skin missing, she now saw, or peeled back, revealing bone. Through a gap in one cheek she saw a row of baby teeth, gleaming like pearls in the gloom. She felt as if she was viewing a picture that went in and out of focus. One moment she saw a decomposed body, a skeleton. Then she saw a little boy. She could barely tell which vision was more real.

Robbie's hands were resting at his sides. In death they had closed up, the tendons contracting. He still had fingernails. Eyelashes. His lids were glued closed, covering shrunken sockets. His lips still held their babyish bow but looked frozen. Hard. A second sandshoe was tied onto a foot, a grey sock clinging to fleshless ankles.

'He has fallen down,' Simon said. He aimed his torch beam up to the source of the faint dribble of light. It was a crack in the roof; perhaps the very one in which Tommy's leg had been snared.

Essie turned back to study Robbie. There was something restful about his posture, she now saw, as if he had just flopped where he'd landed, like a rag doll. Essie felt a wave of relief as she understood what this meant. The boy hadn't writhed in agony after his fall or attempted to crawl away. It was obvious why. His head was at the wrong angle to his body. When he fell, he'd broken his neck.

Essie closed her eyes. All the time the search party was scouring the area, he'd been already dead. There had been no unheard cries, no drawn-out pain. At most, there had been a few seconds of panic – and then nothing. That, at least, was a blessing.

'Someone else is here.'

For a moment, Essie questioned the African's use of English. Some*thing*, surely . . . Then her eyes snapped open. She saw Simon crouching beside Robbie, examining the ground. As she walked towards him familiar patterns came into view – a chain of vertebrae; a rack of ribs; long bones of legs, arms; angled joints of knees and elbows. Lying beside Robbie – partly under him, in fact – was what looked like a full skeleton. It had been here a lot longer than he had. Every fragment of skin, hair, flesh was gone. There were just the bones, half buried in the ground.

Possibilities chased through Essie's head. Had a tribesman, wandering in the foothills, fallen in from above, just as Robbie had done? Was this a burial chamber, where a body had been laid to rest? Maybe there was even some link with the paintings. Essie felt a burst of excitement. In archaeology, context was everything. Imagine if they could put the remains of a person together with the artwork. There might be tools to collect, even grave goods . . .

She moved further around, to where the skull would be. It was obscured by Robbie's arm. For a few seconds she hesitated – the child's body had been resting here for so long she didn't want to disturb it. Then she bent down and grasped the sleeve of the shirt. Pulling against the resistance of dried connective tissue, she managed to gently lift the limb. The rotten fabric tore, letting the arm flop back down. She glimpsed the skull for only an instant before it was hidden again. But the image of the yellowed orb was seared into her mind.

The cranium was bulbous, accommodating a large brain. Yet the overall shape was too oval for a modern human. The forehead sloped back, like an Australopithecine's. But only a little. From all her studies and experience in the field, Essie knew what this meant. The skeleton was nothing to do with the Neolithic people who'd painted the walls of the cave. It came from a completely different era.

It was impossible not to take another look. This time she took hold of the arm itself, and moved the limb to one side, resting it on the earth. She aimed her torch directly at the skull. The brow ridges were clearly visible, yet not too pronounced. The chin did not recede, but nor did it thrust forward like her own. The teeth were prominent, like those of all human antecedents from the ape to the Australopithecine.

Essie felt as if she was caught in a dream: her eyes could not be reading what was really there. She blinked and stared again. In front of her lay a creature that was neither ape-like nor a modern human. He or she was something in between.

'It's an *erectus*.' Her voice was just a whisper. 'Has to be.'

Simon met her gaze. She knew he understood as well as she did what this meant. It was the proof the Lawrences and the Leakeys had always dreamed of finding: that our closest ancestor, *Homo erectus*, had lived here in Africa. The implications of the discovery played out in Essie's head – familiar, but still extraordinary. The news would send shock waves through the musty corridors of universities from Cambridge to Berlin. No one would be able to say any more that Europe and Asia held centrestage in our story. When this skeleton was added to all the evidence of Australopithecines that had been found in Africa – with no traces unearthed anywhere else – it tipped the balance of evidence towards the idea that this continent truly was the cradle of humanity. In the beginning, we were all Africans.

Essie gazed along the full length of the skeleton. The degree of preservation was astonishing – only possible because the cave was so dry and so isolated, set into this arid hillside at the foot of the sacred volcano. Archaeologists founded whole careers on single fragments of bones, or a tooth. Here was a complete specimen. The way the teeth were worn would give clues to this person's diet; the bones would show evidence of wear and tear, maybe injuries as well, hinting at their lifestyle. And that was just the start – there was a wealth of information just waiting to be mined. It would form an unimaginably detailed picture of this groundbreaking species who'd survived on planet earth over a million years ago.

Essie turned to Simon, who was still crouched over the site. He shifted his weight on his haunches, then reached out his hand.

'Don't move anything,' Essie said quickly. She leaned closer, studying the matrix into which the skeleton was set. She brushed the earth with the toe of her boot, leaving a line in the surface. The sandstone dust was only partly fossilised. It would make the excavation much easier, but in the meantime, the remains could easily be dislodged.

Simon didn't seem to have heard. He gestured at the skeleton. 'This one is too old. And we don't know who he is. He's not our responsibility.' He turned to Robbie. 'But he is close to us.'

Before Essie could react, he grasped the child's head with both hands. With a careful movement he set it straight, on the neck. Then he tilted it, just a little, in the opposite direction.

'What are you doing?' Essie frowned with incomprehension. It was as if he hoped to repair the boy's fatal injury.

Simon looked to the far end of the cave. 'His head must be pointed this way – towards the mountain. Otherwise his spirit cannot go back into his body and collect the shadow.'

Essie swallowed. 'Shadow?'

'The shadow is the food of the spirit. When we die, our spirit leaves. It goes away to dig in the earth. Then it returns to gain more strength. It must enter through the head, but if it is in the wrong position, it cannot succeed. In my area there are three sacred mountains. For someone lying here, there is only one – Ol Doinyo Lengai.'

He stood up, his hands resting against his sides. He nodded slowly, gazing down at Robbie. In that moment, Essie was struck by the fact that there was no sense of this place being eerie. The shadows seemed to wrap themselves softly around the two figures nestled together on the ground.

'Now we should go,' Simon said. 'This is not a place where we can be.'

Essie heard something in his voice that reminded her of the straightforward way he'd spoken about the meaning of darkness, and the *epeme*. It was clear, certain; cloaked in awe, yet without any sign of fear. She took a last look at Robbie. A final scan of the bones. Then she turned her torch away, letting the dark close in behind.

She checked on Mara, who seemed on the edge of falling asleep. Then she called Rudie to heel and set off after Simon, making sure Tommy was following behind her. As she navigated the darkness, she kept seeing Robbie's mummified body and thinking of what this would mean to Julia. She pictured the bones protruding from under the boy and had a flash image of herself in the Dining Tent announcing her discovery of a *Homo erectus* skeleton.

She heard Simon's words. *This is not a place where we can be.* They reminded her of what Kisani had said about trespassing in the realm of Lengai. Every image or thought that came into her head seemed to be pulling in a different direction. It was impossible to absorb the enormity of all that had just occurred. She forced herself to focus on finding a safe path over the uneven ground.

Essie was about halfway across the cave containing the bodies when something caught her eye, picked up in the sweeping beam of her torch. It was small, shiny. She couldn't think what it could be. She took a few seconds to pinpoint the location. Then she stood still, staring in disbelief. In front of her lay an old-fashioned mechanical pencil. The tarnished silver glinted in the light.

As she bent to pick it up, she was aware of Simon coming to stand next to her. She turned the object over in her hand, feeling its cool weight. Engraved into the silver, in lacy script, was a name. Lifting it closer, she deciphered the letters.

W. G. Stein.

'The missionary,' said Simon. 'He was in here.'

Essie looked at the pencil resting on her palm, imagining it dropping from the man's pocket. He'd left Magadi a decade before Robbie's death. Stein would have had a clear view of the skeleton; he'd have understood the import of what he'd stumbled across. He'd seen the extraordinary cave paintings, too. And he had chosen to keep news of both discoveries entirely to himself.

Simon met Essie's gaze, his eyes just a gleam in the darkness. As if picking up the unease in the atmosphere, Mara stirred. Essie slipped the pencil into her pocket, then patted the baby's back with her hand. She watched Simon turn away, heading for the tunnel that would lead them out of this place. The jerky movements of his torch betrayed his eagerness to be gone.

SEVENTEEN

Julia peered through a pair of close-up glasses as she scraped at a hunk of rock with a dental pick. A half-smoked cigarette rested in an ashtray on the table beside her. Meg lounged at her feet, idly scratching one ear with her hind leg. In another part of the Work Hut, Ian and Diana were sorting through a tray of specimens. It was late afternoon. The last round of tea for the day had just been drunk; cups and saucers still sat among the scattered rocks and bones.

Essie hovered at a distance, watching the three people absorbed in their tasks. She felt a spike of dismay as she saw how closely Ian and Diana were sitting – the intimate way their shoulders rested comfortably together. But Essie couldn't afford to think about this now. She had to work out how she was going to deliver her news. The impact on Julia, especially, of hearing that Robbie's body had been found was going to be huge. The other discoveries were momentous, too, but in a completely different way. It was impossible to imagine how the two revelations could be absorbed at the same time.

Essie clasped her hands together tensely. She was glad Simon had taken Mara away to the nursery. The baby was hungry and tired; the long day had worn her out. Even if this hadn't been the case, Essie would still have handed her over, along with Tommy. The scene was going to be complicated enough without her having to think about a baby. She felt as if she was standing on the edge of a tranquil pond, about to cause a disturbance that would send waves crashing to its edges.

But delaying was not going to change anything. Taking a deep breath, Essie made herself start walking – just putting one foot in front of the other. When her presence was noticed she'd have no choice but to speak. Then somehow, her words would find their own path.

As Essie neared the hut, Rudie ran ahead to greet Meg, bumping Julia's table with his wagging tail. A cup rattled on its saucer.

'Get out of here,' Julia said irritably. She glanced up. As she met Essie's gaze, her hands stilled. It was as if Essie's thoughts were travelling ahead of her – the look that ran between the two women was instantly potent.

'What's wrong?' asked Julia. 'What's happened?' There was a faint clatter as she put down the stone and pick.

Essie approached her slowly, as one would a wild animal that might startle. In front of the table, she stopped. 'We found Robbie's body.'

Julia's eyes widened. She took in a sharp breath. 'What?'

Essie heard the creak of Ian's chair as he stood up. She tore her gaze from Julia and turned to her husband. He was staring at her, his expression caught between incomprehension and shock.

'He's in a cave,' Essie said. 'He fell through a crevice. It was a long way down. His . . .' Suddenly she felt swamped by the enormity of what she was saying; she had to force herself to keep going. 'His neck was broken – you can tell.'

Julia's lips moved as if she was trying to make sense of Essie's words by repeating them to herself. Ian was frozen, his arms clamped to his sides. Diana was watching him, a puzzled look on her face. Even in the midst of the scene Essie felt a flicker of satisfaction that she clearly had no idea who Robbie was.

'Where is the cave?' Julia gasped out the question.

'Over in the foothills. We've been scouting there.' Essie glanced at Ian. 'We moved up from the lakeshore.'

Ian shook his head, frowning. 'But how could you possibly know it's him? It's probably some African child . . .'

Essie flinched at his tone. Did he think she'd march in here and say something like this, if she didn't know for certain it was true?

'The cave is very dry,' she responded. 'He's like one of those mummies they found in Peru. You can see his blond hair. His clothes . . . He's wearing a checked shirt.' She turned to Julia. 'Turquoise and red.'

Julia's hands rose, trembling, to cover her mouth. A low moan escaped between her fingers. On her face Essie watched shock evolving into pain as old grief – long scarred over – was ripped open. Meg stood up, ears lifted in concern, thrusting her nose towards her mistress's face.

'Oh, my God.' Ian closed his eyes, tilting back his head.

Essie bit her lip, almost drawing blood. She wanted to go and put her arms around him, holding him tight – she could see he was being drawn back into his childhood nightmare. But at the same time she could feel the weight of the other part of her story still waiting to be told. It was like a physical presence in the air. There were two bodies in the cave, their bones literally lying against one another. Their stories were bound together.

She turned from Ian to Julia and back. 'We found something else in the cave.' She hunted for the best words. 'Other human remains.'

Ian looked at her in confusion. 'You mean . . . my brother was with someone when he died?'

Julia's face jerked up. 'Who?'

Essie shook her head. 'The bones are fossilised. Very old. From the skull, I'm ninety per cent certain . . .' Her voice trailed off. The words were too outrageous to be uttered.

'Of what?' Ian demanded.

Essie swallowed. 'It's a *Homo erectus*.'

Ian stared at her in frank disbelief. She didn't blame him. The claim was so unlikely to be true.

'You found a skull?' he said. 'Intact?'

'More than that. A whole skeleton.'

Ian exhaled abruptly; it was almost a laugh. 'That's impossible.'

'I know what I saw,' Essie insisted. In a voice that sounded surprisingly calm, even to her, she explained how Robbie's body was lying on top of the skeleton, but that she'd been able to examine the skull, and had also seen parts of the spine, pelvis and limb bones. As she described the anatomy, the Latin names rolling off her tongue, she was conscious of how incongruous it was to be speaking this way, only moments after the revelation about Robbie. It was like the day of her mother's funeral. One minute people were expressing their sympathy; the next they were talking about the weather, clothes, food, cars – as if reality existed in separate strands that could run alongside one another without touching.

By the time Essie finished talking Ian had begun to nod, almost imperceptibly. She knew he'd had to accept that – at the very least – she might have found something significant. It was not as if she was an amateur, after all, or some semi-skilled volunteer. Most of her field experience had been acquired at her husband's side.

'And there are paintings?' he queried.

'At least a dozen of them. Similar to the ones in the Painted Cave. Maybe even done by the same people.' Essie hesitated for a second, but then pushed on. She was like someone making a confession: she wanted to say everything – get it all out, in one go. 'While I was in the cave I also found this.' She produced the silver pencil from her pocket.

Ian examined the object in stunned silence. Then he spoke in a whisper. 'W. G. Stein.'

'What is it?' Diana asked. She was like someone engrossed in a stage play; she kept looking from one character to another, not wanting to miss anything.

Ian didn't respond to her question. Essie ignored her as well. This was not a time to be dealing with an outsider. She went to stand near Julia. The woman was just staring straight ahead. She'd betrayed no reaction to the information about the skeleton, the paintings, the pencil – but that was not surprising. What mother would be able to think of anything, at a time like this, but the news about her dead child?

Essie bent down to look directly into Julia's eyes, peering past the smeared glass of her spectacles.

'Robbie didn't suffer,' she said. 'He was lying right where he fell. He must have died instantly.'

Essie searched her mother-in-law's face, waiting for her reaction. All the Lawrences' worst fears could now be laid to rest. Robbie had not been abducted or consumed by a predator. He'd met with a terrible, yet simple, accident. Surely it was a huge relief to know this. But if Julia felt this way, she showed no sign of it. Essie wondered if, after her initial reaction, the woman was now struggling to grasp the enormity of what had been said. A sudden thought came to Essie. Reaching into her trouser pocket, she extracted the little sandshoe. She held it out.

Julia remained still, her fingers gripping the edge of the table. Essie peered into the tiny dark cave of the shoe, glimpsing Ian's name written on the back of the tongue. She turned the shoe over. It was so small it weighed almost nothing. After a few moments she placed it on the table. In spite of the yellow laces and blue canvas upper, the object looked oddly at home among the chunks of flint and ochre, and the bits and pieces of bones and fossils. The shoe was a relic, after all – the same as they were. Essie pictured it bagged up and labelled.

Item of footwear.

Juvenile Homo sapiens.

Modern era.

Ian walked across and picked it up. He narrowed his eyes as if straining to see more clearly.

'We didn't remove it,' Essie said. 'Rudie had it in his mouth. That's how we knew to search the cave. It was pitch black in there.'

Ian tightened his hold on the shoe, almost crushing it in his hand. His jaw was clenched, a muscle flickering in his cheek. Words burst from his lips.

'Why didn't I hear him?' His voice cracked. 'Why didn't I find him?'

The table shook as Julia used both hands to lever herself to her feet. She half stumbled towards Ian. Essie stepped back, leaving space for son and mother to come together. But Julia pushed past Ian, heading for the open front of the hut.

She walked across to stand at the edge of the clearing, facing the horizon. In the late light the volcano was a mauve pyramid topped with cloud. Julia's arms rose up, reaching towards the foothills as if the gesture could bring her closer to the place where Robbie lay. Essie was reminded of a puppet whose movements were controlled by strings. If they were cut, the figure would fall in a heap on the ground.

The sounds of the camp punctuated the quiet. A clatter of pans coming from Baraka's kitchen. The strangled squawk of a chicken. The distant thud of Tommy butting his head against the gate of his pen.

Essie looked at Ian. He was immobile, staring helplessly at his mother. Essie wondered if she should go across to her. But the next moment Julia was marching back into the hut.

'I want to see him.'

'Of course,' Essie said. 'I'll take you there tomorrow. Simon and I built a cairn and drew a map, so we can find it straightaway.'

'We have to go, now.' Julia turned in the direction of the storeroom, where the shelves had been freshly stocked with spare torches, batteries and Tilley lanterns. 'Come on.'

'It's too far,' Essie said. 'We can't get there and back before dark. You have to pick your way over the rocks. Even with lamps, it would be impossible.'

'Essie's right,' Ian said firmly. 'We have to wait until tomorrow. We can leave before dawn and be on the mountain at first light.'

Julia shifted her gaze from Essie to her son. A struggle showed on her face, but then her shoulders slumped as reasoning found its grip. She made her way back to her place at the work table.

Ian followed her example. After putting down the sandshoe he collapsed into his chair, covering his eyes with his hand.

Diana leaned over, studying the object. Essie could see her piecing clues together. Before any questions could be asked, Essie made a point of looking away. She didn't want to be the one to tell Robbie's story.

Stillness settled over the scene. There were small meaningless movements: Diana lighting a cigarette – the scrape of a match, the flare of the flame; Ian shifting his weight in his chair, creaking canvas; Julia's foot tapping tensely against the leg of the table.

Essie went to stand outside the front of the hut, resting her hand on one of the support posts. She stared into the distance, the air hazy with dust. Suddenly, without warning, she had a flashback to the instant when she'd first glimpsed Robbie's body. Nausea washed over her as she saw the childish lips, the closed eyes, the partially dissolved cheek baring a section of jaw. It was such a brutal combination of preservation and decay. She imagined the haunting image somehow escaping from her head, flitting across the hut like a bird, settling on Julia's shoulder, entering her thoughts.

Struggling to banish the memory, Essie focused on the sound of her breath, moving in and out of her lungs. Slowly the pictures of Robbie faded away. Inexplicably, images of Mara rose up in their place. With them came a shiver of panic. Essie knew where the baby was – safe in Simon's care. Yet she found herself murmuring her excuses, hurrying away. She needed to bury her face against the soft smooth skin. Hear the gurgling laugh. Press her ear to the warmth of the baby's chest, and listen to the strong, steady beat of her heart.

Ian was pacing the tent restlessly, moving back and forth between the bed and Essie's makeshift dressing table.

'Why wouldn't Stein share what he'd found with the world?' he asked. 'It makes no sense.' He kept looking at his watch as if it would help the night go faster.

Essie was sitting on the edge of the mattress, Mara asleep in her lap. Ian's nervous energy was like a cloud filling the air. He was thinking out loud, using words to keep himself calm. She wondered if he was focusing on Stein to avoid thinking about Robbie, and his mother. Julia was in her tent. Diana had produced a sedative from her purse and given her a double dose.

'I guess he was on the same tack as Kohl-Larsen,' Ian added. 'So he didn't want to find evidence of *erectus* in Africa.'

Essie didn't respond straightaway. Until recently, she'd have drawn the same conclusion. Kohl-Larsen was an anthropologist who'd carried out research expeditions in Olduvai Gorge back in the 1930s, around the time the Leakeys first worked there. He had close ties with the Nazi party, sharing the vision of an Aryan master race. The idea of everybody coming from one source – and Africa, at that – didn't exactly fit with Hitler's picture of the world. Because Stein and Kohl-Larsen were both German, people tended to assume they had some similar ideas. Stein's fascination with the Maasai wasn't inconsistent with this picture – the Nazis funded research into people they termed 'primitive'; they wanted to prove how different they were to themselves. But Essie now had new information about their missionary neighbour – which just showed how wrong it could be to lump people together based purely on where they were born.

'It might not have been anything to do with that,' she said carefully.

Ian paused in his pacing. 'What do you mean?'

'Carl Bergmann knows more about Stein than we do.'

At the mention of the photographer, Ian's eyes narrowed – but he wasn't ready to change the topic. 'How come?'

'He went to the Mission archives in Berlin to do some research, once he knew he was going to be living in the old house. He noticed Stein had stopped publishing long before he died. The explanation of the missionaries was that he'd gone mad. They thought he'd spent too much time living alone with the Africans.'

'What's that got to do with keeping his discovery a secret?'

'The cave is in the foothills of Ol Doinyo Lengai,' Essie explained. 'Stein might have been protective of the Maasai – he got close to them, apparently. Maybe he even took on some of their ideas. They don't believe people should go onto the mountain.'

Ian frowned impatiently. Before he had a chance to say more, Essie kept going. 'Simon was very uneasy about us being in that cave. He couldn't wait to get back outside. He thinks the dead bodies, lying so close to the home of Lengai, shouldn't be disturbed.'

'He's a Hadza. They don't believe in Lengai – or any other god, for that matter.'

'I don't think it's that simple,' Essie said. She wondered what Ian would think if he'd seen the man adjusting the position of Robbie's head, and heard him talking about the three mountains that held special meaning to his people. 'Simon definitely believes in something. But also, he believes in their belief – the Maasai, I mean.'

Ian threw her a look of frustration. 'But what we're talking about here is of huge significance. Doesn't he understand that?'

'Yes, he does. But he's still worried about what we're going to do in there. If the place will be respected.' After they'd left the cave, there had been a long discussion between her and Simon about the issues that would arise from their discovery. It had lasted all the way back down the hillside to where the Land Rover was parked.

Ian waved one hand. 'We can't give in to ideas like that. It would be ridiculous. If Simon doesn't want to be involved, then he can get a job somewhere else.'

Essie felt a rush of defensive anger. 'Without him, nothing would have been found. He feels responsible.'

'Well, that's too bad . . . He'll just have to get over it.'

Essie looked at her husband with incomprehension. He'd been born in this country, like his father before him. Normally, Ian was sensitive to traditional culture – even while usually managing to get his own way. He was critical of Europeans who showed disrespect. Essie had to remind herself that he might not be in a stable frame of mind after the news about his brother.

'Look, we don't have to deal with all this now,' she said. 'You've only just heard about Robbie . . .'

Ian spun around to her. 'I don't care about him.' His harsh tone made Rudie's ears lift. 'I'm glad we know what happened. Now we can finally forget about him.'

Essie eyed him in shock. 'You don't mean that.'

'Yes, I do. Don't you think I've had enough? For God's sake, he's plagued me my whole life. It's like he never grew up. He's been there all the time, trailing behind me like a bloody shadow. Because he's dead, he's perfect.'

The outburst over, Ian bent his head. A few moments passed, then Essie risked speaking again. 'What will happen with his body?'

'It will be removed, of course.' Ian answered promptly, as if his thoughts had already been formed. 'But first we have to document the context of the *erectus*. We'll need to bring in an independent observer – someone from England – just to make sure no one questions anything. So that'll take some time, unfortunately.'

'It might be hard for Julia – leaving him there. Now that he's been found.'

Ian let out a frustrated sigh. 'Look, this goes way beyond what might please Julia or Simon or the Maasai – or bloody Lengai, for that matter.'

Essie threw a glance towards the kitchen hut, as if Baraka might be able to overhear this blasphemy. She had to struggle to remain calm. 'With the *erectus* – we have to think of the best approach. We could do an *in situ* investigation.'

'Absolutely not,' Ian said. 'You said the cave's at the bottom of the volcano. That skeleton needs to come out as soon as possible. It's just amazing the place has never been destroyed by an earthquake or buried in a lava flow.'

'But that's the point!' Essie argued. 'What's the latest date we have for *erectus* – five hundred thousand years? The bones have been there at least as long as that – probably more like a million, or a million-and-a-half. Why should anything change, just because we know that it's there?'

Ian was silent – unable to refute her logic.

Essie continued. 'I don't think we can afford to upset the Maasai. And the Hadza, for that matter.'

'Ah, Essie Lawrence. Defender of the Hadza . . .' Ian smiled grimly. 'Perhaps you've been spending too much time with the natives, too. You'd make a good pair with Stein. He'd probably have approved of . . . this.' He gestured at Mara.

Essie recoiled from his words and his tone. She wanted to object, but knew there was no point. Instead she looked down at Mara, resting in her lap. The baby's lips puckered as if she was drinking milk in her dreams. Ian would not have noticed this, Essie knew. When he looked at Mara he saw only a creature that had caused problems – not a unique and precious little person. A new current of emotion flowed through Essie, displacing her anger towards Ian. She had to search for its name. Then it came to her. Pity. She felt sorry for her husband, that he could look at Mara and not be able to actually *see* her . . .

'But I agree that you've got a point,' Ian added. 'If we get into a confrontation with the local people, the government will be involved for sure.'

Essie watched a new line of thought taking hold. Ian was well aware that since Independence the unqualified support of authorities – the National Museum, the University of Dar es Salaam, the Department of Antiquities, the politicians – could not be taken for granted. It was true that the discovery of a *Homo erectus* was of immense significance to all those groups. Most likely they could be persuaded to side against the Maasai. But there was a risk they might not. The political scene was unstable; the outworking of the new spirit of nationalism could not be predicted.

'So we need to take a careful approach,' Ian said. 'Limit the number of people involved. Consult the elders at the *manyatta*. That kind of thing . . .' He frowned thoughtfully. 'In fact, we could make it a hallmark of our new practice. Let Magadi lead the way in dealing with a culturally sensitive location.'

Essie breathed out with relief. Ian had taken on her suggestion as if it had been his own idea. The next morning she would be able to reassure Simon that his concerns were going to be addressed. As she relaxed, she noticed just how exhausted she was. Images of the day's events trailed through her mind – the flamingos flying over-head in a vast pink stream; Carl saying goodbye to her and Mara; the discovery of the cave; the return to the camp with the news. She was aware of the expanse of the double bed spread out behind her, just waiting for her and Ian to lie down together. With a dull sense of regret she thought of how easy and natural that act would once have been. Now, so much had come between them. She recalled the snide comments Ian had just made about her and Stein, and the way he'd looked at Mara. He was under pressure, she knew, caught up in conflicting emotions. So was she. But perhaps it was still possible for them to turn things around: heal the rift that had formed. After all, something amazing had happened at Magadi, and they were both a part of it. Now that they'd agreed to find an appropriate way to work in the cave site, they should be able to bask in shared excitement and anticipation. Essie glanced over her shoulder at the bed. Throughout their marriage, good news and bad news alike had always been absorbed through the touching of skin on skin . . .

She rose to her feet, ready to place Mara in her cot.

'Good night, then,' Ian said.

Essie looked at him in confusion.

'I thought you'd be sleeping in the nursery,' Ian added. 'It's going to be a big day tomorrow.'

As the meaning of his words sank in, Essie stood in silence. Numbness crept through her body. There was no current of emotion running between them, she realised. Nothing.

Ian came over to her. Bending down, he kissed her quickly, his lips dry and stiff. Essie picked up the smell of tobacco and a faint trace of perfume.

'Good night,' Ian repeated.

'Good night,' Essie echoed.

He sat down on the bed, watching while Essie gathered up the baby's bottle and blanket and prepared to leave. He made no move to untie his shoelaces or take off his shirt. When Essie left the tent, he was still sitting there, fully dressed – as if the day was not yet done.

EIGHTEEN

The hiss of the pressure lantern blurred the thud of Essie's boots as she picked her way along the tunnel. Burnt kerosene fumes wafted through the breathless air. She lifted the lamp up to widen the scope of the blue-white glow. A large spider clung to the wall, legs radiating from its body like the petals of some strange dark flower. Essie glanced only briefly at it, preoccupied with what lay ahead of her. Excitement and apprehension brewed inside her, an uneasy mix of emotion that deepened with each step she took.

She could hear Ian right behind her, and the softer noises of the others further back. Diana was walking with Julia. A discussion had been held the night before about whether the visitor should join the excursion. The first viewing of Robbie's body was a very private occasion, but as Ian had pointed out, the *erectus* was in the cave, too. Diana had made no attempt to hide her eagerness to be one of the first to see it. In the end it had been decided that she would come.

Along with the women there were two members of the excavation team. They were long-serving employees – local Maasai – who'd been carefully chosen by Ian. He believed he could trust them to take a scientific view of the cave and its contents. During a hasty pre-dawn breakfast with Julia, Diana and Essie, he'd explained his strategy: by bringing in some Maasai at the start, and briefing them on each step, he hoped to control the way the discoveries would be viewed at the *manyatta*. The older of the men was called Koinet, 'the tall one'. He was having to crouch over in the tunnel to avoid bumping his head. It was obvious how Legishon – 'the polite one' – had won his name, too: he was softly spoken and had a shy smile. So far, the pair only knew that a promising find had been made near the base of the volcano. Now, as they picked their way through the tunnel, the men were loaded up with extra lamps and torches. They also carried Ian's camera bag and tripod, and the special measuring stick that was marked off in sections of black and white to show scale.

Simon was waiting outside with Mara. He'd helped guide the group to the cave entrance, but had declined to go any further. Instead he'd settled down with the baby next to the marker cairn. He'd spread out the baboon pelt and placed her on it. When Essie had left them, Mara was happily kicking her legs and reaching her hands towards the sky. Rudie was sitting nearby watching over her. It was a peaceful scene, bathed in the soft sunshine of early morning.

Essie's thoughts drifted back to them as she walked. She pictured Simon handing Mara a piece of dried bread to chew on, to help bring through another tooth. He'd keep a good eye on her, she knew, making sure she didn't choke. Essie shook her head at herself. How could she be thinking of such matters, when she was involved in something so important? Suddenly she came to a halt. Ahead was the end of the tunnel – the opening into the cave. She turned around to Ian. His face, lit from below, had a ghostly appearance.

'We're nearly there,' she said.

A look passed between them. Before long, the first paintings would come into view, but they'd agreed not to pause and examine them. They had to lead Julia straight to where Robbie lay. Julia could hardly contain her urgency. When they'd first sighted the cairn this morning she'd climbed frantically towards it, grazing her hands and knees as she scrambled over rocks. It was almost as if she imagined she was part of the search party that had set out decades ago in the hope of being able to find Robbie and bring him home alive. While they were preparing the lamps, prior to entering the cave, she'd paced in circles. She kept pushing back loose strands of her hair, which had not been tied back in its usual neat style. Her dishevelled appearance made her look half mad. How she was going to react to seeing the body was anyone's guess. Julia would know what to expect of a mummified corpse. She'd once accompanied William on a trip to Egypt and must have seen plenty of specimens – removed from their sarcophagi and unwrapped – in the Cairo museum. The Peruvian mummies that Essie had mentioned earlier were closer to what she'd be confronted with today – the remains had been preserved naturally in the open air. Julia was familiar with them from *National Geographic* articles. But nothing could prepare a mother for the moment when she first saw her own dead child.

Essie made her way into the cave. With the light shed by six lanterns she was able to see more of its height and the wide sweep of its walls. She quickened her pace, passing the first of the paintings. It was the long-necked bird – almost certainly a flamingo. An image of Carl's face flashed into her mind. She wished he could be here, to see this. That she could tell him about everything she and Simon had found. She imagined Carl holding Stein's pencil, puzzling over the meaning of it . . . But as she played out the scenario in her mind she was aware that – as had happened before – she was seeing the two of them here alone, or perhaps with Simon and Mara somewhere nearby. There was definitely no Diana and Julia in her fantasy. No Ian.

Essie scanned the other paintings. Under the more diffused light of the lanterns they looked soft and ethereal – barely real. She had a sense that if she tried to examine them in detail, they might disappear. Before long she reached the entrance to the second cave. Ducking her head, she stepped inside.

The lantern light reached out ahead of her. She could see the shape of Robbie's prostrate body, and even a glimmer of colour coming from the checked shirt. She stood to one side, letting Ian and Julia go past. Their steps sounded loud in the stillness as they crossed the short distance to Robbie's side. Diana hovered close to Essie, her perfume clouding the air. Koinet and Legishon stood next to her. Their black skin merged with the shadows, creating the effect of disembodied shirts and shorts. Essie could see the whites of their eyes as they stared around them.

A moth danced in the air in front of Essie's face. Drawn by the light, it dived at her lantern, settling on the hot surface above the mantel. Instantly, the creature became fused to the metal. There was a faint crackle as the wings burned.

Julia came to a halt beside Robbie's body. She set down her lantern, casting light over his features. Her chest heaved as if she was straining to breathe. After a few moments she bent over a little, looking more closely. Essie wondered if she was going to ask how they knew the boy's neck had been broken; Essie hadn't mentioned that Simon had straightened the head. But Julia didn't seem to have noticed. She just stood there, still and silent. Then, without warning, she crumpled to her knees.

Ian crouched next to her, putting his arm around her shoulders. Essie could see the wary look on his face. He was gripping Julia's upper arm tightly, his fingers pressing into her flesh. Whether he was intent on comforting his mother, or on protecting the site from being compromised, it was impossible to tell.

Julia screwed up her eyes as if she was enduring physical pain. She stretched one hand towards Robbie's face. When she touched the hard, dry skin, she froze, then flinched away. Essie thought of how warm and soft a child's face should be – how unbearable the contrast must feel. After a few seconds, though, Julia reached out again. With the back of one curled finger she stroked Robbie's cheek, and traced the outline of his lips. She leaned over to brush some dirt from his brow. Then she carefully adjusted the collar of his shirt. Essie was reminded of a mother preparing to send her child off to school, neat and clean, ready for the day. She felt a lump in her throat. The gestures were so gentle, the expression on Julia's face so tender. Essie glanced at Ian, to see his reaction. His brows were knitted and his gaze intense – but Essie wasn't sure if his focus was on Robbie, or on the fossilised remains that were visible beneath him.

A soft, low moan came from Julia. Essie waited for her to break down, at last, and weep – unleashing the pain of so many years of grief. Instead, she just closed her eyes for a moment, her lips pressed together. Then she shifted closer, pulling against Ian's grip on her shoulder. She ran her fingers through the boy's wispy locks. A hunk of hair peeled off in her hand. She gasped, shaking it off as if its touch had burned her skin.

The strand of blond hair lay on the ground in front of her. It looked like a half-grown feather left behind by a fledgling bird. For a long moment Julia just stared at it. Then she picked it up, folding it inside her fist. With her other hand she grasped Ian's shoulder and levered herself to her feet.

Ian stood up beside her. He looked from Julia, to his brother, and back. He appeared to be desperately trying to work out what he should be doing. Essie felt a rush of sympathy. She understood that this was a predicament he knew all too well. He'd spent half his life trying to meet the expectations of his mother, his father, his colleagues – everyone he met – all because of that one day when he'd run off to play with his brother and returned alone.

The quiet lengthened. Diana shuffled her feet. Koinet cleared his throat. Essie listened to the distant rumble of the volcano. Here in the cave, the sound seemed close, almost as if it came from deep inside her own body.

'I want to go now,' Julia said abruptly. Her voice cracked but was still firm and clear. She began to walk away.

'Wait,' Ian protested. He took a step after her. Essie could see he felt torn – he couldn't let his mother go off alone, but he was impatient to move on to examining the skeleton. His gaze shifted from the two Africans, to Diana, then settled on Essie.

Essie looked at him in silence. She wanted to stay and share the moment when Ian first took in the astonishing details of the skull, the bones. She deserved to be here. But she was his wife, and Julia's daughter-in-law.

'I'll go with her.' The words fell out of Essie's mouth, taking her by surprise. It was almost as if they'd been planted there by someone else.

'Thank you.' Ian threw her a grateful look.

Essie bent down, hiding her face by pretending to adjust her lantern. While she fiddled with the kicker knob, she heard Ian instruct his assistants to bring the camera equipment over. Glancing up, she saw Diana move to stand beside him. She was wearing a special miner's torch on her head – it was her personal possession, the only one of its kind at Magadi. With its help she would make a very useful companion for Ian. All she had to do was follow his head movements with her own, and the strong bright beam would always be shining right where he was looking. With her hands free, she would also be able to hold his camera or take down notes. A perfect team.

Straightening up, Essie headed after Julia. As she left Ian and Diana behind her she braced for a wave of jealousy. Instead what she felt was more like a creeping sense of claustrophobia. It seemed to arise from within her, rather than being triggered by the gloomy confines of the cave. It was as if all the conflicting emotions she experienced whenever she was with Ian and Diana were suddenly crowding in on her. Then there was the pressure of being constantly torn between the professional world she shared with the Lawrences and the one she'd been inhabiting with Mara and Simon and Carl. She wanted to escape from it all.

Overtaking Julia, she hurried towards the entrance. She held her lamp high, so she could walk more quickly. She barely noticed the paintings as she passed them. She couldn't wait to be back outside, breathing fresh air under the wide blue sky.

When she finally emerged from the cave, blinking in the brightness, her eyes went straight to where she'd left Simon and Mara, beside the cairn. They were not there. The place where the baboon pelt had been spread was empty. As Essie scanned the area, her heart skipped a beat. In the short time it took for her to locate the pair – a little further away, sitting in the shade of some bushes – she imagined a whole series of disasters that could have occurred. Yet she should have known that Mara was safe. Essie trusted Simon to take care of the baby as much as she trusted herself – more, in fact. After all, the Hadza man was as much at home in this wild country as an Englishman would be in his own sitting room. Essie blamed her pointless panic on being unnerved by seeing Robbie. But she also knew she had no ability to be rational where Mara was concerned. It was as if the baby had forged some special pathway to Essie's heart, which bypassed large sections of her brain.

Essie was still standing there, looking at Mara and Simon, when Julia stumbled past her. The woman kept going, moving off to sit by herself on one of the broken hunks of rock. Meg approached her mistress cautiously, brow furrowed and ears pricked as if trying to make sense of the intense emotion she detected. As the dog came near, Julia pulled her close, burying her face against the furry neck.

Essie headed over, searching her mind for the right words to say. But then Julia looked up, frowning, and waving her away. Essie paused, eyeing her mother-in-law uncertainly. It seemed wrong not to be at her side, offering comfort. But Julia had made her wishes very clear.

As Essie turned back to the others, Simon got to his feet, holding Mara. When Essie reached them, he threw a questioning glance at Julia.

'She wants to be left alone,' Essie explained.

He nodded, his eyes full of sympathy. Then he looked over at the cave.

Essie guessed at his thoughts. 'She couldn't stay in there.'

Simon nodded again. 'What is happening now?'

'Ian's taking photographs.'

Simon just looked at her, making no comment.

Essie took Mara from him. She kissed the top of her head, her lips lingering on the soft springy curls. Closing her eyes, she breathed in the familiar smell of coconut oil and soap. The sensation drew her into the present moment, distancing her from the events in the cave.

'I've missed you,' she murmured to Mara. It seemed a ridiculous remark; they'd only been parted for a short while. But it was true.

Before long, Mara started to wriggle impatiently. Essie could see she was ready for a change of scenery, or perhaps she needed a sleep. The baby's lips turned down as if she was about to cry. Essie glanced anxiously at Julia. The last thing the woman needed to hear right now was the sound of a baby wailing. Essie quickly began playing a game – one of Mara's favourites. She touched the baby's toes, one by one.

'This little piggy went to market. This little piggy stayed at home . . .' Essie chanted the rhyme that she remembered from her own childhood.

Simon turned to watch, abandoning a stone he'd been rolling over and over in his hand. Essie had the sense that he was keen to find anything that would distract him from his thoughts.

'This little piggy had roast beef,' Essie continued. 'And this little piggy had none.'

Simon raised his eyebrows, then he shook his head. 'That is a strange story to tell.'

Essie paused. He was right. It was an odd thing to say to a child – especially Mara. The idea of some people having food while others went hungry was anathema to the Hadza way of life. Essie just hoped Simon wasn't going to ask her about the meaning behind this rhyme, as he had done after seeing the nursery mobile inspired by 'Hey Diddle Diddle'. She'd have to confess, again, that she had no idea, beyond the fact that it had some connection with English political history.

Essie gently squeezed Mara's toes again, one after another – but now she remained silent. The quiet was not one of peace or contentment; it reflected the emptiness of someone who has nothing to say. Essie envied Simon's vast trove of tribal songs and stories, which he shared so freely with Mara. They were part of the culture of his ancestors, who'd most likely been here in this land for tens of thousands of years. By comparison Essie felt as impoverished as a beggar in rags. She had so little that was truly her own.

Mara didn't seem to mind about the absence of the rhyme. She was smiling in anticipation of what was coming next. Essie walked her fingers up the baby's leg, and on over her body, to tickle her under the chin. As Mara collapsed into giggles Essie glanced over at Julia again. A laughing baby could be as distressing as one that was crying. Julia didn't seem to have noticed anything, though. The look on her face was remote, as if she'd travelled far away in her mind.

After playing with her for a little longer, Essie tried rocking Mara to sleep. She was about to pick up the baboon pelt when she saw Simon become suddenly tense. She turned her head to follow his gaze.

Koinet and Legishon were standing in the entrance to the tunnel. Essie frowned. She hadn't expected the others to appear so soon. Then she realised that the two Maasai were alone. She turned to Julia to gauge her reaction – but she seemed not to have noticed them.

The men marched across, barely glancing at Julia as they passed. Even Legishon offered no greeting. They ignored Essie and the baby, too, focusing only on Simon. When they reached him, Koinet began talking in a vehement mixture of Swahili and Maa. Essie had to struggle with the translation.

Koinet was telling Simon that the Bwana had moved the body of *mtoto wa siri* because he wanted to look at the bones that were underneath where he lay. Koinet's eyes were wide with outrage.

'*Hapukewa heshima,*' he said. He has been disrespected.

Essie looked uncomfortably at Simon. She had interfered with the body herself, by moving the boy's arm. So had he – by correcting the tilt of the head. Even though Essie wanted to know exactly what Ian had done, she didn't like to ask questions that might deepen the tension. Anyway, she felt sure he wouldn't have actually picked up the body. He'd been nervous about Julia just touching it. Even if he'd studied the surrounding sediment and determined that there would be no disruption to the *erectus* skeleton, he wouldn't have committed such a breach of procedure. But even as she thought this through, Essie felt a twinge of doubt. The temptation would be so strong. With neither Julia nor Essie there to protest, and perhaps with Diana urging him on, Ian might have been unable to resist.

Next, Koinet began describing how the Bwana had started taking the photographs. He mimed the way Ian had held out his camera, pressed a button, and somehow triggered an instant flash of lightning. Legishon recoiled visibly at the memory. Essie realised that neither of the Maasai would ever have seen flashbulbs in use before – at Magadi all the work took place outdoors under the bright African sun. She could imagine how shocking it would have been for them to see the blue-white flash being unleashed at close quarters, as if by pure magic, instead of bursting from the sky. And for just one instant they'd have been hit by the full horror of the half-decayed child, the haunting sight of the bare bones protruding from underneath – everything exposed in harsh detail. The scene would have had a truly nightmarish quality.

Koinet fell silent for a while, as if the power of the memory had stolen his words. Then he leaned closer to Simon, turning his back to Essie. When he spoke again his voice was barely audible. Though she didn't know exactly what he was saying, his tone was clear – the fear and awe, and the anger. A few words reached her. She recognised a Swahili phrase used to describe an animal running in panic.

Mnyama anayeishi kwa hofu.

Then she heard the name of the volcano. *Ol Doinyo Lengai.* The home of God.

Lengai. Lengai. Lengai . . .

While he listened, Simon bowed his head. He was ashamed, Essie knew, of his role in the whole chain of events that had led everyone here today. He'd never meant to enter a cave hidden inside the mountain, or to disturb two bodies. He could never have imagined that he and Essie would find the *erectus*. But that was what had happened. She wondered if she should try to offer some reassurances about how Ian intended to approach working on the site. But it was not her place to do that. If she said the wrong things in the wrong way, it would only complicate the situation. She looked across to Julia again, wanting to draw her into what was going on. But Julia was still gazing at the ground, stroking Meg's head mechanically with one hand. The dog's ears were being pulled back, her eyes bulging slightly with the pressure, but Meg remained stoically still.

As the men continued talking, Essie retreated. She felt as if their fear and anger and distrust, permeating the air like a dark gas, might find its way into Mara's lungs. From the rucksack she removed the insulated box and took out a bottle of milk. Mara grasped it with both hands, now expert at the task, and began feeding hungrily. Essie watched the slow, steady decline of the liquid. Then came the sound of the bottle being drained. Before it was completely empty, though, Mara turned her head, letting the last drips fall on her cheek. Following her gaze, Essie saw that Ian had appeared in the entrance to the tunnel, Diana at his side.

One look at his face told Essie that her conclusion about the skeleton was correct. She felt a surge of excitement. But as she headed towards him she could see that his elation was overlaid with anxiety. Instead of meeting Essie's gaze – letting the warmth of gratification travel between them – his eyes were trained on the two Maasai.

He sauntered casually across from the cave. He was hoping to play down the whole situation, she guessed, even though he was concerned that his assistants had walked off the job. Essie watched him veil his emotions. She was reminded of how Rudie behaved whenever she gave him a meaty bone – he'd pretend to be disinterested at first, so as not to signal to any creature looking on that he possessed something worth fighting over. Essie liked to peep back at the dog as she walked away, watching for the moment when he decided it was safe to let his eagerness show, and seize the bone with his teeth.

Ian's ploy was not successful, though. The air remained tense. The men stayed stony-faced while he tried to interest them in a description of the geological features of the cave. When he handed around a packet of biscuits from his bag, even Legishon rudely declined. As Ian stood on his own, munching away, Essie noticed his hand checking his shirt pocket, where several rolls of film made a prominent bulge. She knew he was thinking of the images captured there. She could almost see them running through his mind, like a trail of jewels in the hands of a pirate king.

*

The Land Rover moved steadily across the plains, leaving the foothills far behind. Essie held Mara in her arms. She covered the baby's head protectively with her hand in case it bumped against the window. Along with the usual smells of dust and sweaty bodies, Essie breathed in the chemical taint of new vinyl. The vehicle was the latest addition to the Magadi fleet and had *Diana Marlow Expeditions* written along both sides. Perhaps because it was Diana's car, she was sitting in the front with Ian. Koinet and Legishon were sharing the rear bench seat with Essie and Mara. Simon was in the old Land Rover, with Julia at the wheel. When the group had finally reached the place where the vehicles were parked, Ian had decided who should ride in which car. He was obviously keen to separate Simon from the Maasai, and also, it seemed, from Essie. He was quick to accept Julia's assertion that she was fit to drive, ignoring Essie's whispered concerns that she might not be. He'd sent the first carload on its way as speedily as possible. Essie guessed he was trying to limit opportunities for conversation – though it was much too late for that.

Inside the confines of the Land Rover the atmosphere felt even more tense than it had been back on the mountain. The two Maasai sat stiff-backed in their seats, hands braced on their knees, eyes fixed ahead. No one spoke. Essie gazed out over the scenery, taking in the sun-yellowed grasses, the splashes of pink made by the desert roses, the blue ellipses of the pools. She tried to draw the beauty and peacefulness into herself, but nothing could quell the misgiving that grew inside her. She kept going back over all the things she'd thought about the day before, as she and Simon were returning to the camp. There were so many issues to be considered – all of them unexpected.

Essie had always assumed that the pictures described by the Hadza hunter would be in an open setting like the ones she'd already studied. Now that Simon had given her a new understanding of the meaning of darkness, she grasped the implications of them being deep inside a cave. The site would have to be lit up while she did her tracings. The almost tangible peacefulness was going to be disturbed. Then, there was the fact that the adjoining cave had been the final resting place for two bodies. The proximity to the volcano took on new meaning as well. Essie's research would take place literally inside it. Whether she believed in the existence of Lengai or not was irrelevant. To the Maasai, the mountain was holy.

Whatever Essie might do as part of her work would pale into insignificance, she knew, compared with the invasion that was going to be triggered by the *erectus* skeleton. As soon as news of its existence got out, the attention of the whole world would be focused on the cave. Archaeologists would flock here, along with teams of journalists and photographers. Even though carrying out the research *in situ* was the best option, the disturbance would be both intense and lasting. The age-old silence would be broken by the clamour of voices. And the sacred darkness would be blasted with light – a bright unwavering glare that would go on for years.

If they hadn't discovered Robbie's body, Essie thought, perhaps it would've been better to have simply concealed what they'd found. But they could never have robbed Julia and Ian of the knowledge about where Robbie's body lay, or withheld the clues to how he'd died. Also, Essie didn't think she was brave enough to make the same decision as Stein appeared to have done. The responsibility was too great. She had tried telling herself that in due course someone would surely find other proof that *Homo erectus* had inhabited this continent, but the truth was that lots of people had already been searching diligently for over half a century. In addition to the Leakeys and the Lawrences here in Tanzania, there were the Wilfred-Smiths in Kenya, Broom and Clarke in South Africa, and others elsewhere. All that time and effort had not turned up a single tooth or scrap of a cranium that could be given this classification. Even stone tools like the ones linked with *Homo erectus* remains in Indonesia, Europe and China had eluded discovery. And now, Essie and Simon had stumbled on an entire *erectus* skeleton. The find in the cave was – and always would be – completely unique.

Yet still, as Essie thought it all through again, she wondered if she and Simon should have just returned to the camp yesterday and said nothing. Maybe the benefit to the Lawrences of knowing what had happened to Robbie and the contribution to the world of discovering more about the human story were not the things that mattered most. Maybe there was a reason why this continent, Africa, protected her secrets. Perhaps the enduring mystery – that had captured the imagination of so many people for so long – was intended to remind us that facts and figures, rational thought and scientific theory, were not everything.

Even while she was contemplating this, Essie viewed herself with amazement. She'd devoted her whole life to archaeology, and much of it to the field of paleoanthropology. She was the daughter of Professor Arthur Holland. She was Ian Lawrence's wife. Julia Lawrence's daughter-in-law. For her to be considering following Stein's example, even for a second, was inexplicable. If Ian could read her thoughts, he'd think she had simply gone mad. Like her mother. Or like Stein. Essie recalled how Ian had accused her the night before of being like the old missionary – he'd said they'd make a good pair. Maybe he was right. Essie had exposed herself to influences that had changed her in ways she'd not understood. If that were the case, it had all begun the day she had crossed paths with Nandamara while out collecting flint stones – and come home with a baby in her arms.

Essie looked down at Mara, resting on her lap. She traced the contours of the little face, the subtle tones of black on black. Then she took in the rest of her body, bare but for the string of white beads and the nappy that had been put on in preparation for the return to camp. The white towelling stood out against her darkness. Essie thought of all the times she'd bathed, dried, oiled and powdered every inch of that velvet skin. All the bottles of milk she'd prepared in order to keep Mara well fed and content. The tears she'd wiped away. The hiccups she'd soothed. It was impossible, now, to imagine that Essie might never have had anything to do with Mara. If fate had not brought Nandamara and Essie together, the baby might even be dead by now.

Essie stroked Mara's forehead, feeling the warmth of her. Watching the rise and fall of her chest. Mara was deeply asleep, her limbs flopping loosely. She always felt heavier in this state, somehow, than when she was awake. Essie had given up the obsessive ritual of weighing her on the nursery scales; she could tell by the feel of her body that flesh had filled out, firm yet soft, cushioning her bones. She was around four months old now. The fragility of the newborn was long gone. She'd claimed her place in the world.

A lump formed in Essie's throat. She stared out at the landscape again, searching for reassuring evidence that – even though the pools and springs created patches of green – the land was still deep in the grip of the dry season. If she were to walk across the grasses, the brittle stems would crunch and shatter underfoot. The leaves on the bushes were tough and old. The place was still empty of large game – the sand would be marked only with the prints of small, scurrying creatures; lizards trailing long tails; slow-moving, sun-sleepy snakes. The sky above was clear and blue – safely empty of any hint of cloud. It should be around two months before the Short Rains came.

There was no need to think of the future. Not yet.

'Nearly home.' Ian's voice rose over the drone of the engine, his tone still insistently bright.

Essie watched the camp come into view. There were the lines of tents and thatch-roofed huts, the shade trees huddled in groups, and the barren swathe of the parking area. A tendril of smoke rose up from Baraka's cooking fire. Usually Essie felt a sense of homecoming when she caught sight of the place after a day out in the bush. But today, it was as if her perceptions had been distorted. The settlement didn't seem to belong there on the hillside any more. Set against the background of the *korongos*, its grip on the environment looked fragile. It was so easy to picture it just disappearing – an unwanted smudge, wiped away. As she watched the camp draw nearer, Essie had a vision of the land as a living creature, the humans who lived and worked there no more than an unwanted infestation. She imagined it stirring into life, rising up and giving its body a great shake, like a huge wet dog shedding water from its fur.

NINETEEN

The yellow plastic moon swung wildly as Mara batted it with her hand. A few days ago Essie had lengthened the cord from which the mobile hung, so the nursery rhyme characters would be in reach of the change table. It meant she had to be careful while she was standing there in case she was hit on the head, but the distraction stopped Mara from wriggling in protest as she was being dressed. The baby didn't understand why sometimes she was allowed the freedom of being naked, while on other occasions – like now – she had to wear a nappy, pants and frock.

Essie pulled the two corners of the folded cloth together, binding them firmly over Mara's hips. She tried to keep her movements steady and relaxed to avoid transmitting the tension that simmered inside her. Mara was so quick to pick up on Essie's emotions that it seemed there was an almost physical connection between them. The last thing Essie wanted this morning was for Mara to be unsettled.

As soon as she was finished here she'd be heading for the Work Hut, where Ian was waiting to talk to her. The meeting had been set up at breakfast time. There was a formal air to the arrangement as if she and Ian were just colleagues, now, instead of husband and wife. They'd slept apart again last night. Essie had gone straight to the nursery when she'd eaten her dinner. After the events of the day – the visit to the cave, and all that had then ensued – she simply didn't have the energy to face the question of whether she and Ian would, or would not, be sharing the same bed. Nor did she want to risk a confrontation about where else her husband might have preferred to be sleeping. When she thought about Ian and Diana – and the truth of what might be going on between them – she felt like a moth hovering around a lantern. If she moved in close, she would be burned. Unbearable emotions would overwhelm her and she wasn't sure how she would cope. And there was more than her own survival to consider. There was Mara. With a baby in the camp, life could not be turned on its head.

Essie didn't know if Ian had been upset about her choice to sleep in the nursery or relieved. Perhaps he'd been glad to be alone in their tent. Perhaps he'd not even been there. This morning he'd made no comment on it. Instead he'd been preoccupied with scribbling notes on his pad, writing and chewing toast at the same time. Any attempt to conceal his feelings about the contents of the cave had been abandoned. He radiated an intense, almost uncontainable, excitement.

Yesterday, when they'd all finally returned to the camp, his demeanour had been very different. He'd watched on in silence while Simon, Koinet and Legishon walked off towards the staff camp, and Julia retired to her bed, wanting solitude. When he'd joined the others in the Dining Tent his mood had remained subdued. Essie knew he was not grief-stricken about Robbie – he'd made that clear – but the experience of seeing the boy's body, and witnessing his mother's distress, was obviously raw and close. On top of this, there was the conflict with the Maasai workers. A report on the events at the cave must have travelled around the staff camp quickly. There was no sound of singing or drumming coming from that end of the settlement – only an eerie quiet. Kefa had served the meal but hadn't lingered in the tent. The after-dinner cup of tea had been slow to arrive.

Diana had been determined to lift Ian's spirits. She started talking about the *erectus* – teasing out what the discovery would mean. Then she had a bottle of champagne brought to the table, and opened it herself, aiming the cork out through the doorway. The familiar popping sound created an atmosphere of celebration, but it had not lasted. Even as the wine frothed over the edges of the glasses, it was fizzling away. Ian's toast to the future of Magadi sounded hollow. Every now and then, as the evening progressed, his excitement had flared up like a pocket of oil burning in a piece of green firewood. With Diana's encouragement he would discuss the position of the skeleton, or speculate about how the *erectus* came to be there, and how the remains had been so perfectly preserved. Then he would fall suddenly quiet again, though Essie could sense thoughts still racing behind his eyes. Diana had smoked constantly, lighting a new cigarette from the stub of the one before. She hadn't spoken much herself, aside from prompting Ian. Perhaps she real-ised that the undercurrents of emotion were too complex for her to understand. Or else she, like Ian, was thinking and planning in silence.

Essie pulled a pair of pink plastic pants over Mara's nappy and smoothed down the skirt of a pink-and-white dress. Then she paused, gazing down, almost wishing Mara would begin to cry, hold-ing Essie hostage to the task of meeting her needs. But the baby kicked her legs happily, as if she'd forgotten she didn't like being clothed. Essie smiled, momentarily distracted from her concerns. Playfully she reached for Mara's feet. Though still so small they felt firm and strong in her hands. If Hadza babies were like their Maasai counterparts, it was likely that within a few months she'd begin standing up. Essie pictured the sturdy feet planted on the ground. The soft pink soles pressed into the red earth. Skin dusty with ash. Dirt under the toenails. Her imagination was like a roving camera lens, pulling back, revealing more. A tuft of yellow grass. The spiky thicket of a thornbush. There was a burnt stick, one end charred with a black pattern of squares. A woven basket, the insides stained red by berry juice. Sounds went with the scene – women talking to one another, their words punctuated with the constant clicking that Essie had once found so strange. The voices floated, disembodied, in the air. There was a lilt of laughter, the hiss and crackle of a fire. Then one woman's voice could be heard rising above the others. She was calling out to the baby, Mara – but not using her name.

Essie tried to add to the vision – summoning Giga's face, the way she spoke, the string of beads she'd been wearing that day at the Painted Cave. But nothing came to her. The Hadza woman was like a wraith from a dream. The essence of 'mother'. The one who would take Essie's place.

Bending her head, Essie brought the captive feet towards her face. She kissed the twin lines of toes, tasting warm salty skin. She felt the sting of tears in her eyes. Mara laughed and reached out with her hands as if they must be tickled as well. But after just a few seconds she became very still, as if sensing that this was not just a light-hearted game. Essie held the feet against her lips, pressing steady and hard as if she might somehow staunch the pain that welled inside her like blood from a cut vein.

A sudden rustle of canvas made Essie turn around. In the doorway Ian's body was a dark shape backlit by bright early sun.

'There you are,' he said. 'I've been waiting for you.'

'Sorry.' Essie picked up Mara, holding her against one shoulder. She averted her face while she collected herself. When she turned back, Ian was scanning the nursery, looking baffled, as if he still didn't understand how the old guest tent had come to be so transformed. In all the time since it had happened, he'd barely set foot in the place.

'Shall we go to the Dining Tent?' Essie asked.

Ian ran his hand back through his hair. He didn't appear to have heard her.

'I've been on the radio,' he said. 'Talking to people in Dar es Salaam. And Cambridge. Telling them what we've found.'

Essie stood still. '"We"?'

Ian looked at her for a second. 'Well, you. But you know how it is.'

Essie nodded slowly, absorbing the realisation that she and Simon were not going to be personally recognised for their work. In the past, this would have upset her. However much she pretended otherwise, she'd have resented the fact that as Head of Research, Ian would enjoy the limelight. And now there was the added factor of Diana, the benefactor, being right there beside him. But these last months had changed Essie. Even though the admiration of others would have been nice, she could manage without it. She knew what she and Simon had done. She knew why it mattered. And that was enough.

'No one can believe it,' Ian continued. 'Well, who could blame them? I just told them to wait until they see the pictures.' He gave a triumphant smile. 'The camera never lies.' He began pacing up and down between the door and bed. 'I'll get the film developed and printed in Dar es Salaam – blown up into a large format. I'll show them around at the museum and the university. Then I'll go to the Department – the Minister will be there on Tuesday.'

'You're going to Dar es Salaam?' Essie asked. 'Straightaway?'

'It's all organised,' Ian responded. 'I've chartered a plane. I want face-to-face, top-level meetings as soon as possible.' He paused in front of Essie. 'One thing is very important. The location must remain a secret until I have all the right agreements in place.'

Essie nodded. It was probably the best way to keep control, and make sure the work was done with the minimum disruption to the site.

'Publicity has to be managed carefully as well. I've got a call booked with the BBC for later today. They'll need detailed briefing notes.'

As he walked, Ian picked up random items and then put them down again – a pink hairbrush, the grey plush elephant, a plastic rattle. They were discarded after only a moment's attention, like stones from a specimen tray that showed no potential. Essie recognised Ian's habit of quelling nervous energy through constant movement.

'We'll fly straight on from Dar es Salaam to London,' he continued. 'There we'll hold a press conference.'

Essie didn't need to ask where this event would happen. Back in 1948, Mary Leakey had held a press conference at Heathrow Airport after being met by a pack of journalists and photographers when she arrived on a BOAC flight from Africa. She'd shown off the skull of the ancient primate *Proconsul*. It was proposed that the creature could have been the common ancestor of both apes and humans – occupying a place in the family tree before the two evolutionary strands were split. The skull, with its hints at human characteristics, had been painstakingly assembled from thirty fragments of bone. It had been packed inside a biscuit tin, which Mary had famously nursed on her lap throughout the flight. The airline had offered a free ticket to the Leakeys – but only one. Since Mary was the person who'd made the discovery, she had taken the trip, exchanging her work clothes for a smart woollen suit. Essie had seen some of the press photographs mounted in frames, over at Olduvai. Mary had been at the centre of a frenzy of attention, surrounded by men wielding microphones and cameras. Though she must have loved sharing the discovery with the world, she looked stunned and forbidding – completely out of place. Back in Africa, Louis Leakey had been hard at work managing the publicity. The conference had been the family's first step towards international fame.

'So the next thing is . . .' Ian tossed aside a ball made from velvet, which jingled as it rolled across the bed. 'We need to name our *erectus*.'

This was something else the Leakeys had done, over the years. Nicknames were much catchier and easier for people to remember than combinations of numbers and letters. Olduvai Hominid 7 – a *Homo habilis* – had been dubbed Johnny's Child since the fossil came from an immature specimen and had been found by the Leakeys' own son Jonathan. Olduvai Hominid 5, or OH5, went by the name Dear Boy. There was even a Twiggy and a Cinderella, though they were less well known.

'Do you have any ideas?' Essie asked Ian. She wondered if Diana would step in with a name – immortalising a relative, an old boyfriend or even a pet.

'I haven't had time to think about it much yet,' Ian replied. 'There's so much to arrange. Flights. Accommodation. Meetings. We'll have to bring along a couple of Tanzanians – probably from the government. We'll collect them in Dar es Salaam on our way. So that will make six of us altogether. At least we aren't short of money to pay for it all.'

'Wait,' Essie broke in. 'What do you mean? Who's going?'

'Julia, me, you, Diana . . .'

Essie stared at him. 'But I can't come.'

'What on earth do you mean?'

'I can't take Mara away from here.'

'No, of course you can't.' Ian spoke slowly, as if to an uncomprehending child. 'The baby will stay here with Simon.'

Essie shook her head. 'No.'

'Why ever not? You trust him, don't you? He often babysits for you.'

'Of course I trust him. But I still don't want to leave her.' Essie instinctively held Mara more tightly. 'It's okay. You all go. I'll just stay here.' Even as she was speaking, Essie was struck by the fact that she felt no ambivalence about her statements at all. The thought of leaving Mara here at Magadi and flying to another country was simply impossible for her to entertain.

'Essie.' Ian said her name firmly. 'This is about the Lawrence family. When we're all seen together at Heathrow, people won't just be thinking about us. It'll be as if my father were there as well. It's . . . what we're known for. Julia and William, the first couple. Then you and me. The whole thing won't look right without you.'

'You've got Diana.' There was a spike in Essie's voice.

'She's not a member of the family.'

A tense quiet filled the air. This would be the time for Essie to ask exactly what status Diana did have in Ian's life – to demand to know if he had been unfaithful. But as before, Essie's thoughts kept turning back to Mara. She pressed her lips onto the crown of her head.

'You need to think very seriously about this,' Ian said. 'In a couple of months you'll be handing that baby over to her real family. Then you'll be free to get back to work. You'll regret that you didn't seize your place in all this. After all, you were the one who made the big find. You deserve to be part of the team.'

Essie shook her head. 'What I'd regret would be if I gave up even one day of the time I have left with Mara.'

'But your own family comes first!' Ian's hands formed fists at his sides as if he was about to explode with frustration. Instead he bent his head, looking down at the ground. After a few moments he lifted his gaze. In the soft light of the tent his eyes burned with the intense blue of a kerosene flame. 'In Cambridge I'll be visiting Arthur.'

'Dad?' Essie caught her breath. She had a flash image of herself running into her father's arms, feeling the prickle of his tweed jacket, taking in the smell of his pipe tobacco. They'd sit at the kitchen table and drink tea from the blue-and-white pot with the cracked spout. After that, they'd tour the damp garden, peering into mossy corners to see what had grown and what had died away. There were so many things Essie longed to discuss, in a way that was not possible in letters. Practical topics, like his health, were just the start. She wanted to learn all the small details of his life and share stories of hers. And even though part of her didn't want to think about it, there were the serious questions she wanted to ask him. This was her chance to try to learn the truth about Lorna. Perhaps, face to face, she could push Arthur to be honest about whether her mother's family had Aboriginal heritage – whether an ancient bond with the island home could have been the reason

Lorna literally couldn't survive in England. If that were the case, Essie could ask Arthur why he had never taken his wife back to her home, her family, when she'd been so desperately unhappy. Perhaps – as Diana had insinuated – there was some other issue at play in their marriage. Arthur wasn't all that old, but the future could still not be taken for granted. If Essie didn't go with Ian to England, now, leaving Mara behind, she might never find out what had really gone on in Lorna's life. She'd be letting her mother down.

Ian waited in silence, wearing a small, forced smile.

Essie tried picturing Lorna's face as if this might be able to guide her decision. Instead, she saw her own image, as if she and her mother were one person, and Mara, in some way, a baby version of herself. Essie focused on the warm sleepiness of Mara's head nodding against her shoulder. She thought about the fact that Lorna had once held her own baby in her arms, just like this. Lorna knew what Essie was feeling. She'd want her daughter to remain right here where she belonged.

'I'm not coming with you.'

Ian pursed his lips. He was quiet for a while, as if hunting for a new line of argument. 'You're pushing me towards Diana. You do know that?'

Essie eyed him in silence, her gaze unwavering. She saw him struggle with the realisation that his wife, his assistant – the one who'd always followed his instructions – was not going to be swayed by anything he could say. He looked angry, confused, hurt – but more than anything, defeated. He had no cards left to play.

With Mara on her hip Essie walked along the stony path that ran through the middle of the staff camp. The Lawrences didn't enter the area very often – it was an unnecessary invasion of the workers' privacy – but when they did, they always received a warm welcome. Today, though, the mood was different. As Essie moved between the tents, avoiding the crisscross of fly lines and the pegs in the ground, she felt people watching her every step. When greetings were called, they had a grudging edge.

Essie paused at a tactful distance from the unzipped door of Simon's tent.

'*Hodi!*' she called out.

There was no reply – yet Essie sensed that he was there. With a stab of pain she realised Simon might be trying to avoid her. When they'd returned late yesterday afternoon there had been no chance for them to talk in private, but she knew Simon deeply regretted the part he'd played in finding the cave. It would be hard for him to trust Ian's reassurances about how the research was going to be handled. After what Essie had just heard about Ian's plans for publicity, she felt uneasy herself. She couldn't blame Simon if he held her responsible for the dilemma in which he now found himself. It would be understandable if he needed some time to process the situation before he was ready to face her; she was his friend, but she was also a Lawrence.

The polite thing, Essie knew, would be for her to withdraw – but she just couldn't bring herself to walk away. Of all the people in the camp, Simon was the only one she wanted to be with.

'Hello? Simon?' she called again.

After a short delay the man appeared in the entrance. He was wearing clean, pressed khakis, but his feet were bare. His posture was upright and stiff, his face impassive. He might have been a stranger to Essie. When he saw Mara, though, Simon's expression softened. The baby reached out for him with her chubby arms.

He hesitated, then took her from Essie. Mara nestled her head beneath his chin.

There was a brief silence. Essie cleared her throat. 'The others are going away – to Dar es Salaam and then England. Ian's got meetings planned. But I'm staying here.'

Simon inclined his head to show that he'd heard. He was looking past Essie's shoulder to the other side of the camp, where the Europeans lived. 'I cannot work at Magadi any more. I must leave.'

Essie felt a lurch of dismay. Her worst fears were confirmed. 'Is everyone blaming you for finding the cave?'

'Not everyone. Some are congratulating me. They know there will be more work to do, now. More jobs. They are considering their relatives. But the Maasai are angry. Not just Koinet and Legishon. Everyone.'

'I'm really sorry.' Essie could hear the pain in Simon's voice. Since Mara's arrival, and his reconnection with his Hadza origins, he had gone from being an outsider to a figure of respect among the Maasai. This was not just due to his display of hunting skills, and the provision of meat; his pride in himself had elevated him in the eyes of others. Now his new status was under attack.

'Ian could go to the *manyatta* and talk to the elders,' Essie suggested. 'You were working with me. It's our responsibility.'

Simon shook his head. 'I am leaving for my own reasons. I do not want to work for Bwana Lawrence any more.' Essie opened her mouth to plead with him to reconsider, but he raised his hand. 'I have decided.'

Essie gazed bleakly into the tent. With a jolt of alarm she saw that Simon's clothes were laid out on the bed – two shirts, two pairs of trousers, long socks neatly rolled into balls. 'Are you packing already?'

'No. I am making repairs, replacing buttons. To find a new job I must be smart.' Simon's voice sounded heavy, as if the words were being hauled up from somewhere deep inside him. 'I should leave straightaway. But I will wait until the rains come.' His expression softened again. 'You will need me then.'

As the meaning of his last words sank in, Essie's heart clenched. She just nodded, unable to speak. He was right. She would need Simon then. He was the only person here who knew how to speak and translate Hadza. Someone had to be able to tell Nandamara and Giga everything about Mara. How she preferred to sleep with a light cloth covering her. How she enjoyed a change from being carried in the sling, and that when she was tied onto Essie's back she had to have her arms and legs sticking out from the cloth so her fingers could reach her toes. Someone had to say that she was fascinated by spiders but was afraid of flying bats. And that when she made beckoning gestures with both hands she wanted some milk. She'd be eating plenty of solid food by the time the Hadza came for her, and Giga would also breastfeed her again. But still, Mara would miss her bottle.

She will miss me.

Essie stared mutely at Simon.

She will miss you.

In the man's eyes she saw a foretaste of the pain that he, too, was going to feel, when it came time to be parted from Mara. She knew it was mirrored in her own expression. And now, on top of the agony she'd rehearsed so often was this second blow. Essie would be saying goodbye to Simon as well. Words formed on her tongue, but then evaporated, leaving emotion to flow silently between them.

Finally, Essie managed to speak. 'Where will you go?'

'I have heard they like to employ Hadza guides in the national parks,' Simon replied. 'We can tell stories about all the plants and animals.'

'You'd be very good at that.' Essie tried to sound encouraging. But even if she had to accept that Simon was leaving Magadi, she hated the thought of him sharing his knowledge with tourists who probably only wanted to tick off seeing the 'Big Five' – elephant, lion, buffalo, leopard, rhino – and might very well be sorry that no hunting was allowed.

'Will you write me one of those letters?' Simon asked. 'Where you say that I will work hard. I will not be late. My clothes will be clean. I will obey —'

'Stop.' Essie held up one hand, cutting him off. She couldn't bear to hear him speaking about himself in these terms. Since arriving at Magadi she'd seen plenty of letters presented by would-be staff that included just these kinds of comments – but the words sounded different to her now. The thought of them being applied to Simon was ridiculous. At the same time, though, she understood that if he was going to get a new job, he'd need a solid reference.

'Of course I'll write you a letter,' she said. 'I'll say that you are the best assistant anyone could ever have. That you know everything, and you can do everything. That you're kind . . .'

Her voice suddenly stuck in her throat. She looked down at Simon's feet, toughened from walking barefoot over the rough volcanic stone. Not long ago he had been proudly wearing his pointy blue shoes around the camp, yet now she could hardly imagine him in the sturdy desert boots that were issued to game scouts and rangers. She didn't blame Simon for wanting to leave Magadi, and him getting a job in one of the national parks made sense – but it didn't seem the right future for the Simon she now knew. But then, who could say what path anyone's life would – or even should – follow?

Essie thought about how the next years were going to unfold for her. She forced herself to look past the yawning gulf that would be left by Mara. To skip over in her mind an image of the nursery, stripped bare of all the baby's things and returned to its former status as a guest room. The question of Diana Marlow's place in Ian's life – her life – she ignored as well. She imagined the woman somehow magically removed from the scene. She focused instead on picturing herself at work documenting the cave art, manoeuvring around the people who were studying the *erectus*. She'd have to employ a trained assistant to help with the tracing, in order to reduce the amount of time they were at the site. In the evenings she would play hostess to a long tableful of academics and journalists. With all the visitors around the camp, something would have to be done about Tommy. His growing horns would soon pose a real danger to the unwary. He needed to be transported to a game reserve – returned to the wild where he belonged . . .

It was possible for Essie to conjure all of these things in her mind – even the process of letting Tommy go, with all the accompanying worry about how he'd survive. When she turned her thoughts to Ian, though, Essie was instantly at a loss. She tried to picture the two of them working together again as a team, like they always had, or chatting in bed after a long day in the field. But the vision would not come into focus. Everything remained stubbornly vague and blurry – as hidden from her as the distant peak of the volcano, shrouded in dense cloud.

TWENTY

Essie stood in the parking area beside the Land Rover holding Mara in her arms. Daudi was in the driver's seat, ready to take the travellers down to the airstrip, where a charter plane was waiting to collect them. Ian and Diana were by the front passenger door, their heads bent over a notebook as they checked off items on a list.

Essie peered into the back seat of the Land Rover, with its smart new seats. Two large Louis Vuitton suitcases bearing Diana's monogram had been stowed there. She assumed one of them contained Ian's clothes since she couldn't see his old cardboard case. There was no other luggage in the vehicle – but this was not a surprise. There had been a change of plan; Ian and Diana were going to be setting off from Magadi alone.

Essie was still trying to absorb the news. Right up until the plane had landed half an hour ago, she'd thought her mother-in-law was leaving with the others. Kefa had prepared Julia's suitcase. He'd even aired out the lace evening gown, hanging it from the branch of a tree. But when the time came for all the luggage to be carried to the Land Rover, Julia's belongings had been left behind in the Dining Tent, and she was nowhere to be seen.

Essie wasn't sure who had decided that Julia should remain at home. She presumed Ian had reached the conclusion that his mother wasn't in a fit state to travel, let alone attend important meetings and front up to a press conference. During the days following the visit to the cave, Julia had barely eaten anything, and on the brief occasions when she'd emerged from her tent it was only to sit in a trancelike state at her table in the Work Hut. All her tools and artefacts had been pushed aside. In the empty space she'd laid out Robbie's rubber shoe and his lock of wispy hair. Now and then she would touch one of the items, or turn it over, but mostly she just stared at them, her arms folded over her body, rocking faintly in her chair. Essie and Ian, as well as Diana, Baraka and Kefa, had all tried to draw her out. They'd talked to her, offered her food and drinks, created distractions. Ian had even tried to engage her in planning Robbie's eventual burial, but his efforts were in vain. No one had been able to reach her.

Essie suspected this disturbing behaviour wasn't the only thing that had been of concern to Ian, though, in the lead-up to his departure. In the Dining Tent, she'd seen him eyeing the wall where Mirella's paintings had once hung. He must have felt unsure that he could rely on his mother to play her role in the celebration of the Lawrence family heritage. But all this was just conjecture. For all Essie knew, Julia may have been the one who'd decided to stay here at the camp. Essie hadn't wanted to involve herself by enquiring; her own refusal to join the tour had caused enough trouble already.

'Okay, we're ready.' Diana's voice drew Essie's eyes back to her and Ian. Diana flipped shut the notebook and slid it into her pocket, then she approached Essie with a smile. 'I'm sorry you're not coming with us. We'll miss you.'

'I'm sure you'll manage without me,' Essie responded. There was a sarcastic edge to her voice, but Diana showed no sign that she'd noticed. She stepped closer. Essie forced a fleeting smile and then pretended to be occupied with Mara. She didn't want to receive the kiss she could see coming – she recoiled from the thought of it – but neither did she want to provoke conflict by refusing. At the back of her mind was the idea that if she behaved like a jealous wife, it would only become more certain that she'd been betrayed. The ploy with Mara worked. From the corner of her eye she saw Diana turn back and climb into the Land Rover. Essie watched her slide into the middle of the front seat, leaving space for Ian to join her.

The next moment, Essie felt a hand on her shoulder. Ian was standing beside her. She breathed in the smell of his shaving soap. The familiar perfume caused a dull pain to stir inside her.

'Goodbye, Essie,' Ian said. 'I'll keep in touch.'

Essie nodded. They'd already arranged for regular radio schedules during the time he was away. How many weeks that would be was unclear; it depended how long it took for all the meetings to occur.

A brief embrace followed, hampered by the presence of the baby. Ian gave Essie a hurried kiss, his lips brushing hers, dry and hard. Then he turned away.

As she watched him leave Essie was torn by conflicting emotions. She was the one who'd decided to remain here – yet now she felt abandoned, once again. The thought of Ian boarding the plane with Diana, the two of them flying away on their own, made her stomach churn. Ian was right: Essie *had* pushed them together. Yet if she had the chance to reconsider, she knew she wouldn't change the choices she'd made.

As Ian settled himself beside Diana, he looked around to Essie, giving her a final wave. She stepped forward – suddenly wanting to feel a sense of connection with him in this last moment before he was gone. She almost ran up to him, seeking another kiss. But she could see in his eyes that his focus had already shifted from her and their home. In his mind, he was airborne already, and speeding away to another place.

Essie waited for Daudi to drive off, then walked back towards the main part of the camp. She wondered if Julia was now in the Dining Tent. When she pictured her sitting there, gazing into a cold cup of tea, her heart sank. She'd been expecting a time of solitude, once the plane flew away. Her step slowed. On top of the turmoil of seeing Ian and Diana depart she simply couldn't face dealing with Julia's distress.

Veering off the path that led to the Dining Tent, she aimed instead for the nursery. In the shady interior, the air tinged with the smell of milk, baby powder and nappy cream, she picked out a couple of toys and a blanket. She took them to a spot at the edge of the camp, where she sat cross-legged under a thorn tree. There was a view down to the plains, but the landing strip was hidden. Essie imagined the scene – Kefa unloading the suitcases; the pilot stowing them in the hold; the passengers taking a last stretch of their legs and casting final looks back up at the camp . . .

Essie focused her thoughts on the baby. She watched as Mara grabbed her favourite toy – the plush elephant – and began chewing on the trunk. Perhaps another tooth was coming through. Mara devoted herself intently to this task for a few minutes, then decided it was time for a new occupation. She started playing with Essie's shoelaces. Next, her attention was caught by a pattern of shadows cast onto the blanket. Mara's eyes were wide with interest. Essie never tired of watching how the baby – still so young – constantly absorbed the details of the world around her, storing up every little thing that she learned.

All the while, Essie listened for the sound of the plane. It seemed to take a long time, but finally she heard the propellers kicking into action. Then came the whine of the engine, building into a roar. Moments later the plane could be seen: a moving shape climbing in a slow arc against the sky. Essie followed it with her eyes as it grew smaller and smaller, then finally vanished from view.

The smell of raw onion permeated the air of the kitchen hut. Essie glanced at a chopping board where thick slices of the vegetable lay beside a mound of sweet potato peelings. She wondered where Baraka was – it was unusual for him to leave the kitchen with food preparations in progress. After taking a bottle of formula from the fridge she set off for the workers' camp. She planned to visit Simon again. She told herself she should talk to him some more about finding a new job. But the truth was, she just wanted his company.

As she was walking, something drew her gaze in the direction of the *korongos* that rose up behind the camp. On the slopes were odd splashes of bright colour amid the natural tones of grey and ochre. She must have noticed them almost unconsciously, at the edge of her vision. Red. Orange. Purple. There were at least two dozen of them. It took a few moments for Essie to realise what she was looking at: Maasai men, draped in their *shukas*. They were moving slowly but steadily away from Magadi Camp. Frowning, Essie quickened her pace.

When she reached the staff quarters she picked up an air of unease. The place was too quiet. There were not enough people around. Simon was standing outside his tent, looking across to the hillside. As Essie neared him she called ahead.

'What's going on?'

Simon spoke without shifting his gaze. 'They are leaving.'

Essie shook her head, struggling to absorb his meaning.

'News was passed around the camp,' Simon added as she came to stand next to him. 'Someone heard Bwana Lawrence say that all the bones were going to be removed from the cave. Then they would be packed into boxes and taken away to another country. It made the Maasai very angry. They refuse to stay here any longer.'

'But that's not what's going to happen,' Essie exclaimed. 'They have to come back!' She began striding towards the gullies, with Simon coming behind her.

Soon, more of the landscape was visible. At the base of the nearest hill, Essie could see the Maasai workers clearly. She handed Mara to Simon so she could pursue them more quickly.

But after a few steps, she came to a halt. In her mind she ran back over all that Ian had said and done since he'd heard about the *erectus* – and how their conversation about a carefully controlled *in situ* procedure seemed to have been forgotten. There was a ring of truth about the story Simon had reported.

She gazed helplessly at the departing men. Then she turned to Simon. 'Are all the Maasai going?' She estimated that would represent at least a third of the workforce.

Simon nodded. 'They have to.'

Essie tried to form a timeline in her head – working out when the exodus might have begun. 'Did they wait until Ian was gone?'

'No. They are not thinking about him,' Simon stated. 'The first of them left at dawn.'

'Why didn't they say something?' Essie murmured. But then, she asked herself – why would they? Nothing Ian could have said in response would have made any difference. He'd lost their trust.

A thought came to her. 'Baraka . . .'

'He has gone, too,' Simon confirmed. 'But he will be living at the *manyatta*. We will see him again.'

'Did he say goodbye to Mrs Lawrence?'

Simon shook his head. 'I said I would explain everything in his place.'

'Baraka has worked for the Lawrences nearly all his life!' Essie said wonderingly.

'It was a hard decision for him,' Simon said.

Essie remembered the unfinished tasks in the kitchen. Perhaps the old man knew that if he didn't act straightaway he would not be able to do what he believed was right. She watched the hillside in silence, imagining the depth of feeling that had spurred each one of these men to make such a huge change in their lives. Their decision would affect not just themselves, but the extended families that relied on their incomes. If anyone was having second thoughts, though, it didn't show. Magadi Camp had been home to most of these Maasai for years. Yet not a single person paused to look back.

'They don't want to turn their faces towards the volcano,' Simon commented, as if sharing the same thought. 'They are too ashamed.'

Essie watched the tall figures, cloaked in their red-and-purple blankets, as they climbed up the slopes of the *korongos*. When the land flattened out, they moved more quickly – settling into the steady, loping gait that would carry them on effortlessly over vast tracts of land, with barely a need for rest.

TWENTY-ONE

Two weeks later

A tiny bubble of glue oozed from between two fragments of fossilised bone. Essie scraped it away with a toothpick before wiping off the last traces with a cotton bud. Then she picked up a pair of tweezers ready to select the next piece of the *Sivatherium* skull. She'd barely begun scanning the specimen tray, however, when her attention drifted down to where Mara was lying on the floor nearby. A small Persian rug had been rolled out for her there. Her white smock stood out against the tapestry of vibrant colours. She was resting on her belly; Essie had removed her nappy so she could kick freely. The baby was ignoring the tow-along wooden duck that had been brought from the nursery and was instead plucking bits of crimson fluff from the rug. Essie watched the way the baby used her thumb and pointer finger to grasp the woollen fibres. The manoeuvre was so delicate and precise; it seemed a momentous achievement.

Focusing again on her work, Essie located the piece she wanted and began scraping off a residue of sandstone. Behind the rhythmic scratching of the dental pick, she could hear the sound of cards being dealt out and then turned over one by one. It was Julia, playing a round of Patience on a table set up in the entrance to the Work Hut. Her chair was placed so she could pick up the wind that eased the stifling heat, without being blasted with airborne dust. She'd dragged her suitcase – still unpacked – over from the Dining Tent, placing it at her side where it served as a table on which to rest her ashtray, cups and glasses. For the last few days she had been playing card games obsessively – almost as if it was important work, and not just a waste of time.

The change had occurred without warning. Essie had been trying to draw Julia back to her work – setting an example by continuing with the assembly of the *Sivatherium*. It seemed the best hope of easing her torment. But Julia had shown no interest. Then, one morning, she had suddenly removed Robbie's shoe and the lock of hair from her table, adding them to a tray stacked on a shelf. Essie had watched on, hoping it was a sign that her strategy had worked. But instead of getting out her tools and notebooks, Julia had located the pack of playing cards. It was then that she'd begun the endless rounds of Patience, occasionally interspersed with other games in which Kefa or Daudi were required to take part. The activities seemed mechanical for Julia, rather than enjoyable. She expressed no satisfaction when she won or dismay if she lost. It was as if she was filling a void with pointless action, being no longer able to find meaning in doing anything else. It wasn't the development Essie had hoped for – but it seemed better than her just sitting around staring into space. And somehow the simple act of card playing had prompted Julia to begin talking again. There were no actual conversations, just short comments or queries – but it was a start.

Simon was spending his days here in the Work Hut as well. Instead of assisting Essie, however, he was studying the *Field Guide to the Birds and Animals of East Africa*. He had to concentrate hard, lips moving as he absorbed the dense text. Now and then he'd frown and shake his head. There were inaccuracies in the text, he claimed, and gaps in the knowledge. Some of the illustrations looked wrong. He marked the errors with a pencil. He was determined to learn all the false information, so he'd be able to pass any tests he might be set when applying for a job. Essie wanted to tell him this wasn't necessary – the knowledge of the Hadza, honed over millennia, surely carried greater authority than the observations of a foreign ornithologist. But when it came to the preconceptions of potential employers, Essie wasn't certain that she was right.

Whenever she looked up and saw Simon poring over the field guide, she felt struck afresh by the knowledge that he was preparing for a new life. Soon, he'd be leaving, like the Maasai had done. She might never see him again. There was a sense of unreality about this fact, as there was with many other things at the camp. So much had happened in the small world of Magadi, so quickly.

Over the time that had elapsed since the mass departure of staff, the subdued mood in the camp had gradually lifted. In its place, the optimism of the remaining workers – many of whom weren't so concerned with the beliefs of the Maasai – broke through. They talked constantly about the future employment prospects for themselves and their relatives. Though there were now lots of empty tents in the staff quarters, daily life seemed set to return to normal. Essie had consulted Ian's foreman about what work could be done in the *korongos*. But with the Bwana absent, and such big changes looming on the horizon, he could not see the point of continuing the usual tasks. A feeling of hiatus set in. It was as if a holiday had been declared. There was noisy drumming and dancing every night; during the day, music from transistor radios blared out. Essie listened to it all from the Lawrences' end of the camp. She told herself the Africans were making the most of the chance to relax. But there was something extreme about the constant celebration, as if the workers were trying to fill a void with sound and movement – a whole community of people whistling in the dark.

Essie turned to the *Sivatherium* project as a distraction from her unease about the situation. Now, as she removed the remnants of sandstone, she tried to give the task her full attention. It was not very long, though, before her gaze shifted away from the skull again. Over on Ian's table she could see the neat stack of his notebooks; his bush coat was hanging over the back of the chair – there were reminders of him everywhere. Essie couldn't help wondering where her husband was, right now; what he was doing – and who he was with. She pictured him in university quadrangles, television studios, taxis, hotel rooms . . . Her fingers tightened their grip on the dental pick; she found herself scraping so hard that a fragment of fossil sheared away.

'Damn.' She swore under her breath.

The slap of cards on the tabletop suddenly stopped. 'Don't you hate that sound?' Julia asked.

'What sound?' Essie looked up.

'Scratch. Scratch. Scratch.' Julia gestured at the tool in Essie's hand. 'For God's sake. It just goes on and on.'

Essie stared at her in confusion. Removing sediment like this was something the Lawrences spent a lot of their time doing, whether they were in the field – often lying on hard earth, in the hot sun, painstakingly exposing a fossil – or at work back here at the camp, cleaning what had been harvested.

'I've always hated it,' Julia added. 'It gets on my nerves. Like fingernails scratching on a blackboard.'

Essie eyed the tool in her hand. Now that she thought of it, she understood what Julia meant. When you paid attention to the sound, it was harsh and irritating.

'Anyway, I'm finished with all that,' Julia said.

She spoke firmly, as if announcing a decision. Essie's lips parted. She couldn't imagine what the comment might actually mean.

Julia turned over another card. 'Red Queen,' she stated. After placing it down she sat back, rolling her shoulders as if to release stress. 'I could do with a cup of tea. Where's Kefa got to?' She peered around the space and the area outside, looking anxious. 'He hasn't disappeared now as well?'

Essie shook her head. 'He's getting something from the store-room.' She put down her work. 'I'll make the tea,' she offered. She didn't want Julia to have to dwell on the fact that even though Kefa was still around to deliver the tea tray, the cook was gone. Whenever Essie thought about Baraka, she felt a wave of dismay. But she knew the feeling of loss would be much more intense for Julia; he had been part of her world for such a long time.

She pushed back her chair, intending to collect Mara and hand her to Simon before going to the kitchen. As she stood up she saw that Tommy was approaching the baby. His head was lowered; there was a look of intent in his eyes. The gazelle had never shown any aggression towards Mara – though he'd occasionally appeared offended by the sight of her being bottle-fed, as if he remembered that this had once been his prerogative. However, now that his horns were emerging, he was experimenting with new ways to assert himself. He'd caused an upset in the Dining Tent recently by chewing at the corner of the tablecloth. When he was chased away he didn't let go until several items of crockery had toppled behind him.

Essie watched Tommy warily. The baby was already reaching one arm eagerly towards him. Separating the two of them now would indicate to Mara that the animal was suddenly to be considered dangerous – which would make no sense to her. It would be much better to let the interaction play out, just as long as Mara was safe.

As the gazelle came within reach, the baby dropped her collection of carpet fluff and grasped his front leg. Tommy stood motionless, snorting softly. While Essie was hovering uncertainly, trying to read his mood, Julia appeared at the animal's side. She squatted next to him, putting her hand on his collar, stroking his neck. Essie frowned in surprise. She couldn't think what had prompted Julia to take an interest in the gazelle – she'd never approved of his presence at Magadi. But then Essie remembered it was because of Tommy that Robbie's body had been found; the two must have become linked in Julia's mind.

'Be careful now,' Julia was murmuring. 'There's a good boy.'

Essie could hardly believe it was her mother-in-law speaking – her manner was so gentle. Tommy sat down beside Mara, folding his legs under his body. He nuzzled her face with his quivering nose. Mara giggled with delight. She focused her attention on one of Tommy's hooves that was protruding from underneath him. Essie watched her exploring it with her fingers, feeling every detail of the shape like a blind person. Tommy remained perfectly still. Essie waited until Mara had finished her investigation, then she picked her up.

She turned towards Simon, ready to give the baby to him – but he looked deeply engrossed in his book. She began to walk away; she'd become used to doing tasks with one hand while holding Mara with the other.

A voice came after her. 'I can hold her.'

Turning back, Essie saw Julia spreading her arms. She faltered, mid-step. A memory came to her of the day when Julia had burned the paintings on the fire. When Essie had returned from looking for Baraka, and found her clutching Mara against her chest, she'd felt an urgent desire to get the baby safely back into her own hands. Julia wasn't in a half-crazed state now – she seemed very steady and relaxed – but only recently she had been emotionally unhinged again. Essie didn't want to let her hold Mara. Yet she didn't feel she could just walk away. She knew the offer was more than a casual gesture on Julia's part – it suggested that something was shifting inside her.

After hesitating just a few seconds more, Essie walked over to Julia. Leaning close to her, she smelled the familiar hint of *eau de cologne*. A wiry strand of grey hair brushed her cheek. The next moment, Mara was in Julia's hands. The action had felt smooth, natural. Julia hoisted the baby expertly onto her hip. She didn't seem bothered about the bare bottom, only thinly veiled by the cotton smock. She pulled back her head, chin pressing into her wrinkled neck, so she could watch Mara's face. There was a gleam of light in Julia's faded blue eyes, the beginning of a smile on her lips.

The tune of a popular song carried across from the workers' camp. Essie thought she recognised something by The Beatles, but wasn't sure. Stepping into the kitchen, she wrinkled her nose. Something must have gone rotten – it didn't take long in the heat. One of the field staff had been asked to take over cooking duties but he hardly spent any time in here. He served basic meals of boiled rice and beans that reminded Essie of the days before Diana Marlow had arrived at Magadi with all her supplies of luxuries.

Glancing around the small space, Essie took in the blackened pans and hanging spoons, a lamp with a shattered mantle, a dead cockroach on the table. Her gaze settled on the bare nail where Baraka's *shuka* used to hang. She remembered the day she'd used the plaid blanket to wrap Mara tightly so she would calm down enough to drink her very first bottle of milk formula. Essie thought of how encouraging Baraka had been, back when she was new to the role of looking after a baby. And now – spurred by fear, anger, shame – he'd been driven from his home.

She crossed to look out through the small window, screened with dense wire mesh to keep out mice and rats. Through the haze of tiny squares, she stared towards the volcano. She pictured Baraka doing the same – trying to read the mood of Lengai. As she trained her eyes on the distant peak, she thought the plume of smoke looked bigger, darker. Her hands tightened on the narrow window ledge. She imagined the incessant grumbling of the mountain taking on a new note of urgency – the restless activity beginning to build, and build, until finally an eruption was unleashed.

Lowering her gaze to the lake, just below the foothills, Essie scanned the deserted shores that should have been painted pink with flamingos. Could the birds have known, somehow, of the events that would unfold at Magadi – not just the discovery of the cave and its extraordinary contents, but the plans that Ian would make? Did they see, in the future, the threat of an invasion by foreigners? And the fury of Lengai? Essie remembered the picture of time – as a circle with no beginning and no end – that Simon had tried to describe to her. You had to imagine the viewpoint of a bird in the sky, he'd said. The story of the world is laid out below. You can look forward and backwards and see everything at once. There seemed no other explanation for why the flamingos had left this place – with its protected island nesting ground where they had always hatched their young – to take their chances elsewhere.

There had been no news yet, via the Ranger at Serengeti, of where the flocks had gone. They hadn't settled at the soda lake over the border in Kenya where they'd nested that year when the one at Magadi was flooded. It was thought they were probably some-where else – less known; more remote. The Ranger was expecting a report any day. Essie pictured Carl flying over the countryside in a small plane, like a bird himself, looking down over the land. Or perhaps he was already standing on the shore of some far-off lake, observing a parade of flamingos high-stepping across the crystal glitter of the saltpan – beaks waving, heads dipping, wings stretch-ing and folding as they each played their part in the time-old dance of attraction and desire.

Cups rattled on their saucers as Essie carried the tray back towards the Work Hut. She bent her head against the dry season wind that always sprang up as the day wore on. She could feel the grit stick-ing to her sweaty face and collecting in her hair. She knew she'd have to wipe the dust from the cups before she could pour the tea.

The path ahead was marked by white-painted rocks. As she passed them, one by one, her head bowed, Essie recognised their individual shapes and the size of the spaces between them. Soon she was nearing the hut. As she ducked around into the shelter, she looked up, shaking her head to dislodge a loose strand of hair that was stuck to her lips.

She saw Julia still standing where she'd left her, holding Mara. Simon had joined them, his book dangling in his hand. Essie picked up the tension in their bodies, her own muscles tightening in response even before she had time to wonder at its cause. They were both looking out through the front of the hut. There was something protective in the way Julia's arm was covering Mara's body. A shiver travelled up Essie's spine as she turned slowly round, her gaze following theirs.

Standing beyond the fireplace at the edge of the clearing, almost blending with the backdrop of bushes and red earth, was the dark slender figure of a woman. She wore nothing but a leather apron around her loins and a necklace of red-and-yellow berries. In one hand she carried a small woven basket decorated with feathers. If she noticed Essie, she gave no sign of it. She was staring at Mara with wide eyes and a focus almost fierce in its intensity – as if there was nothing else in the whole world for her to see.

TWENTY-TWO

Essie gripped the tray with rigid hands. The figure was like an apparition conjured from one of her dreams. She thought it was Giga standing there, unflinching in the wind. But then, with a flash of relief, she saw that this woman was much taller than Mara's foster mother.

Keeping her eyes trained on the motionless figure, Essie moved further into the hut. Questions raced through her mind. What was a Hadza tribeswoman doing in this area, at this time of the year? And what had brought her to the Lawrences' camp? Essie scanned the surroundings – the bushes, sisal plants and clumps of desert roses that grew around the clearing – but there was no sign of any companions. That was strange as well. The Hadza lived in close-knit communities and rarely travelled alone. Yet it seemed unlikely that one of these expert hunter-gatherers would ever become lost. Essie wondered if the woman could have been cast out by her people; Simon had explained that this was the worst punishment a Hadza could receive, reserved only for the most serious of crimes. She didn't look hungry or sick. But from the way she stood there – tense, silent – something had to be wrong.

Essie deposited the tray on a table, tea slopping from the pot as it settled at an angle. She crossed to Julia, exchanging puzzled looks with her as she took Mara into her arms. She held the baby tightly; the stranger's intense focus on Mara made her uneasy. The presence of an African child in a European family always aroused attention, but this was much more extreme. Essie turned to Simon with raised eyebrows.

'What does she want?'

'I will talk to her,' he said.

Tucking his field guide under his arm, he took a few steps towards the woman, while beckoning her to come closer. She hovered uncertainly for a moment, then began walking over to him. She was still staring at Mara, her gaze unwavering. As she stepped cautiously into the shelter of the hut, Meg ran up and sniffed her hand, but she didn't even glance down.

Now that she was closer, Essie saw that as well as being taller, the woman had finer features than Giga. And on her prominent cheekbones, the flesh was marked with dark lines of decorative scars.

Simon began offering greetings. He'd barely begun, though, when a second figure emerged from behind one of the sisal plants – an old man with grey-speckled hair. He was panting with exertion, but still strode on until he reached the fireplace. Then he bent over to catch his breath, bracing his hands on his knees. A baboon hide covered his back. Hanging down from it were two strips of fur – once legs – swaying in the wind. Essie recognised the distinctive waistcoat. Her stomach twisted in alarm.

'Nandamara.' She breathed his name.

The old man approached the hut. He was looking at Mara, his gaze as intense as that of the young woman. Essie turned to Simon, her heart beginning to pound.

'Why are they here?' Her voice was edged with panic. 'It's too early.'

Simon lifted one hand towards her – a hunter's signal to be

quiet, still. He continued with his greetings, now addressing both of the visitors. He looked calm, but Essie could tell that he, too, was shaken by Nandamara's unexpected appearance.

The woman didn't respond to Simon, but Nandamara began smiling, pointing at Mara, talking quickly. Simon translated, throwing words to Essie, but not looking at her.

'He is very happy. He is amazed to see his granddaughter. She is so big. As fat as a zebra.'

Essie had to smile at the comparison.

'And she is very beautiful,' Simon continued. 'Like her mother.'

Mother. The word seemed to hover in the air. It took Essie a moment to realise Nandamara was referring to his dead daughter. She saw a shadow of grief pass over the old man's face.

'Why are they here?' Essie asked Simon again.

More words were exchanged. Then there was a pause. The silence felt suddenly dense.

'They have come.' Simon's voice was heavy and flat. He didn't need to say any more.

Essie's arms tightened around Mara. 'But we've got six more weeks, at least. Tell him . . . we're not ready.'

While Simon was speaking, Nandamara watched Essie's face. He scratched his head, looking confused.

'He thought you would be pleased to be relieved of your task,' Simon explained. 'You did not want to look after a baby.'

Essie eyed him blankly. She could hardly remember that she'd once been reluctant to accept responsibility for Mara – that Nandamara had more or less tricked her into agreeing.

'Tell him . . . my feelings about her changed,' Essie said. 'I've loved looking after her.' Her voice felt strained. 'It's the best thing I've ever done.'

Nandamara nodded slowly as Simon relayed her words. As he looked into Essie's eyes, she had the sense that he was able to picture everything that had happened: how the whole story had been played out – beginning in one place and ending somewhere completely different. He frowned with indecision, turning from Essie, to Mara, to the young woman and back. Finally, he spoke again, pausing now and again for the translation.

'You have protected my granddaughter, and given her good food, and kept her healthy. And you have given her love as well. For that I will always be very grateful.' Nandamara's eyes, wreathed in wrinkles, were full of compassion. 'But still, the time has come for us to take her back.'

'Why has the time come?' Essie asked. 'It's still the dry season.' She looked up at the sky as if asking it to bear witness to the lack of any sign of impending rain.

Another conversation took place between the two men. Simon's voice sounded firm, almost interrogative. Essie guessed at what he was saying.

You can't just turn up here and change the plan. It's not fair on the baby. Or on this white woman who agreed to care for her.

Nandamara spoke in response, moving his hands to add weight to his words. As he did so, Simon's expression softened. Then he began nodding his head. Essie studied Nandamara's lips as if she might be able to read the meaning they conveyed. She was aware of Julia moving closer and doing the same.

Eventually, Nandamara fell quiet. Simon turned to Essie.

'This woman is called Milena. She is from another Hadza tribe. The two families met in the hunting grounds in the north and began sharing the same fireside. She had a baby son, about the same age as Mara.'

Essie glanced sideways at Milena. Her belly looked firm, giving no hint that she had ever been pregnant, but on a closer look Essie saw pale stretch marks on the dark skin.

'A few weeks ago the baby became ill,' Simon continued his translation. Even though Milena couldn't understand what he was saying, he lowered his voice. 'He could not be cured. She has buried him.'

Essie's lips parted as she took in the meaning of the words. No wonder the young mother was looking at Mara. She must be thinking of her own little one.

'*Pole sana,*' Essie said. I am very sorry.

She didn't know if Milena understood any Swahili; she just wanted to say something directly to her. But even as she spoke, Essie shook her head helplessly; the words were inadequate for the compassion welling up inside her. She could feel the emptiness of those arms, hanging so limply by the woman's sides.

'They have walked a very long way,' Simon said. 'They slept only in the heat of the day. The journey took many, many days – at least one cycle of the moon. All of that time, Milena drew out the milk from her breasts so that they would not become empty.'

A chill spread through Essie's body. She knew where this story was leading. It had been obvious, she saw now, from the instant the Hadza woman had appeared – but Essie had refused to let the idea settle in her head.

Nandamara continued speaking. His voice slowed down as if he was reaching a conclusion. Simon mirrored his tone.

'And now, two things have come together. Milena's sadness will be healed. And Mara will have a mother.'

Essie shook her head again. For a long moment she could find no words. But then they came bursting out, desperate. 'But she's so happy here. She loves me. She loves Simon. And lots of the others who work here . . .'

As Simon passed on what she'd said, Nandamara nodded. 'She will come to love Milena. And me, as well. We are her people.'

A voice inside Essie reminded her that she'd always known this time was coming. But words of protest came to her lips. 'No. I can't let her go. I can't.'

Milena stared at Essie. Her eyes were wide with alarm. She hugged her arms across her chest, fingers pressing into her biceps.

Simon came to stand in front of Essie. He switched to English, his voice suddenly sounding stilted – as if in this short time Hadza had become his preferred tongue.

'Nandamara says he has found out everything about Milena. She is gentle and kind. She laughs a lot. She is good at finding food and making baskets. Her mother has died, but there are many sisters and aunties to help her with her responsibilities. And she has no other children. All her care and attention will be for Mara. She will love her with her whole heart.' Simon paused, looking straight into Essie's eyes. 'Becoming the daughter of Milena is the best future for Mara.'

Essie bent her head over the baby. Everything Simon had just said was true. It had always been a concern that Mara was going to be fostered again by Giga, whose first loyalty would always be to her own child. Whenever times became hard, Mara would be vulnerable. This mother, Milena, had lost her own baby. In time, she would probably have another – she was only young – but by then she'd be closely bonded with Mara. And Mara would be older and weaned off the breast. Leaving aside the tragedy of the death of Milena's baby boy, it was an ideal scenario.

'He's right, Essie. You have to do this.' Now it was Julia speaking.

There was a surprising softness in her tone that ran counterpoint to her firm words. 'Let her go with them.'

Essie gazed blankly ahead. She could not think, speak; her feelings were a tumult. Then she took a deep breath, struggling for clarity.

'Are they camping at the Painted Cave?' she asked Simon. 'Tell them I will bring Mara there. In a few days' time. Maybe a week?'

She waited for Nandamara to agree; perhaps he would offer to stay in the area for a while so the transition could be played out slowly. The Hadza weren't a people who lived their lives in a hurry. But when Simon finished speaking, the old man shook his head.

'He is sorry,' Simon explained. 'It is not possible for them to stay around here. Some other Hadza came with them on the journey. Nandamara and Milena must meet up with them at a certain place. Then they must return to the rest of the tribe.'

There was a short silence, then the old man signalled to Milena. She moved towards Essie as if in a trance, keeping her eyes on the baby. Her foot caught on the fringe of the rug. She almost tripped, but barely seemed to notice.

When she was right in front of Essie, she stood still. Tears ran down her cheeks. Then she began to sob, silently, her chest heaving. Rudie appeared at her side, gazing up at her with a wrinkled brow. Essie could feel the mother's grief for her own baby radiating from her. But then, as Essie watched, something else broke through – a look of almost reverent wonder, blended with pure joy.

Milena turned to Simon, letting out a stream of words, smiling through her tears.

'She is thanking you,' Simon said. His own eyes had a sheen of tears. 'She says that she will love Mara and take good care of her.

And she will always remember you. You are her big sister, her aunty. In the time of the *epeme*, when there are voices in the dark, she will imagine that you are speaking to her, and to this child.'

Milena spread her arms, ready to receive the baby. Essie stared at the outstretched hands, her whole body rigid. She watched herself as if from outside. She knew she had to push all her emotions back down inside, where Mara could not feel them. Her one task was to convey to Mara that she was safe. She had to be warm, steady, confident. She felt a spasm pass through her. It was impossible. She couldn't do it. She'd rehearsed this moment in her head so many times, but now it was happening she felt completely unprepared. Yet for Mara's sake, she had to succeed.

She took a step back, shaking her head. 'Wait. Just a minute.' She saw Milena stiffen, then heard Simon reassure her.

Essie blotted out everything around her, except for Mara. She cradled the baby in her arms, letting her eyes travel over her, memorising every detail. The roundness of her cheeks; the curve of her rosy-purple lips; the tip of her tongue peeping between her gums. There was a crust of salt, left by dried tears, in the corner of her eye . . .

The image blurred as Essie's own eyes swam with unshed tears. She bent her head over the baby, hugging her close, feeling the supple body moulding into hers. When she finally spoke, her voice little more than a whisper, she pictured her words reaching deep inside Mara, lodging in her heart.

'I love you, my little one. I will always love you.' Essie broke off, gasping back a sob. 'Be safe. Be good. Be happy.'

Simon came to stand next to her. He stroked the baby's head, talking softly to her. He sounded calm, almost bright. Essie knew that he, like her, was being brave for Mara's sake.

Essie walked back to Milena, each step like a blow to her soul. The woman, though tall for a Hadza, was shorter than she was; Essie had to stoop to transfer Mara into her arms. The women's shoulders bumped together; their heads touched. Essie breathed the Hadza's musky, smoky scent.

'Mara, this is Milena.' The words were torn from Essie's throat, but she managed to keep her voice steady. 'She is going to look after you.'

Mara gave Milena a broad grin. Her face displayed the brimming confidence of a child accustomed to being loved and admired. Milena smiled back, a light burning in her dark eyes. For what felt like a long time, she just gazed down at the baby. Essie was aware that Kefa and Daudi had arrived, along with some other people from the workers' camp. There were soft murmurs as subdued conversations were held.

Milena shifted Mara into the crook of one arm, then began trying to remove the white dress.

'She can keep it,' Essie said to Simon. 'And tell her she can take what she wants from the nursery.'

'A Hadza baby does not need anything,' Simon responded.

'I know, but still . . .' Essie wanted, suddenly, to send Mara off with at least some of her possessions. It would make Essie feel that she was taking a piece of her life at Magadi along with her.

'Milena will tie a string of plaited grass around her waist,' Simon said gently. He pointed to where Mara's baboon pelt and sling were lying on a chair. 'That is all she needs.'

Essie turned to Milena, who was now struggling to undo a set of hooks and eyes. Essie reached automatically to take Mara back and help remove the dress. But she knew that if she had the baby in her arms again, she might never let her go. She hesitated, her hands outstretched, her mind a haze of distress. Then Julia stepped forward. Undoing the fastenings, she eased the open neck up over Mara's head. The soft fabric snagged on the tough skin of her hands as she pulled it free. She folded the dress and pushed it into her trouser pocket.

Essie gazed at the baby lying in Milena's arms, naked but for her string of eggshell beads. Mara was still smiling happily. With one hand she reached for Milena's ear; the other rested on the mound of her breast. A faint smile touched Essie's lips. It was so obvious that Mara belonged there, with this woman who looked like a grown-up version of herself. The two had the same skin, the same hair. They were part of the same world.

Nandamara approached Essie. He reached for one of her hands, enfolding it in a leathery grasp. As she looked into his eyes, lids drooping and the whites yellowed with age, thoughts swarmed in her head – plans, suggestions, promises. She wanted to ask if the family would definitely still be returning to the Painted Cave when the rains came. If perhaps they could stay there for a while. But she already knew the Hadza didn't plan their lives like this. And she'd always promised herself, and Mara, that when this day of parting came, she would let go completely and freely – so they could both move forward into their own futures.

Essie held her breath, keeping all these thoughts in their place – locked inside her. She didn't trust herself to speak. She bowed her head. She could hardly bear to look at Mara. If she was going to hold her composure, she knew this farewell could not be stretched out.

'Tell them . . .' she said to Simon, choking on the words. 'Tell them to leave.'

As he passed on what she'd said, Milena reached out, touching Essie's arm. The contact was light, brief. Then the hand pulled away.

Nandamara stepped back outside the Work Hut, bending his head against the wind. Milena picked up the fur and the sling. As she was about to turn away, Mara's face spun round, seeking Essie – the baby reached out her hands, grasping at the air.

When Essie didn't respond, Mara's eyes widened with anxiety. She began to struggle in Milena's arms.

Essie managed a smile. 'It's all right,' she said. 'Milena will take good care of you.'

Inside her heart was breaking. Every fibre of her body wanted to take her baby back.

She's not your baby.

Simon murmured something to Milena; she began walking away.

Mara started to cry. At first it was just a whimper of protest but with each step Milena took the sound grew louder and more urgent. It wasn't the cry of annoyance Mara made when she didn't get what she wanted. The baby was afraid.

Essie turned to Simon. All her emotions were mirrored on his face. The screams ran on, floating back to them. Rudie bounded after the departing figures, but then stopped and looked back, his head tilted in confusion.

Essie stared around her, almost in panic. The sound of Mara screaming was too much to bear. Yet she could not intervene. She turned to Simon.

'I can't bear this . . .'

Her voice trailed off as she saw that he was holding something out to her: the field guide he'd been studying. Essie's hands rose automatically, taking hold of it. With his own hands now free, Simon started unbuttoning his shirt. The look on his face was one of surprise, as if his actions were running ahead of his thoughts.

Soon he was wearing only his shorts. From his belt hung a sheath, holding his hunting knife. With his chest bare, and no shoes on, he resembled the departing Hadza much more than he did a Magadi Research Camp worker.

Simon called out to Nandamara. The old man stopped, then turned around. Milena followed his example. They'd only gone a short distance and Essie could see the torn emotions on their faces: they didn't want to bring Mara back; but to them, too, the baby's distress was intolerable. Simon called to Nandamara again. Words travelled between them. At the sound of the voices – one strange, but one deeply familiar – Mara's cries quietened. Next, a discussion took place between the old man and Milena. Essie sensed that Simon, standing next to her, was holding his breath as he waited to hear their response.

Finally, Nandamara raised his hand in a welcoming gesture. Simon turned to Essie. They didn't hug or shake hands. A stillness enveloped them, dense with the memories of all that they had shared. The moment passed quickly; Simon shifted his gaze in the direction of the Hadza. As he said goodbye to Essie, she could feel that a part of him was already on his way towards them – leaving behind his old life and joining Mara in hers.

Soon, Simon was walking in between Nandamara and Milena, heading past the orange tent, aiming for the *korongos*. He was holding one of Mara's hands, Essie saw, her short chubby arm forming a link between him and the woman at his side. No sound carried back from the baby. Everything was quiet. The three were like figures in a slow-motion film, their bodies almost suspended in time. Clinging to the last glimpse of them, Essie walked out of the hut. She kept them in view for a little longer. But finally they blended into the landscape, and were gone.

Essie stared in disbelief. The whole episode had taken place so quickly and without warning. It felt like an aberration that would soon be corrected. Everything would go back to normal. But then the harsh truth broke through. Her baby was gone. She might never see her, touch her, hear her, ever again.

Essie sagged to her knees as if all her strength had departed along with Mara. She bent over, her hair hanging down, shrouding her face. Her hands pressed into the ground. She felt she was disintegrating, falling away into nothing. There was no boundary between herself and the earth beneath her. The pieces of her would merge into the particles of sand and be lost forever.

Then, as she gave in to the sensation of falling, she felt two arms wrapping around her, lean but strong – pulling her back to reality.

Julia knelt beside Essie, rocking her gently, stroking her hair. She didn't say anything. She just held her, as if she understood that there could be no words, at least for now – no comfort or advice. All Julia had to offer, and all that was needed at this moment, was her presence.

Essie turned her face to the older woman's chest and sobbed. As Julia tightened her arms around her shoulders, Essie clung to her. Julia began to cry as well – a high keening sound, like the call of a bird on the wing, broke from her lips. Grief flowed between the two – old pain and grief meeting fresh, sharp loss. Their bodies heaved together, faces pressed skin to skin, tears blending with tears.

TWENTY-THREE

Essie walked slowly around the nursery. Each step she took was an effort – like wading through mud – but she pushed herself to keep moving. She was collecting up toys, clothes, bottles, tins of unused formula – everything that was connected with Mara. It was unbearable to have these things still here, now that the baby was gone. Even with the door zipped shut and the window coverings folded down, Essie could sense their existence from the most distant corners of the camp. So far this morning she had already packed two large baskets and placed them by the door. A third stood half full by the bed. Once the tent was stripped bare she hoped to feel stronger and more able to concentrate on her work. There was a lot to be done before Ian and Diana returned with the first entourage of visitors. Their trip had been extended twice already – but now, within a week, they would be back.

Essie wasn't sure exactly how much time had passed since Simon and Mara left. The first few days had been a blur. She and Julia had spent many long hours together – neither of them could face the isolation of their tents. They talked about Mara and Robbie, but their conversations were disjointed, often fading into painful silence. Time moved slowly, as if life itself had wound down. Essie felt numb inside; when she bumped her elbow against the table edge, she was almost surprised to feel pain. She felt as if she was wrapped in a dense cocoon, half prison and half refuge.

The nights were the hardest. As Essie lay awake listening for the soft rhythm of Mara's breathing, or a whimper sparked by a dream, she heard instead just the lonely call of the night birds. Hot tears trailed back over her temples and into her hair. When she finally slept, there was no waking cry to send her fumbling for the lamp and reaching for the bottle. And when the morning finally dawned it brought with it the harsh knowledge that what might have been just a nightmare was true.

But with each day, the sense of loss receded a fraction. Essie glimpsed the horizon beyond the dark cloud that filled her consciousness. She could see that Julia was making the same progress. The pair began to eat again, and to talk in longer bursts. They were like dancers moving together to the same music, taking turns to lead. Two steps forward, before the one that led them back.

Now, while Essie was packing up the nursery, Julia was up behind the parking area, preparing the ground for a garden plot. She'd announced her intention that morning after breakfast. Instead of instructing staff to do the work, she was wielding a pickaxe herself. Essie had watched her for a while, observing her firm grip on the handle and the bunch of her arm muscles. She appeared younger somehow, carrying out this hard labour, than she usually did, as though her body was thriving on the new challenge. Looking on, Essie had a sense that the act of turning the soil might be linked in some way with Robbie. Julia didn't want his body to be buried at Magadi beside his father. She said that if the *erectus* had not been in the cave – soon to become the centre of research activity – she'd rather he could just stay in the place where he'd rested peacefully for so long. She wasn't preoccupied with Robbie's physical remains, Essie realised. What mattered to Julia was that she now knew his story. So far she'd shown no interest in finding an alternative site. Essie wondered if this garden plot was the memorial she had chosen, perhaps unconsciously, for her son – instead of a grave, a place for burying seeds and looking towards new life.

Standing at one corner of a large rectangle marked out with string, Julia had told Essie what she intended to grow. She was going to irrigate by piping water from one of the pools. It sounded so simple that it seemed surprising no one at Magadi had ever bothered to plant crops before. But then, there had been no spare time or energy to spend on something that wasn't vital. After all, it was perfectly possible to live on tinned and dried food, plus the supplies from the Maasai, and for everyone to spend their days in the *korongos* digging for buried fossils.

Essie collected up a pile of nappies, trying not to think of how she'd folded them, ready for use – achieving that perfect kite shape that was now second nature to her. As she carried them to the basket, they were heavy in her arms. She felt a deep sense of exhaustion. At the same time, though, she was wide-awake; some part of her on full alert. She was sure there were important things she'd forgotten to do. The question of what they were nagged at her. Then she remembered. There were no urgent, vital tasks that she'd neglected to carry out. The responsibilities that had filled her days had evaporated away. There was just a gulf of nothingness left behind.

A feeling of panic rose up to fill the void. Essie had to pause, taking a breath.

'She's fine. Simon is with her. She's okay.'

She repeated the words like a mantra. As she did this, she conjured an image of Simon holding Mara in his arms. She focused on the details – the way the baby's head rested against his chest; the swing of her arm, flopping down; his steady, foot-sure step. She recalled the look she'd seen in Milena's eyes as she gazed at Mara – the raw longing, giving way to relief and hope. Essie imagined Mara feeding at her new mother's breast. She didn't let herself wonder whether the adjustment had been easy or difficult – she dwelled on the fact that Mara was always happy and accommodating; and that when she was hungry, she'd want to drink. Essie guessed Nandamara's group would have met up with their other travelling companions by now. Simon may have been introduced to them by his real name, Onwas. She pictured a line of people trailing across a hillside, talking to one another, pointing out landmarks, perhaps choosing a place to spend the night. A scene from Mara's life, as it was always meant to have been.

Essie stacked a nest of cubes, one inside another, and put them in the basket. Next, she found the grey plush elephant. As she turned it over in her hands, she felt a rush of pain. She imagined that the misshapen trunk might still feel damp to the touch. One eye was gone. Essie remembered the frantic search that had taken place after she'd discovered the button was missing. She was so afraid Mara might have swallowed it. She'd been forced to ask Julia what it would mean if she had.

'Nothing,' Julia had replied. 'Babies are tougher than you think.'

Though the remark sounded harsh and uncaring, Essie had found it reassuring. She'd glimpsed, in that exchange, a vision of how life with a baby was meant to be: a young woman turning to her mother, sharing skills and knowledge that had their roots in her own first years. She had allowed herself a fantasy in which Lorna was here at Magadi. It was not the sad, sick woman who'd lived in England that Essie pictured. It was a different version of her mother: happy, alive; like the person in the swimming costume, rising from the sea.

Essie placed the elephant gently in the basket, nestling it into position as if it was something alive. The next item she picked up was the nursery first-aid kit. Inside, she knew, was the box of sticking plaster she'd torn open one morning when she discovered Mara had a cut on her leg – somehow it must have been caught on a thornbush. Again, Essie had been in a mad panic. Caring for a baby seemed to be as much about anxiety and fear as it was about smiles and cuddles. She had washed the cut over and over, applying iodine so generously that it spilled onto the ground. The injury had looked, to Essie, so much bigger than it was. She felt negligent and guilty – she'd been given a baby who was perfect and precious and had failed to keep her safe. After dabbing the cut dry, Essie had covered it with some sticking plaster. The pink strip was eye-catching against Mara's black skin. It immediately captured the attention of the Maasai women when they came to sell their eggs. At first they thought it was some kind of talisman – a white woman marking her black baby with a piece of her own skin. When the purpose of the plaster was explained, they were bemused. How will the skin heal, they asked, when it's hidden from the sunshine? As it turned out, they needn't have worried; the plaster wasn't in place for very long. Dust started to cling to the sticky edges. It soon looked so dirty and ragged that Essie had pulled it off. Baraka, watching on, had grabbed the relic from her and tossed it into the fire. Looking back now, Essie knew that the accident would never have happened in more recent times. She'd developed a sixth sense about exactly how much space the baby took up. It was as if Mara's body had become an extension of her own. No wonder she now felt as if part of herself was missing.

Essie dropped the first-aid kit into the basket. Taking a breath, she looked around the nursery. She was making very slow progress. Every object she came upon seemed to have a story to tell. She would have to take control of herself – this was not the only task she had to achieve today. She needed to go over to the staff camp and try to mobilise the workers. She would have to get someone to turn off the radio and summon people from their tents.

'The Bwana is returning,' she would announce. 'Make certain you are ready to begin work.'

She wouldn't linger there. She didn't want to get drawn into the question of what kinds of jobs they were going to be asked to do.

As she gathered up cot sheets and pillowcases, Essie thought back over last night's scheduled radio call. The wind had dropped and conditions had been perfect for a clear transmission. It was just as well, since Ian had a lot of news to convey. His contact at the BBC had finally confirmed that a film crew was going to fly back to Magadi with him and Diana. The negotiations were one of the reasons the trip had been extended. The crew was going to record the excavation of the *erectus* from the very start. It would be like when the Leakeys found the skull of Johnny's Child; the television audience, watching from their sitting rooms, would feel as if they were right in the midst of the action.

Essie didn't interject to remind Ian that he'd promised a different approach to the work in the cave. The whole issue was overshadowed in her mind by the loss of Mara. When there was a moment of space, she told Ian what had happened. The facts, broken up into pieces for transmission, had sounded as bald and brutal as they felt.

'The Hadza came back early. They've taken Mara away.'

There was a short silence – just static on the airwaves. Essie could feel Ian struggling to shift his focus.

'I'm so sorry, Essie. It must have been a shock,' he'd said eventually.

He was full of sympathy, then. He understood how bereft Essie must feel. He was sorry that he wasn't there to comfort her. But behind his words Essie could hear the note of relief. A baby at the camp – black or white – didn't fit into the scene Ian wanted to present to the world. He hadn't lingered on the subject for long; he thought it was best for Essie not to dwell on her distress. He'd moved on to an account of visiting Cambridge.

'Your father is doing well.'

'That's good.'

'Of course, he was disappointed you didn't come, too.'

Now it was Essie's turn to be silent. She bit her lip as Ian added that he'd told Arthur his daughter would come next time.

'And you will,' Ian said. 'Now that you are free again.'

Essie stared at the receiver as if she could see, and not just hear, these last words.

'Diana's doing a wonderful job.' Ian switched topics without a pause. 'She's completely at home with all the university people, the press – everyone.'

Essie listened to him with a sense of unreality. They were discussing a woman who was now her husband's constant companion; probably his lover as well. What was going to happen when the pair got back here? Was Essie supposed to maintain the façade of a happy husband-and-wife team, in front of the visitors, with Diana watching on? It was impossible to imagine. Essie had no intention of being like Julia, accepting a marriage in which her husband was involved with someone else. Yet she seemed, already, to be doing just that. She thought of saying something to indicate how she felt, but she knew these transmissions weren't private – anyone from the Ranger at Serengeti to the radio operator for St Joseph's Mission could be listening in.

'We'll be home next Tuesday, then,' Ian said next. 'You need to make sure everything's ready. Brief the staff.'

'Yes. Sure, of course,' Essie responded. She knew this was the time to let him know that at least a third of the Africans had left, and the ones who remained were not doing any work. But she simply didn't have the energy to absorb his reaction. She decided she'd tell him during the next radio call; she might feel more ready for it then.

Fortunately, Ian hadn't dwelled on this topic. He began enquiring about Julia – whether she was looking after herself. Eating. Working. Dressing properly. Essie couldn't help thinking that his main concern was not so much his mother's wellbeing as the issue of how Julia Lawrence was going to appear to the team from the BBC. Listening to Ian talk, Essie wondered if he'd changed during these last months. Had he been influenced by Diana? Or had he always been so focused on his own goals and his own feelings? It occurred to Essie that perhaps she'd been so intimately involved with her husband – every strand of their lives entwined – that his thoughts and actions were like her own. She had been too close to actually see what was in front of her.

Crossing to the change table, Essie stood still, gazing at the mobile. The hanging shapes looked so still, with no waving hands to set them in motion. Essie nudged the black plastic cat with her finger, watching it collide with the fiddle, then swing away. Baraka loved the mobile as much as Mara had. Several times Essie had seen him standing in here, looking at it. He was not interested in the nursery rhyme; he just liked the fact that the cow was jumping over the moon. The symbolism was powerful to him. Lengai had given the Maasai ownership of all the cattle in the world. Once, a Texan rancher had turned up at Magadi as part of a hunting safari. Baraka had overheard him boasting about how many heifers and steers he owned. The cook had informed the visitor that he was mistaken in his claims. The herds that grazed on his land actually belonged to the Maasai. Essie smiled at the memory. She understood why Baraka liked the nursery mobile. That a cow could be seen to dominate the moon – as much a source of life as the sun – ascribed ultimate power to his tribe's most precious asset.

Essie untied the mobile and laid it on the bed. Instead of packing it away, she decided, she would give it to Baraka. She and Julia were planning a visit to the *manyatta* some time soon. As well as seeing the old cook, Julia wanted to meet up with Kisani. There was a lot for the two to talk about after all these years: not just the recent discovery of Robbie's body, but also their shared memories of the little boy himself.

Upturning a basket onto the change table, Essie spread out an array of frocks, singlets and shorts. Among the pastel tones a splash of colour caught her eye. It was the bright-patterned dress that mirrored the one she had hanging in her own wardrobe. As she picked it up, memories came to her of the day the Maasai women had come to the camp, full of curiosity about the Hadza baby that had been taken in by the Bwana's wife. She relived the moment when they had given her a new name, translating it from Maa into Swahili so she'd know what it meant.

Mama Mzuri.

The Beautiful Mother.

Essie held the miniature dress up to her face, feeling the soft fabric against her skin. It didn't smell of Mara – only of the soap Tembo had used to launder it – yet it still seemed to carry with it some essence of the baby. She didn't want to part with it.

With the dress in her hand, she left the nursery. She headed along the path that led to the tent she shared with Ian. Rudie followed her, sticking close on her heels. Ever since the departure of Simon and Mara, he'd been uneasy. Essie wanted to convey to him that the two were not lost somewhere, in need of rescue. All was as it should be. But she knew a dog was not easy to fool. Even if she managed to sound convincing, Rudie would pick up on her mixed emotions. All she could do was stroke his head, easing the lines from his brow.

Unzipping the tent, Essie breathed the familiar smell of the place – shoe polish, canvas and a hint of Imperial Leather soap. She hadn't been in here since the evening of the day she and Simon had found the cave; she'd already moved some clothes and other items into the nursery so she hadn't needed to return. Now, as she stepped inside, she saw evidence of Ian's speedy departure – Kefa hadn't found time to tidy up in here; he had too much to do, helping cover Baraka's workload. There was a single shoe in the middle of the floor. A pair of socks rolled into a ball lay on the bed. Beside it was a flared tie with a lurid paisley pattern. It had been a thank-you present from a visitor, Essie recalled. The female historian had said she'd bought it in Carnaby Street, and it was the very latest fashion. Ian had shoved the tie into his bottom drawer; it was the last thing he would ever want to wear. Essie was surprised to see it had been unearthed now. He must have considered taking it to London.

Her gaze passed over a formal shirt with a stiff collar, and then settled on an odd-looking hunting vest – too neatly tailored and made from fine cotton instead of sturdy twill – that she'd never seen before. Next to it was an array of bits and pieces that must have come from the pockets of Ian's work clothes: a broken pencil, a scrap of paper, a piece of string and the sunglasses Diana had bought him when they'd met up in Arusha. Essie found herself viewing the collection of objects with the eyes of a stranger. They didn't look as if they all belonged to the same person. She was reminded of her mother's wardrobe – the way there was no sense of cohesion about the things that had been chosen. Perhaps Ian, too, had no idea of who he really was.

Essie walked over to where her suitcase was stowed on top of the wardrobe. Bracing to take the weight, she dragged it down onto the chest at the end of the bed. After struggling with the corroded locks, she lifted the lid. The smell of stale lavender and wool escaped. She looked at her old grey jumper with its coloured band of Fair Isle knitting. She trailed her fingers across a pretty, sleeveless dress that she'd brought from England but never worn. Then she touched a blue silk wrap of Lorna's. It was too big to be used as a neck scarf but Essie hadn't been able to bring herself to cut it up; the fabric looked so expensive. Her hand came to rest on the orange gown she'd put on for the Marlows' visit. She pictured herself all dressed up, sipping champagne, talking to the visitors – trying to appear calm, when all she could think of was the baby she'd just deposited in the kitchen. She remembered putting on her leather apron before sitting on a stool by the fireplace and giving her flint-knapping demonstration. She'd made a replica of an *erectus* tool – a pear-shaped, double-sided hand axe. Ian had explained to the guests that not a single example of the Acheulean style had yet been found anywhere in Africa. But with extra funding, he'd hinted, it was only a matter of time before this deficit was corrected. Imagine if they could have known back then, Essie thought, that instead of digging up *Homo erectus* artefacts, the Lawrences would find a whole skeleton – perfectly preserved – that was representative of the species. The discovery was beyond their most optimistic dreams. Yet it had brought disharmony and division to Magadi, instead of joy.

Essie returned to the wardrobe, this time reaching inside it, locating her own version of the little dress she'd brought from the nursery. Taking it back to the bed, she pushed Ian's clothes out of the way and then laid the two garments out, side by side. One big. One so tiny. At the sight of them lying there – the sleeves just touching – a wave of grief swept over her. She rubbed her eyes, warding off tears.

Placing Mara's dress on top of hers, she folded them up together – the two merged into one, cloth lying against matching cloth, and seams against seams. She placed them in the suitcase beside the jumper and the evening gown. As she did so, she noticed her document wallet tucked into the corner. Her eyes lingered on the slim tan shape. Inside it – along with her passport and Tanzanian work permit – was the piece of card on which Carl had written his agent's address.

You can always find me.

She pictured him standing on the shore of a lake, his tripod set up beside him. He was surrounded by the hectic sound and colour of a vast congregation of flamingos. She felt a longing to be with him that was so intense it was like physical pain. She wanted to tell him about Mara and Milena, and Simon. And hear him convince her that though it hurt so much, what had taken place was the best possible ending for the story.

Even if Essie had been able to find out where Carl was, she knew there would probably be no means of communicating with him. He wouldn't return from the field until his assignment was either abandoned or completed, and there was no way to guess when that might be. There was also no way of knowing where he'd then go. One thing Essie was certain of, though. As soon as Carl had the chance, he'd print up all the portraits he and Essie had shot at the Mission house and send copies to her. The thought aroused a feeling of relief. She'd have an image of Mara's face, then – every detail recorded on paper in tones of black and white. Something tangible she could hold in her hand.

Essie was about to close the lid of the suitcase but then she paused, scanning the contents. Aside from more articles of clothing, there were a few books, a pair of high-heeled shoes wrapped in brown paper, some unused medicines, spare stationery. The suitcase was almost full – yet these possessions were just the ones Essie didn't actually use. Spread around various areas of the camp there were so many more things that were hers. Essie thought of how Simon had been able to simply walk away from this place. There was not a single item, back in his tent, that he really needed. What he valued – his bow and arrows – he could make or find again.

She remembered the Maasai workers – how they, too, had left the camp in a hurry. They owned more belongings than the hunter-gatherers, but still, not much. They'd carried just a few things tied up in a spare blanket. Their spears were angled over their shoulders; knives swung at their hips. Like Simon, they'd been free to depart, as soon as they decided to.

Essie pictured the way they had headed off into the *korongos*, moving with such a resolute step. Every one of the men was clear on where he was headed. They were returning to their tribe. The local Maasai knew where their *manyatta* was, since it had become a long-term base. The others would just aim for the region where their relatives were last known to have been. They'd ask around until they discovered where their homes were now located. When they finally reached the family *manyatta,* they'd be welcomed with singing and dancing. A goat might be killed for a feast. As greetings were exchanged, the new arrival might discover that a face was absent. Someone might have moved away. There could even have been a death, news of which had not yet travelled as far as Magadi. But the extended family – the tribe – would be there. And the sense of belonging was to be found wherever they were.

Essie gazed around her, not seeing the tent walls or the space beyond the entrance – but instead, scenes from her life. It was as if she was viewing a film played in reverse: the sequence began here in Magadi and reached back to Cambridge – to university halls; soggy camping grounds near archaeological sites; the cosy kitchen of the cottage, Arthur stooped over the stove. An empty bedroom; the stained yellow walls of the hospital; a gravestone daubed with moss . . .

The pictures were vivid and clear – but they weren't what Essie was focused on. She was chasing a vision of another place, from much further back in her life. It was like trying to find snatches of a fading dream. There was the detailed memory of the muttonbirding that had been evoked by Carl's photograph – but the rest of her recollections were a blur. As she homed in on them, they pulled away. The moments were so few, as well. Each fragment was already familiar – the crackle of a fire, a swell of laughter, the murmur of breaking waves, the lilt of voices in the dark. What Essie could grasp felt warm, intimate. There was a sense of comfort there. She trailed the impressions through her mind, straining for detail.

There had to be more . . .

She looked down at the contents of the suitcase. Almost without thought – on impulse – she picked up Lorna's silk wrap and spread it out on the bed. She began forming a small pile of things in the middle. First came the folded mother-and-daughter dresses. The document wallet landed alongside them. Next was the jumper – warm and comfortable. And a novel she'd not found time to read. Moving away from the suitcase, she added some work clothes from her drawers; a nightie; some underwear. From beside the bed she chose a spare pair of shoes.

When she was done, she gathered the ends of the cloth together and tied a knot, forming a bundle that would fit inside her field rucksack. Lodging it under her arm, she took a last look around the tent, and walked out the door.

As she stepped into the mid-morning heat, a sense of relief washed over her. She was not going to be here when Ian and Diana returned with their entourage. She wouldn't have to watch while the film crew invaded the cave, and feel caught between the Africans and the outsiders – responsible, somehow, for Ian's actions. She'd never again have to look across to the orange glow of the Palace at night and wonder about the shadows she could see. And she would not have to find a way to face still being here, in this place, now that Mara was gone. If she was running away, she didn't mind. She wasn't thinking about what she was leaving behind, but where she wanted to go.

She found Julia sitting in the Work Hut, smoking a cigarette. Her shirt was damp with sweat and there was a streak of red earth on her cheek. She looked up as Essie entered. As her

eyes slid to the blue cloth bundle, she raised her eyebrows questioningly.

'What have you got there?'

'I've packed up some things,' Essie said. 'I'm going away.'

Julia looked mystified. 'To London – to join Ian?' She seemed
unconvinced by her own question; she didn't wait for a reply. 'Where
to, then?'

Essie took a breath. 'I've decided to go back to where my mother
came from. Rocky Bay. I want to find her family and ask them about
her. I want to understand who she really was. Who I am . . .'

There was a short silence. Essie waited for Julia to start arguing against the plan. There were practical barriers to making a trip
from Magadi to Tasmania. But that was not all. Julia would be
able to give voice to a whole list of doubts – ones that were already
brewing in Essie's own head. She knew Essie hadn't been back
to the island since she was a child, and that her mother's illness
and death had cast a shadow over her past. Julia could point out
that any relatives Essie found would be complete strangers to her.
She might find they had nothing in common. And who was to say
that Lorna's family would want to make any space in their lives for
Essie? If everything turned out badly, Essie would be completely
alone, far from anyone she knew . . .

Instead of raising objections, though, Julia just nodded slowly.
She stubbed out her cigarette, then placed her hands on her knees
as if ready to spring into action.

'There's money,' she said. 'Diana gave it to me to run the place
while they were gone. We can get more at the bank.'

Essie looked at her in confusion. 'We?'

'I'll drive you to Nairobi,' Julia stated. 'It makes more sense than
going to Arusha and catching a train to Dar es Salaam. The border

is only a three-hour drive from here if you take a shortcut. And I need to go over to Kenya, anyway.' She gestured towards Tommy, who was sitting on the rug nibbling at one of the fringed ends. The sun glanced off the shiny tips of his horns. 'I've been thinking about him. I want to take him to a wildlife sanctuary I've heard about, before this place fills up with visitors.'

Essie frowned, struggling to absorb Julia's train of ideas. Then she stared mutely at the gazelle. A lump rose in her throat. The plan for him was right and necessary, but picturing it happening was painful. It would have been comforting to know that even though she was leaving Magadi, Tommy would still be here. Now he, too, was moving far away.

'The dogs can come with me,' Julia added. As she spoke, she looked to the north-east – the direction in which they would travel. Her eyes brightened. 'I might stay a while. The garden can wait till I get back. There are people I could visit. They might still remember me.' She got to her feet, suddenly energised. 'We'll go in the new Land Rover. Kefa and Daudi can take over here. Between them they know how to run the place.'

Essie felt a rush of excitement, the reality of the scenario filtering through. But then anxiety stirred. She knew that if she didn't go now, she could easily lose her nerve. Just one more radio call from Ian might be all it would take. 'I don't want to wait.'

'There's not much to organise,' Julia responded. She was bending over her suitcase, which was still serving as a makeshift side table. She removed an empty whisky glass that was resting there, as well as a saucer sprinkled with crumbs. She planted them both in the middle of an abandoned card game. Grasping the handle of the suitcase, she lifted it up.

'I've got what I need in here.'

As Julia tested the weight in her hand, Essie remembered what she had said – days ago, when Essie was working on the *Sivatherium*: 'I'm finished with all this.' It was almost as though the suitcase had been kept here, still packed, ready for this moment. Could it be that the idea of leaving Magadi had begun with Julia and found its way to her? Essie imagined the thought alighting on her shoulder like a bird, whispering in her ear. It didn't seem completely impossible – if time went in circles, who could say where an idea had first been born?

Crossing to stand at her work table, Essie looked down at the skull, still missing some key fragments. The reconstruction would not be high on Ian's agenda, she knew; all the focus would be shifting to the cave. Perhaps some student volunteer would take over the task. Essie waited to feel a pang of jealousy, but it barely registered. After taking a last look at her handiwork, she picked up a couple of tools and tidied them away. Then she brushed a dead fly onto the floor.

She walked over to Tommy and bent down to pat his head, her hand lingering on the smooth warmth of his coat. Then she moved on past Julia. Emerging from the hut, she skirted the fireplace and went to stand at the edge of the clearing – the same spot where Milena had appeared. She looked towards the *korongos*, where Simon, Mara and the others had headed. In the far distance she could just glimpse the edge of the plateau where the flint factory was located. She thought back to the morning, just a few months ago, when she'd encountered the two Hadza hunters there, and been led off to the Painted Cave.

Essie remembered the moment when she'd seen Mara for the first time – a small curled shape, asleep on a baboon pelt. It was only a dim impression; she hadn't known, then, the import the memory would one day have. The backdrop to the scene, though,

Essie could visualise in intricate detail. She'd studied every brush mark and dab of pigment that made up the paintings on the wall of rock.

Now, as she pictured the place in her mind, Essie imagined her own story recorded there. The figure of a woman drawn in white clay. A baby formed from black pigment. The tribe gathered around them, lean bodies carrying long bows – men, women and children – all captured in sparse but powerful detail. What would an archaeologist make of the image, Essie wondered: the story of a woman who was given the gift of a baby and became – for one season – a mother.

Essie turned back to the eastern horizon. She traced the pyramid shape of the mountain set against the crystal sky. There was no wind this morning – smoke and steam rose straight up from the crater forming a tall pillar of cloud. She could feel the brooding power of the place. There was a strange, taut stillness, as if time had been suspended. A breath drawn in and held. Like the Maasai who'd walked away from Ol Doinyo Lengai with their faces averted, she lowered her eyes.

Essie looked instead towards the silver gleam of the lake with its curved white shoreline. Then she picked out the rooftop of the Mission house nestled among the trees. Finally, her gaze settled on the plains. As she scanned the wide swathe of stony land – from the Steps to the grass-ringed pools – the scene transformed in her mind. She saw the vast stage of an ocean – steely blue, white-capped, wind-scraped. Thousands of birds formed a dense black pattern against a pastel sky, flying so low that their wingtips skimmed the tops of the waves. She heard the seabirds calling to one another, and the rhythmic hush of their wings as they floated on currents of air – returning from the far end of the earth, heading home.

POSTSCRIPT

Ants abandon their castles of dried mud, swarming over the stony ground. Snakes emerge beady-eyed from their burrows, writhing towards open spaces. The ground begins to move – a tiny tremor leading to a rolling shudder. In the foothills of Ol Doinyo Lengai, boulders shift and stones topple.

Within the volcano, molten rock seethes. A fierce energy builds, rising to a crescendo. With a roar of thunder the lava bursts out – not from the crater at the peak, but through a chasm that opens up halfway down the side of the mountain.

Lightning dances against the sky as the torrent of lava flows. It slides down into the foothills and on, lining the gullies, settling in the gaps between the broken rocks. It fills the spring-fed pond, anointing the standing stones on its banks. The opening to the cave is sealed over, the tunnel choked with rubble.

In the new world that is created, no map holds meaning. There are no landmarks. What has become hidden can never be found.

The rivers of lava reach all the way down to the lake. They pour onto the abandoned shores, hissing as they meet the tranquil, salt-oily water. Clouds of steam rise into the air, like prayers.

AUTHOR'S NOTE

At the time when this novel is set, Tasmanian schoolchildren were being taught that the island's Aboriginal people had 'died out' and disappeared. In fact, the unique culture and identity of the first Tasmanians was still being handed down from generation to generation, in the way it always had been for tens of thousands of years. Many decades passed before this truth became widely understood. Today, in the thriving Indigenous communities across the island, Aboriginal languages are being revived and the state's landscape officially renamed. Lots of gatherings and events, private and public, now begin with an acknowledgement of Aboriginal people as the traditional owners and ongoing custodians of the land.

The archaeology explored in this story reflects what was known in 1970. Later discoveries of fossils and stone tools pointed more and more to what the Lawrences and Leakeys had always believed: that Africa was the first home of all humans. DNA evidence has finally proven this to be true. *Homo erectus* migrated from Africa, moving up into Europe and beyond. Over time, the species evolved further. Exactly how this played out is still the subject of research, with the picture becoming increasingly complex as new discoveries are made. What used to be called the human family tree is now more aptly described as a tangled bush. It is known that there were at least three distinct human species living on the planet at the same time: Neanderthals, Denisovans and our own kind, *Homo sapiens*. They interbred with one another and today nearly all of us have a small percentage of Neanderthal and Denisovan DNA in our genes.

The Hadza are the last surviving hunter-gatherer people in East Africa. Only a few hundred of them still maintain a fully traditional lifestyle. Gene mapping has supported what has been long supposed: that the Hadza people have one of the oldest human lineages on earth. They are not closely related to any other peoples. Their ancestors may well have been living in their current territory for tens of thousands of years. Hadza oral history contains no stories of migration from another place. It was only around ten thousand years ago that *Homo sapiens* began settling down in villages and farming the land. Since our journey as the *Homo* genus began around two million years ago, this means that for ninety-nine per cent of our history we lived as hunter-gatherers. Most of the qualities we possess evolved in that setting.

The Lawrences of Magadi Gorge live only in these pages; however, the Leakey family is real. Louis and Mary Leakey began excavating in Olduvai Gorge in the 1930s and continued working there for most of their lives. Their sons grew up spending lots of time in the camp at Olduvai and were skilled fossil hunters. The passion for archaeology has lasted through three generations of Leakeys so far. Olduvai continues to be a centre for exploration, with the work now being led by Tanzanians.

Wolfgang Stein was not a real person, but was inspired by my readings about missionaries and other visitors to Africa who bucked the conventions of their era. Some of them ultimately found more meaning in the traditional cultures they encountered than they did in their own.

Ludwig Kohl-Larsen was an amateur anthropologist and explorer. After joining the Nazi party in 1931 he undertook government-sponsored expeditions to what was then German East Africa in search of 'primitive man'. He excavated for hominid remains in the Olduvai area and also collected folklore from the Hadza people. As a result of his politics and beliefs, as well as his poor scholarship, his research is not highly regarded by modern academics.

The Painted Cave is imaginary, but was inspired by the caves at Kondoa in Central Tanzania, which were studied extensively by Mary Leakey in the 1950s. The caves are of spiritual significance to local communities, including the Hadza. I have memories of visiting the caves with my family as a young child.

The Steps site is fictitious, but inspired by a discovery made in 1978 by Mary Leakey at Laetoli, about 45 kilometres south of Olduvai. The Laetoli Steps, a series of fossilised footprints that have been dated to 3.6 million years ago, are believed to have been made by our first upright-walking ancestors, the Australopithecines. Other fossilised footprints estimated to be between five thousand and nineteen thousand years old have also been discovered at Engare Sero next to Lake Natron. In one section of this site there are so many prints that the space has been dubbed 'the dance hall'.

The lake that lies at the foot of Ol Doinyo Lengai is actually called Lake Natron. In the novel the Swahili name for any soda lake – *magadi* – is used in connection with both the lake and the nearby gorge. There is another soda lake called Magadi in the Ngorongoro crater in Tanzania, and also one in Kenya.

My fascination with the area around Ol Doinyo Lengai and Lake Natron began with a visit I made there ten years ago with my parents and brother. Although the landscape is very different to the Ugogo plains where I was born, I felt an immediate connection to it, and the powerful presence of the place lingered with me long after I left. It became the setting for my book *The Lioness*, and I was drawn back to it in search of this new story as well.

The setting of *The Beautiful Mother* in a paleoanthropologists' camp is the result of a family preoccupation with the topic that was originally inspired by my husband, Roger Scholes. Twenty years ago he directed a television series called *The Human Journey*, which explored the origins of our species. He filmed in key locations around the world, including museums, caves and excavation sites. Re-enactments were staged abroad and also here in Tasmania, where the ancient flora is reminiscent of earlier eras in Europe. I found myself playing the part of a Neolithic hunter-gatherer in one of the scenes, along with my then young son. Many props from the shoots – including replicas of hominid skulls, stone tools and early artworks – have been on display in our home ever since. With all this surrounding me, and Tanzania being both the 'cradle of humankind' and my own country of birth, there was every reason for me to explore this world in a novel.

The full meaning of the way in which Tanzania and Tasmania are linked through Essie's story only emerged during my research. Within eyesight of my writing desk – on the clifftop at the end of the beach – is a tall sandstone shot tower. While studying European prehistory, I learned that in the early 1900s the building attached to it was home to Joseph Moir, a renowned collector of Tasmanian stone tools. This sparked the idea for Arthur Holland's famous collection. As I continued my investigations I learned of the unique place both Tasmania and Tanzania have always held in the imaginations of paleoanthropologists across the world. As the connection between my two homelands deepened in unexpected ways, the question of Essie's personal heritage came to the fore. The topic is a potent one for me, as a writer who was born in a land far from where I now live. The story gave me the chance to pursue questions that lie within us all. Who am I? Where did I come from? Who are my people? For Essie, the search for answers takes her beyond the boundaries of this novel – to another adventure.

From a long list of research sources used in the writing of *The Beautiful Mother*, I would like to acknowledge in particular:

Rebe Taylor's fascinating book *Into the Heart of Tasmania: A Search for Human Antiquity*; Mary Leakey's detailed autobiography *Disclosing the Past*; and *Ancestral Passions – The Leakey Family and the Quest for Humankind's Beginnings* by Virginia Morell.

ACKNOWLEDGEMENTS

In tackling the research for this book, I relied very much on Roger Scholes' vast knowledge of paleoanthropology. As the field is so complex, he had to explain many things to me over and over, yet somehow never ran out of patience. He helped with plotting and read all my work as it was being written. He also advised me on Tasmanian history. I am deeply grateful for his professional contribution and unending personal support.

I am fortunate to have a wonderful, talented publisher in Ali Watts of Penguin Random House. This is the fifth book we've worked on together and each one has been an absolute pleasure. My thanks go to all involved in the publication of *The Beautiful Mother*, especially Julie Burland, Justin Ractliffe, Lou Ryan, Amanda Martin, Deb McGowan, Madison Garratt, Louisa Maggio, Saskia Adams and Sonja Heijn.

As always, I am grateful to my agents Fiona Inglis and Kate Cooper at Curtis Brown for finding perfect homes for my work. Thank you to my overseas agents, publishers and translators as well.

Many people supported me during the writing of this book. Much love and thanks go to Jonathan Scholes, Freya Sonderegger (to whom this book is dedicated), Linden Scholes, Charlotte de Jong and my whole fabulous extended tribe, especially my parents,

Robin and Elizabeth Smith. Hilary Smith, Clare Smith and Freya Sonderegger all read the work in progress, and their insights were much appreciated. A particular thank you to Hilary for taking on the delicate task of reading the first drafts, and responding with such enthusiasm and love. Andrew, Vanessa and Lachlan Smith, along with Martin Kennedy, Hamish Maxwell-Stewart, Tim and Kate Bendall, Olivia and Nick Hitchens, and Jordan and Gemma Smith all helped in other ways.

Thank you also to my dear friends and colleagues who are always there for me when needed, offering encouragement, advice and fun. You allow me to disappear into my eyrie for months at a time – and then welcome me back. I am extra grateful for the support of Melanie Sandford, Julian Northmore, Anna and Tim Jones, Joce Nettlefold, Claire Konkes, Stephenie Cahalan, Libby Lester, Stefan Visagie, Heather Rose, Brian and Elizabeth McKenzie, Jane Ormonde, Bill Pheasant, Lynda House and Tony Mahood.

Finally, a huge thank you to my readers from near and far, especially those of you who read all my books as they are published, and get in touch to convey your response. It makes for a shared journey, which is very precious to me.

BOOK CLUB NOTES

1. Did Essie have any real choice when she was handed the baby by Nandamara?

2. Ian becomes frustrated to see his wife acting in unfamiliar ways, yet in his work he believes that *Change is the only constant*. In what ways does change come to affect their marriage?

3. Do you understand Julia's decision to live the rest of her life in Magadi, 'the heart of their agony', where the closest thing to happiness was a day of good, hard work and the satisfaction of seeing the camp run smoothly?

4. Simon believes himself to be a 'modern Tanzanian'. In what ways is this so? What has he rejected of his Hadza past, and what does he reclaim?

5. Carl travels the world taking photographs but still feels a pull back to a single place he calls 'home'. Discuss the notion of home as it is explored in the novel.

6. In a world where our extended families may not be all that close, emotionally or physically, how do we find 'our tribe'?

7. What makes someone a mother?

8. How does Essie's time with Mara transform her?

9. What roles do possessions play in our lives? Are there lessons to be learned from the Hadza, in a world on the brink of environmental crisis?

10. Do you agree with Kisani's statement: *The past had to be left behind, so that something new could begin.*'?

11. The Maasai women tell Essie, 'You are her mother at this moment. The future is another time.' What do you think this means?

12. At the conclusion of the novel, Essie says 'though it hurt so much, what had taken place was the best possible ending for the story'. Do you agree?